WELCOME TO THE FAMILY

KATE GRAY

MLP

First published in 2026 by Mountain Leopard Press
An imprint of Headline Publishing Group Limited

This paperback edition published in 2026

1

Cataloguing in Publication Data is available from the British Library

Paperback ISBN 978 1 0354 2353 8

Offset in 10.56/14.52 pt Sabon LT Pro
by Six Red Marbles UK, Thetford, Norfolk

Printed and bound in Great Britain by Clays Ltd, Elcograf S.p.A.

MIX
Paper | Supporting
responsible forestry
FSC® C104740

Headline's policy is to use papers that are natural, renewable and recyclable
products and made from wood grown in well-managed forests and other
controlled sources. The logging and manufacturing processes are expected
to conform to the environmental regulations of the country of origin.

Headline Publishing Group Limited
An Hachette UK Company
Carmelite House
50 Victoria Embankment
London EC4Y 0DZ

The authorised representative in the EEA is Hachette Ireland,
8 Castlecourt Centre, Dublin 15, D15 XTP3, Ireland (email: info@hbgi.ie)

www.headline.co.uk
www.hachette.co.uk

Praise for *Welcome To The Family*

'Gripping'
Daily Mail

'The perfect destination thriller . . . a beautiful Italian villa, a messed-up family with devastating secrets and a twisting murder mystery. A stunning summer page-turner'
C.M. Ewan

'An absorbing and atmospheric summer thriller that is sizzling with twists'
Heidi Perks

'Oozing with suspense, this fiendishly twisty thriller is guaranteed to keep you guessing'
Heat

'I was transported to Italy in this utterly addictive thriller. The twists are whip-smart and kept me guessing until the very last page'
Nikki Smith

'A sticky, sun-drenched thriller to rival *The White Lotus*, rich with suspicion, deception, and characters you'll love to hate'
Abigail Dean

'Simmering tension turns deadly in this twisty and addictive summer mystery – a cracking family thriller'
T.M. Logan

'A fast-paced, twisty thriller where everyone's a suspect. I raced through this – the perfect holiday read'
Tariq Ashkanani

'Oozing with tension, this complex sizzler of a thriller delivers on every level. Brilliant!'
Isabelle Broom

'A red-hot thriller, which simply demands to be read by a pool. I didn't know who to believe; lies, betrayal and buried secrets ensured I read *Welcome To The Family* in one weekend'
Jo Murray

'A destination to die for – quite literally. Kate dials up the heat in this tense, claustrophobic, addictive thriller – that will make you think twice about going on a family holiday'
Ruth Kelly

'A masterfully plotted, beautifully written mystery that's tense, treacherous, and utterly unputdownable'
Katy Brent

'A rollercoaster read'
That's Life

Also by Kate Gray

The Honeymoon
The Summer Party

To my family – including my in-laws.

PROLOGUE

The police officer's gun is aimed at her chest. Her eyes dart between the weapon and the deep frown sliced in his brow.

She can't breathe.

The small interrogation room is too hot. Too cramped. Filled with fear. Her legs shake as adrenaline zips across every tense muscle.

Another officer fires rapid Italian words in her direction. She squeezes her clammy hands. Again and again. Needing to feel something real to prove this is happening. The movement brings a faint waft of the coconut aftersun she rubbed over her skin before she got dressed, reminding her how differently this day had started.

The holiday was never supposed to end like this.

Her eyes fall to the blood stains on her dress. The many rips in the delicate silk material. Once the colour of early-morning sunshine, now smeared with mud and splatters of deep crimson. If she tried to explain the past twenty-four hours, would they believe her? Where would she begin?

The officer's unarmed colleague steps closer. He looms over her. His eyes are dark and expressionless. She needs to tell them what she knows, but her words escape her. Shock steals her sentences.

He clears his throat and begins again in English. 'You are under arrest . . .'

A rush of nausea leaps in her stomach. She shakes her head, blinking rapidly.

'Under arrest? For what?'

Her heart pounds with every second it takes for him to answer. When he speaks again, the world stops turning.

'Murder.'

1

ROSIE – DAY 1

Kill them with kindness, that's Rosie's plan. She needs to do everything she can to get Theo's family to like her. Starting with chocolate. He insists she doesn't need to bring a gift, but she can't show up empty-handed. First impressions are everything.

Her plan was to pick up a box in duty-free, but time is running out. They will be boarding soon. The enthusiastic dance music blasting from a speaker above isn't helping.

Make a decision.

But what do you buy for someone you've never met before? Why didn't she ask Theo to be more specific? She needs something thoughtful but not too over-the-top. Chocolate liqueurs or truffles? Dark, milk, or white? With nuts or without? Triangle-shaped bars or individually wrapped shiny jewels? Choice paralysis takes over. Their flight is announced over the tannoy. She's stood here for long enough.

Pick something.

She grabs a box of Belgian chocolate balls, praying Theo's mother doesn't have any allergies – accidentally killing her would not be a good start – and tries to find her way through the fog of clashing perfume samples to the check-out.

Theo is waiting for her outside the shop, leaning against a concrete pillar, unaware of the stressful last ten minutes. He glances up from his phone screen and the look of recognition as he spots her in the crowd melts her heart. The laughter lines around his brown eyes crinkle under his floppy, sandy blonde fringe. He steps forward with an enthusiastic spring in his step.

Five months in and the honeymoon stage shows no sign of fading.

Theo laces his fingers through hers. Instinctive. Protective. Leading her past the huddles of holidaymakers to check out the departures board. She wonders if he's nervous, too; after all, this is a big deal for both of them.

'Gate four,' he says.

There's nothing in his chilled demeanour to suggest he's apprehensive about this trip. It's their first official holiday, and also the first time she'll meet his family.

Please let this go well.

Theo has done something no other boyfriend has been able to do; he's made Rosie feel special. In return, she has embraced his love of fitness – reluctantly at times, but it's paying off as she's the healthiest she's been in years. Her colleagues might tease her for bringing Tupperware filled with nutritious greens and grains to the staff room, but they also admit that it's nice to see her happy again. She remembers the look on her teaching assistant's face when she told her about her summer plans; she found it unfathomable that Rosie was about to go on holiday with a family she hadn't properly met.

'It'll be fine.' She'd laughed. 'How bad can they be?'

***

Rosie locates their seats on the plane. The stuffy cabin air is uncomfortable after the chill of the departure lounge. She fiddles with the controls above their seats to allow more air flow, and quickly writes a text to her mum, telling her she'll be in touch soon. Her earlier messages remain unread. She knows her mum's signal is patchy, but it's frustrating not to hear from her more. Perhaps it's a good thing. She would interfere otherwise.

Theo offers to help an older lady struggling to lift her scuffed travel case into the overhead locker. His arms flex to reveal toned biceps, the result of dedicated gym sessions. Rosie tears her eyes from him and takes out a bottle of mineral water from her backpack, spotting the notebook she tucked behind a copy of *Heat* magazine.

She quickly zips the bag shut.

'God, I think she's packed a dead body judging by the weight of that bag.' Theo laughs, slipping into the seat beside her. 'Do you want me to put that up too? Give you more room?' He nods at her backpack resting on her knees.

She gulps a mouthful of water.

'No. I mean . . . no thanks,' she adds quickly.

The words written inside the notebook zoom to the front of her mind. She should have left it at home.

She shoves the bag under the seat in front.

He keeps his eyes on her. 'You ok, babe?'

'A bit nervous,' she admits, truthfully.

'The flight will be fine.' His bright smile helps calm her racing heart.

'I wasn't thinking about the flight . . .' She wafts her boarding pass at her face.

'Oh, I see. You don't need to worry, they're going to love you.' He plants a reassuring kiss on her forehead. 'Nothing's going to go wrong. Trust me.'

2

FENNA – DAY 1

'This holiday will do you good,' Luke says, reaching over the handbrake and squeezing his wife's upper thigh, leaving a clammy hand resting there. She's told him enough times that he needs to have both hands on the steering wheel, especially with the kids in the car, but she bites her tongue. She can't face another row before they arrive. 'Hopefully bring the old Fenna back.'

The old Fenna. The old Fenna is strutting down a catwalk in Paris, partying until three in the morning, surviving on Malboro Gold's and espresso, laughing and dancing, oblivious to her unbridled freedom and pert breasts.

The old Fenna is not sitting next to her husband in a stuffy and sensible Italian hire car. This version feels a hundred years old, survives on minimal broken sleep, and has a newborn who painfully tugs her nipples when he feeds. She's ruled by a petulant 'threenage' toddler, who hasn't taken to her new baby brother as seamlessly as everyone told Fenna she would. Not to mention the stretchmarks across her fleshy stomach, the swollen ankles, and the postpartum thinning hair that comes out in clumps in the shower.

She knows he's trying to be positive, but she can't help but be irritated.

'Yeah, maybe.' She lets out a yawn. It's been a long day. The tense moment in the crowded check-in hall leaps to the front of her mind, when they were told they had exceeded the baggage weight limit and needed to cough up an extra £45. Luke paid with gritted teeth, moaning loudly that he didn't understand why they needed to bring So. Much. Stuff.

Fenna snapped that since *he* didn't pack the cases, *he* didn't know how much of a military operation it was to reduce the sheer number of things the children needed down to one hold suitcase. If anything, *he* should be congratulating her on her packing skills. So what if the case was a little heavier than allowed? She'd forgone the things *she* wanted, the many outfits she would have bought pre-kids.

The marital row was diffused when Fenna bought them both over-priced lattes as an apology. A frivolous expense. They are supposed to be tightening their belts until she's back to work from maternity leave and Luke is able to pay himself a decent wage from his company's accounts. Every new business has teething problems; she just didn't realise they would be budgeting for things for this long.

'Daddy?' Alba pipes up from the back seat.

'Yes, poppet?' Luke asks, pulling down his trendy sunglasses to see his daughter in the rearview mirror.

'Where's Binky?' Alba asks. The bright sunlight catches those baby fine wisps that curl around the edge of her heart-shaped face.

'I don't know, darling. Is he not next to you?'

Fenna twists in her seat, the seatbelt cutting into her, to

search for their daughter's ratty comforter. 'I can't see it. Did you put it in the boot?'

For a few moments, the click of the indicators is the only sound in the car.

He swears under his breath. 'I might have left it on the plane.'

The relentless clicking goes through her.

'Luke!' Fenna cries. 'I asked if you had everything.'

One job. He had one job to check they hadn't left anything behind. Why didn't he check the seat pockets?

'I'll find it for you when we get there, poppet. Ok?'

Fenna bites down the urge to ask him where he is expecting to find a replacement Binky in the middle of the Tuscan countryside.

Alba starts to cry.

'Don't worry. Daddy won't let you down. Let's listen to some music, hey?'

Luke turns the radio on. An uplifting dance song from a TV advert blares in the car. The noise somehow calms Alba, and she burrows back to her tablet.

Fenna crosses her arms. Their daughter's screen time is something else to add to her never-ending list of Things To Worry About. She tries to push it to the back of her mind and focus on good things instead. The thought of spending two free weeks in Tuscany has kept her going during many long, lonely night feeds. Marianne and Gerry's holiday house is her dream home. And, despite the stress of travelling with two young children, she knows it's going to be good for them all to have a change of scene.

Marianne had summoned everyone on this family holiday in her hectic, whirlwind way. A style Fenna still struggles to get used to after five years of knowing her mother-in-law. Marianne is getting worse. More emotional, more forgetful, more highly strung. If that's possible.

The car in front suddenly brakes.

'Remind me why your mum asked everyone to visit in peak season?' Fenna asks as they come to a stop yet again.

The motorway traffic has been near-gridlocked since leaving the airport. Not to mention the debacle of the hire car – Luke was determined to persevere with the Italian salesman, despite Fenna offering to translate everything.

'Something to do with Theo's new girlfriend. She's a teacher, so we've had to fit in with her summer holidays.' He wafts a hand. The one that's still not on the steering wheel. This is the first time Theo has introduced someone he's dating to the family. It's a big deal.

She reaches to find the dial for the air-conditioning, needing a blast of icy air. There is a faint but distinctive smell wafting from Raffi's nappy. He's not complaining about it yet so she doesn't mention it, praying that Luke will change this one. Or maybe it can be a welcome gift for Marianne.

'What's so funny?' Luke asks. Fenna hadn't realised she was smiling to herself.

'Nothing.'

He looks relieved to see her relaxing.

'How does the air-con work?' she asks.

'Try turning that.' He reaches over and flicks the dials. The radio gets louder. The windscreen wipers come on.

Back in the day, when they were dating, she would have found this funny; they both would. But with sweat dripping down her swollen breasts and the heat from his gaze still upon her, she's not in the mood. The car swerves while his eyes are off the road.

'Jesus, Luke!'

'I'm trying to help. How am I supposed to know how to work it? I've never driven this before.'

'Let me deal with it. You concentrate on driving.'

Her phone chimes with a reminder from Alba's nursery to settle the outstanding balance. Luke was supposed to set up a direct debit. She's about to ask him why he's not done it when she spots a sign from her window that makes her heart skip. *Laprezia.*

Coming here feels like coming home.

Villa Speranza. The name literally means peace. Set among five acres of land and built in the fifteenth century, it is to die for. From the first day she pulled up and saw it all those years ago, it's never failed to make her catch her breath. The big wooden shutters, open balconies, tall ceilings, and stunning Italian tiled floors; it is utterly beautiful.

It's the only place in the world where she can fully relax, even with her in-laws nearby.

'We're almost there,' Luke says in a sing-song voice for the children's benefit. 'I bet Uncle Theo will be excited to see you, Alba.'

Alba ignores him. Her pudgy finger drags streaks across the screen of her tablet.

'How are things with you and Theo?' Fenna asks, her voice low and cautious.

Luke's been quiet about spending a fortnight with his younger brother. As an only child, she struggles to relate when he moans about Theo. There isn't any bad blood between them; they prefer to live their lives separately from one another, unless family circumstances call for it.

Theo hasn't met Raffi yet, but he did send a 'Welcome to the world' greetings card and a plush stuffed giraffe, which Luke took great delight in googling the price of, grumbling about how over-the-top it was.

The brothers are close in age and share the same competitive streak. Fenna knows Marianne wishes they were best friends, but instead, it's more of a love-hate relationship. You never know if they'll blow hot or cold.

'Things are fine.' The inflection in his voice sounds forced, but she's too tired to question what he really thinks.

It's a shame the brothers don't have a closer relationship. She would like to be a little close-knit foursome with Theo and his partner. Who knows, maybe this holiday will change things. The air will be cleared and a budding friendship will be born.

'You'll get so much help,' Fenna's mum friends chimed when she told them about her summer plans.

Fenna had nodded and smiled, saying how lucky she was. But her smile was forced. They've not met her mother-in-law. Marianne has different ways of doing things. And it's her way, or the wrong way.

If she's honest, it will be a miracle if they all survive the fortnight.

3

ROSIE – DAY 1

The taxi cuts through the narrow mediaeval lanes, which are punctuated every few metres by tall, elegant cypress trees. Rosie wasn't prepared for the wall of oven-like heat that hit them the moment they stepped off the plane and hasn't eased off since. The last thing she wanted was to arrive with sweat patches under her armpits, but it's too late now.

They've swapped a grey strip of motorway for winding roads through terracotta-tiled villages, steep hills, and vast farmers' fields filled with drooping sunflowers. They venture further into the countryside, past a derelict old farmhouse with spindly trees poking from holes where the roof once was. The Mediterranean sunlight hits the weathered stone buildings so they glow.

It's a world away from her life in a market town in North Yorkshire, where summer has been a total washout. She pictures the grey, rain-drenched streets, the familiar smell of boiled vegetables at the primary school where she works, and the early-morning alarm that forces her to start the day with her class of seven and eight-year-olds.

'Are you nervous?' she asks, looking at Theo's handsome face, his earnest brown eyes, those long blonde lashes.

He's grown quieter as the journey from the airport has gone on.

'Me? No.'

'Really?' She nudges him.

'Really! Why would I be? I know they're going to love you.' He grins.

She crosses her fingers.

'You didn't tell me how gorgeous it is here.' She nods at a hand-painted road sign, yellowed from the sun, with an arrow pointing left. 'What's *Lago Parrocchetto*?'

'It's a lake not far from here. It used to be a nesting place for green parakeets, hundreds of them, but they've all vanished. Like the tourists. Back in the day this town was different, it's not that popular now . . .'

She's about to ask what made them disappear when there's a sound from the front of the car.

The driver mumbles something.

'What's that, mate?' Theo asks.

There's no response. The driver shakes his head, flicking his attention back to the road.

'Is he listening to our conversation?' Theo drops his voice to a whisper. His breath tickles her ear.

'I hadn't noticed,' she lies. She's been aware of him watching them with a furrowed brow since he picked them up at the airport and Theo gave him the address of where they wanted to go.

'Could you turn up the music, mate?' Theo asks loudly.

The driver doesn't say a word but he must understand the request as a pop song fills the car.

Shortly after, the taxi turns a corner and sweeps down a long gravel driveway towards a farmhouse made with apricot-hued bricks. Neat flower boxes sit under every one of the second-floor windows, a splash of pink petals and trailing vines against the worn, wooden shutters. The sun bounces off the terracotta roof. Lush, glossy green ivy spreads itself across the faded facade. Clay urns and pots hold bushy fat olive trees and spiky herbs.

It's almost like a child's drawing has come to life. The wide-open door in the centre, the same number of windows on either side, a neat chimney sticking up from the middle.

Villa Speranza has been in Theo's family for thirty-plus years. For him, being here is like coming home. However, to Rosie's eyes, this place looks like something you'd see in a film.

'We're here.' Theo glances up from his phone, quickly silencing it. 'What do you think?'

'It's not exactly how you described it,' she says, her pulse quickening.

Most of her childhood holidays were on the west coast of England in a budget holiday park, playing solitaire as rain pounded the roof of their mobile home and her parents bickered in the cramped master bedroom. In later years, she was dragged away by girlfriends to cheap sunny resorts full of lairy men and lurid shots of booze. She's never been anywhere like this.

Theo's brief description of where they would be staying rushes to her mind. *It's like a hundred years old. Not exactly modern. But it's homely.*

Homely is not a word she would use to describe this enormous farmhouse. The driveway alone would fit ten cars, easily. There is another building further to the right, of a similar age but half the size. Well-maintained gardens hug the main house from all sides, the lush green grass stretching as far as she can see. There's not a neighbour in sight.

'There must be like twenty bedrooms.'

Theo laughs. 'No, there's only six. The rooms are large to keep it cool; there's no air-con but there are loads of fans. Like I said, it needs updating.'

A short, pear-shaped woman in her early sixties bustles out of the open door. She waves her arms at the driver as if guiding a jet to land.

'There's Mum.' Theo smiles, raising a hand. 'Park anywhere near those big planters, mate.'

Rosie takes in the bright, welcoming smile of Marianne, his mother, and the spike in anxiety simmers a little. She looks approachable and friendly.

Marianne turns, calling something to someone inside the house. A tall, rakish man with a neat white beard stoops slightly through the dark doorway and emerges into the sunlight.

'Gerry, my stepdad.' Theo shifts in his seat. 'Let's hope he's in holiday mode.'

Gerry Fraser. A retired photographer, and, according to Theo, 'a bit of an arse'.

'No sign of Luke yet . . .' Theo peers around.

It's not just Theo's mum and stepdad to impress. She needs to get his brother and his sister-in-law on her side this fortnight, too. No pressure. It will be good to meet the mysterious Luke. Theo rarely talked about him, despite her attempts to find out more about his older brother. At least she's more confident about winning their children over. The gifts she bought them should help.

The taxi stops and the driver jabs at the electronic display showing the cost of the fare.

Theo leans forward to pull the right euro notes out of his wallet. 'Keep the change.'

The driver's face doesn't break from the permanent scowl he's worn all journey.

There's a knock on the car window next to Theo, making Rosie jump. Marianne waves from the other side of the glass and Rosie plasters on her brightest, widest smile.

'Here we go. Good luck.' Theo leans to give Rosie a reassuring kiss on the cheek before opening his door. High-pitched shrieks fill the space he's left behind.

Rosie swallows and wipes her sweaty palms against her thighs. She steps out into the dry heat before she can overthink those final words.

The taxi driver pops open the boot and throws their cases to the ground. He clears his throat and steps closer. The smell of stale nicotine hits her.

'*Stai attento.*' His voice is raspy. His weathered brow is knotted in concern.

'Sorry, I don't speak Itali—' she starts to explain before realising that he's gesturing to something.

He's glaring at the high brick walls that edge around the house. Or, more precisely, at the many CCTV cameras dotted about. A shiver rolls across her.

'*Stai attento*,' he repeats, quieter this time.

Before she can ask him what he means he burrows his head out of view and leaps into the front seat. He races up the driveway, skidding over the gravel, churning up a cloud of dust in his wake.

What the hell?

Rosie tucks her hair behind her ears and presses her crumpled sun hat further down on her head, praying that her cheeks aren't too flushed.

'Ah, and this vision in pink must be the famous Rosa. *Ciao bella*!' Marianne wraps her arms around Rosie. She smells of lemons and something sweet and buttery. Rosie is aware of her own less-than-fresh smell and the clammy, recycled air of the aeroplane coating her skin.

'Rosie,' she politely corrects her, unsure if that 'vision in pink' was a compliment or not.

A hand flies to Marianne's mouth at her error. 'Sorry, Rosie.'

Theo shakes his head at his mother but there is a broad smile on his face.

Rosie can instantly see the similarities between the pair of them. They both have the same big, expressive brown eyes and neat chin. At first glance, she thought Theo's mum was more of a homebody but closer up Rosie can sense the money. Marianne's shoulder-length blonde hair looks like it's had an expensive blow-dry and her polished nails suggest a recent manicure. Delicate gold bracelets studded with clear diamonds dance on her tanned wrists as she waves her arms, punctuating every sentence with a soft chime. The oatmeal linen shift dress hugs her curves, the neckline open to reveal a chunky gold necklace with two gold stars; one is engraved with an 'L' and the other with a 'T'.

'How was your flight? Have you eaten? Was the traffic ok?' Rosie tries to follow Marianne's continuous barrage of questions. She doesn't take a breath. Is she also nervous? The thought makes her feel a little better. 'Luke and Fenna and the babies haven't arrived yet. They should be here soon. Luke's my big boy,' she says for Rosie's benefit. 'His wife, Fenna, is half Italian, so you never know when they'll turn up. She follows her own schedule.' She gives a slight eye roll and claps her hands. 'I can't wait to have my boys back together. We're going to have the best time.'

During this conversation, Gerry has joined them. Rosie glances over to see Theo saying hello. Gerry looks like a tourist in knee-length khaki shorts, a shirt covered with lime green pineapples and a camera with a worn leather strap draped around his neck. His dark, square sunglasses hide his eyes. The older man jerks out a stiff, robotic arm and vigorously shakes Theo's hand for a painfully long couple of seconds. Neither meets the other's gaze.

'You've lost too much weight.' Marianne clasps a hand against Theo's face. 'I'll be getting Julietta to fatten you up, mark my words.' She steers Theo into the house, leaving Rosie and Gerry alone.

'I'm Gerry.' He offers a hand. It's cool and bony with a firm, authoritative grip. 'Welcome to the family.'

4

ROSIE – DAY 1

The last half an hour has been spent traipsing after Gerry as he led the 'unofficial' tour of the house for Rosie's benefit.

'Glad to see Gerry's his usual chirpy self,' Theo says to Rosie as they walk down a corridor, just the two of them.

Villa Speranza is breathtaking. Every high-ceilinged room oozes warmth, style, and personality. And money.

Theo puts his hands in his pockets to find a key. 'Luke says Gerry likes to wear those bright shirts to overcompensate for his lack of personality . . . That's one thing I agree with him on.'

'He is passionate about this place,' she replies, tactfully. There's something about his stepdad's rigid body language and tight smile that does little to calm Rosie's nerves.

'It's best not to encourage him or else you'll be listening to him drawling on for days.'

Rosie had clocked Theo yawning as Gerry revealed the historical features of the restored fifteenth-century farmhouse. He must have heard the same story countless times. Marianne had to take a phone call so apologised for missing the tour. Before she went she hugged Rosie and thanked her for the chocolates. She told her they were her favourites. Rosie appreciated the compliment, but there was something in Marianne's eyes that made her question if she was telling the truth.

'This house is amazing, I'm genuinely interested,' she says as they move past a textured oil painting of a washed-up ship hanging from a picture rail that runs the length of the honey-coloured corridor.

'I thought you were doing it to be polite.' Theo laughs.

'No.' She blushes. 'There's clearly so much history to this place and he was keen to share it with us.'

Maybe she went OTT with the questions. But Gerry didn't seem like he minded.

You never get a second chance to make a first impression.

'I find it annoying how he acts like he put every brick here when the truth is it's not even his home. Mum bought it with Dad back in the early nineties and it'll be left in a trust for me and Luke when she dies. Gerry won't get a look in. We may all be Frasers in name but that's it.'

Rosie remembers Theo telling her about Gerry taking her mum's surname when they got married in the early noughties. Marianne refused to give up her identity. Even before meeting her, Rosie understood Marianne Fraser to be a woman who knows her own mind.

They stop outside a closed wooden door.

'There was one thing I didn't ask . . . What's with all the security?'

'Huh?' Theo struggles with the key in the lock.

Some of the rooms downstairs were locked too. One stands out in her mind. Down the hallway, leading off the vast farmhouse-style kitchen, was a door with a padlock and thick metal chain. When she'd asked Gerry what was behind it, she was sure she'd seen a flicker of something pass his eyes.

'That leads to the basement,' Gerry had answered after a beat of hesitation. 'The laundry rooms and larders and other boring places like that. The gardener stores his tools down there. It's locked so Alba won't accidentally wander in.'

Rosie watches Theo struggle with the lock. She remembers the CCTV cameras watching the property, and the way the taxi driver had looked at her. What was he trying to tell her?

She takes a breath. 'I noticed the cameras outside. They look pretty high-tech.'

'Gerry's paranoid about someone breaking in when the house is empty. It's over the top if you ask me.' He mutters under his breath at the stiff lock. 'Mum likes things to stay as they are, which means never updating these old heavy doors.'

She's about to ask if he needs help when there is a loud click. It echoes.

'And this is where we'll be staying.' Theo smiles, pushing open the door.

Bright sunlight makes her blink. A king-size bed stands in the centre of the enormous room, lit from the wide windows. The duvet cover is a pale forget-me-not spring blue. Oversized voile drapes hang from a wooden rail, the ends trailing into a sheer puddle. The white-washed stone walls are rustic. There is a wooden chest of drawers underneath an oval mirror. The décor is simple but full of Mediterranean charm.

There's a shelf with a collection of photographs. She's drawn to one of Theo with some famous footballer taken when he was a young teenager. Next to it is a framed certificate from when he took part in a football competition in 2010, and a polished silver trophy.

He looks embarrassed and goes to turn the frames over. 'I didn't know Mum still had these.'

'No, don't. You look so young.' Rosie pulls his hand away.

'I was sixteen and thought I knew everything . . .' he says with a poignant sigh. 'Seeing them reminds me of what I could have achieved. I was this close to making it, getting signed to a professional club.' He pinches his fingers together.

She can't imagine him in that world.

'You've never told me that before. What happened?'

He takes one last look at the shelf. 'Life.'

Rosie steps towards the large oak wardrobe. It has fancy curved handles and looks about a hundred years old. The doors creak with age as she opens them.

'Julietta will have done it,' Theo says, watching her shake her head in awe.

All of her clothes are hanging neatly from hangers, colour-coordinated.

'Julietta?'

'She's worked here for years. You can't leave anything lying around for a second without her tidying it up.'

He says it like it's a bad thing.

'You didn't tell me about the place having staff,' Rosie says.

'You didn't ask.' He laughs. 'It's not a big deal, baby. It sounds grander than it is.'

Maybe not to him.

She moves towards the open window, breathing in the fresh summer air. The land around the house goes on for miles. The neighbours, some distance away, are hidden behind tall trees. It's a lot more remote than she'd pictured. Rosie had hoped that once she'd arrived and completed the initial introductions she would start to feel less on edge. If anything, she is even more anxious.

'There's Julietta, who's the chief housekeeper.' Theo comes and stands behind her, pressing gently against her. 'There's kitchen staff to wash the pots, local teenagers usually, and the groundskeeper, Paulo.'

Rosie's gaze follows to where he's pointing. An older man dressed in green has his back to them, bent over an iron trough full of flowers.

'And all this land belongs to this house?' Rosie asks.

'Yeah. You can't see the pool from here, but it's pretty nice.'

There's a patchwork of low bushes that separate the olive grove and the orchard, individual smaller gardens with ornate stone statues dotted in between. Her eye lands on one that looks out of place, full of wildflowers and long, stringy grass. It's a contrast to the manicured lawns of the others.

Theo follows her gaze. 'That's Mum trying to save the planet or something. Gerry hates that it's such a mess; ruins the aesthetic, apparently,' he says, deadpan. 'It's best not to go there.'

She takes one final look at the view, unsure what to say, before Theo pulls the drapes shut and tugs on her waist.

'Come here.' He leads her towards the bed. She knows what's on his mind.

'No! I need a shower. I'm gross.'

'Not to me you're not.' He gives her a look that melts her heart. 'Mum and Gerry are heading out. I told them we were having a nap. The others haven't arrived yet. We've got loads of time before dinner . . .'

***

Half an hour later, having been unable to resist his advances, she walks into the ensuite to have a shower and freshen up for dinner. The contents of her make-up bag are displayed like a counter in a department hall. Everything is laid out in size order, silver lids glinting under the spotlights. It's a little unnerving to think of a stranger going through her things. Thankfully she didn't pack any sex toys. A rush of heat washes over her at the thought.

She takes her mind off it by connecting to the Wi-Fi and opening her messages. The WhatsApp she sent her mum at the airport remains unread.

'Everything ok?' Theo asks.

'Fine,' she replies, minimising the app.

She goes to unpack her carry-on rucksack and frowns. *Where is everything?*

'If you're looking for your passport that'll be in the safe.' He shrugs, eyes back on his phone screen, playing snippets of tinny pop music she's heard on TikTok.

'The safe?'

'Yeah. Gerry has this thing about making sure all the valuables are locked away.'

She clenches her jaw at her things being rifled through, decisions made on her behalf.

She realises what he's said. *Locked away.* Another security precaution. What is there to be scared of?

He must see the look on Rosie's face, picking up on her apprehension.

'Don't worry. He's being overly cautious. Nothing ever happens around here. I promise.'

5

ROSIE – DAY 1

Rosie's flip-flops slap across the polished Italian tiles in the dining room. She hovers behind the patio doors, watching the family through the glass, drawing up the courage to join them on the large terrace. The festoon lights that trail across a long wooden table sway in the evening breeze. A silver tray is covered with small bowls of nuts, plump black olives, and crisp breadsticks. Slender flutes of bubbles are topped with thinly sliced strawberries hanging over the edge of the glass. Aperitivo. Everyone is outside apart from her.

They are all at ease and relaxed. Rosie is not.

Marianne is rocking a pushchair; the thick rubber tyres gently move back and forth over the terracotta tiles. A little girl – who looks about three – sits on Gerry's knee entranced by an iPad. They must be Theo's niece and nephew.

His sister-in-law, Fenna, is beautiful. Her dark brown hair is braided in a long, intricate plait that falls over her slender shoulder. She's wearing a floor-length midnight blue skirt, a relaxed cotton vest top, and a cream belt that cinches in her waist. Rosie has seen some of her modelling shots on Instagram, and considering she's recently had a baby she looks fantastic.

Theo and Luke are sitting on an outdoor rattan sofa drinking pints. Luke has one leg cocked over the other, flashing a sockless ankle in his tan deck shoes. According to Theo, Luke looks most like their father who died when the boys were young. He has much darker features compared to Theo and Marianne's light complexion. His deep, brooding eyes and sharp, angular face shape is less welcoming than his relatives. He throws back his head and chucks a handful of nuts into his open mouth.

It's all convivial and easy.

Rosie steels herself.

Get out there and be yourself.

Her stomach growls with hunger. She wishes she could get Theo's attention so he would walk over to her. He'd asked if she wanted him to wait with her whilst she finished getting ready, but she told him she'd be ok, wanting to take five minutes alone to psych herself up.

She'd left their bedroom in a fluster, unsure if she was supposed to lock the door behind her. But as Theo didn't leave a key, she left it open. Hopefully she won't get in trouble for not knowing 'the rules'. She has her phone on her and her other valuables are locked in the safe – well, all of them except her notebook, which she'd slipped in between the pages of a magazine. Julietta hadn't tidied that away at least.

A burst of laughter from outside pulls her attention. They will be wondering where she is. Rosie takes a deep breath and plasters on a bright smile. She pushes the patio door but it's stiff and refuses to budge. For a horrifying split second, she panics that she's broken it, but then the wood gives and a loud creak heralds her arrival.

They all turn to face her.

Rosie wipes her sweaty palms against one another. Luke lets out a snigger from the side, and Fenna shushes him.

'Ah, here she is! Fenna, Luke, this is Theo's girlfriend – Rosie,' Marianne says with a wide smile, spreading her arm out as if heralding the main act.

Heat rushes to Rosie's cheeks. She's not used to being in the spotlight like this. She knocks into a side table. The glasses wobble dangerously.

'Hi.' She's unsure whether to go and hug them or shake their hands. She feebly lifts her left arm and gives a pathetic wave.

'Hello, I'm Fenna, Theo's sister-in-law.' Fenna steps forward and gives her a light kiss on both cheeks. Rosie isn't expecting a double kiss so awkwardly bumps her nose to Fenna's cheek.

'Oh, gosh, sorry.'

'She's half Italian, that's their way. I'm Luke.' He leans forward with a polite handshake. His aftershave smells delicious and expensive.

'Hi, nice to meet you both.' Rosie smiles.

Marianne bursts with pride as she introduces her grandchildren. Rosie allows herself a moment to relax. They are both adorable.

'Here.' Theo hands her a cold glass of Prosecco from the rattan coffee table once Marianne has finished. 'You look beautiful by the way.'

She feels underdressed in her jean shorts and plain white cotton t-shirt but she appreciates his compliment and nestles into him. The bubbles pop up her nose when she takes a sip. It's not a great idea to drink but she's craving something to take the edge off.

'So, Rosie, I hear you were given Gerry's famous tour?' Luke says. 'You should get a badge. "I went on the tour of *Villa Speranza* and survived".'

Marianne throws him a look.

'Come on, you know I'm teasing.' Luke grins. He's got the same broad smile as Marianne. Dazzling teeth. Rosie tries to find similarities in the brothers' appearances but there's not many. 'I'm sure Gerry wowed her with his facts.'

'It was a pleasure,' Gerry replies, not picking up on Luke's tone. 'Rosie was asking lots of great questions. She kept me on my toes.'

'Your house is amazing,' Rosie says to Marianne and Gerry.

'Thank you, darling. It was a project. A labour of love.' Marianne turns to face the building as if greeting an old friend. The up-lighters throw a golden glow against the chunky Italian stone. 'I'm sure Gerry would love to show you his photos. You'll be able to see all the work we've done on this place over the years. We've got so many photo albums in the library here. I must dig them out.'

The fact they have a library blows her mind. There's also a drawing room with a piano and an ornate chess-set, laid out as if someone paused mid-game. This is a world away from what she's used to.

'I'd love that. Now?'

Everyone laughs and she realises how eager she sounds. Her cheeks flush.

'There's plenty of time whilst we're here, darling.' Marianne smiles fondly. 'I have to say, it's refreshing for one of my boys' girlfriends to take an interest. Most of the others were empty up here.' She taps her head.

'Charming.' Fenna sniffs.

'I don't mean you, dear. We all know that not all models are airheads.' Marianne laughs but Fenna doesn't crack a smile. 'Have you been to Tuscany before, Rosie?'

Theo puts a warm arm around Rosie's shoulders. 'This is her first time to Italy.'

They look at her with pitying glances.

An uncultured slug in their midst. Her northern accent sets her out as different from everyone here with their soft, southern-clipped consonants. Theo's 'posh boy' tones were what caught her attention when they first met. He could be the main British character in any American movie. She finds the way he pronounces certain words endearing, but now the shoe is on the other foot and she's the one who stands out.

Gerry looks as if Theo told him Rosie has never drunk water before.

'Oh, lucky you. You're going to love it here; we might be biased but Tuscany is the best part of the country. It's so peaceful. And the light. It's wonderfully inspiring.' Marianne nods to her husband. 'Gerry photographs the landscape and I used to paint it.'

'Theo said that you're an artist?' Rosie asks, hoping her question sounds innocent.

To look at her this evening, in her freshwater pearls and pashmina, she doesn't have the air of a bohemian artist, but Rosie knows exactly who Marianne Fraser is. She's read articles in *The Times* about her influence in the art world. Her paintings are worth thousands of pounds. Marianne is a celebrity in her own right. Or at least she was. She hasn't exhibited anything for the past fifteen years. She never gave a reason for her sudden departure.

'Gerry used to own a gallery in Soho many moons ago. It's where we met. He was in charge of my exhibition,' Marianne explains.

'Ah yes. The Dursak Gallery; it's on Bold Street, around the corner from the big Starbucks. Easy to find. It's a beautiful space. The good old days of the Soho set. They wrote a book about us, you know – *The Light Within*,' Gerry says, sounding equally proud and nostalgic. 'Elton John bought one of your pieces at the publisher's launch, didn't he? Told us he hung it in one of his guest bedrooms.'

Luke lets out a dramatically loud yawn, patting his open mouth.

'You must miss it? Painting I mean,' Rosie asks Marianne.

'No.'

There's a painful beat when nobody talks. Has she said something wrong?

Marianne picks up her glass, her bracelets jangling on her thin wrist and takes a long, slow sip. 'I retired a long time ago.'

'I wish you would pick up a paintbrush,' Luke pipes up, breaking the strange tension. 'We all know how much you could sell your art for.'

'Anyway, enough about me,' Marianne forces a smile, ignoring her son. 'You must try the sun-dried tomato tapenade. It's from Monterchi. Julietta picked it up at the market this morning. Sadly, the one in Laprezia has finally closed as there are simply not enough customers. It was heading that way for a long while but the locals didn't want to admit defeat.'

'Another nail in the coffin for this place,' Gerry says wistfully. 'Such a shame and all because of that girl.'

'Who?' Rosie asks Fenna. She nibbles a spindly, salty breadstick, dropping fine confetti-like crumbs on her lap.

'Danielle Dixon,' Fenna leans across and whispers, darting her eyes to her mother-in-law. 'Bit of advice, don't let her hear you say that name.'

Rosie is about to ask her why when a clay dish of olives is passed around. She politely takes one, despite being hungry enough to eat the whole bowl.

'What are you two whispering about?' Marianne asks, dabbing a napkin to her mouth.

Fenna shifts in her chair. Her cheeks redden. 'Nothing.'

'You were talking about something.' Marianne flashes her perfect teeth. 'Go on. There's no secrets here.'

Rosie glances at Theo but he's not listening to this conversation. She tries to decipher what the women are saying with their eyes.

Fenna takes a deep breath. 'Rosie was asking about Danielle.'

At the sound of the name, the others stop their conversation and turn to face her. She immediately feels like she's done something wrong, without realising.

'I wasn't. I mean, well, I was. I wondered who you were talking about and—' She starts, coughing on the olive.

Theo rubs a reassuring hand across her shoulder and passes her a cold glass of mineral water. Heat flames across her face.

'Theo's not told you? Well no, I suppose he wouldn't. It's not much of a selling point for the town,' Gerry says, over Rosie's splutters. 'There was a foreign exchange between an all-girls school from Surrey and a high school not far from here. During the trip, a British student called Danielle went missing. She was maybe sixteen or so, and—'

'No. She was younger than that,' Luke interrupts.

'Not by much. Fifteen perhaps? Yes, that's it. She was a year younger than you, Theo, if I remember rightly,' Gerry replies. 'Anyway, it's the fifteenth anniversary of her disappearance this week. They're still hoping that people might remember something. Clutching at straws if you ask me; everyone knows she's dead.'

Marianne dabs her napkin at the sides of her mouth. 'Last week, an Italian TV news programme filmed a reenactment by the lake, which was terribly upsetting.'

Gerry nods. 'They still think her body might be in there. That's where a Polaroid camera and a denim jacket that belonged to Danielle were discovered.' He adds for Rosie's benefit, 'Sadly, that's the only trace of her.'

'Is that the same lake where the birds vanished?' Rosie asks. 'Something to do with parakeets?'

'Yep. *Lago Parrocchetto*. People say the birds left because of Danielle,' Luke whispers in a ghoulish tone.

Rosie grips her wine glass.

'Ignore him.' Gerry rolls his eyes. 'There's a lot of local superstition as to why the birds chose a different nesting place. Not everyone listens to facts about climate change, instead believing what they want to believe.'

Luke leans back in his chair, a toothpick angled in his mouth.

'But they're still looking for her?' Theo asks.

Marianne takes a deep breath. She straightens, brushing her hair from her face. 'Do we have to talk about this now?'

'The strange thing about the Danielle Dixon case is that—' Gerry starts.

'Let's leave it there, darling.' Marianne pats Gerry's hand firmly. 'It's not exactly dinner party conversation.'

Gerry's response is cut off by the sound of glass cracking.

Rosie looks down.

The stem of her wine glass has broken in two.

6

FENNA – DAY 1

'Oh gosh. Careful, darling,' Marianne leaps to her feet, calling to Julietta for a cloth.

Red wine slowly drips onto the ground and resembles a crime scene. Rosie comments on how she doesn't know her own strength, followed by a nervous laugh.

It's not long before the mess is cleaned up and the atmosphere returns to normal. The conversation moves on. Fenna flicks her eyes to the new girl. Her broken glass was replaced and refilled. It's like it never happened.

A chorus of excitable Italian flows over the terrace and breaks the tension.

Fenna is relieved to see Julietta jogging over, her neat, gold-rimmed glasses held on a metal chain bouncing upon her ample chest, tears in her eyes, arms wide open. There is a flurry of kisses and fast-flowing Italian.

'It's so lovely to see you.'

The older woman stands back, a beaming smile on her rosy cheeks. She reaches out to stroke Alba's hair, shaking her head with an adoring look. In her mid-fifties, she is a substitute *nonna* to Fenna's children.

'Yes, she's growing up,' Fenna replies.

Marianne and Gerry have made several remarks about how rude it is when Fenna speaks to the staff in Italian, saying they feel excluded. But it is unnatural for her to be talking to an Italian in English.

She's not talking about them.

Not now, at least.

Marianne clears her throat. 'Rosie, this is Julietta. She's worked here almost twenty years. A valued member of *Villa Speranza*.'

'*Benvenuta*. Welcome!' Julietta takes both of Rosie's hands and gives them a shake. 'I'm so happy to see the family all together. It's been a long time.'

'Too long.' Marianne nods wistfully.

Another woman emerges from Julietta's shadow.

'Oh and this is Carla, she started a few months ago. Julietta has done a wonderful job training her,' Marianne tells the table. 'I think only Luke has met her before?'

Luke looks up from his phone screen and nods hello to the young woman. She flutters her long feathery lashes and lets out a light giggle.

'*Buonasera*.' Carla must be in her mid-twenties. She's dressed in a dove grey tabard and black skinny-fit trousers. She looks like a puff of air will blow her away, a contrast to Julietta's broad shoulders.

'*Mamma mia*. What a beauty,' Julietta says, beaming at Raffi in his pushchair.

Carla strokes Raffi's cheek with a pointed fingernail, the tips painted a glossy red. Their coos and exclamations swirl over Fenna. Blood rushes in her head at how easy it would be for Carla to accidentally scratch him. One millisecond is all it would take. After a minute or so, the women walk away to get on with their work. Fenna lets out the breath she was holding.

'Theo, darling, did I hear you say you were running a marathon? Don't let me forget to sponsor you. Ask Richard and Evelyn too. They're also around this week and next. They would love to see you boys.' Marianne turns to Rosie. 'They've been dear friends for so long and are wonderful company.'

'And they're stinking rich,' Luke pipes up.

'Luke, that's not very polite of you, but yes, they aren't short of a few bob. They don't have children themselves; missed the boat as it were. See, money can't buy you everything.'

Luke leans in closer. His breath smells of dry-roasted peanuts. 'But it can buy you a super yacht and a villa in Monaco.'

Fenna rolls her eyes at her husband's obsession with money.

'You're going to love them,' Marianne says.

'I can't wait to meet them.' Rosie smiles.

Carla silently moves around them and lights the candles. The warm evening air is perfumed and sweet from the bougainvillaea trailing over their heads. Raffi is in his pushchair, entranced by the shadows cast from the delicate flowers climbing the pergola. Occasionally there's a waft of luscious mint and rosemary coming from the tall clay planters. Birds and crickets hum from the nearby fields. Every time Fenna's here she remembers why she loves it so much. The solitude, the nature, the chance to take a full lungful of fresh air.

Nothing like their life in London.

The view from the terrace is like a painting, even in the

fading daylight. Rolling hills and skinny cypress trees, farmers' olive groves and churned earth crisscross the land. It's breathtaking.

She's on a high from the conversation she'd had with Luke earlier. Landing back in Italy felt like a familiar hug. This is where she belongs. She misses her Italian roots, the language, the weather, the food, and the lifestyle. She wants her children to have the childhood she had. London was the place to be in her twenties, and she doesn't regret it – it's where she met Luke after all – but now, as a wife and mother, things have changed. She doesn't want to be squashed on the Tube, rushing to casting calls, being judged, measured, dismissed. How many more years does she have left in her anyway? Whenever she glances in the mirror she sees another fine line that wasn't there the day before.

She pictures them at *Villa Speranza*, running holistic retreats; Luke's new business means he can work from anywhere, and she can learn to teach yoga. The house technically belongs to Marianne, but will eventually go to Luke and Theo. She wonders how much they would need to pay Theo for his share and whether Marianne would go for the idea of them taking ownership early.

'I'm serious. We could make this dream come true. Not many couples have this chance to start a new adventure,' she'd reminded him.

Luke huffed. 'Fen, we've got enough on our plate.'

'Think about it whilst we're here, please. Maybe talk to Theo and your mum about it? It would be good for us, for our marriage,' Fenna said quickly, crossing her fingers.

He promised he would. It might not be a firm yes but it was

a start. A zip of adrenaline flies through her. For the first time in ages, she is hopeful that she might make this dream come true.

She allows herself a moment to breathe it in. Her shoulders drop a fraction. The only cloud that hangs over this stunning place is Danielle Dixon. Fenna wondered how long it would be until someone mentioned the schoolgirl's name. As a teen herself at the time, Fenna remembers the story making the news when she disappeared. The nation was gripped by the many theories of what might have happened to her. But after a while, and with no updates, the news agenda moved on and so did the rest of the world. She didn't realise they were still actively trying to find her. People usually move on. People usually forget.

Fifteen years is a long time to be searching.

7

FENNA – DAY 1

Following a call for dinner, the family move from the comfy sofas to the long outdoor dining table. It is dressed as if styled by a professional for a magazine shoot. Fenna has told Julietta many times that her tablescape talents are wasted but she chuckles and ignores the compliment. Matching sage-coloured vintage porcelain sits on rustic rattan placemats, adorned with linen napkins in antique jewelled napkin rings. An impressive centrepiece of seasonal foliage and velvet olive leaves is lit by individual tealights. Italian jazz music plays from an outdoor speaker and fairy lights twinkle.

'Fen, when are you back to work?' Gerry asks with his mouth full. A grain of rice flicks out and gets stuck in his beard.

'I'm not sure.'

The truth is, she's at a loss with her job. Her agency has said they would put her forward for 'mum brands' until she lost the baby weight, but even the thought of attending a casting makes her panic. Then again, a reason to leave the house, to go to the toilet alone and have someone else making her a cup of tea – that she can drink while it's still hot – sounds like heaven.

'Have you picked up many hobbies whilst you're on your nice break from work?' Gerry asks.

'Hobbies?' Fenna repeats to make sure she's heard him right.

She's been awake for two months solid whilst taking care of a toddler and a newborn. Her body is broken.

'Erm no. No time for *hobbies* . . .' She jabs her fork into her chicken breast. Garlic sauce oozes around her plate.

'I couldn't bear to leave my boys. I didn't officially get back to the studio until they were well into primary school,' Marianne clucks, adding reluctantly, 'but I suppose every mother is different.'

Fenna nods to her mouth full of food as if that's the reason she can't answer.

'And Luke, how about you?' Gerry asks, wiping the piece of food from his beard with his finger before examining it and eating it. 'The new business going well?'

Luke sits back in his chair, the glow from the uplighter behind his head casting a halo around his hair. 'Yeah, fantastic, thanks.'

She watches him lie so effortlessly, taken aback by how convincing he comes across. Only she knows how tough it's been with the business is in its infancy. She's tried her best to support his decision to go freelance but they've never argued about money so much as they have recently.

'The food was delicious, thank you,' Rosie says politely, as Carla passes by to clear her plate. It is still half-full. Perhaps it's nerves.

She's pretty, very English rose. Her pale complexion will surely struggle in the heat. Her mid-length light brown hair is in a neat half-up-half-down style and she has big, expressive eyes, like one of Alba's dolls.

Marianne's dig about intelligence didn't pass Fenna by. She's heard it all before. The airhead model. Beauty, not brains. People underestimate her all the time; she just wishes she wasn't related to them.

Based on tonight's initial impression, Rosie seems harmless. A little jittery but that must be the pressure of meeting her boyfriend's family. Theo is sitting beside her, their hands clasped, skin velcroed together. He looks besotted. Fenna smiles at the memory of her and Luke like that. Funny how quickly that phase can fade.

'You're near York, aren't you?' Fenna asks Theo and Rosie.

'Yep, not too far.' Rosie fidgets as she speaks. She has gone quiet since breaking her glass. Everyone told her it was fine, it wasn't the family crystal, but she must be embarrassed.

'Hopefully we'll be moving in together soon,' Theo says with a bright smile. 'Did I mention my promotion, Mum?'

Theo tells them all about his new role as a sports therapist for disadvantaged teenagers, and the podcast he's launching soon. They are chalk and cheese. Luke is Mr Corporate whereas Theo wants to help others.

'Ugh,' Luke groans loudly. 'Surely the world doesn't need any more podcasts.'

Theo kindly picks up a teddy that Alba has knocked to the floor. 'Yep, another one,' he replies, not rising to the bait.

'How did it go when your parents first met Theo?' Fenna asks, changing the subject.

'My dad's not with us anymore,' Rosie says sadly.

'Oh, I'm sorry to hear that.'

'Thank you. It was a long time ago . . .' She mouths the word 'cancer'.

Rosie and Theo have got that shared experience. Luke barely talks about his dad. He died when the boys were young. Fenna's tried to get him to open up but it is very much a closed-off subject. Uncle Richard, who isn't officially an uncle, had been more of a father figure during the boys' adolescence than Luke lets on. Perhaps that's why she often gets the sense that Gerry feels second best.

'And Theo hasn't met my mum yet.'

Theo's planning to move to live with her. Yet he's not met her mum? Fenna's face must have given away how confusing it sounds.

'She's abroad. She works on a cruise ship so it's tricky trying to pin her down to Facetime and stuff,' Rosie adds quickly. Her knee dances up and down. Theo moves his hand to calm the jittering leg.

'I hope we'll get to meet her soon. So, tell us about how you two met? Theo is terrible at sharing the details,' Marianne encourages.

Rosie smiles and looks over at Theo affectionately. 'It's not an understatement to say that he saved me from the world's worst Tinder date. I'd travelled to London to meet this guy, who was nothing like his picture—'

Theo winces. 'She was catfished.'

'Big style.' Rosie picks up her glass. Fenna notices the slight tremble in her hand. 'I was drowning my sorrows in a pub in Soho when Theo walked in. He heard my accent and we got chatting.'

'We realised we work twenty, minutes from each other. The rest is history.' Theo beams.

'Well, you must be doing something right as Theo's never

brought a girlfriend to *Villa Speranza* before,' Fenna says. No wonder the poor girl looks like a rabbit in the headlights, this is clearly a big deal for both of them.

'I feel very lucky. This holiday came at the right time.' Rosie smiles.

Luke burps. Fenna elbows him, embarrassed on his behalf. 'Whoops, excuse me. Compliments to the chef. Dinner was delicious,' Luke says. 'Much better than the food last time I was here.'

'I'm surprised you can remember what you ate then,' Gerry sniffs. 'You know the neighbours are still cross about it?'

'It wasn't my fault.' Luke rolls his eyes. 'Jonno can't handle his drink.'

'Well Jonno's still not paid for the damage,' Gerry huffs.

'What happened?' Theo asks.

Fenna has no idea what they're talking about.

'Nothing. Drop it,' Luke says, pouring himself another glass of wine.

Fenna grits her teeth, wanting someone to tell her what's going on. Of course she knew that Luke had come here with a few mates for a lads' weekend at the start of May, but he'd said it was pretty low-key, something about how they all couldn't party like they used to. She'd not given it a second thought at the time but clearly she's been kept in the dark.

'Go on . . .' Theo smirks.

Luke crosses his arms. 'Jonno got pissed and set off fireworks, which went into the neighbour's land. The police were called. It was all blown out of proportion and everything was fixed and repaired like new.'

Fenna stares at her husband. Why didn't he tell her this?

'Boys will be boys,' Marianne clucks. 'Could you turn that down please, darling,' she asks Alba who lets out an excitable giggle at whatever Bluey is doing on her tablet.

Alba ignores her grandma's request.

'Tomorrow I will ask Julietta to give the children an earlier dinner. It's far too late for Alba to be staying up at her age.'

'Oh? It's only eight o'clock,' Fenna says. She knows she should try and wrestle the screen from her daughter but she is enjoying the peace.

'Exactly. It must be her bedtime soon? Routine is key at this age.'

She stares at her husband, waiting for him to chip in. He is too busy examining the wine label to pick up on his mother's passive-aggressive tone.

'It's their holiday too,' Fenna replies as politely as she can despite the knot of irritation forming in her stomach.

Fenna knows that her style of parenting is different to Marianne's, who believes children should be seen and heard at times when it suits her. Fenna wants her children to have the childhood she did – long, balmy nights, being part of the dinner table conversation, involved in family time, not rushed to bed and forced to stay out of the way. Her relaxed 'European' views are a bone of contention.

'If you want her to sit with the grown-ups, it might be an idea to work on her table manners?'

Fenna wants to scream that Alba is only three. How impeccable does she expect her grand-daughter to be? *It's the first night. Bite your tongue.* Every time Marianne interferes with her parenting it makes Fenna feel like she's failing. She takes a deep breath and nods. She needs to keep the peace. For now.

8

ROSIE – DAY 2

Rosie self-consciously tugs her cotton kimono cover-up across her stomach and follows Theo to the swimming pool. Her tropical leaf print swimming costume is a little more snug than she'd like. She wished she'd skipped dessert last night but Julietta had kept generously adding more *torta della nonna*, a vanilla and lemon-filled tart topped with toasted Tuscan pinenuts, to her plate and she couldn't resist.

The pool is a little way from the main house, down a stone path, littered with fallen pinecones from the tall firs above. She grips onto a wooden railing when she reaches the uneven steps.

'So, you survived your first night,' Theo says, ahead of her. 'Thirteen more to get through.'

'It is a test?' She laughs.

'No. Not a test. Although spending time with grumpy Gerry can be an ordeal, but everyone else is alright. Luke has mellowed out since I last saw him . . .'

Rosie remembers Fenna side-eye Luke as he uncorked another

bottle of Italian red at dinner, that might have something to do with it.

'. . . Fenna had better watch out.'

'Hmm?'

'I mean she needs to be careful. I think my mum has a new favourite.' He nudges her gently.

Rosie laughs. She had picked up on a hint of friction between the two women. In fact, there seemed to be a lot of things going unsaid at the dinner table last night, but she hadn't had a chance to ask Theo about any of it. The travelling had caught up with both of them as they collapsed into bed after dinner and he was soon fast asleep. Along with the pent-up nerves she should have been equally wiped out, but she barely slept. Her head buzzed with names and details, trying to build a picture of this family. The locks and the cameras and the disappearance of that schoolgirl spun through her mind.

There were so many questions she wanted to ask.

It's the first night. There will be plenty of time.

There is a happy shriek of a child and a splash of water. A few more steps past a wall of leafy bamboo and suddenly they are greeted with a picture-perfect vista.

The swimming pool is set against the backdrop of rolling hills that go on for miles. A lone stone church sits in the distance. Uninterrupted shades of green fields are punctuated with skinny, pointed, cypress trees. Clusters of olive groves follow the curves of the hillside. It doesn't look real. She's so absorbed by the breathtaking view that she doesn't hear Alba calling her name.

The little girl's face lights up seeing them. She's bobbing on the surface of the turquoise water in a unicorn inflatable.

'Here they come, the lovebirds.' Luke heaves himself out of the water and onto the pool's edge. 'You missed breakfast. Alba's been waiting for you to get out of bed and play with her.'

Rosie tries not to look at the smattering of brown hair on his chest or the tight red trunks that have bunched up around his thighs. He has the physique of a man who once religiously went to the gym but has now gone soft. A classic dad bod. There is a faded tribal tattoo on the underside of his left bicep.

'Morning, trouble!' Theo calls to Alba. 'Sorry, I had to go for a run but I'm ready to play now.'

'You planning on running every morning?' Luke looks up from the pair of neon pink sparkly goggles in his hands that he's trying to fix.

'Yeah, most days. I've got a training plan to follow.'

'Doesn't sound like much of a holiday.' Luke hands the goggles to Alba.

'I know, tell me about it,' Rosie says. He's sprung this new challenge on her not that long ago.

'I did a marathon once. Never again.' Luke groans.

'Thank goodness for that,' Fenna calls from a padded sun lounger, an arm stretched over her head. Rosie does a double take. It looks like she's posing for a fashion magazine shoot in her classic black all-in-one. Raffi is asleep in the pushchair under a parasol, the fringed edges dancing in the occasional whisper of a warm breeze.

'You coming in, babe?' Theo asks Rosie, pulling his t-shirt off. She catches Luke watching them before darting his eyes away and slipping under the surface of the water.

'I need my suncream to sink in first.' She's not ready to lose her kimono yet.

'No problem.' He turns to the pool. 'Right, Alba. Count to three.'

Cool droplets of water flick across Rosie's bare legs as he dives into the pool. There's a rush of chlorine in the disturbed air. Alba asks Theo to do it again and again.

Fenna smiles as Rosie walks over. 'I'm glad Theo's here to entertain Alba; he's a natural with children. I think she was getting bored of just Daddy.'

Rosie perches on a padded lounger, tugging her cover-up tighter, and watches Theo lift Alba in the air, pretending to make her fly. A pang of pride blooms inside her. He would make a wonderful dad. She brushes the thought away. It's not healthy to think too far into the future.

'I still can't get over this place. It's amazing.'

She's never had a holiday like this before. It's like she's on a film set. An extravagant fruit platter sits on the table beside them. Juicy pink watermelon slices glisten invitingly. There's a large bottle of chilled lemon-infused water and a bowl of fat green olives with sharp wooden cocktail sticks.

'We love it here. And the food . . .' Fenna mimes a chef's kiss. 'Julietta was here picking herbs for whatever she's knocking up for lunch.' She nods to the fragrant rosemary bushes nearby. 'I never want to leave.'

Luke is baiting Theo to do his best belly flop into the pool. It's all good-natured but Rosie can see the brothers' bravado starting to show. Alba has lost interest in the men and is dipping a Peppa Pig toy in the water.

Rosie clears her throat. 'I was going to ask about the missing girl that was mentioned at the dinner table last night. I didn't want to seem rude by asking loads of questions, but I can't stop thinking about it.'

'If I'm honest, I was surprised by how open Marianne was. Normally she shuts down any conversation where Danielle Dixon is mentioned. Clearly, she trusts you,' Fenna says. 'Do you not remember the story? It made the news back home, but you're a few years younger than me so maybe it wasn't on your radar.'

'I vaguely remember something about a British teenager vanishing in Italy.' Rosie fiddles with her sunglasses, wishing the sudden butterflies in her stomach would calm down. 'I had no idea it was here. You wouldn't expect it in a place like this.'

'I know. It goes to show, it can happen anywhere.' Fenna leans across to adjust the clip-on stroller fan that's blowing softly over Raffi. 'I can see why Marianne wanted to change the subject last night; she won't want you thinking this is an unsafe place.'

The locks. The security cameras. The missing girl.

'Do people think she's still alive? Is that why they're appealing for witnesses?'

Fenna checks no one is listening. 'The general consensus is that she was murdered but who knows. They've never found her body. She vanished into thin air. Some say she ran away – by all accounts she was a tearaway, problems at home – but I suppose we'll never know what she was going through. People keep secrets for all sorts of reasons. I heard a rumour that she's living with a new identity. Others even say she's being held somewhere—'

'God, you're not still talking about Danielle Dixon are you?' Luke steps in front of the sun, casting a shadow.

Fenna sits taller. 'Rosie was asking if people think she's still alive.'

'No chance.' There is a satisfying hiss as Luke pulls the ring pull from a can of Italian beer. 'The pervert teacher killed her.'

Rosie frowns. 'Her teacher?'

Luke sits on the lounger opposite Rosie, his legs spread. 'A few weeks after the traumatised class returned home, minus Danielle, the fella who had organised the exchange, the Italian language teacher, took his life. God, what was his name?'

'Alba – come and get a snack, honey,' Fenna calls, before turning to Luke. 'I thought that was a rumour? We don't know if he killed himself because he had something to do with Danielle's disappearance.'

Luke stares at his wife as if she's deluded. 'Err. Don't you remember he had her phone? He claimed it was an innocent mistake and that he "forgot" he had confiscated it. Pfft. Sounds like the guilt got too much for him, if you ask me.'

'I'd forgotten about that part . . .' Fenna muses. 'Alba. Snack time.'

Luke throws a plump black grape into his mouth. 'This new appeal is pointless if you ask me. I don't know what they're expecting to find after fifteen years. Everyone knows she's in the lake and that's why the birds vanished. And so did the tourists. The locals think that if the mystery is solved they can clear the town's reputation and bring money back to the area. But the damage has been done. Plus, who wants a load of tourists taking over? The roads will be gridlocked and it'll be a nightmare when we come on holiday.' He stands up and clicks a muscle in his back. 'Anyway, at least the sicko teacher did the world a favour so no other girls could be hurt.'

He nonchalantly wanders back to the pool, challenging Theo to a diving competition.

'The whole thing makes my skin scrawl.' Fenna closes her eyes and angles her face to the sun. 'I know that the town suffered after she disappeared. The locals became wary of everyone who was here at the time; that's why Marianne isn't keen to dwell on it. It must have been hard staying here that summer. Luke once told me that they had journalists at their door most days . . . well, until the teacher was linked to it. I bet Theo was grateful he was away when it all happened.' She fans her face. 'I don't know if Danielle's family will ever get answers and—'

'Ah, here you all are.' Marianne emerges from the steps. She looks fabulous in a wide-brimmed sun hat, silky mint green Palazzo trousers and a pretty cream-coloured scalloped-edge t-shirt.

Fenna stops talking immediately.

'What's everyone's plans for this week? A vineyard tour? Olive oil tasting? We must take a visit to Florence and Lucca . . . oh, and Siena. What about Pisa? That's not too far away,' Marianne says, without taking a breath, sinking to the sun lounger beside Rosie. 'Or we could have a girls' trip to a spa one day? That would be wonderful.'

'We don't need an agenda, Mum. This is meant to be a holiday,' Theo calls from the pool. 'What's that saying? *Dolce far niente* – the sweetness of doing nothing.'

'Alright, show off.' Luke grins. 'But yeah, who the hell wants to taste olive oil?'

'I want us to make lots of lovely memories. I'm so happy to have you here. All of you,' Marianne says. 'Fenna, why isn't

Alba wearing her sun hat? Tell me that you've not forgotten to pack one for her?'

'Nope, she just doesn't like wearing it. I've asked her three times already to put it back on,' Fenna replies.

'Well if she refuses she should be inside. Tell me she's got factor fifty on? Ideally she shouldn't be in the sun during eleven to three anyway. I wish you would make her put her sun hat on.'

Fenna sighs and gets to her feet, muttering to herself.

'Good. That wasn't hard, was it?' Marianne lies back, her hands behind her head, her lips pulled into a satisfied smile. 'Ah, this is the life, isn't it, Rosie? Or should that be *la dolce vita*!'

Rosie mumbles in agreement. Clearly Marianne didn't hear what her daughter-in-law called her.

9

FENNA – DAY 2

Fenna leans over the toddler bed and brushes her fingers through Alba's curls. 'Night night, darling. Daddy will give you a kiss when he gets in.'

God knows what time that will be.

Luke got to his feet as soon as they'd finished dessert and announced he would be going for a drink with Theo and Rosie. Irritation curled inside her. She's still annoyed that her husband didn't tell her what he and Jonno got up to when they were last here. When she brought it up, Luke claimed he forgot to transfer the cash from his idiot mate to Gerry. He said he would sort it straight away.

His group of friends could get lairy at times, especially without their wives to calm them down, but she'd thought that kind of behaviour was in the past. Since they all started having children, 'the squad' – as Luke embarrassingly referred to them in the WhatsApp group – didn't hang out together as often. Fewer golf days, poker nights, and beer-filled European weekends away. So their taking the chance to blow off steam, get drunk on Italian wine, and make fools of themselves shouldn't be a total surprise to her.

Julietta offered to stay late and help get the children to bed but Fenna hugged her tightly and said it was ok. The poor woman had been at work for hours. If Fenna's honest with herself, it's easier to get things done this way. Her way.

Fenna zips up Alba's thin sleep bag as quietly as she can. She's had to put her back in her bed twice already.

'Sweet dreams.' The sound of Alba gently sucking on her dummy makes her smile. No doubt Marianne will have something to say about her still having one when she sleeps.

Fenna thinks about her conversation with Rosie earlier by the pool.

Luckily Marianne didn't overhear them talking about Danielle Dixon. Her mother-in-law likes to pretend everything is perfect. She thinks she's doing the right thing by shutting any difficult conversations down. That's what the Frasers do. Luke is the same. Any time there's something that needs to be discussed, he retreats into his shell and acts like it will go away. But you can't run from your problems forever.

Rosie clearly had a head full of questions. And Fenna doesn't have all the answers.

Danielle disappeared many years before Fenna met Luke, but whenever her name was mentioned Marianne struggled to remain dry-eyed. At first, Fenna thought it was strange how teary she got for a complete stranger. Now she's a mother she gets it. She can't imagine the pain and anguish of your child going missing. Danielle is someone's baby. The fact that her family hasn't given up hope after all these years is remarkable but understandable.

Before she leaves the nursery, she pulls open the wardrobe doors. No one is hiding inside. She drops to her knees and sweeps a hand under Alba's bed, using the light from her phone to see into the far corners. No one underneath. She angles the beam of light up to the corners of the room and around the window frames. Everything looks ok. She steps back, making sure the monitor is plugged in and working, and that there is nowhere else she's missed.

The daily checks on the children are a hangover from home. Luke wants the monitors to go. He thinks it's overkill in their narrow terraced house, but it makes Fenna feel better to be able to watch them at all times. It's a necessity, after what happened. She's not a paranoid mother, but until they can afford to move it's the compromise he has to live with.

Satisfied, she leaves Alba's door slightly ajar and pads across the hallway. Her and Luke's bedroom is one of her favourite rooms in *Villa Speranza*. The views from the wide floor-to-ceiling windows are spectacular. Right now glinting stars illuminate the expanse of patchwork fields. Utter peace. Such a contrast from the noise of London.

Raffi is fast asleep in his cot beside their king-size bed. She has about twenty minutes until he will wake for his next feed.

Whilst brushing her teeth, she taps open the monitor app on her phone. The grainy black-and-white screen shows the room temperature and a view of Alba's toddler bed. Her daughter's chest moves softly, rhythmically.

Fenna remembers a moment during bathtime. Marianne had offered to help, making a dig that perhaps an earlier bath would make Alba sleepier as she was 'full of beans at dinner again'.

'That was thoughtful of Rosie to bring a gift.' Marianne had nodded to the plastic doll Alba was thrashing in the lavender-scented water. 'It must be overwhelming meeting us all in one go. Poor girl.'

'I thought you'd met her before?'

'Nope.'

A bubble of anxiety rose in Fenna's throat. Alba's happy squeals tore through her. 'So, she's a complete stranger?'

Fenna's certain that Luke had told her that Theo and Rosie went for dinner with Gerry and Marianne. Didn't he? Maybe she'd misheard him thanks to her sleep-deprived brain fog. The other day she found the remote control in the fridge. She must have put it there when getting the milk out for a cup of tea.

Marianne picked up on this glimmer of panic. 'Not everyone has an agenda, Fenna. What happened was a one-off.'

Suddenly she wasn't perspiring in the wet heat in the bathroom, her knees pressing into the Italian stone tiles, her heart pounding. She was back at home in London. A place of sanctuary, until it was shattered a month ago when someone broke into their house.

Luke's laptop was stolen along with his expensive golf clubs and one of his mum's original paintings. She's grateful that he has taken on the headache of sorting out the insurance claim. The police gave her a number for a generic national helpline for victims of crime. She never called it. The officer she spoke to also made a vague promise that they would try and catch the perpetrator, but she'd had no updates.

Whoever did it is still out there.

Marianne had asked her to pass the baby shampoo, breaking the spell. Fenna swallowed the spike of panic down, blinking away the heart-stopping moment she came downstairs in the early hours of the morning and found the back door smashed in. They'd slept through it all. Thankfully no one was hurt, but she can't help playing the *what if* game. What if the burglar had come upstairs? What if they'd harmed the children? What if one of her family had been seriously hurt? Her GP prescribed low-strength sleeping pills – because she was breastfeeding she couldn't take the strong ones – which helped remove the night terrors, but the fear of another break-in – a stranger in their home – still hasn't fully gone away.

Fenna climbs into the enormous king-sized bed, savouring the softness of the sheets and the scent of the fabric softener Julietta uses.

Perhaps Luke is right that coming here will do them good. Being at *Villa Speranza* is the first time her anxiety has lifted. There's something about the Tuscan farmhouse that soothes her. Perhaps it's the reassuring solidity that comes from the old building, the peace and stillness, or the connection to her Italian ancestry; she doesn't know, but she feels safe here.

She glances at the time on her phone. It's almost eleven o'clock. Her finger hovers over Instagram, pulled by a desire to do a deep dive into Rosie Riley.

Raffi lets out an adorable snuffle from the cot beside her.

With a yawn, she taps open the white noise app instead and puts her phone on the bedside cabinet. Luke said he did a thorough background check, and she trusts him. He wouldn't put his family in danger.

10

ROSIE – DAY 2

Rosie tries to match the men's footsteps. Their long legs stride effortlessly ahead causing her to scurry breathlessly behind them up the hill. The night sky chitters with crickets and a dog barks from somewhere. The temperature has dropped for the first time all day.

'You ok?' Theo asks. 'Not much further to go. There's a path but we always take this shortcut through the grounds to get to the village.'

'Fine,' she pants. The porcini mushroom risotto she ate rolls in her stomach.

Luke leans against a tree, pausing for them to catch him up. He was the one to suggest they go for a nightcap after knocking back most of a bottle of red wine with dinner. There's nothing wrong with him letting his hair down on holiday, she reminds herself. But there is something about his energy tonight that is different to the first night.

Fenna huffed about being left on baby duty. Rosie threw her a well-meaning smile, but she didn't catch it. Marianne, on the other hand, looked pleased when the brothers said they were going for a drink. She practically ushered them away from the dinner table before they had finished their last mouthful.

Rosie worries she's imposing but Theo promised she isn't.

The torch on Luke's phone zig zags as he steps forward, swaying slightly. The 'grounds' they are walking through are more like a wood than a garden. A stretch of dark, evergreen-filled land between their holiday house and the small village centre. A gnarled wooden handrail guides the way up deep stone steps. There is little light through the leafy canopy above their heads. She reaches for Theo's hand.

As they emerge from the winding woodland path, Rosie catches her breath and tries to get her bearings. The taxi drove them through the village when they arrived two days ago and it wasn't exactly heaving with life then, but at nighttime it's even emptier. Uninviting sleepy corners are hidden down dimly lit lanes. An imposing red brick church peers over the marketplace . . . or at least what remains of a marketplace. A couple of locked-up shops are plastered with faded posters for a circus that passed through two years ago, another board says '*Vendesi*', and a tatty metal sign points the way to '*Lago Parrocchetto*'.

The trio walk down the deserted main street, past a cafe and a circular grey stone water fountain that's long dried up. Television sets blare from behind half-closed shutters. A skinny tabby cat prowls by. They wander past a bus stop with a large noticeboard full of posters and timetables. Tiny metal birds are sitting on the top of the bus shelter. Green parakeets.

Luke tears something off the board. 'Whoops.'

A sheet of A4 paper flutters to the ground.

'Luke, man. Don't be like that,' Theo snaps.

The paper rests in the gutter, near a dusty drain cover. Rosie tries to see what's going on, but Theo blocks her view of what his brother has torn from the board.

'What? My hand slipped.' Luke holds up his hands in defence and walks backwards a few steps.

Theo makes a noise between his lips. He picks up the crumpled poster and tacks it back onto the bulletin board as Luke carries on walking up the street, veering into the empty road, muttering to himself. Rosie glances at the board and spots which poster caused this reaction. It's hanging slightly haphazardly compared to the other pieces of paper.

She blinks.

A young woman in a school uniform smiles back. Her ash-blonde hair with a strip of unforgiving roots hangs in a sheet around her slender face. She's wearing silver hoop earrings and has a bright, toothy smile. Alongside the photograph is a blur of text. It's all written in Italian, but she can guess what it says. An appeal for information; fifteen years on. A local phone number is printed in bold at the bottom.

'I think that was an accident,' Theo says to Rosie, a flash of embarrassment on his face.

Rosie doesn't know what to say. It didn't look like an accident.

'Come on. Let's make sure he doesn't get into any more trouble,' Theo says, rolling his eyes, leading her away.

***

Luke has made it to a bar at the top end of the town. It looks like someone's house; the sand-blasted bricks are worn and tired, and an amber glow spills from the windows. A couple of round, wrought-iron tables and plastic chairs are laid out on a driveway. Inside the bar is a small shop selling pastel-coloured gelato from a chest freezer and packets of cigarettes lined up like dominoes. There is a smell of spilt beer, sweat and stale smoke. There's no music. It isn't like any bar she's been to on holiday before.

Drinkers pause their conversations and glare at them. Rosie tells herself it's their English voices, but she realises that no one is looking at her. It's the two brothers they're staring at.

'Is there a problem?' Rosie whispers to Theo.

'God, what is wrong with these people?' Luke cuts in, slurring his words. 'Xenophobes, the lot of them.'

'Luke,' Theo chides.

'None of them can understand English; I can say what I want.'

'Please ignore my brother,' Theo says to Rosie, rubbing her hand with his. 'The locals are still, for some reason, pissed off that Mum and Dad bought the house back in the day. They think it should be owned by Italians.'

'They loved tourists when it made them money. Since the businesses at the lake closed down – which has nothing to do with us, by the way – they treat us like *we're* the problem.' Luke shakes his head. 'These people think they know everything about us.'

If they know the locals don't like them, why did they come here?

Theo reads her mind. 'It's the only bar in the village. Desperate times and all that.'

'You can say that again.' Luke pops a piece of gum into his mouth.

Chairs scrape across the scuffed stone floor. The other

drinkers peel their eyes from the trio and their conversations slowly pick up again.

Luke calls over the barman, ordering in English. 'Two pints of lager . . . and?' He turns to Rosie.

'Erm, a glass of *vino rosso*, please.'

The barman nods. His face is on the wrong side of friendly.

The three of them take their drinks and sit at one of the outside tables. The air isn't much cooler, but there's fewer people to stare at them.

'Thanks for the drink,' Rosie says, lifting her glass from the sticky tabletop.

'No problem.' Luke has gulped half of his, wiping the frothy moustache from his upper lip.

'So, how's work?' Theo asks his brother.

Luke launches into a long-winded story about how he decided to quit his steady office job in order to start his own recruitment consultancy, and how much he's expecting to make in the first year.

'Isn't that the new girl? Carla?' Theo says, nodding at two young women when Luke finally pauses for air. Rosie turns to see Carla wave shyly at them. Her friend leans over and whispers something in her ear. She giggles.

'Anyone want another?' Luke asks, standing up and finishing his pint.

Rosie shakes her head.

'I'm good, thanks,' Theo replies, swatting away a mosquito.

'Lightweights,' Luke says as he wanders off towards the bar, stumbling into a table on the way.

'God, sorry about him.' Theo groans.

'What was that about before? With the poster?' Rosie asks,

dropping her voice. Danielle Dixon's young face leaps to the front of her mind.

'Luke's under pressure juggling his new job and the baby and stuff. Maybe he needs to let off steam.'

'Yeah, maybe . . .'

Theo picks up his pint. 'That's Luke's sense of humour. He pretends like everything is a big joke. It's all masking. He was here that summer when everyone was searching for Danielle. Mum's told me before that she felt completely helpless. I guess this is his way of dealing with those tough memories.'

'Fenna said you were away when Danielle disappeared?'

'Yeah, I was playing football in Croatia; competing, trying to get spotted out there. I'd completely forgotten the anniversary was around this time of year. I hope it hasn't put you off being here,' he says with a sheepish grin.

She leans over to kiss him. 'It'll take more than that.'

'Phew.' He smiles.

Rosie looks at Luke through the doorway. He's standing at the bar. One of his shirt buttons has come undone. Carla is laughing at whatever he's saying, her eyes fixed on him as one hand wraps a dark strand of her hair around her slender fingers. Over and over.

'I didn't know he spoke Italian,' Rosie says, overhearing their chat.

'Non è bravo quanto me,' Theo purrs.

'What? You speak it too? What does that mean?'

'It means he likes to show off. We both know a little, though I've forgotten most of it. He's probably chatting nonsense. The booze makes him think he's bilingual but he's not.' He pulls her closer, running his lips across her bare shoulder. The sensation makes her tingle. *'Dov'è il mio astuccio?'*

'That's pretty sexy,' she whispers into his ear. 'What does it mean?'

'Where is my pencil case?' he breathes, trying to keep a straight face.

She laughs.

'Oi, Theo. You got cash on you?' Luke yells from inside the bar, ruining the moment. He's oblivious to the looks he receives from the other drinkers.

'Hang on.' Theo gets to his feet, planting a firm kiss on Rosie's head.

She pulls her phone out once she's alone. She can't shake the feeling that Theo was making excuses for his brother's strange behaviour. Why did Luke really tear down that appeal poster? She types Danielle's name into Google. A list of English and Italian news sites pop up. She clicks on the most recent article.

MISSING SCHOOLGIRL'S GRIEVING FAMILY STILL SEARCHING FOR ANSWERS

The mother of missing schoolgirl Danielle Dixon urges people not to forget about her daughter, fifteen years on . . .

She jumps when a heavy hand presses down on her shoulder and flinches at the sting of her sunburn being touched.

'You ok? I was calling you for ages,' Theo says.

She quickly turns her phone face down. 'Oh? Sorry, I was checking the weather. Everything ok?'

'You ready to head back? I'm not sure I can handle another.'

'Sure. Let me nip to the loo. I'll be right with you,' she says, relieved that he's happy to call it a night.

Before she can get to her feet, an older man strides over to the table and slaps Theo on the back. 'How the devil are you? Long time no see.'

Theo leaps to his feet. 'Hello, Uncle Richard.'

They embrace in a bear hug.

'And who's this?' Richard leans over and takes Rosie's hand.

'I'm Rosie,' she says, trying to remain polite despite the man's clammy hand gripping hers too tightly. This must be the family friend that Marianne mentioned.

'Ah, yes. Theo's mother said he was bringing a date. Welcome.' Richard chuckles. He looks like a bald Father Christmas with a sizeable belly, ruddy round cheeks and a deep, warm laugh. 'Is Luke out, too?'

Theo glances around and Richard follows his gaze.

'Of course your brother's propping the bar up. Who's that he's with? I think I recognise her . . .'

'Carla. She works for Mum. Luke launched himself into the poor girl's night out with her friend.'

Richard pulls out a chair, shaking his head with a smile. 'So how long are you here, Theo? You didn't reply to my last email.'

'I know, I've been busy, sorry.'

Rosie politely excuses herself, leaving the two men to catch up.

On her way back from the bathroom, Rosie walks past the entrance to a narrow alleyway that runs down the side of the bar. There's a couple sharing a cigarette in the darkness. Luke's booming laugh makes her stop and take a better look.

He's leaning against a rough granite wall, near a stack of

metal beer barrels and a heavy-duty black bin, talking to Carla. He stubs a cigarette against the bricks.

There's a tinkle of a flirty giggle. Rosie's sure she hears Theo call her name but she can't tear herself away. Luke takes an unsteady step forward. She watches as he trails one hand down Carla's back and uses the other to tip her jaw to his, leaning in for a kiss.

11

FENNA – DAY 3

Sunlight and birdsong stream into the dining room through the open double patio doors. Alba is singing to herself, swinging her pudgy legs under her highchair, a circle of crumbs at her feet. She's on her second breakfast of the day; after demolishing cereal and a sliced apple, she is now munching honey toast fingers.

Fenna tears a warm almond croissant apart, needing the sugar hit to keep her awake. Luke barrelled in drunk at one o'clock in the morning, waking Raffi, who she'd just got back to sleep. She was awake for another hour listening to Luke's snoring, debating how she could get away with murder.

She tried to force him to get up with the children so she could sleep in, but he mumbled incoherently into a saliva-damp pillow, blasting foul beer breath at her. It's safer for the kids to be with a responsible adult right now. She blinks away the tears that press the back of her sandpaper-like eyes. Alba's singing grows louder. She clatters her plastic spoon against the table and throws it to the polished wooden floor. The sound makes Fenna jump. Raffi lets out a frustrated cry, his startled arms leap in panic.

She shushes him and tries to resettle him against her breast.

Carla, the young housekeeper, rushes across and picks up Alba's spoon. She pulls a funny face and pretends to make the spoon dance across the table. Alba shrieks in delight. Fenna tries to rearrange her buttoned-up nightshirt that is half-open as she feeds Raffi. The poor girl doesn't want an eyeful so early in the morning.

'*Caffè*?' Carla asks Fenna in a timid voice, her Italian accent heavy.

'*Sì, grazie*,' Fenna replies.

She'd made herself a cup a while ago, but Raffi needed feeding and it now sat tantalisingly out of reach growing cold. Marianne's remark yesterday evening about how long Fenna was planning on breastfeeding returns to her.

'Express some milk. Let someone else feed him,' she'd said. 'It's the only way you'll get a decent chunk of sleep. My friend's daughter-in-law does that and her baby sleeps for twelve hours a night.'

Fenna was too tired to defend her choices.

'*Prego*.' Carla wobbles a large cappuccino over and places it before her.

Fenna smiles gratefully. She burps Raffi and places him gently in his bassinet, turning on the mobile above his head, and takes a sip. It's delicious.

'It's like a sauna in here,' Gerry announces as he bursts through the door dressed in his gym kit, followed by Marianne, wearing a chic white blouse and linen A-line skirt with a full face of make-up. She beams at the kids. 'Hello, my little loves.'

Soon the room is full of noise and kisses for the children.

Fenna answers questions about how they slept, what the plan for the day is, and what they've had to eat.

'You ok, Fenna? You look ever so tired. Tough night?' Marianne asks.

If she was truly honest, she would reply that she could say the same to Marianne. Clearly she's hiding the effects of a hangover. They must have had a nice evening with a bottle of wine, or two, as her skin looks sickly despite the blusher she's applied. Flecks of her taupe-coloured eyeshadow sit in the many creases under her eyes.

'I'm fine. I simply need a steady supply of coffee,' Fenna replies, taking another sip.

'Have the rules changed about caffeine and breastfeeding? I remember when I fed the boys it was very strict – one cup a day, or at least certainly no more than two. I know it was a long time ago, but I didn't think they'd relaxed the rules so much.'

Fenna puts her mug down and tries to hold back the tears that unexpectedly arrive.

'This is decaf,' she lies. What she wants to yell is how this is her only vice. How else would she function? She doesn't need an old bag making her feel guilty about it.

'Oh, good.' Marianne smiles. *Correct answer.* She starts to peel a satsuma, digging her long, painted nails into the flesh. 'Where are the boys?'

'Luke's still sleeping. I've not seen Theo or Rosie yet,' Fenna says.

'I'm so pleased they went out last night. It will do them good to spend time together. I dreamt they would grow up to be the best of friends as that wasn't always the case when they were younger. Gosh, I remember their squabbles over the same toy. Each wanted what the other had. It was exhausting. You've got all that to come.' She nods at the children. 'Do you want cereal, Princess Alba?'

'She's fine. She's already had a bowl, and a round of toast,' Fenna says.

'One more won't hurt her, she's a growing girl.'

Fenna bites her tongue as her mother-in-law pours an adult-sized portion of Coco Pops for her grand-daughter.

The door to the dining room opens.

'Here he is.' Marianne beams as Luke slopes into the room in his silk kimono robe that has a toothpaste stain near the frayed collar. 'Morning, darling, how did you sleep?'

He lets out a noise between a hello and a groan and drops into an empty chair. 'Any breakfast going? Where's Julietta?' He rubs his bleary, bloodshot eyes.

'I was thinking the same thing,' Gerry says, glancing around the room as if the members of staff are hiding.

'Carla was here a moment ago,' Fenna says.

Luke covers his mouth and lets out a deep yawn.

'You should go back to bed by the sounds of it. What time did you come home?' Marianne asks her son who is morphing further into a teenager by the second.

'Not too late. About midnight maybe.' He shrugs.

Fenna makes a noise between her lips. 'It was later than that.'

'I don't think so.' Luke frowns.

'It was.'

Gerry and Marianne share a look, evidently not wanting to get involved in this marital dispute.

'I'm going to go and have a shower.' Fenna gets to her feet. 'You ok to watch the children? I've fed Raffi.'

Luke waves a hand, wincing when Alba loudly cries that she wants the green spoon, not the pink one Marianne is offering her. His hangover is going to be tested today. Fenna leaves the room but not before he asks his mum to make him some food. Marianne replies that she'll 'do anything for my little prince'.

Fenna's stomach churns.

The doorbell chimes. Fenna hesitates, waiting for Julietta to emerge to answer it, but no one appears. She reluctantly plods down the hallway and pulls open the front door.

She's momentarily lost for words at the attractive police officer on the other side.

His pale blue shirt stretches over his muscular frame. Sunlight bounces from the glossy peak of his black hat. A leather belt across his waist holds a handgun.

She automatically tugs her robe closed, hoping to hide the milky stains around her breasts, and with the other hand, she flattens down her bed head hair.

'*Buongiorno . . .*' she stutters.

'Where's Julietta? Has Fenna opened the door? Next, she'll be opening my post,' Marianne's voice echoes down the corridor. 'Hello? Who is it? Oh. Good morning. Can I help you?' She purses her lips and looks the policeman up and down slowly.

Fenna notices that he is holding something.

'Giovanni Salvatore. I'd like to speak to your sons, please,' the officer says, pulling himself taller.

'Luke and Theo? Why?' Marianne asks.

A second later, Luke barrels down the corridor, a slice of toast in one hand, a wriggling Alba in the other arm. He must have left Raffi with Gerry. 'Did you call me, Mum?' He tenses when he sees who is at the door.

'Nee naww.' Alba makes a siren sound when she sees the officer.

Giovanni flashes a brief smile at Alba, revealing a dimple in his dark stubble. The lightness fades as he makes eye contact with Luke. 'Did you go to *Tre Sorelle* last night, sir?'

Three Sisters. That's the name of the bar in the village. Why is he asking about that?

'Yeah, why?' Luke grunts.

Giovanni shows them what's in his hands. 'You were seen tearing this down.'

Fenna and Marianne gasp at the same time. It's a poster appealing for information to find Danielle Dixon. Luke swears under his breath and hands Alba to Fenna. He lets out a steady exhale. Can the policeman smell last night's alcohol on her husband's unclean breath?

'Firstly, I didn't *tear down* any poster. One accidentally fell as I walked past. My brother stuck it back up again. No harm done. And secondly, haven't you got better things to be doing? What about catching real criminals?' Luke scoffs.

Giovanni's brows knot in displeasure. 'You didn't damage the poster on purpose?'

'No. Of course not. Why would I do that?' Luke replies.

'So you won't mind me placing one of these outside this house, like many of your neighbours?'

Luke folds his arms. Fenna waits for him to say something more, but he presses his lips in a tight line.

A knot of unease stirs in Fenna's stomach at his childish behaviour. Why is he being so defensive? Before she can say anything, Marianne sparks to life, taking the poster from Giovanni, one hand on the door frame to put an end to this little chat.

'Of course, officer. We're happy to help.' Marianne smiles at him, it doesn't meet her eyes. 'I'll make sure this is put up as soon as possible.'

'*Grazie*,' Giovanni replies, his gaze firmly on Luke.

Alba wriggles, bored of the grown-up chat. Fenna struggles to hear what they are saying over her daughter's frustrated shouts.

'Sorry, officer.' Marianne inches the door closed. 'Boys will be boys, I guess!'

12

ROSIE – DAY 3

Rosie is half asleep when she leaves the bedroom. Her head is tender after the wine last night. She's annoyed at herself for accepting the booze. She needs to keep a clear mind. This isn't the time or place for her to lose her inhibitions. She rubs the sleep from her eyes and nearly trips over what's waiting on the other side of the door. A stack of photo albums rests by her feet, topped with a handwritten note on a piece of creamy paper torn from a notepad.

Rosie, you mentioned you were interested in these the other night. There's loads more in the library downstairs. Help yourself. It's nice to have someone take an interest. They usually gather dust. Marianne x

Rosie quickly flicks through the top album dated 'Summer 2010', pausing to look at teenage Theo. She smiles to herself; he had a blonde mop that was clearly inspired by Justin Bieber.

The doorbell chimes and the sound of voices erupts from somewhere in the house. She hurriedly puts the albums down. She'll go over them properly later once she's got caffeine in her system.

She goes downstairs, past the locked door to the basement. There must be a window open down there as cold air escapes through the gap at her bare feet, blowing onto her toes. She shivers and hurries to the kitchen. The house is silent once more. She expects to see Julietta but there's no one here. Where is everyone else? What is she supposed to do?

Suddenly a voice comes from behind her. Standing next to the window, looking out over the drive, is the gardener, Paulo.

'*Ciao*,' he says gruffly, tearing his eyes from the view, unaware of the fright he gave her.

He looks to be in his mid-fifties, wearing a scruffy, bottle-green shirt and grubby cargo trousers. Wiry grey hairs stick up at different angles on his head and there are bags under his wrinkled eyes.

'*C-Ciao* . . .' she stutters awkwardly.

'Coffee?' Paulo offers, nodding to the sleek barista-style coffee machine.

'Yes, please.'

The smell of ground coffee soon fills the warm air as Paulo moves around the kitchen and prepares her drink. He looms over her. His rough, tanned hands are massive. She remembered Theo saying he had been working here for years. He clearly knows his way around the place. A large set of keys jingle as he clomps to the fridge to get the milk.

'Did you have a nice night?' he asks in stilted English, over the sound of the frother. 'I saw you going to the bar.'

She nods. Was he there too? She didn't see him, but then again, only one thing plays on repeat in her mind from last night. Luke and Carla in the alleyway. She pictures his hand sliding across her waist, tugging her closer.

What happened after Rosie ran away? Did the kiss lead to something else or was it a drunken moment of madness?

'The Three Sisters. It used to be a good place. It's tired now. Old. Like me.' He winks. Despite his intimidating height and stature, there is a kindness about him.

'Theo told me you've worked here for a long time. I wonder if—' she starts to ask but is interrupted as the door opens.

Marianne sweeps in, looking ready and made up for the day, holding a rolled-up piece of paper in her hand. 'Ah, Rosie. Sleep well?'

'Erm, yes, lovely, thanks,' she lies. She had tossed and turned, wondering whether to tell Theo about Luke and Carla's brief embrace all night. He was unusually quiet on the walk home from the bar. His early-morning runs must be catching up with him. Even if he had been in the mood to talk, Rosie was still in too much shock to mention his brother's infidelity.

Paulo hands Rosie a cappuccino, breaking her thoughts. The cream-coloured cup looks miniature in his large, soil-stained hands. '*Prego*.'

She brings the cup to her lips and carefully blows on the steam, the smell of roasted coffee unfurling up her nose.

'Theo still in bed?' Marianne asks.

'No, he's in the shower. Thanks for the photo albums, by the way.'

'You're welcome, dear. Like I said, it's lovely to have a guest take so much interest.' Marianne smiles. A clock chimes. 'I'm glad to see Paulo has prepared you a drink. The others are in the dining room finishing breakfast, if you want to go and join them. Julietta and Carla are around somewhere if you'd like to request anything particular to eat. If you'll excuse us? Paulo?'

The older man bobs his head to say goodbye before trailing after Marianne, ducking under the door frame as he leaves.

***

Luke and the children are in the dining room. The patio doors are flung open, bathing the wood-panelled room in golden sunlight. The antique oak table is covered in pastries, home-made preserves, a gleaming fruit platter, and a tall, silver cafetière. By the looks of the crumbs and half-finished bowls of cereal, they've been here for some time. Raffi is in a wicker bassinet, entranced under a mobile playing a soothing nursery rhyme.

'Morning,' Luke croaks. He's wearing an open, flowery robe that reveals his bare chest and designer boxer shorts.

'Hi,' she replies, struggling to keep eye contact, grateful that the children are there as a distraction. She can't shake the kiss in the alleyway from her mind. 'Morning, Alba, how are you doing today?'

The little girl smiles shyly at her, burrowing her head into Luke's armpit. He downs his drink in one gulp. As he does his robe opens further. Rosie looks away but not before she catches his lips curling into a wry smile.

Is he doing this on purpose?

'How's your head?' she asks, filling the awkward silence while tentatively reaching for a croissant from under a polished glass dome.

'Fine.' He lifts up the cafetière. 'Well, I will be after this. Would you like some?'

'No thank you. Paulo sorted me out.'

He rolls his bloodshot eyes. 'Course he did. He's probably acting like he owns the place. He's worked here for donkey's years. I bet there's some clause that he came with the house and will end up being buried here.'

Before she can reply, the door opens and Theo walks over to Rosie and kisses her on the cheek. He smells of the expensive body wash she saw in the ensuite. Relief at having him in the room floods her body.

'Morning, babe. You should have woken me. Did you find everything you need?' he asks.

'Paulo looked after her. Watch out, she told me she likes older men.' Luke winks.

'I didn't say that, I . . .' Rosie stutters.

Theo pulls a funny face at Alba and settles into the seat beside Rosie. 'So, Paulo, hey? Do I need to be worried?'

'No! I mean, he made me a drink,' she exclaims, taking in the playful look on Luke's face and realising he's winding her up.

'What time did you get back last night?' Theo turns and asks Luke.

'Dunno. Not too long after you.'

They'd left Luke at the bar, despite Theo's best efforts to get him to go with them. Luke had staggered over, smelling strongly of booze and cigarettes, slurring that he was staying out. Theo had rolled his eyes and told him he was old enough and ugly enough to make his own decisions.

There was no lipstick mark, no smell of perfume, nothing at all to suggest he'd kissed a woman who wasn't his wife moments before.

'Anything happen after we went?' Theo asks.

Luke shakes his head. 'Nope. Richard bought another round and disappeared with someone he knew and left me on my own. Nothing exciting.'

Rosie's insides tighten. He doesn't know that she knows. Flashbacks of the kiss flicker through her mind as Luke talks. She can't concentrate on what he's saying.

That's not the only churning thought that bothers her. *Do the family like her? What do they really think of her?* She knows Theo says she's doing great. They laughed at that joke she told. The one she remembered from a Christmas cracker. The one about a hamster that goes on holiday. Childish, yes, but it raised a smile on his stepdad's rigid lips. But were they doing it merely out of politeness? She re-lives conversations, analysing the way their faces tightened or softened, trying to understand her place in this perfect family. But no one is perfect, are they?

The dining room door opens and Carla steps into the room. '*Buongiorno*,' she says brightly.

She's wearing a muted grey tabard over a plain black t-shirt and trousers. A waft of sweet tropical perfume surrounds her. She silently picks up the crusts that Alba has dropped to the ground and hands Luke a soft toy that's fallen. There's nothing to suggest anything illicit happened between them.

Rosie sits up straight, hoping her heart rate will return to normal. She steals a glance at Theo who is frowning at a message he's received on his phone. He's completely unaware of what's running through her mind. She is alone with this secret. Maybe it was a silly drunken kiss. That's all. She takes a breath. Perhaps Fenna knows. They could be one of these open-relationship sort of couples. Luke was pretty brazen about it, given that anyone could have walked past.

Luke and Carla are both brilliant at acting like they barely know one another, but the atmosphere in the stuffy dining room tells another story.

'You're quiet this morning, babe.' Theo's concerned voice brings her back to the present.

'Just a bit tired,' she replies.

Theo keeps his eyes on her for a second to make sure she's ok. 'Was someone at the door earlier? I thought I heard the bell.'

Luke nods, a mouth full of food. He waits until Carla has left the room, closing the door behind her before he speaks. 'Yeah, it was Giovanni.' His voice is low.

Theo's cup clatters against the saucer.

'What did he want?' Theo asks, reaching across for a napkin to mop up the coffee he's spilt.

'To stick his neck in. Same as always.' Luke grimaces. 'Apparently, someone complained about me messing with the poster of Danielle Dixon. Bloody snakes. What is wrong with these people? It was a joke. It's funny, right, Rosie?'

Both men turn to look at her.

She wants to say that she found it disrespectful and uncalled for, but instead she smiles politely and ignores the question.

'Who's Giovanni?' she asks.

'A local policeman who has a vendetta against us,' Theo explains. His voice is calm but there is an edge.

'A vendetta?' she repeats.

'Maybe that's the wrong word. He's never liked us. He's still annoyed that Luke stole his girlfriend when they were teenagers.'

Luke leans back in his chair. 'I didn't *know* she was his girlfriend. It was a holiday romance that ended years ago. Anyway, he's never forgiven me. It's true that Italians hold a grudge. We're blamed if it rains here.'

He gives a nonchalant shrug and the conversation moves on to the plan for the day. Giovanni's name isn't mentioned again. Rosie tunes out of what's being said, focusing instead on Luke's body language. He's trying hard not to seem shaken up by the police officer's visit.

Maybe he's not such a great liar after all.

13

ROSIE – DAY 3

The sun beats down on Rosie's shoulders. She knew Italy in August would be hot, but she didn't expect it to be so uncomfortable and oppressive. None of the Frasers complain about how sweltering it is, whereas she is constantly damp with sweat and hunting for shade. She needed fresh air, though it's not much cooler out in the garden than in the house.

What should she do about the kiss? Should she tell Theo? The brothers seem to be getting on and she doesn't want to rock the boat. Why did she have to stumble into this situation? She wishes she could call her mum or her best friend; they would know what to do. She can pretty much picture Lydia's pursed lips ordering Rosie to confront Luke. The idea makes her stomach churn.

Surviving the first holiday with her boyfriend's family is stressful enough, let alone with this added dilemma on top. Perhaps it's best if she wipes what she saw from her mind. After all, it was dark, she'd had a drink and it's none of her business.

She's too busy worrying to realise where she is. The morning heat rises from the gravel path, licking her bare legs. She stops walking and takes in the olive grove, which has been left to nature. The eco garden. Colourful wildflowers are everywhere. The rest of the extensive grounds are immaculate, except this space, which hasn't seen a lawnmower in years.

A little further ahead is a marble statue of a woman, hedged in by a thicket of laurel leaves. Her limestone face is partially shrouded by the folds of a veil. A chunk of her exposed shoulder has gone. There's a forest green stain across her milky bust. Her almond-shaped eyes rest on the house with an insolent gaze. Her rosebud lips are pinched in a frozen half smile. Rosie spends a long time staring at the mesmerising statue and fails to notice that she's not alone in the wild garden.

Half hidden behind a narrow Tuscan Cypress tree, is Marianne. She sits at a stone bench and is writing something in a notebook. Her right hand moves with alarming speed, as if she can't jot the words down fast enough. There is a pensive look on her drawn face.

Rosie freezes. What should she do? She doesn't want to disturb this moment. Marianne hasn't seen her yet. Theo told her his mum was funny about people coming into this wildflower garden. Indecision plagues her. She holds her breath and doesn't move a muscle.

Marianne is too engrossed in her work to realise she's being watched. Every so often she stops writing to wipe the tears from her cheeks, but she doesn't once glance up. She looks like a lost little girl with a weight of secrets zipped into the folds of her lips.

What could Marianne Fraser cry about? She lives a life many dream of.

Rosie doesn't know how much time has passed but she is sweaty and dehydrated. She debates turning around and retracing her steps, but Marianne senses someone is there and turns with a start.

Rosie instinctively crouches down behind a spiky thorn bush.

Now what?

She thinks someone shouts her name but she doesn't want to turn her head and risk being seen. How would she explain this compromising position? She focuses on the procession of woodlice scuttling in the cracks of the paving slab and ignores the pins and needles that fizz across her legs. Sweat trickles down her neck.

When the pain in her thighs gets too much, she stands, furtively glancing around to check that she's alone. It's just her and the statue. Marianne has vanished.

She walks past the empty bench and spots something glinting from the ground, caught in the petals of a weed. A bronze-coloured key. It's small but solid. It looks antique.

A memory rushes back. Her first mini-break with Theo was to Bath where they wandered along a bridge covered in love locks. Theo produced an engraved ruby-red lock from his pocket. He had carried it around all day and she'd had no idea. He clicked the clasp shut and threw the key into the murky brown water.

'We're locked in forever,' he'd told her with a wink. Her heart soared with a rush of love, ignoring the unwanted negative emotions that bubbled under the surface.

Marianne must have dropped the small key.

Rosie quickly looks around, expecting to see a locked box or chest hiding somewhere amongst the knee-height wildflowers that scratch her bare legs. There's nothing here. A bee buzzes past and she instinctively jerks away.

'Rosie?' Theo calls her name from a distance.

She puts the key into her pocket and scurries out of the wildflower garden. Her head pounds with questions.

'I thought that was you. What are you doing here?' Theo jogs over, panting. There's mud on his tomato-red cheeks.

'I got lost on the way to the swimming pool. I must have taken a wrong turn,' she says, her tongue thick in her parched mouth. Her top has stuck to her back with sweat.

'Sorry, I forgot to tell you there's another path down here that takes you straight there.' He pushes open a low wooden gate. He's limping a little.

'Are you ok?' she asks.

'Yeah, I took a tumble.'

'Theo, you're bleeding,' she says.

His t-shirt has a rip in it. There's another smaller tear on his running shorts. His knees are grazed and muddy. Blood seeps through the thin fabric.

'I tripped over a tree root and fell. Don't worry; nothing is broken, except my ego,' he says with a laugh.

He uses his sports top to wipe the sweat from his face, flashing his toned stomach. He's losing too much weight in his training. The little fat he had before appears to be melting before her eyes. It's like he's becoming a different person.

'Let's go and find Julietta. She must have a first-aid kit?' she offers.

'I'm fine, I'm made of strong stuff.' Theo brushes off her concern, making light of the injury with a bicep flex. The gesture makes her laugh. 'Don't you worry about me. Are you ok? My family aren't getting on your nerves yet?'

'No. They're all lovely.' She takes his clammy hand and their palms glue together. 'Well, there was something I wanted to mention—'

'*Buongiorno*,' Paulo calls, interrupting Rosie. He's standing next to a ride-on lawnmower, a black plastic trug filled with wood chippings by his feet.

Theo raises an arm in acknowledgement. He leans closer and whispers, 'There's something about him that gives me the creeps. Always has done.'

Paulo gives them the thumbs up and says something else but it's drowned out by the sound of his mower.

'Sorry babe, what were you going to say?' Theo asks her as they walk away.

She thinks about telling him about Luke and Carla and what she saw at the bar. But she stops herself. Gossiping is not going to help her win this family's affections.

'I can't remember,' she lies.

14

ROSIE – DAY 4

Rosie lies on the sun lounger and watches Marianne pull out a teal-coloured soft-cover Moleskine journal and an expensive ballpoint pen. It's the same one she was writing in when Rosie saw her yesterday in the wildflower garden. Marianne clearly didn't see her, or if she did, she's not mentioned it.

'We had a retreat here a few months ago, and a bunch of authors came to stay. They were friends with Richard and Evelyn,' Marianne tells Rosie. 'They've also got a place here. You'll get to meet them in a few days, I hope. Anyway, these authors start the day with morning pages. A way to clear your head. The older I get the more I forget. So I decided to give it a go. It's probably a lot of nonsense but I'm finding it helpful. You might like to do this for the children, Fenna? Start a journal.'

'Mmm, maybe . . .' Fenna replies. She's trying to doze in the sun beside them but keeps getting interrupted with Alba's many questions.

'Have you put Alba's name down for swimming lessons? Both my boys could swim at her age.'

'Not yet,' Fenna replies.

'It's so important.'

'I know but she's got time,' Fenna says. Rosie picks up on the tone of irritation. 'She's got armbands on and Luke's in the water with her.'

The baby lets out a loud cry from his pushchair and Fenna gets to her feet with an exasperated sigh. Marianne looks like she wants to say something else, but Paulo appears.

'Ah, Paulo. Any news?' Marianne asks.

He stands with his hat in his hands, moving it quickly between his fingers. 'No, I'm sorry.'

Marianne sits up. 'What? I was sure I'd left it there. Did you look properly?'

Paulo nods.

'Fenna, Alba didn't pick up anything she shouldn't have this morning, did she?' Marianne asks.

'No. Why?'

'Nothing,' Marianne flaps her hand.

Fenna shrugs in confusion.

The key rests in her shorts pocket. Is this what Marianne is searching for?

'Have you lost something?' she asks.

'No. I mean, it's nothing to worry about,' Marianne replies, her voice higher than usual. 'I'm sure it'll turn up.'

Paulo takes a breath. 'If you allowed me to cut the grass . . .'

Marianne holds up a hand. 'I've told you that garden is not to be touched. Gerry knows this. I can keep on top of it. The children don't go in there.'

'I know, *Signora*, but . . .'

'Paulo. I won't tell you again.'

Rosie is taken aback by Marianne's no-nonsense tone. Her

demeanour has changed in an instant. 'Go and have another look for me. I'd appreciate being left alone with the family.'

Rosie tenses. A loud bark of laughter from Theo and Luke in the pool drowns out whatever Marianne says next.

Paulo leaves and Marianne declares that she's going for a dip in the pool, muttering something under her breath as she takes off her cover-up.

'What was that about?' Fenna asks, nodding at Paulo sheepishly walking away.

'No idea,' Rosie lies.

A slow prickle starts at the back of her head. Should she tell her that she's found the key?

'I wonder what it was. She can get territorial about her things. But Paulo's right. That wildflower garden needs a good tidy up. I've always thought it would be perfect for a tennis court. If it was up to me, I'd rip it down and start again.'

'Theo mentioned that his mum doesn't like anyone going there. Do you know why?' she tentatively asks.

'It's so the wildlife isn't disturbed, but who knows. It's easier to do what she says sometimes. The place is so full of weeds and God knows what else. I wouldn't want to spend time down there. Poor Paulo clearly was in the wrong place at the wrong time as usually she gets Gerry to run around after her.'

'Speaking of Gerry . . . Where is he?' Rosie hasn't seen him much in the daytime.

'God knows. I think he finds it easier to keep his distance when the brothers are together. Marianne gets caught in the middle.'

She's still not sure why there is a coolness towards their stepdad as he's been in the boys' lives for years now. She's about to ask Fenna why they're not particularly close when a cascade of water hits the sun loungers. Luke is trying to use Alba's inflatable unicorn ring as a basketball hoop, dunking Theo in.

'Watch it. I'm soaked!' Fenna cries.

Luke raises a hand in an apology. 'It was Theo's fault.'

'Hey.' Theo splashes his brother again.

'They're so competitive. Always been like this, ever since they were little,' Marianne says from the other end of the pool where she's sitting on the low steps, laughing. 'They must get it from their father.'

Fenna swears under her breath. Rosie tries to give her a smile in solidarity as she dries her legs with a towel, but it's clear that cracks are starting to show.

15

FENNA – DAY 4

Fenna lies back on the sun lounger. Perhaps if she stays still the tension in her skull will disappear. Marianne has to nitpick everything she's doing with the children. She's fed up with these unwanted opinions. Can no one else hear how she talks to her? Perhaps she's overly sensitive at the moment but she can't do anything right.

It's not just Marianne who is getting on her nerves; Luke has been hungover every day so far. It's like having another child to look after. She thinks of the row they had earlier this morning, which started from an innocent text message that pinged on her phone as she was changing Raffi's nappy.

'Who is it?' Luke had asked.

Fenna glanced at her phone. 'It's Nish; she wants to send me something about a job.'

'What is it?'

'It's an online campaign for a small company based in St Ives, to promote their vegan hair conditioner. Starting a couple of days after we get back,' she read aloud. 'She wants me to video call them tomorrow. I'll tell her I'm on holiday.' Her fingers started to tap out a polite reply.

'Hold on. It sounds good. You should take it.'

Fenna looked at Raffi lying on his changing mat, all scrumptious and scrunched up. She's not ready to go back to work. 'I don't know. The shoot will be an all-day thing . . .'

'Do it. I'll babysit.'

'Babysit?' It came out of nowhere, the dart of white rage tore through her. 'They're your children!'

He pulled his shoulders back. 'I'm trying to help here. You say you're tired, you moan that I don't do enough . . . well, here I am offering to help, and you still throw it back in my face. I don't know what more you want from me.'

She fastened Raffi's striped cotton romper and picked him up, leaving the full nappy for Luke to clear up, and stormed out. They've not spoken since.

Fenna has been trying to doze beside the pool and shake the row from her mind. They never used to be this snappy with one another. She doesn't know why Luke is so keen for her to get back to work much sooner than they'd discussed. She carefully budgeted to take a year off. As long as they aren't too extravagant, they've got enough in the bank, so what's the rush?

Gerry pulls out a camera and breaks her thoughts. He emerged from the bushes ten minutes ago proudly showing off an interesting shot of an unusually coloured butterfly. 'Say cheese.'

'Remember not to post the photos online,' Fenna says.

'We know, we know. Don't worry.' Marianne replies sharply. She presses her fingers into the Scout's salute.

Fenna bites down the irritation. There's a reason she doesn't show her children's faces on social media. Everything is artfully curated to only show the backs of their heads. She knows Marianne thinks it's ridiculous. Her mother-in-law doesn't understand the way the world works now.

Marianne sweeps to her feet and announces that she's heading back to the house as it's 'too hot!'. The chunky jewels on her embellished flip-flops cast rainbows on the wet tiles. Gerry trails behind her. A succession of clicks sound from his camera.

Alba has got out of the water and is running across the wet tiles towards Fenna.

'*Stai attento*!' Fenna calls.

Alba dutifully slows her pace and flops onto the sun lounger next to her, picking up her doll.

Rosie darts her gaze to Fenna. 'What did you say?'

'Hmm?'

'What did you say to Alba?'

'Ah, sometimes I slip into Italian without thinking. Marianne has complained in the past that she finds it rude, but I can't help it. I told her to *be careful*, why?'

'No reason.'

She rubs her daughter with a soft hooded towel. 'Are you ready to have a break, poppet?'

'No,' Alba giggles, scurrying away, her damp towel falling to the floor and landing in a puddle.

'Ten more minutes then you need some time in the shade,' Fenna calls. Theo scoops Alba up and gives Fenna the thumbs up. She picks the towel off the ground and catches Rosie staring at her. She looks confused. 'Everything ok?' she asks.

'Yeah . . . fine,' Rosie says, blinking, plastering on a smile.

Fenna sinks back onto the sunbed and sighs. The sky is a brilliant blue. There's not a cloud to be seen. 'I meant to ask you, what happened at the bar the other night?'

Rosie sits up. 'What do you mean?'

'The whole pulling a poster down thing. Was it really as innocent as it sounds?'

None of the family have mentioned the handsome police officer randomly knocking at the front door to warn Luke. Another thing brushed under the Fraser carpet.

'Erm, yeah, that was nothing. He was messing around. Sorry, I thought you meant something else . . .' Rosie coughs.

'Why? What else happened?'

Her back is taut. 'Nothing.'

'You said something else happened . . .' Fenna says slowly, frowning at Rosie's sudden change in demeanour.

'Nope. No. I mean, nothing interesting,' Rosie adds, her eyes darting to the pool.

Theo is pretending to be a shark nibbling Alba's toes.

Rosie flashes Fenna a tight smile and performs an overly dramatic stretch. 'I need a break from the sun. I think I'll go inside and get a drink.'

It's like she can't get away quick enough.

Fenna watches her scurry over to say something to Theo. Her gut twists. The longer she spends with Rosie the more something about her feels off. There's a fine line between being keen and earnest, and being sneaky. Rosie says all the right things but it's like she's playing a part.

Luke, Theo and Rosie walk away from the swimming pool, leaving Fenna and the children alone. Alba is happily singing to herself under the parasol, playing with her teddies, making up little songs and feeding them chunks of watermelon. Pink juice dribbles down her fingers.

Fenna leans over for a baby wipe and spots something out of the corner of her eye. Rosie has left her bag by her sun lounger. A sturdy, waterproof, canvas beach bag covered in wide navy blue and white stripes.

What secrets is this primary school teacher hiding? Even her job seems too perfect. And what was that about interrogating Fenna over what she was saying to Alba in Italian? Her demeanour changed in an instant. It's all a little weird.

Fenna places one hand on the straps and double-checks the coast is clear. She knows this is wrong. She should put it back. Luke would be horrified if he knew she was thinking of rummaging in another woman's belongings.

But there's something about Rosie that she can't put her finger on.

She unzips the bag. The sound is louder than she expected. What if someone comes down the steps and sees her? What will she say? Her heart beats faster. She doesn't know how long she will be left alone.

Inside is a tube of lip gloss with SPF, Rosie's mobile phone – the background a selfie of her and Theo in front of a blossom tree – her purse, and a magazine. Fenna pulls it out and flicks through the glossy pages. Her fingers land on something hard. Hidden inside is a black, A5-sized wire-bound notebook. Is this Rosie's diary?

There is a bang. Fenna jerks her head at the sound. It's Paulo moving a wheelbarrow full of cut branches. The metal handles clanged on the stones. He apologises for making her jump.

Sweat drips behind her knees. She shouldn't be doing this.

She wipes her clammy fingers on the beach towel and opens the notebook.

Her stomach flutters with unease.

It's not a diary. The paper is thin and tinged brown with age. Fenna frowns. It's a scrawling mess of scribbles, unreadable words and abbreviations. There are doodles in black biro on the lined pages. A scruffy drawing of a big house. A child-like pencil sketch of a church. There's some sort of crossed out map. Words scratched through the paper. A couple of pages have been torn out leaving strips of ruffled paper trapped in the wire binding.

What the hell is this?

There's so much she can't decipher. Much of the writing is illegible and the ink has faded over time. However, on one of the pages is an address that she can read.

It's a local address.

10/12 Via Della Chiesa, 53010, Laprezia, Italy.

She checks the children are still occupied and unaware of what Mummy is up to, and grabs her phone. Her fingers race to open Google Maps but she struggles to connect to any signal.

'Come on,' she mutters.

There is the sound of footsteps. She doesn't have time to wait for the page to load.

She quickly takes a photo of the address and starts to put the book away. As she does, the pages flutter and something catches her eye. One word that is sharp and vivid compared to the rest of the bizarre scribbles.

Fraser?

Rosie and Theo's voices grow louder. They're almost here. Her fingers are damp with sweat. She hurriedly arranges the items in the bag so it doesn't look suspicious. Which side of the sun lounger did Rosie leave it? Alba's singing isn't helping her think. She drops the bag to the floor at the exact moment Rosie comes down the steps holding two glasses of sparkling water. Theo is right behind her.

Fenna plasters on a bright smile and unclenches her jaw.

'I thought you might want a cold drink,' Rosie says, padding over in her flip-flops. 'Cheers.'

16

ROSIE – DAY 4

Rosie steps out of the house, closing the front door behind her. A voice from below makes her jump.

'Afternoon, you look nice.' Marianne smiles. She's crouched down by a trug of ruby red flowers, a spade in her hand and an audiobook playing on her phone. She tugs off a garden glove and mutes the clipped narrator's tones. 'Where are you going, darling?'

Rosie tugs the puffy sleeves of her gingham pink sundress. 'Theo's giving me a tour of the local area.'

Theo had suggested an afternoon away, just the two of them. It sounds perfect. The house is starting to feel claustrophobic. It was torture lying next to Fenna at the pool all morning, pretending that everything was fine, that she didn't see her husband have an illicit kiss with a young member of staff two nights before. Her stomach was in knots any time Luke's name was mentioned. Sweat dripped down her temples when she batted off Fenna's questions about their trip to the bar the other night. She'd had to get away and cool down.

Marianne stands, wincing as her knees loudly click. 'I wanted to ask you something.' Her mouth is drawn in a tight line.

'Hmm?'

'Has Theo said anything to you about Luke?'

'Luke? No. Why?'

'I think they might have had a little tiff. Apparently Luke threw Theo's protein shake away because he wouldn't give him one?' Marianne rolls her eyes. Roise allows herself to exhale. 'Well, that's what I've heard. They're grown men, surely they wouldn't be bickering about something as silly as that. Hopefully, it'll blow over. They need to know how important they are to one another. Family is everything. I'd thought they'd grown out of this possessive stage. Seriously, all that money I've wasted on therapists.'

'Therapists?'

'Yes. After what happened to their dad it made sense they both saw a grief counsellor, and, over the years, Theo has needed to have some extra support. Seeing him smile again is wonderful. I can tell he is besotted with you.'

Theo had never confided to Rosie that he'd seen a therapist. But she hasn't revealed that she has, too.

Their attention is pulled by Gerry standing in the shade of a nearby tree. He waves his arms wide, amid a phone conversation that the two women only catch the end of.

'. . . I was trying to do the right thing and give her a job. They moan about us having this place, so we try to help the economy and hire local workers to keep it running, but they take the piss.'

'Carla's not turned up today,' Marianne adds for Rosie's benefit. 'He's tried to get through to her but she's ignoring his calls.

So now he's moaning to Richard, our friend I told you about. He recommended Carla to us. Gerry thought he might know someone else who can help us out. But by the sounds of it it's not going too well.'

Perhaps Carla is lying low?

'What's wrong with expecting employees to have a sense of loyalty?' Gerry grumbles down the phone.

'I'm sure she'll be here soon,' Marianne says, fanning her face with a gardening glove. 'Oh, before you go. Have you made plans for tomorrow? I thought we could all have a day out. Florence? Or Siena? Both have lovely galleries, and we could get a spot of lunch, maybe a glass of wine or two? It would be nice for the whole family to do something together.'

'Sounds great.' Rosie nods with a tight smile.

'Wonderful. Have a good day, darling.' Mariane leans over to kiss Rosie on the cheek, imprinting her heavy floral perfume on her clothes. The smell suffocates her. 'Remember, if you can't be good, be careful.' She laughs.

A shiver rolls over her.

Be careful. Stai attento.

This is what Fenna said to little Alba by the pool earlier, warning her not to run in case she slipped. The same thing the taxi driver told her. Rosie remembers the look on his face. Her stomach twists. What did he mean? Why would a stranger bring her to *Villa Speranza* and tell her to be careful?

***

'You took your time,' Theo gets up from a bench beside the double-fronted garage.

'Sorry. I got held up talking to your mum. She wants us all to go on a day out tomorrow.'

He looks handsome today in his cute straw sun hat, pale blue linen shirt and navy shorts. The sun has lightened his blonde hair and his skin is healthy and tanned, compared to the blisters on her sunburnt shoulders and the angry, red mosquito bites on her calves.

'What?' he says, self-consciously.

'Nothing.' She smiles.

There is a low rumble as he slides the garage door open, the metal wheezes on its hinges. A double-height space filled with boxes and tools is revealed. It smells of sawdust and oil.

'I thought we'd do a tour of the countryside . . . in style,' he says.

Her eyes land on the baby blue Vespa in the corner.

'We're going on this? Can you drive a moped?'

'Course, I'm a man of many mysteries,' he says with a wink. 'When in Rome . . . or should that be Tuscany?' Theo grins, handing her a polished cream helmet.

The Vespa zips past fields of drooping sunflowers. They've left Laprezia and joined a busy A road. Her arms are tight around his waist, her chest is nestled against his warm back, feeling the beat of his heart through his shirt.

After about twenty minutes, they come to a stop and he parks under a pointed cypress tree. She gets off as graciously as she can, unsticking the leather seat from the back of her thighs, and looks around. Her hair is sweaty from being pressed into the helmet.

'This is Monterchi,' Theo says, handing her a bottle of mineral water. 'The views this high up are pretty awesome.'

Rosie gulps the tepid water and hands the bottle back. It must be about thirty-three degrees today. Other tourists have had the same idea for a day trip, as car after car revs up the hill looking for a parking spot. She marvels at the view. It's like stepping back into the past. Cats sunbathe in patches of sun on cobbled streets. Italian gentlemen chatter as they play dominoes on a folded-out table, gesticulating wildly with hands and slamming of palms. Limp cigarettes dangle from their mouths. There is the smell of hot diesel from dusty convertible Jeeps that drive past. An accordion player sits below a walnut tree. What little hair he has left is slicked back, black threads shimmering in the sun. His calloused knuckles dance over the ivory keys.

It is a world away from Laprezia. There's life here.

The mediaeval walls of the village snake out below them. It's an incredible vantage point. Theo goes to pay for parking. Rosie holds her phone up to take a photo, but her attention is pulled from the view.

There's an appeal poster tacked to a rusty red post box, near where she's standing.

The ghost of Danielle Dixon is everywhere.

Theo strides over. 'The machine wasn't working.' He shields his eyes from the sun, trying to see what's caught Rosie's attention. A cloud passes over, dimming the light for a second.

'What do you really think happened to her?' Rosie nods to the poster.

There's a long, drawn-out silence.

'I don't know, it's complicated, but sometimes people don't want to be found.'

'You think she's run away?' She's surprised. Everyone else seems to be so certain the poor girl is at the bottom of the lake. 'Fifteen years is a long time to be missing. To leave no trace behind.'

He shrugs. 'What do I know? I'm not a detective.' He moves to the side to let a group of determined tourists pass.

The click-click of their hiking sticks goes through Rosie.

Theo wraps a heavy arm across her sunburnt shoulders. 'Come on, you. Let's get a drink. I'm melting here.'

***

After a couple of hours exploring Monterchi, they stop off for a handmade gelato. It's hard to choose from the mouth-watering selection of ice-cream flavours. She eventually picks artisanal fig and honey in a wafer cone, served by a man with a booming laugh and a glint in his eye. They sit in the shade of an olive tree, far away from the bin clouded with wasps, and she brings up the conversation she had with Marianne.

'Your mum told me you'd had therapy?' Rosie says, licking a dribble of ice-cream that's trailing down her hand.

Theo has finished his tub of lurid green pistachio ice-cream. 'I didn't realise she was sharing so much so soon.' He shakes his head with a smile. 'It's good, it means she trusts you.'

Rosie lets out a sigh of relief. 'Did something happen?'

'What do you mean?'

'I mean, for you to get therapy?'

'It was a while ago. Mum was big into getting me and Luke to talk about our feelings when we were kids. She made us both have counselling when Dad died.'

Rosie and Theo lost their fathers when they were younger but it's not a subject they dwell on, for many reasons.

He pauses for a moment. The sparkle dims in his eyes. 'She thinks we bottle too much up.' Theo looks as if he's about to say something else, but he pulls himself up. 'Come on,' he says with a smile, shaking himself out of his reverie. 'We should make a move.'

***

They arrive back in Laprezia but instead of turning towards *Villa Speranza*, Theo unexpectedly parks on a side street.

'I thought we were going back to the house?' she asks, glancing around as he turns the engine off.

'I lost one of my AirPods when I was running the other day. You don't mind if I have a quick look for it?' he says.

Yes, she does mind. She's thirsty and her feet are aching from walking up and down the cobbled hills. She wants to get changed out of her sweaty summer dress and lie in a cool, dark room.

'Nope, it's fine.'

'Wait here. I'll be five minutes.' He plants a quick kiss on her head, and jogs away, not picking up on her irritation at this unexpected stop.

Rosie wishes Theo had at least parked under a shady tree. She wanders further down the road into the town to find somewhere cool to sit. On her way, she sees vibrant green parakeets with a distinctive red beak, yellow throat and long tapered tails. They appear in faded murals on the side of old buildings, and as moulded metal shapes as if perching on road signs. She's not seen an actual bird yet.

She peers in the window of a closed-down shop. Her eyes land on a small parrot ornament covered in a thick layer of dust. There's a framed print behind it. She blinks. It's a photo of the lake, and reflected in the still water is a mass of vivid green as hundreds of parakeets take flight into the sky above. It must have been an incredible sight. The birds by the lake were once a huge draw for the area. Now tourists spend their money in other towns, away from the place linked to a young girl's disappearance. She thinks of how busy Monterchi was. No wonder people here are upset and want answers.

'Found it.' Theo holds a white AirPod in the air, breaking her thoughts.

'How did you know where it would be?' she asks.

'That's my running route.' He nods to the footpath through a metal gate. Thorn bushes line the sides. That's where he must have fallen the other day.

As he walks ahead to the scooter, she glances back at the cheerful images of the exotic parakeets. Like Danielle, will they ever return?

17

ROSIE – DAY 5

Rosie's back is warmed by the sun. She picks up her glass of freshly pressed orange juice. The citrus smell fills her nose. Morning sunlight streams across the long wooden dining table, illuminating the jugs of fruit juice and steaming cafetières. Noisy birds chitter in a high tree. Marianne wanted everyone to eat breakfast together outside this morning before they head out for the day. Julietta rushes around, her arms laden with heavy plates. Rosie has offered to help but she is kindly shushed.

'Still no Carla this morning, Julietta?' Gerry glances up from his camera screen. He has been showing off his nighttime shots of an owl to anyone who will pay attention.

Julietta sighs in exasperation. 'No, I don't know what's going on with that girl. She has never done this before.'

'If she changed her mind about working here, she could have had the decency to tell us,' Gerry tuts.

Rosie analyses Luke's reaction hearing Carla's name. He is sitting at the far end of the table. There is nothing in his behaviour to show that the absent member of staff is a concern to him. Did he tell her not to come to work? Or was it her decision to take time off?

Raffi's cries fill the air. Fenna is standing a little away from the table, swaying gently, patiently trying to calm her son. Marianne fusses around the pair of them, telling Fenna to think about going dairy-free as it might be causing tummy upset in the baby.

There is the sound of tyres on gravel. The slam of a car door.

'Anyone expecting a delivery?' Gerry asks, placing his camera beside his mug.

Everyone shakes their head. Julietta goes to see who the visitor is.

Marianne finally leaves Fenna and the baby alone and sits at the head of the table. She asks Luke to pass the milk, oblivious to the look on Fenna's face.

Julietta rushes to the terrace.

'It's the police. They want to talk to you,' she says, her eyes darting between Gerry and Marianne.

They exchange confused looks and start to stand. The scrape of chairs over the stone tiles goes through Rosie.

'What now?' Luke groans, a tiny espresso cup cradled in one hand. 'If it's that jumped-up loser Giovanni come to complain about bloody posters again, I'll lose my mind.'

Before Gerry and Marianne can investigate, the police officer who was here the other day emerges from the house. Luke exhales loudly at the sight of him.

'*Buongiorno,*' Giovanni says. Judging by his stern expression, it's something more serious than posters.

'Everything ok, officer?' Gerry asks.

'Sorry to interrupt *Signore* Fraser,' Giovanni says, glancing at the decadent breakfast spread before them. He clears his throat. 'I need to find out when you last saw Carla Conti?'

'Carla? We were just talking about her. She left her shift early on Monday and hasn't turned up since. She's not answering her phone and hasn't returned any of my calls,' Gerry answers, crossing his arms.

Giovanni notes it down in a palm-sized notepad. 'So you last saw her two days ago . . .'

'Is she ok?' Theo asks the question everyone is thinking.

Giovanni looks up and holds Theo's gaze. His expression remains tight, giving nothing away. His brown eyes are so dark they are almost black. 'We don't know.'

A shiver dances across Rosie's arms. Alba bangs a spoon against her bowl.

'What? What do you mean?' Marianne asks, sitting forward.

Bang, bang, bang.

He clears his throat. 'She's missing.'

Bang.

Julietta drops a plate. It shatters on the stone tiles. The sound is drowned out by the rush of blood in Rosie's ears. Alba bursts into tears at the unexpected noise. Julietta rushes to get a dustpan and brush, apologising for being so clumsy. Her cheeks are flushed.

'She's missing?' Marianne repeats, fumbling to put on her designer sunglasses.

A prickling sensation starts at the base of Rosie's skull.

'What time did she leave here on Monday?' Giovanni asks Gerry.

'Well, she was supposed to be here until seven but she went

before lunchtime and left poor Julietta in the lurch.' Gerry blinks rapidly. 'Julietta? Do you know any more?'

Julietta looks up from the shards of ceramic in her hands. 'She told me she wasn't feeling well. I don't know if she was sick or not. Perhaps it was something to do with her boyfriend? Maybe they'd had a row? I know they have problems sometimes.'

'Have you spoken to him, officer?' Marianne jumps in. Her fingers play with the gold chain around her throat. 'The boyfriend?'

Carla has a boyfriend? Rosie turns to Luke to see if his face is giving anything away, but he is picking up a toy that Alba's dropped.

Giovanni nods. 'He was the one who reported her.'

Julietta wrings her hands together. 'I told her she could go home early. When she didn't turn up for work the next day, I spoke to Mr Fraser, who said he would speak to the agency.'

Gerry nods. 'They told me someone would call me back but no one has done. Our friend Richard Taylor-Warner was going to suggest a replacement as—'

'Do you remember exactly what time she left here on Monday?' Giovanni asks Julietta, interrupting Gerry.

Julietta blinks. 'It was before lunch. Eleven, maybe eleven thirty. I'm not sure . . .' She looks uncomfortable having everyone's attention on her. 'Do you think something has happened to her?'

'Her family say it's unusual for her to not come home so we're keeping an open mind. We have a witness who says they saw her at midday, heading towards the town. Alone. Upset. Wearing her work uniform.' Giovanni nods to the CCTV cameras. 'I will need to take a look at the recordings from those. It will help give us an exact timestamp of when she left here.'

'Of course,' Marianne says.

'Carla often takes the shortcut home through the woods and we don't have cameras all along that way,' Gerry chimes, cutting into a tomato with his knife, watery red liquid oozing across his plate. The sight of him eating makes Rosie's stomach turn. Her appetite has completely vanished.

She flicks her eyes around the table, trying to gauge what everyone is thinking.

Giovanni looks as if he is about to say something to Gerry but stops himself.

'Perhaps it's a lovers' tiff and she's gone to get some space?' Marianne suggests. 'Have you checked if she's gone to stay with family or friends? I'm sure others will tell you that she can be emotional; she's only young after all. Isn't that right, Julietta?'

Julietta nods.

'We're doing all the checks we can,' Giovanni confirms.

Rosie sits on her hands. Should she tell him about the kiss? Luke hasn't said a word. Perhaps it's the light, or his hangover, but he looks paler than normal.

Sweat beads down her back. The sun that was previously warming her is now burning her skin. Her eyes focus on her breakfast plate and the slice of melon she has half eaten. The bite marks in the pale orange flesh.

'Does anyone else have anything to share?' Giovanni pushes.

There is a collective shake of heads. Rosie bites her lip.

'Can I ask you where you all were around that time on Monday morning?' Giovanni asks, breaking the tense silence.

Rosie casts her mind back. She was hiding from Marianne in the wildflower garden. She doesn't know where everyone else was.

'This feels like an interrogation, mate,' Luke growls.

'Luke . . .' Marianne warns.

'No, no interrogation. *Mate.*' Giovanni's jaw tenses. 'We want to find Carla. Her family are extremely concerned, as you can imagine.'

'Of course, but we've told you what we know,' Theo says.

No, we haven't.

'I heard you were with her in *Tre Sorelle.*' Giovanni points at Luke.

Rosie forgets to breathe.

'And?' Luke bristles, darting a furtive look at Fenna. 'Chatting to someone at the bar is not a crime.'

Raffi's cries break the tension.

Giovanni snaps his notepad shut and asks Julietta to show him where Carla keeps her personal items. Marianne offers to come with them. Gerry says he'll join them when he's finished his breakfast. He looks in no hurry.

'I hope Carla's ok. It must be serious if the police are involved?' Rosie finally finds her voice the moment Giovanni has gone.

Theo dances his fingers across her arm. It's supposed to be comforting but it sends a shiver down her spine. 'I mean they're probably covering their backs after what happened before, with Danielle, I mean.'

'They cocked up not arresting Danielle's teacher when they had the chance and they're now going overboard and treating everyone like suspects over the smallest of things,' Gerry says with his mouth full. He mops up the oily residue on his plate with a slice of sourdough.

'It's not a small thing – Carla's been missing for two days,' Fenna says, rocking Raffi. 'They're right to be concerned. Can you imagine what her family are going through? They must be thinking the worst.'

Luke lifts his glass of orange juice and takes two quick gulps. 'Can we please stop being morbid?' he snaps. He leaves the table without another word. The back of his neck has broken out in red blotches.

'He's right. Carla will turn up,' Gerry says, filling his cup of coffee, in no rush to move. 'Hopefully.'

18

FENNA – DAY 5

Siena is teeming with tourists, bikes, art, and architecture. As soon as they arrived, Marianne steered Fenna to *Galleria Lombardi*. Despite not picking up a paintbrush in years, her mother-in-law clearly can't escape the pull to be surrounded by art. She explained how the collection of Italian Renaissance art is tiny compared to the vast gallery around the corner, but the space was air-conditioned and deliciously cool. Luke and Gerry took Alba to get an ice-cream after her noisy protests attracted too many tuts and glares from other visitors, and Theo and Rosie went off somewhere. She's not sure where. Rosie has barely spoken a word to her all morning since Giovanni's visit. The scribbles in her notebook that she found in her beach bag play on her mind. What does it mean? She hasn't had the chance to google the address yet.

Marianne and Fenna have meandered silently around the peaceful space, pausing now and then to look at portraits from the sixteenth century that caught their attention.

'Do you see how they've captured the light? It's spellbinding.'

Marianne muses, shaking her head in awe at an oil painting of a vase of colourful flowers.

'You paint better,' Fenna says. Her mother-in-law might be lots of things, but she can't deny her talent.

'Oh, shush.' Marianne lets out a tinkle of a laugh.

'Do you miss it?' Fenna asks.

'Every day. It wasn't a job to me. It was my passion.'

'So why not paint again?'

She remembers Luke telling her his childhood stories of his mum locked away in a paint-splattered studio, emerging with unwashed hair and bags under her eyes after working on a painting for days. He is proud of his mum but once confided to Fenna that he could never understand why people used to pay so much money for her pieces.

Marianne stiffens beside her. 'No. That's all in the past.'

Raffi wriggles in his pushchair and lets out a mewling cry. Lunchtime. There is a bench in front of a wide fresco and Fenna settles on it with Raffi in her arms. It's a scene of a woman and a man, side by side, his head against her ample, curved bosom. Fenna peers closer at the shiny plaque underneath. Saint Monica. Patron Saint of Mothers. This seems like the perfect spot to subtly whip out the muslin and feed her baby.

There is an occasional squeak of soles padding around, a polite cough and whispered Italian voices as visitors respectfully file past. Fenna reads the plaque below the painting once Raffi has latched on.

> A paragon of enduring love, patience, and persistent efforts. Saint Monia was a mother who believed her son was capable of good.

She prayed tirelessly for many years for her wayward son, Saint Augustine to convert to Catholicism. Eventually, he rejected his immoral life and found his faith.

Seen by many as a model wife and parent, but others believe she submitted to her volatile husband's abuse, meddled in her son's relationships, and violated boundaries.

Marianne comes to sit beside her and clears her throat. 'Why don't you and Luke go out tonight? We don't mind watching the children.'

'Well, Raffi will need to come with us,' Fenna says.

'No he won't, give him a feed and he'll be fine. Even if you only go for one drink. You need to leave him one day, you know.'

Fenna pushes her hair from her face. Luke has been in such a strange mood recently, she's not sure she particularly fancies spending one-on-one time with him. 'I'll see what Luke says.'

Marianne smiles as if she was expecting that reply. 'I've already asked him. He said it would be fine.'

Fenna clenches her jaw. She doesn't want to seem unreasonable. It's kind – and unexpected – of her mother-in-law to offer, but Raffi is still so dependent on her there's no way she's ready to leave him. It's not just his age. The horror of the break-in still hangs over her. Fear pulsates inside her at the thought of it happening again. Until someone is caught she won't rest easy.

'Thanks but I might have an early night.'

'You're on holiday,' Marianne says, rummaging in her handbag for a bottle of mineral water. 'Well, the offer's there if you change your mind.'

Fenna flashes a tight smile and focuses her attention on her son, rubbing a finger over his velvety soft cheek.

'I hope Theo and Rosie are having a nice time. It's good for her to see the sights. I can't believe she's not been to Italy before,' Marianne muses.

'Mmm.'

Fenna can't shake off the things she saw in that notepad she found in Rosie's beach bag yesterday. What do the chaotic scribbles mean? Why would she have a local address written down, and a note saying '*Fraser?*'

'What do you think of Rosie?' Fenna asks.

'Oh, she's wonderful. She's a positive, calming influence on Theo. Having a nice girlfriend like that will do him the world of good. Why? What do you make of her?'

Fenna chews her lip. 'Erm . . .' How can she explain what she saw without confessing that she went through her bag?

'Go on?'

Fenna exhales. *Here we go.* 'There's something about her.'

'Like what?'

'Don't you find that she asks a lot of questions?'

'You were the same when we met you.' Marianne chuckles. 'We need to cut her some slack. She's meeting all the family in one go, there's lots to take in. Plus, the police knocking on the door every five minutes isn't exactly welcoming.'

Thankfully Fenna was dressed when Giovanni visited at breakfast this morning, and not in her pyjamas this time. Not that he gave her a second glance. He was more focused on delivering the worrying news about Carla.

Gerry and Marianne don't seem too concerned about the missing member of staff and Julietta thinks it's a lovers' tiff. She remembers what Luke said to her on the way here. 'The local police need to be seen to be taking these things seriously, given the town's history.'

What was Giovanni getting at singling her husband out like that? She was sure she saw Rosie's eyes widen. There's something about her. Something she can't put her finger on. Her gut is warning her to keep her at arm's length.

'This is one of my favourites here,' Marianne says, nodding to the painting in front of them. Clearly wanting to change the subject. A Fraser family trait. 'She's also known as the saint of "trying your best". She dedicated her life to the salvation of her son. She wept every night for him to change his ways. When yours are teenagers, you'll understand.'

Fenna shakes her head. 'That's a long way off.'

'It'll come before you know it.'

People love to give advice about 'enjoying the moment' and 'being present' and 'once it's gone, it's gone', but after another terrible night's sleep Fenna isn't in the mood for a lecture about making the most of every second.

'Sometimes we're not the parent we want to be,' Marianne says, her voice low. 'All you can do is your best.'

A silence settles between the women. Fenna concentrates on her baby, milk-drunk and puckering his pink lips with sleepy eyes. She clicks her feeding bra back in place. Marianne gazes at the piece of art, head tilted, a faraway glaze on her eyes. She looks like she might cry.

'Are you ok?' Fenna asks. The silence of the gallery weighs down on her.

Marianne nods. 'You're doing a great job, you know. Being a mother is the hardest thing in the world. You try to keep them safe and protect them. It's heartbreaking knowing that you won't always be there beside them. Time is so precious.'

A rush of goosebumps covers Fenna's skin, and not from the gust of cold air coming from the air-conditioning vents. She's never had a heart-to-heart with her mother-in-law like this. Never heard praise from her. But there's something Marianne is alluding to. Something more she wants to say but is holding back.

She's about to ask when a noisy American couple enters the space, the man recording himself on his iPhone, with a loud running commentary. 'And here we have the next awesome room . . .'

Marianne pulls herself together. 'Right, it's high time for a glass of something cold.' She stands and attempts to brush the creases from her linen trousers. 'Shall I meet you out the front?' She doesn't wait for an answer and walks away, saying hello to the couple as she goes, leaving Fenna sitting alone wondering what that was about.

She carefully places Raffi back in his pushchair and tucks a thin blanket over his turned-out pudgy legs. A rush of love washes over her. Perhaps she's too harsh on Marianne for molly-coddling her sons; the fierce maternal love may shape and change over the years, but it never fades.

Her phone lets out a message chime. A member of staff tuts from behind her. Phones are supposed to be silent in the gallery. She mouths an apology and checks her text with a frown. It's from their mortgage company.

. . . Insufficient funds. Please call us urgently.

She blinks and reads the message again.

What? Insufficient funds? The mortgage is paid from their joint account. They're usually very good at keeping it topped up. There must be a mistake. She sits back down, her legs tingling, and logs into her online banking.

Her eyes dart down the screen. There's a lurch in her stomach. She might be sick.

Where the hell is all of their money?

19

ROSIE – DAY 5

Rosie tries to listen to the tour guide's voice filtering through her headphones. They are in the *Duomo di Siena.* Theo insisted that visiting the beautiful cathedral was a bucket list activity, 'We can't come to Siena and miss this.' She didn't want to tell him that she wasn't particularly interested.

It's packed with clammy tourists craning their necks to gaze up in bewilderment at the majestic dome that soars overhead. The looming Gothic architecture gives her the creeps. Statues of long-dead philosophers and prophets are tucked into alcoves beside towering black and white striped marble pillars like huge sticks of liquorice. She would have preferred to wander around the city's vibrant streets, which looked to be filled with artisan boutiques, heaving pavement cafes, and clouds of sugar from the many patisseries, but she didn't want to appear uncultured.

She hasn't stepped inside a church in years. *Not since the funeral*, her subconscious mind reminds her. She blinks that horrible day away. The tightness in her chest is an unwanted memory of the pain that she once was in. It's amazing how it lessens over time like everyone says it will, but the guilt and grief never fade completely.

Theo keeps giving her the thumbs up. He somehow manages to pull off the black plastic headset they were handed by the tour guide. She didn't realise he was so into architecture. Despite her grumbles, he went out for another run this morning. His training is starting to become a bone of contention. When she asked him to skip today's run, he insisted he would be quick but was still gone for forty-five minutes. He's going to get an injury if he keeps pushing himself so hard.

She tries to listen to the voice of the guide sharing details of the Baroque sculptures created in the thirteenth century, but her mind is elsewhere. After Giovanni's visit this morning, it's hard to relax.

Another girl has disappeared.

Rosie tells herself that it's a coincidence, nothing more. Yet something in her gut refuses to believe this. Another girl is missing in the same town. And not any girl. Carla. The one she saw kissing Luke. He didn't flinch when Giovanni spoke. And everyone else carried on eating as if they'd been told the weather forecast. She wonders if Gerry handed over the footage from the CCTV cameras. He seemed reluctant, but why would he not want to help the investigation?

That's not the only thing playing on her mind. Should she have told Giovanni about Luke and Carla? What if it's relevant?

'Rosie?' Theo is giving her a funny look. His headset round his neck. The tour guide has finished speaking.

She realises she's completely tuned out.

'I said, are you ok?' he repeats.

She decides she'll talk to Theo about her concerns as soon as they get out of here. They can find a nice cafe, preferably with air-conditioning, and come up with a plan.

'Great!' she replies.

He looks baffled at her over-exuberant reply but is pulled away to follow the group as they move on to the next room. It's much smaller but still breathtaking, decorated with five-hundred-year-old frescos dedicated to the Virgin Mary. Rosie tries to appreciate the painstaking hours each piece took to complete, but she can't concentrate.

Is she being watched? She glances around at the rest of the group. About ten or so other tourists are also on the midday tour. All are wearing headsets, and most have cameras around their necks or their phones in their hands. No one is looking at her.

Theo has his hands in his pockets, tapping his feet on the intricately laid tiles.

'Are you bored?' she asks.

'No.' He breaks into a wide smile. 'I'm with you, so of course I'm not.'

She smiles at the cheesy line.

Another tour group has joined them. A steady gush of people fills the small room. Bodies all around her. A nervous itch starts at the back of her mouth. A warning sign for a panic attack. She wants to pull Theo aside and ask if they can leave but he's wandered to the far side of the room, in his own world. A man with sharp sideburns and a mop of brown curls gives her a polite smile as she fans her face with a pamphlet.

Saints and gargoyles peer down from the walls and ceiling. She's spooking herself out for no reason. She takes a deep breath, pressing her fingernails into her palms to remain centred.

Thankfully their tour guide tells them to follow her through a brick archway for the 'pièce de résistance'. Rosie has no idea what this might be but excitable chatter breaks out. Theo glances down at his phone and looks up again. He's swallowed up at the front of the room, trying to fight the tide to rejoin her.

They move en masse to an entrance to a circular stone staircase.

'I hope you've saved your energy,' the tour guide says. 'Only three hundred and fifty steps to go.'

Everyone else bustles to push to the front. Theo manages to make his way over to her. She clasps his hand, surprised by how clammy it is, and holds on tightly.

'Three hundred and fifty steps?' she groans. 'Are you kidding me? This is supposed to be a holiday!'

'You'll be fine. The view is meant to be amazing. After you.'

She reluctantly enters the narrow staircase, muttering under her breath. Huge blocks of bricks surround her. Like a tomb. She blinks away the thought and focuses on putting one foot in front of another to climb the worn stairs. Theo follows her, playfully giving her bum a tap every few steps. This might not be how she would choose to spend her free time, but he's organised this visit for her. None of her other boyfriends ever went out of their way to plan things. It's romantic. Or at least it would be if her mind didn't keep wandering back to Carla.

And Danielle Dixon.

She's not seen any appeal posters for the schoolgirl in this city. The further away they drove from Laprezia, the more her youthful face disappeared.

'Not too much further to go,' Theo says.

She prays that he's right.

'I hope it's worth it,' she mumbles, sweat puddling in her bra. Before long, it becomes too hard to keep a conversation going.

The stairs are never-ending.

'It will be,' he promises her.

Eventually, the light in the stairwell changes. Excited voices and shrieks of delight filter down to them. They've reached the top.

'Wow.'

She momentarily forgets everything else and takes in the impressive landscape before her, suddenly feeling very small and insignificant. The slate grey roofs, the red terracotta tiles, the doll-house-like buildings that stretch into the distance. Theo was right. It was worth the effort. She wipes the sweat from her brow and drinks in the hustle and bustle of Siena spread out before them. A warm breeze licks her flushed cheeks. There is a flash of light. A camera startles her. It's a man from the tour group, the one with the sideburns. But he's not taking a photo of the view.

He's taking one of her.

What's going on?

She spins to find Theo but she can't see him anywhere. She's about to call his name when suddenly there's another flash.

People are clapping. She realises why she can't spot Theo in the crowd. Because he's kneeling on the ground.

On a bended knee.

'Rosie, will you marry me?'

20

FENNA – DAY 5

Back at *Villa Speranza*, everyone crowds around on the terrace to see the ring. Theo stands, chest out proudly like he's caught the catch of the day. Rosie looks starstruck. A tray of Negronis sit on the low table, a row of celebratory sundowners as the sun sets.

They're joined by Richard and Evelyn. The last time Fenna saw them was at her and Luke's wedding. Richard, a balding man in his mid-sixties with the round stomach of a privileged solicitor, gifted them a ridiculously expensive but horrendously ugly vase. If it hadn't broken when they last moved house she would have sold it to get some extra cash whilst she's on maternity leave.

'Another wedding!' Evelyn lets out a whoop, flicking her glossy, curly black hair. Richard's wife is a lot younger and slimmer than her husband. She comes from Barbados and is full of warmth and smiles. Fenna forgot how much energy Evelyn has. She likes to be centre stage whereas Richard prefers to stand on the sidelines and observe. She's always wondered if there has ever been a thing between him and Marianne. They seem a lot better suited.

'Congratulations,' Fenna says, coming to kiss Rosie's cheek.

'You'll be sisters-in-law.' Gerry smiles, a camera in hand to capture their brief embrace. 'A new addition to the Fraser family.'

Rosie Fraser – it doesn't sound right.

'It belonged to my great-great-grandmother, and survived two world wars,' Marianne clucks, angling Rosie's hand for everyone to see better. The deep blue sapphire and gold ring glints in the golden evening light.

Evelyn squeals, proclaiming it to be 'the most beautiful thing' she's ever seen.

Fenna swallows the sudden bubble of jealousy. She wasn't presented with a family heirloom. Not that she dislikes her engagement ring, but there is no story behind it. Luke picked it up at a local jewellers – she knows because he got the wrong size and she had to get it altered. Saw the receipt. Saw how it was bought the day of the proposal, in the sale. She's always sensed it was a rushed decision and seeing it printed in black and white confirmed her suspicion.

She waits for Julietta to finish setting up the aperitivo. She needs a drink after the rollercoaster of emotions of the day.

She was convinced their bank account had been hacked. The moment she saw the low funds she'd called Luke, but it had gone to voicemail. She'd left a hysterical garbled message, pacing the stone steps opposite the gallery, ignoring the concerned looks from tourists enjoying a gelato. She was calling the bank to tell them to block their cards in case more money vanished when Luke had rushed around the corner to find her. Alba was covered in chocolate ice-cream stains and Gerry trailed behind the two of them, looking frazzled.

'We've not been scammed. I did it,' he'd said under his breath so Gerry couldn't hear.

Fenna cancelled the call.

'What?'

'I moved the money. It's fine. It's in the business account. I completely forgot to tell you; it slipped my mind.'

'But . . . what about the mortgage?' she'd stuttered.

Her heart had slowed a fraction as she'd listened to him explain that his accountant had advised it, something to do with the rate of inflation and tax purposes. He offered to send her a screenshot of the money in this different account to prove it was safe if she wanted him to. She'd felt embarrassed for being so dramatic. Sleep exhaustion was clearly affecting her ability not to catastrophise.

'Fenna? Hello, earth to Fenna.' Marianne waves her hand. 'Gosh, you do look tired. I was asking if you could move along so Rosie can sit down?'

Fenna does as she's asked, blinking away the thoughts about money. Luke seemed calm about it; she knows he will have been advised to do the right thing.

'So, tell us everything.' Marianne turns towards Rosie.

'I'm still in shock.' Rosie lets out a high-pitched giggle. Her cheeks are flushed and she keeps twiddling the ring.

'You didn't suspect anything?' Theo asks.

'Nope,' Rosie blinks.

'Did you know he was planning this, Mum?' Luke asks Marianne.

'I might have done.' His mum beams. There is a sheen where her foundation has slipped. The powder of her taupe eyeshadow sits in creases. She's pretty drunk already. 'It was a giveaway when Theo asked for Grandma's ring to be cleaned.'

There is the sound of a cork popping.

'Half a glass for Fenna,' Marianne says to Julietta who pours the expensive Champagne into gleaming flutes. 'She's breast-feeding, remember.'

A glass of pale pink bubbles – barely half filled – is handed to her. Fenna tries not to be wound up by the miniscule measure. Why does Marianne insist she knows what's best?

'Congratulations.' Gerry leads the toast. 'To Rosie and Theo. Welcome to the family.'

Fenna lifts her flute and gulps the bubbles, which fizz at the back of her throat. She finds it hard to swallow.

'You know, Rosie, I feel like we've met before,' Evelyn says, coming to join the women on one side of the terrace. The pearls around her neck are the same shade as her incredibly white teeth.

Rosie politely smiles. 'I don't think so.'

'Were you at the celebration for Marianne's lifetime achievement in March? The one at the art gallery on Bold Street? That was the last time I was in the UK.'

'Nope. Not me . . .'

'Hmm. Strange. Maybe it's because you remind me of that actress . . . you know the one? With the lovely big brown eyes? Fenna? Do you know who I'm talking about?' Evelyn asks.

Fenna shakes her head. 'You need to be more specific.'

'Darling, do you know who I mean?' Evelyn loudly calls to Richard, pulling him from his conversation with Gerry. 'Doesn't Rosie look familiar? Who am I thinking of? An actress. Brown hair. Wide stare-y eyes. Neat chin.' Richard's face is scrunched in thought. She wafts a hand. 'Perhaps she's not an actress.'

'You're not getting confused with Theo's ex-girlfriend, are you? She was also very pretty,' he says, his voice baritone deep.

Evelyn lets out a tinkle of an embarrassed laugh. She fidgets with her shoulder-length curls. 'Richard! You tease. Please ignore him. He's terrible.' She wafts her husband away. Rosie presses her glass to her lips and holds her fixed smile in place.

Marianne claps her hands to get everyone's attention. 'Now this might sound premature, but I was hoping to get plans underway for your engagement party. You will want to do something official when you get back home, but it would be wonderful to celebrate together here before you leave, and I've got lots of ideas.'

'Calm down, Mum,' Theo laughs.

What's happened to her relaxing holiday? The ring *and* an engagement party? Why are they treating this new girl like she's royalty? No one even knows her! Fenna coughs on her Champagne.

Everyone turns to check she's ok.

'It went down the wrong way.' She pats her chest.

'What about getting married here?' Marianne asks, ignoring Fenna's splutters. 'We could help organise everything. Destination weddings are en vogue you know. It would be easy to get a licence; I'm sure we know someone in the village who can help us out. Oh, imagine this place fit for a wedding,' she breathes, beaming up at her house. 'Gerry could do the photos. Julietta could make the cake. Evelyn can help with the wedding favours. You always give the most thoughtful gifts.'

Marianne and Evelyn start mentioning names of people they could call on to help organise marquees and catering and airport transfers for the guests. A dart of jealousy strikes Fenna. She was never offered *Villa Speranza* for their wedding.

'It's all coming together.' Marianne clasps her hands. 'What do you think? Wouldn't it be great?'

Rosie puts down her glass and is about to reply.

'If it gets that far.' The words spill out of Fenna's mouth before she realises she's said them out loud.

Everyone twists their heads to face her. Evelyn gasps. Luke and Richard give her an amused look. Rosie shifts on her feet.

Her stomach lurches. She needs to quickly backtrack.

'What I mean is that . . . erm . . . marriage is hard work, and some people change their mind. Cold feet and things,' she adds, flushed at the way they're looking at her.

'Nothing will go wrong,' Theo says, protectively wrapping an arm around Rosie's shoulders. 'Nothing.'

21

FENNA – DAY 5

'So . . .' Luke says, standing in front of the mirror, squeezing a dollop of hair product onto his hands. A wide grin is on his face. 'Rosie and Theo, getting married. Mum's over the moon. She bloody loves a wedding.'

'Clearly,' Fenna replies, deadpan. She was surprised by how ecstatic Marianne seemed. It took her ages to win his family's affection, but it's being handed on a platter to Rosie. Does no one apart from her have reservations about this new girl? 'They barely know each other, they're not living together, and she told me that her mum hasn't met Theo yet . . .'

'It's a bit of a shock, I guess, but you're clearly not a fan judging by your outburst earlier.'

Fenna bristles. She doesn't want to be reminded of the way Theo threw daggers at her. She usually thinks before she speaks but sleep exhaustion has clearly removed her filter.

'It seems rushed. Don't you agree?'

'Yeah, it's quick, but when you know you know.' Luke concentrates on his reflection. 'He's moving in with her when they get back from this holiday and isn't her mum on some cruise? It's not that suspicious.'

'Hmm. You're sure this is all Theo's decision?'

'What do you mean?'

'Well, your mum has a lot of money. This house for one thing—'

'You think this has to do with money?' Luke turns to face her. 'Theo will get a pre-nup sorted.'

'We didn't.'

'That's because I trust you.'

There's a pause. She knows Marianne tried to push Luke to sign a legal contract but he refused.

'Anyway, a lot can happen between now and their wedding day. Don't stress about it,' Luke says, checking the time.

Richard had insisted the men continue the celebrations at the bar in town and Luke said he'd join Theo and Gerry once he'd helped get the children to bed. Evelyn and Marianne seemed happy to be left alone to catch up and Rosie said she wasn't feeling great, blaming a bad headache on the Champagne that Marianne kept pouring for her.

Fenna pulls her hair back into a ponytail and catches her tired reflection in the mirror. 'Something feels off about her.' She starts to take her make-up off with a cotton pad. 'It's like she's playing a part.'

'You'll need to give me more than that.'

She takes a breath. It would be good to get his take on things. 'I found her notebook. It had these strange notes in it.'

'What? Where?'

She can't say that she rummaged through another woman's handbag.

'It was on the table outside,' she lies.

'And you went through it?' He gives her a look.

She drags the cotton pad over her eyes. 'That's not the point.'

'What did it say?'

She remembers the scribbles, the map, the heavy-handed lines through words; she wished she'd had longer to try and work out what it all meant.

'It was weird. There was loads of stuff crossed out so it was hard to read. What jumped out at me was the name Fraser, followed by a question mark, and an address in Laprezia.'

'Ok . . .' he says slowly, in a slightly patronising tone. 'Have you searched for this address?'

Fenna shakes her head. 'Not yet but—'

He sighs and checks his watch. The gesture irritates her. She wishes she'd not mentioned it. Clearly he wishes he was out with the boys. 'Do you remember where it was? I'll look now.'

She picks up her phone and reads it aloud. He doesn't ask her why she took a photo of it.

'It's the address of a shoe shop in the town.' Luke frowns a second later. 'Well, it was. It's closed down now.'

'Shoes? Let me see.'

He turns his phone screen towards her. Google Street View shows an ordinary-looking house. A faded sign is painted on the side of the bricks. *Mario's Shoes*.

He snatches the phone back when it pings with the sound of a message.

'Err, I was looking at that.' Fenna pouts.

'Sorry. It's Richard. He's asking what's taking so long.'

Luke types out a message, a dart of concentration between his eyebrows.

Fenna lifts the lid of her lavender-scented night cream. *A closed-down shoe shop? Why would Rosie be interested in that?*

Luke glances at her, picking up on the look on his wife's face. 'Maybe she just likes Italian leather shoes?'

'Maybe . . . Something feels weird to me. I'm telling you, there's something about her that I can't put my finger on.'

'You jealous?' he says playfully, reaching across and tickling Fenna in the side. 'Worried she's going to be the new favourite daughter-in-law?'

'No, I'm not jealous, I'm concerned. There's a difference. I'm thinking about our children's safety. I mean, none of us know this woman and she's around our kids every day. If I'm totally honest, what happened at home has made me wary of new people. Is that such a bad thing?'

They've never properly spoken about the break-in and how it made them feel.

The smile vanishes from his face. 'Babe, I told you I already checked her out. She's really normal and boring. And besides, she's going to be family now. You need to forget about the burglary. It's one of those unlucky things. Nothing more. You can't let it warp how you see people. Unless you're telling me that you think she's the scumbag who broke into our house?'

'No. I'm not saying that, I—'

He cuts in. 'Are you ok though?'

'Me? I'm fine,' she says, pulling back the bed sheets. She's had enough of this conversation and needs to sleep before Raffi wakes.

'No.' He steps towards her. His arms hold hers so she is forced to stay put. He tightens his grip. She wants to wriggle from his grasp but he's stronger than her. 'Are you *sure* you're ok?'

A strange rush of emotion falls over her. It must be the way Luke is looking at her, asking if she's ok for the first time in what seems like ages. Suddenly she wants to tell him all the spiralling thoughts she has in the dead hours of the night. The ones when she feels like she's the only person awake in the world. It's like they leak under the gap of the closed bedroom door and swirl around in the darkness. Mostly she stresses about feelings of guilt and regret, and concern for her children. Sometimes it's the news – the terror, the injustice – or the chores she's not finished, the messages she's not replied to, the events she's missed. She panics about how it's all going too fast and too slow at the exact same time and how is that possible? How she wants this exhaustion to end but knows she will crave this chapter of her life in years to come.

'I'm fine.' She pulls away.

Maybe this isn't about Rosie.

It's just a phase. I'll sleep again one day.

Luke keeps his eye on her for a second or two. 'I mentioned what you said about moving to Italy to Mum.'

'And?' Her heart picks up.

'And she said we're welcome to come here for holidays if we want, as long as there are no guests booked in. She could give us mates' rates.'

Fenna bites her tongue. *Mates' rates?* Marianne's practically offered to pay for Theo's wedding and all they get is mates' rates? She remembers to breathe and follow what Luke's saying.

'. . . She's worried about you.' He drops his voice. 'Is this idea to relocate a cry for help?'

'No!'

'She thinks you might need to talk to a doctor as you're not managing the transition going from one to two. You are ok, aren't you?'

'I'm fine. What else did your mum say?' She crosses her arms, trying to stay calm.

'Maybe it's time to stop breastfeeding and get Raffi on formula so other people can help. So it doesn't all fall on you.'

Not this again. She exhales. 'He's thriving as he is. I don't want to change anything.'

'But when you go back to work you'll have to leave a bottle for him. I mean, what about that job Nisha mentioned? You won't be able to stop the entire shoot to feed him, will you? Wouldn't it be easier to introduce formula now? Mum says it's called combi-feeding . . .'

'Stop, please.' Fenna doesn't want to hear another thing about what Marianne thinks. It's exhausting. 'Forget it. Moving to Italy can stay as a dream. I'm fine, don't worry about me.'

She wishes he would wrap his arms around her. Instead, he puts on his shoes and tells her not to wait up. Leaving her alone with the baby, again.

22

FENNA – DAY 5

Fenna has tossed and turned in bed for around twenty minutes since Luke left. It's no use. She's too restless to sleep. She pulls on her robe, pads down the corridor and knocks on Rosie's bedroom door. It's time for a chat. She needs to get over this niggling doubt that something is wrong with Theo's girlfriend. *Fiancée.*

'Rosie?' Fenna knocks again.

Perhaps she was abrupt earlier, suggesting things may go wrong before the big day. Rosie hasn't done anything wrong. Ok, the scribbles in her notebook are odd and the eagerness to be liked is irritating, but Luke's right, she's going to be part of the family now. Fenna needs to get over this weird gut feeling that she can't put her finger on.

Things have been stressful back home since the burglary and the difficult birth and the stretched family finances, so it's no wonder she's overthinking things. Fenna is here to enjoy a much-needed holiday, not convince herself everyone is out to get her.

She knocks a little louder this time. There's still no answer.

She presses her ear to the wood to see if she can hear the shower running from their ensuite. Silence.

'Rosie?' she calls again and pushes the door open. The wood scratches against the floor with an ominous creak. 'Rosie? I wanted to check if you were ok . . .?'

Fenna stops.

There's nobody here.

The bed is made up from the morning. The plump pillows are waiting to be used. A side lamp is on and Rosie's shoes, the patent black sandals that she wore to dinner, are kicked off near the antique mirror.

'Rosie?' Fenna knocks on the ensuite but the door moves open with her touch.

Where is she?

Did she change her mind and stay downstairs drinking with Marianne and Evelyn? Fenna strains to see if she can make out women chatting but all she can hear is the faint hum from Alba's white noise machine that helps her to sleep. Rosie definitely complained that she didn't feel great so perhaps she's gone to get some painkillers or maybe she had a miraculous recovery and went to meet the men at the bar. Either way, she's not in here.

A sound from down the corridor makes Fenna jump. She automatically checks her phone. The monitor app shows both children are sleeping. Fenna pulls her dressing gown tight.

Something catches her eye as she turns to leave. There's a stack of family photo albums shoved under her side of the bed. Why are those here? Hidden away like this? Does Theo know?

Fenna returns to her room. But no sooner does she slip into the soft sheets does a light brown coloured moth hop around the bedside lamp, flittering erratically above the bulb. Grumbling under her breath, she gets up to open the window to let it out. There's no way she will be able to sleep otherwise, imagining the paper wings and furry body trapped in the bedroom with her.

They sleep with the fan on and the windows shut to keep any bugs out, but it's nice to have a sudden waft of the nighttime air. She inhales the smell of the sun-scorched earth and honeysuckle from the climbing plants. The stars are twinkling overhead. She turns off the lamp and the moth obediently flies out through the open window.

She's about to close the shutters when she sees a figure in the garden.

Paulo? No. It's too late for him to still be here.

It takes a second for her eyes to adjust to the darkness. The person is lit by a small torchlight.

Rosie?

Fenna presses herself closer to the glass and holds her breath.

What is she doing? The beam of light, from a phone, moves as if whoever is holding it is walking quickly. It disappears behind a wall. A chill dances over Fenna.

She leaps from her skin when an alarm rings out. Raffi's due his night feed now. She hurriedly turns the sound coming from her phone off but when she looks back the figure is nowhere to be seen. She scans the empty gardens one more time and then closes the shutters and scurries back to her bed.

Luke said he'd checked Rosie out but there's still something about this woman that doesn't sit right. Call it women's instinct. She should have done it herself, not taken his word for it.

Raffi isn't stirring for his feed so she's got time. Fenna sits upright with the glow from her phone screen lighting her face and opens her internet browser. She types two words: *Rosie Riley.*

The only social media profile she can find is on Instagram. Nothing comes up anywhere else. Her feed is like Rosie in real life. Quiet. Unassuming. Boring. Her photos are mainly linked to the primary school where she works or arty shots of nature. There are a couple of older photos from Christmases long ago with her mum and dad and a young Rosie in a dated sweater and nineties hairstyle. She celebrated her last birthday at a chain chicken restaurant with a friend; a woman called Lydia is tagged in the post.

Fenna clicks on Lydia's profile. This feed is bright and busy, full of people and smiling faces and trendy brunch food. There's a photo of her leaping onto a blow-up flamingo in a swimming pool, a wide, cheesy grin on her face. This is a girl who likes to have fun. Fenna keeps scrolling, wishing Lydia was here on holiday instead. She wouldn't put Rosie and Lydia together as friends.

A cry from Raffi pulls her back to reality.

She blinks, her eyes tight and gritty from the light on the screen. She's been searching online for the past twenty minutes. She's not discovered anything suspicious, and yet . . . Something in her gut refuses to accept that.

Something is going on with this girl.

She's determined to find out what.

23

ROSIE – DAY 6

The smell of fresh lemon hits Rosie as she passes the door of the nursery. Julietta is running a dust cloth over the windowsills.

'*Buongiorno.*' She smiles.

'Morning.' Rosie takes a few steps into the room.

Julietta squirts cleaning spray across the glass and quickly buffs away sticky fingerprints. Sunglasses that hang from a chain around her neck dance as she moves.

'Congratulations, *cara*.' Julietta nods to the engagement ring.

Rosie self-consciously clasps her hand. 'Thanks.'

'So exciting. I know when Carla comes back she will be so happy for you, too.'

'Have you heard from her yet?'

'No. Not yet.' Julietta's smile falters. 'Can I help you with anything?'

Rosie chews her thumbnail. 'I wanted to ask you something actually—'

'Me? Of course. I'm happy to help.'

She takes a deep breath, unsure how to phrase the questions on her mind. *Be careful.* 'Do you know if—'

The doorbell rings and cuts her off. Julietta quickly grabs her cleaning products and loads them back into a plastic caddy.

'Sorry, *tesoro*, I have to go. I'm waiting for a delivery. Come and find me in the kitchen later if I can help with something?'

Rosie sinks to the padded rocking chair when Julietta has gone. The arms and back panel are upholstered in a neutral oatmeal-coloured fabric with tiny white birds. She closes her eyes and gently rocks back and forwards. What a whirlwind twenty-four hours. She can't catch her breath.

Theo's called her 'wifey' all morning. Was he planning to propose to her this whole time? The Frasers will be her official in-laws! It's all happened so fast.

Too fast?

Everyone is excited about the wedding. Not that they've thought about a date yet, despite Marianne pushing for them to 'not waste a second'. Clearly she wants more grandchildren.

Rosie twirls the ring around her finger, getting used to the weight of the gold against her skin. Fenna could barely hide her irritation that she wasn't offered this beautiful piece of antique jewellery as she pretended to extend her congratulations. Rosie could tell that she didn't mean the kind words she was saying. She doesn't blame her. If the shoe was on the other foot, she'd also feel upset that a new girl has come in and threatened the status quo. She wanted to take her to one side and tell her that she didn't *ask* for this ring, and in all honesty, she's not sure it's her taste, even if the sentiment is breathtaking. She suspects it to be worth an absolute packet. But she wouldn't know how to say all this without rubbing it in Fenna's face.

In all honesty, she's in complete shock. The proposal came from nowhere.

Theo said he couldn't imagine his life without her, and she feels the same, but a niggling voice at the back of her mind reminds her how quick this is. There's still so much they don't know about one another. Are they ready to vow to stay together till death do they part? She thinks of her precious notebook and the secrets it contains.

Will he still want to marry her once he knows the truth?

There is the sound of laughter from outside. Rosie peers out of the window. Fenna is barefoot and chasing Alba on the lawn. The little girl giggles and squirms when her mum catches her. Rosie sinks back in the rocking chair. The familiar smell of the window spray reminds her of home; it's the same scent that her mum used. A sudden rush of emotion squeezes her chest. She wishes she could hear her voice.

As she takes out her phone, she notices how the stones in her engagement ring sparkle in the sunlight, creating a glitter ball that bounces against the nursery walls. She taps open her messages. Her finger hovers over the microphone icon, ready to record a voice note.

It's been so long since she's spoken to her mum. She's not sure where to start. She wants to tell her that she's engaged, but there's so much more that she needs to say. Things she needs to explain.

She remembers Theo's face, his bent knee, and the tremble in his hands as he held out the most expensive ring she'd ever seen. Was she blinded by the gem that's worth more than what she's ever had in her bank account? Maybe. The word 'yes' flew out and she couldn't take it back. She's not sure if she *wants* to take it back.

The headache last night was an excuse for her to have some

time alone to process everything. After a brief chat with Marianne and Evelyn, who were tipsy and getting carried away with plans for the engagement party, she went for a walk around the gardens, thinking with every step. She was out there for ages, unsure if she's made the right decision.

She loves Theo, that much is true. She didn't expect *this* so soon.

'Alba, come and put more suncream on, please,' Fenna's voice from outside breaks her confused thoughts.

Rosie sits up and winces as pins and needles tingle in her right foot. There's still so much they don't know about each other. The taxi driver's cryptic comment rushes to her mind.

Be careful.

The rocking chair lets out a long, slow creak across the wooden floorboard. The sound travels through her. She clears her throat and lifts her phone to her lips, pressing the microphone icon.

She takes a deep breath and starts to talk.

24

FENNA – DAY 6

Fenna wanders into the house, breathless from chasing Alba, trying to remember where she put her phone. She retraces her steps and goes to the downstairs bathroom. Not there. Where is it?

She is about to move to a different room when she hears a low buzzing sound. Her phone is half hidden behind the fruit bowl on a console table in the hall. The screen is lit up with an alert from the baby monitor app. Fenna squints in the sunlight. There is a figure moving in her daughter's bedroom. The volume indicator is tilting up and down. She frowns and sits down on the bottom step of the stairs. Everyone is outside.

At least she thought everyone was.

Rosie appears like a ghost on the black-and-white camera screen. She's talking to someone on her phone.

It might be Fenna's imagination but earlier she's sure that Rosie stiffened when she questioned her about where she was last night.

'I went to get a glass of water,' Rosie had said, unconvincingly.

Marianne was quick to leap with an answer. 'She joined Evelyn and I for a chat in the kitchen.'

'Oh? I thought I saw you in the garden,' Fenna said, intently watching Rosie's reaction.

'In the garden?' Marianne laughed. 'I know you're shattered, Fen, are you sure you're not seeing things?'

Rosie laughed too, as if this was an absurd suggestion.

Fenna's hand had curled into a fist under the table. She knows what she saw. Doesn't she? What if her mind is conjuring up images? There is no reason why Rosie would be wandering around in the garden alone. At night. And yet . . .

Fenna holds her phone closer to her ear.

'I hate lying to him . . .'

Paulo whistles as he drags something heavy through the back door, the sound cutting out whatever Rosie said next. Her voice is low, as if she's whispering. Clearly she doesn't want anyone to hear this conversation. Doesn't she know there's a baby monitor in the room?

Who is she talking to? Or more to the point, who is she lying to? Fenna turns the volume up and holds her breath to hear better. Every muscle is tense.

Paulo's whistling gets louder. She grits her teeth.

'. . . Maybe I should never have come here. This wasn't supposed to happen.'

There is a crackle then silence.

***

Fenna gets herself a glass of water from the kitchen. Rosie's 'admission' has unsettled her. Raffi is nestled in the stretchy wrap baby sling attached to her chest, she hoped it would help him drift off. He has been cranky from the moment he woke this morning.

Plinky, plonky melancholy classical music echoes down the hallway. She thought the piano in the drawing room was for show. Who's playing it? She steps closer to where the sound is coming from, each note growing louder. Raffi blinks his eyes, alert to the song.

The door is slightly ajar. Fenna pushes it open. Her footsteps are drowned out by the crescendo. Sitting at the piano – head bent, eyes closed – is Marianne. She must sense that she's no longer alone as she snaps her hands away from the keys.

The silence is worse than the music.

'That was beautiful,' Fenna lies, taken aback by how exhausted her mother-in-law looks.

Marianne pushes her stool away to stand. It makes a painful scraping sound over the tiles. She turns her back to Fenna, pulling a tissue from her pocket to wipe her nose.

'I didn't mean to disturb you. I wondered if I could have a word, but if you're busy . . .' Fenna trails out, wishing she'd not interrupted what is clearly an emotional moment. 'I'll leave you alone.'

'Is everything ok? The children alright?' Marianne asks, nodding at Raffi, her voice stringier than normal. She coughs. 'Excuse me, my hay fever is playing up again.'

'Yep, they're fine. But don't worry, I'll catch you later.'

'You're here now.' Marianne pushes open a window. It cracks the tension and brings in welcome fresh air. 'What did you want to talk about?'

'Rosie,' Fenna says.

'Rosie?' Marianne frowns. 'Has something happened?'

'No, well, I . . .' She takes a breath. 'There's something about her that makes me uneasy.' Fenna folds her arms. 'The family photo albums are in her room and—'

'Yes, I gave them to her. Why? Is that a problem?'

'No . . . I . . .' she stutters.

Should she tell her about Rosie's notebook? But she'll have to lie about *how* she found it. Marianne doesn't believe that Fenna saw Rosie wandering around the garden last night. She probably won't listen to her concerns about what she overheard on the baby monitor. She presumed Roise was referring to Theo with the comment about how she *hates lying to him*, but she didn't catch the start of the conversation. It could be completely innocent. The thing is, she didn't say *anything* that can be used as evidence. And yet . . .

'Fenna,' Marianne sighs. 'Not everyone is out to get you. Remember how eager you were to impress us when we first met? You were nervous, exactly how Rosie is now. It doesn't mean there's any malice. Unless she's done something specific to make you *uneasy*, I can't help you.'

There's a drawn-out pause. Raffi wriggles against her chest. A tiny foot kicks her ribcage.

Marianne tilts her head. 'This isn't about Rosie, is it?'

'What? Yes—'

'Luke told me you were finding things tough, going from one to two. Maybe you're projecting this onto Rosie. Feeling threatened a little?'

Fenna shakes her head. 'No . . . it's not that, I—'

'There's been a lot of change in your life recently. It's ok to feel out of control.' She simpers. 'Don't take this the wrong way, but you look exhausted. It's not fair on the children to get yourself in this state.'

'I'm fine.' She clenches her jaw. 'I'm not *in* a state.'

Why isn't she listening to her?

'Go and have a lie down. Raffi needs his mother to be rested. This is your holiday too. Alba's with Luke, she's fine.'

It's infuriating that Marianne won't take her seriously but perhaps she is right. Maybe if Fenna had more sleep she would have a clearer head. She could figure things out easier?

'Fenna? Earth to Fenna?' Marianne waves a hand in front of her face, making her jump. She was miles away. 'You're spilling your water.'

She looks down at where she's pointing. A wet patch has appeared on the hem of her maxi skirt from the glass that's tilted in her hands. Raffi blinks up at her and she is overwhelmed with guilt that she's letting him down.

'Maybe you're right,' she reluctantly agrees.

A nap does sound good.

'Good girl. I'll help Luke watch the children.'

'Are you sure you don't mind?' Fenna chews her lip. 'Raffi will need feeding in about an hour or so, but I'll be back before then.'

'Please, go and take all the time you need. Don't worry about us.'

Fenna hands over Raffi and his changing bag. She wants to leave a list of instructions, but Marianne tells her she will be offended if she thinks she can't manage to look after a baby when she raised two herself. So Fenna gives her son a kiss and does as she's ordered. Everything inside aches. No wonder terrorists use sleep deprivation as a form of torture. Though Fenna hates to admit it, Marianne might be right. Sleep could be exactly what she needs.

She walks upstairs, hovering outside Rosie and Theo's room. Part of her wants to go inside and have a look for clues. *Stop being paranoid. There is nothing wrong with his fiancée.* She carries on walking to her bedroom, the enticing crisp white sheets drawing her in.

It's a matter of seconds before she's fast asleep.

25

ROSIE – DAY 6

Rosie slips on her sandals and heads down the corridor that takes her outside. She wants to be alone with her thoughts. But as she turns the corner she sees Luke slumped on a plush, plum-coloured velvet chair. The bags under his eyes are the same colour as the fabric. He's eating an apple and looking at his phone. He thrusts it away when he sees her coming and quickly positions himself as if admiring the painting on the opposite wall.

'Afternoon, Rosie. God, it's a hot one today. Where's Theo?'

'He's gone for a run.'

'He's insane. In this heat?' He shakes his head.

Every day he seems to be out longer. She told him he should have a rest day, especially after his fall the other day, but he brushed off her concern, reminding her that running is good for him to clear his head, and will keep him on track to hit a PB before the race.

'He said Richard had suggested a new route? One that he wanted to try?'

'No idea. I was pretty wasted last night. He must love being

Uncle Dickie's favourite.' He lets out a hacking smoker's cough then takes a noisy bite from his apple. His phone starts to ring. The jaunty tune echoes. He pulls it from his pocket and cancels the call. 'So, how does it feel to be "the chosen one"?' he asks with his mouth full.

'Sorry?'

'The wearer of Grandma's ring?'

'Well, I mean . . .'

'You hate it, don't you? Well, don't worry, I won't mention anything. My lips are sealed.'

'I love it. Seriously,' she says, hoping he can't hear the white lie.

'If you say so. Big week for you guys with the engagement party too.'

'It's so kind of your mum to organise something. She doesn't have to; I wasn't sure if we should maybe have something quieter. You know, with Carla still missing . . .'

She trails off and waits for his reaction. It might be her imagination but she's sure he stiffens at the mention of her name. The memory of them kissing in the alleyway zooms to the front of her mind.

'Carla's gone to see family, that's what the police think. You heard Giovanni.'

She tries to summon the courage to confront him. 'So you're not worried about her?'

'No. Why? Should I be? Carla's not Danielle Dixon. She's not some stupid schoolgirl.'

'You were here that summer when she disappeared, weren't you?'

He nods and takes another bite of the apple.

'What was it like?' she asks.

There's a long pause as he swallows. She thinks he's going to change the subject but to her surprise he draws a breath.

'It was mad. At first, the Italian police didn't do much, then, once the Foreign Office was involved – well, and the papers – that was when it went wild.' He rubs a hand across his neck. Is that growing red blotch sunburn or something else? Stress? 'The town was overrun with reporters and detectives. You couldn't sleep because of the helicopters. I was here for a week or so, but had to get back to go to get ready for uni.'

'Did you meet Danielle? Before she vanished, I mean.'

He lets out a brittle laugh. 'No.'

'You know, Laprezia is small and, as a teenage boy knowing an all-girls school was staying in the village at the same time, I figured that . . .' She trails off at the change in his body language.

The atmosphere has suddenly cooled.

He crosses his arms. 'No. I didn't *meet* her.'

She knows she shouldn't push any more. It'll get back to Theo. *Why was Rosie asking these questions?* But she can't let it go.

'What were you doing on the night she disappeared?' she asks.

'Jesus, Rosie.' His eyes widen. There's a lightness in his voice but that doesn't hide the steely undertone. 'Are you interviewing me?'

'I'm curious.' She smiles as sweetly as she can.

'I was stuck watching football with Gerry. I don't know why you're so interested in this all of a sudden, but I have nothing to do with Danielle Dixon. None of us do.' He spits out a brown apple pip into his cupped hand. A string of saliva trails after it. 'You need to watch out, you know.'

Her chest thrums under her summer dress. 'Sorry?'

'If Fenna could hear you talking like this, digging into all this Danielle nonsense, she would think you had an ulterior motive for being here. It's ridiculous, I know. I told her to chill out, said there was nothing to worry about. We don't need to be wary of you.'

She knew Fenna was suspicious of her.

He leans closer. 'You're not lying to us are you, Rosie?' He keeps his eyes on her for a second longer than necessary.

She swallows.

'I'm teasing. Anyway, I've got to go and drop the kids off at the pool, if you know what I mean.' He throws his apple core into a wastepaper bin with a loud clang.

As he starts to walk away she blurts out, 'I know what you did.'

He turns. 'You know *what*?'

She drops her voice. 'I know about you and Carla.'

'What? There is no me and Carla.' He looks genuinely amused. 'Are you ok, Rosie? You've not had too much sun, have you?'

'I saw you when we went to the bar. You *kissed* her,' she hisses.

He shakes his head with mirth. 'A word of advice? I've learnt it's best not to get involved in other people's relationships.' He looks her right in the eye. The smile fades. 'You never know what's going on behind closed doors. Right?'

He walks towards the downstairs bathroom without another word.

26

FENNA – DAY 6

Fenna doesn't know how long she was asleep for – an hour, maybe two – but she feels so much better. Her body isn't as achy. Her brain is less mushy. For the first time in a long time she's able to think clearly. Screw going to the spa for the day; a solid chunk of sleep was all she needed. She could have slept for longer, but her breasts are full with milk. Raffi is due his next feed. She pads downstairs to find the others.

Marianne is sitting on the terrace, writing in her journal, as Raffi dozes in his pushchair beside her.

'Ah, here she is. Sleeping beauty.' Marianne smiles, handing Fenna a cold glass of iced tea.

'Thank you. I needed that.' Fenna sits down. She's pleased to see her son is in the shade with his sun hat on.

'Good, glad to hear it.' Gerry looks up from the newspaper he is reading and smiles.

'I don't want to say I told you so, but . . .' Marianne laughs.

'How long was I gone for?' Fenna asks. Everything is a lot clearer. The colours from the many plants on the terrace and the bright blue sky appear more vivid.

'A few hours,' Marianne replies.

That's the most uninterrupted sleep she's had in weeks.

'I've had a text from Richard,' Gerry says to Marianne, his arm outstretched, peering at his phone through his reading glasses. 'Him and Evelyn are inviting us all for a day out on their yacht.'

Fenna's seen photos of this yacht. It looks unbelievable.

'He says to bring the whole family. They've got a chef for a barbecue, too' Gerry adds.

'That sounds amazing,' Fenna can't help but chime in.

'Say thanks but sadly we've got plans,' Marianne replies, tartly.

'No we don't? Ah, look, they've got lifejackets that friends use for their grandchildren.' Gerry tilts his phone to show them both an image.

'Hmm. It's still a no,' Marianne says.

What is wrong with her? Why doesn't she want to go on the luxury yacht?

'I'm happy to take them,' Fenna says. 'It would be a good idea to have a family day out. All of us together.'

'That's true,' Gerry says.

'Ok, fine,' Marianne says eventually.

'I'll text them back.' Gerry holds his phone out again, jabbing the screen with his index finger.

'Is Alba with Luke?' Fenna gently picks up Raffi, surprised at how content he is. Perhaps it's the heat.

'No, Julietta offered to watch her,' Marianne says.

'Why? Where's Luke?' Fenna asks, preparing to feed Raffi. Gerry awkwardly coughs and picks up a newspaper, holding it high to block the view of any exposed nipples.

'He said he needed to pop out. Julietta didn't mind. She was happy to spend time with her. Theo and Rosie have gone for a walk and we've been relaxing here,' Marianne replies.

Fenna frowns. Raffi isn't latching on. He keeps nudging his head away, uninterested.

'Did you put more suncream on Alba?' Fenna asks distractedly, trying to coax Raffi to feed. *Why isn't he hungry?*

'Yes,' Marianne says. There's a steeliness to the word. A *don't mess with me* tone. 'This isn't my first time around children, you know.'

'Sorry.' Fenna lightens her tone. She needs to relax.

Marianne sighs. 'It'll be good for you to let your hair down at the engagement party. Plans are coming together now.'

Fenna can't help but pull a face.

Marianne spots it immediately. 'What?'

'Nothing. They've only been dating for five minutes.'

'Almost as long as you and Luke were when you got engaged.'

That's because I was pregnant.

'You don't think she's pregnant, do you?' Fenna decides to try Raffi on her left breast instead.

Marianne shakes her head. 'People get engaged because they're in love.'

'I know, but there's something about Rosie . . .'

'Oh, for God's sake, Fenna.'

Fenna is taken aback.

'Life is too short to be so negative all the time.'

Gerry sinks further down his chair as if wishing to be invisible. There is a crinkle of newspaper as he turns the pages.

'I-I . . .' she stutters, blinking back the tears that have arrived from nowhere.

Marianne gets to her feet and paces across the tiles. The swish of her skirt fills the sudden silence. 'I don't know why you're still so untrusting of newcomers. Not everyone has an agenda. The burglary was a one-off. I know it was scary, but you need to get over it.'

Fenna is too shocked to speak. Raffi isn't interested in feeding. Her breasts tingle with the need to empty, but she doesn't know what to do if he won't latch on. This has never happened before. He's always hungry, so what's wrong with him?

'I'm just saying we don't know this woman,' Fenna says, hearing the wobble in her voice, covering herself up, panicking that Raffi's not well. 'Come on, precious, have some milk.'

'He's probably not hungry.' Gerry peers over his paper. 'He absolutely devoured the bottle we gave him. Loved the stuff, I said to Marianne that—'

A wave of anger flares across her. 'What bottle?'

'A bottle of formula. These ready-made ones,' Gerry says. 'Ever so good, so simple for on-the-go and—'

'You gave him a bottle?' Fenna stares at her father-in-law.

A snap of adrenaline shoots through her. Every nerve suddenly lit.

So that's why he's not taking her breast milk.

'I . . . I . . . I didn't,' Gerry stutters.

'I did. It's fine. Raphael's a growing boy. You shouldn't take it personally if he needs more than you can give him.' Marianne puts her hands on her hips. 'Anyway, Luke said it was ok.'

She wants to cry. Scream. Both.

'I thought you'd be happy?' Marianne tuts. 'It means you've had a good chunk of sleep.'

'You had no right!'

It's the first time she has ever raised her voice with Marianne. There is a second or two of stunned silence that follows.

Julietta walks out onto the terrace. She flicks her eyes between the two women. 'Everything ok?'

'Fine,' Marianne says tightly.

Fenna can't speak. Why would Luke go behind her back like this? She told him she wasn't ready for Raffi to take a bottle. She presses her thumbs to her temples. She scans behind Julietta. 'Where's Alba?'

'Alba? I haven't seen her.' Julietta frowns.

Her stomach loops. 'What?'

Gerry coughs. 'Luke said he was leaving Alba with you so he could pop out?'

'No . . .' Julietta wrings her hands together. 'Yes, I saw him go out, but no one asked me to look after the children.'

'So then where's Alba?' Fenna's voice rises in pitch.

'I don't know, *cara*.'

Voices compete. Marianne says she'll call Luke to check he didn't take Alba with him. She tells herself to stay calm. This will be a mix-up. A case of crossed wires. That's all.

Marianne hangs up. Her face ashen. 'He says he left her with Gerry.'

Gerry's eyebrows lift. 'No. I heard him say he would leave her with Julietta.'

A pounding beat thumps in Fenna's skull. A bolt of adrenaline shoots through her. No one has been watching her toddler this whole time?

'Who's by the pool?' Fenna demands.

No one answers.

Fuck.

Visions of her daughter submerged, alone, in the water flash through her mind.

'Stay with Raffi,' she yells to Gerry as she races away.

Tiny shards of gravel slice her bare feet and bushes scratch her ankles as she leaps across borders. It takes forever to run down the hot stone steps towards the swimming pool. She nearly slips on the rocks as she takes them two at a time. She can't see properly, sweat and sunscreen sting her eyes. A zip of pain shoots up her left ankle but she barely notices it. All she cares about is her daughter.

She rounds the corner. The sun glares in her face. Her heart pounds in her chest.

Oh God.

No.

The world tilts.

There's someone face down in the water.

27

FENNA – DAY 6

Black spots cloud Fenna's vision. Her mind leaps to a nightmarish place that no parent should ever be forced to confront.

'Alba,' she yells, sprinting closer.

Relief floods her body when she sees a plastic limb at an angle, a painted-on smile and big eyes staring up at the sky.

Alba's doll is floating on the surface.

She stumbles against a sun lounger, hitting her shins, her legs unable to hold her up any longer. Tears make her vision blur.

The pure joy that her baby girl hasn't drowned is replaced with another terrifying thought. Where is she?

Carla is missing. Alba is missing.

Theo appears on the steps.

'I've come back from a run and I heard shouting. Mum said you've lost Alba?' He pants. Sweat patches under each armpit. His face is puce pink.

Lost her.

Fenna wants to scream that *she* hasn't lost her. *She* wasn't in charge of her.

She cups her mouth with her hands. 'Alba!'

'Luke's on his way back. We'll find her. Stay calm.' Theo places a sweaty palm against her bare shoulder. The touch makes her jolt.

'Alba? Alba!' The side of her lips split as she stretches her mouth wide enough to bellow her daughter's name.

'Let's spread out. She can't have gone far,' Theo suggests.

'No one's been watching her for hours. Who knows where she could be,' Fenna cries.

She pats down her pockets to find her phone. She needs to call the police and get them to put out an alert for a missing child.

Marianne trots down the steps, holding Raffi in her arms. 'Julietta's gone to have a good look in the house. We need to stay calm. Oh hello, Theo. Is Rosie not with you?'

'No. I went for a run.' Theo answers. 'Rosie's having a lie down.'

'Are you sure that she's having a lie down?' Fenna spins to face Theo.

'What? Yes, why?' Theo wipes his face on a towel from the sun lounger.

'Your mum thought you had both gone for a walk.'

'I must have misheard.' Marianne chimes. 'It's hard to keep on track of everyone.'

'Something is going on with your weird fiancée,' Fenna replies through clenched teeth.

'What?'

'She's been creeping around the garden at night, writing cryptic notes. Saying how she's lying about something.' Rosie's whispered voice picked up by the baby monitor comes back to her. 'We don't know this woman.'

'Fenna?' She turns at the sound of Luke's voice, but not before catching the look of confusion on Theo's face.

Her husband races over. Gerry follows close behind.

Luke wraps his arms around her and the tears she was trying to hold back erupt. She tries to tell him what's happened. Her voice is shaking. Whilst they're all standing here, Alba might be in trouble.

'Take a deep breath,' Luke orders, rubbing her clammy back.

Fenna gulps air as Marianne explains how there has been a mix-up with who was watching Alba. '. . . And I thought Rosie and Theo were out together but apparently she went for a lie down.'

'Rosie told me she was going for a walk,' Luke interrupts. 'Perhaps she's in one of the gardens with Alba?'

'Has anyone checked the outhouses?' Gerry suggests.

The old outhouses down the valley are still pretty much the death trap they were when the house was built. There's a river that runs at the far end of the olive grove. The danger is endless.

Everything Fenna thought about Rosie swirls around her mind as she watches the men race off. She stumbles to her feet to follow them.

Rosie's got something to do with it. She's sure of it. She hates herself for not trusting her gut. What if something has happened to her daughter? How will she live with herself?

28

FENNA – DAY 6

Fenna is about to call the police when Luke yells.

'She's fine!'

Fenna doesn't stop running until she has her daughter in her arms and can check her over herself. Tears streak down her cheeks. She breathes her in, pressing her face against Alba's skin. She will never take an inch of her for granted ever again. It's only when Alba complains that she's being squished that she pulls away.

Grass stains are smeared across Alba's summer dress. There's a tear near the hem. One of the embroidered bunny rabbits has been decapitated by a rip in the fabric.

Theo has his arm around Rosie, inspecting her right hand. A neat gash of red runs across the palm.

'What happened?' Fenna gasps at the sight of the blood.

'I must have caught myself on a thorn. Alba was looking for a ball in the bushes near the outhouses, so I tried to help.'

A yellow ball that Fenna's not seen before is resting by Theo's feet.

'What were you doing down there?' Fenna asks.

'I went for a walk and saw Alba on her own, struggling to get her ball . . .' Rosie flicks her gaze between Theo and Marianne, her bottom lip wobbling. 'I didn't mean to get in trouble. I was—'

'No one's in trouble,' Marianne chimes. 'Thank goodness you were there.' She claps her hands. 'Time for cake. Or how about ice-cream?'

Alba shrieks with joy at this suggestion. She appears unharmed by her adventure.

'I don't know about you, but I could do with a vodka.' Luke shakes his head, taking Fenna's hand.

'All's well that ends well,' Gerry keeps saying as they walk back to the house.

'I don't understand how Alba got down there,' Fenna says. 'She doesn't know where the lower gardens are. She could have fallen in the river or . . .'

'Don't worry about it now,' Luke soothes.

Fenna keeps playing it over and over again. 'There's a latch on the gate. She couldn't have opened it herself.'

'Paulo could have forgotten to close it.' Luke shrugs. 'It's an innocent mistake, Fen.'

'Why was no one watching her?'

'You heard what Mum said about crossed wires, everyone thought someone else was with her. No one did this on purpose. I know it was scary but Alba is fine.'

'But—'

'She's fine. That's the main thing.' His jaw clenches. There's no point hammering the point home. He doesn't know the nightmares that raced through her mind when her daughter was out of her sight.

'Bye, horse,' Alba says, waving an arm.

'Horse?' Fenna repeats, eyebrows raised at Luke.

'There's horses down by the outhouses.' He turns to Alba. 'Is that where you went, poppet? Did you go to see the horses?'

Alba starts making a neighing sound.

Fenna zones out as Luke tells Alba that she shouldn't wander off and if she wants to see the animals she needs to be with a grown-up. She takes a look back at the outhouse. An old rusting wheelbarrow sits on its side next to a stack of bricks and a few overgrown plants. A weathered blue wooden door hangs on its hinges. One question runs through her mind. Why the hell was Rosie down here in the first place?

29

ROSIE – DAY 7

Rosie has come to the church in Laprezia. It must be around thirty degrees today but she is hit with a refreshingly cold wall of air as she pushes open the door. The creak of wood against stone heralds her arrival. The simple brick facade is nothing like the ornate architecture of the cathedral in Siena, but as many weighty confessions hang over the wooden pews, clouded by centuries of deep exhales.

A looming marble Jesus peers down as she pads across the faded tiled floor. His eyes bore into her. She lets her hands trail across the backs of the benches, looking at the Italian names and dates of the dead etched into small golden plaques. Her hometown church, the one she would visit every Nativity and Harvest Festival with her school friends, smells like a school hall. This smells of patchouli and heady floral incense.

She sits in a pew, head bowed, hands clasped together. Her throat constricts with a rush of emotion as her dad's face appears in her mind. His memory is never far during moments of stillness like this. Her fingers trail the sign of the cross over her chest. She likes the cocoon-like feeling this place is giving her. The cool, musty air, the sacred stillness.

The events of the past few days wash over her.

Rosie had hoped to have some time alone yesterday, so she'd wandered down to the lower garden knowing she wouldn't be disturbed. But it was too hot to think. It's so muggy it's like the weather has got a hand wrapped around her throat. Choking her.

The collection of crumbling grey stone outhouses, used for cattle back in the day, provided shade. She'd perched on an old railway sleeper and massaged her temples. That's when she saw the lock. It looked to be the right size for the key she'd found in the wild garden the other day. She'd taken to carrying it with her and drew it from her pocket, putting it in the metal opening. It fit. She tried to turn it but nothing happened. That's when she'd spotted Alba toddling down the garden towards her. Alone.

'Are you ok, sweetie? Where's Mummy and Daddy?' she had asked, her voice naturally turning into a sing-song style, stepping into teacher-mode.

Alba had stared up at her with large eyes.

'Shall we go back to the house?'

'Ball.'

'Sorry?'

'Ball.' She'd pointed a pudgy finger at a thorny bush. A small flash of yellow was buried within.

'Let me try and get it for you.' She'd pulled the key from the lock and put it back in her pocket. The little girl eyed her curiously.

Underestimating how sharp the prickles were, Rosie had

reached into the bush and bit down the flash of pain as she caught her skin. 'We need to find a stick and then—'

'ALBA!'

A chorus of panicked cries echoed in the air before Rosie saw Luke speed down the garden, racing towards her.

'Oh my God, where did you find her?' He'd panted as he scooped up his daughter. Alba giggled in glee.

'She was . . .' Rosie started to stutter.

'Rosie? I thought you were in bed?' Theo had emerged behind his brother, looking less out of breath.

'Thank God you were here.' Luke placed a firm hand on her sunburnt shoulder, his palm pressing into the blisters. 'Anything could have happened to her. Did you not hear us calling?'

'No.' She'd shaken her head.

Luke carried his daughter towards Fenna, racing from the house, leaving Rosie and Theo alone.

Theo had turned to face her. 'Be careful.'

A prickle of anxiety had tingled across her hearing Theo repeat the taxi driver's warning.

Her head pounded from the bright glare of the sun. 'S-s-sorry?'

'I mean, this is pretty much a building site down here, babe.' He'd nodded to the dilapidated stone outhouses. 'What are you doing this far from the house?'

She'd thought of the key in her pocket. How would she explain that?

'I must have taken a wrong turn,' she'd lied.

The church door opens, flooding the atrium with a bright strip of daylight as an elderly couple enter, both making the sign of the cross on their chests. The sound and light pull her from her thoughts. Rosie stands, unsure why she's here. Perhaps it was going to the Duomo in Siena, or maybe she wanted to find some inner peace, but either way, she needs to be making a move.

She absently looks at her phone. Theo will be up soon, wondering where she's gone. Something catches her eye on the way out. Tucked in one of the alcoves is a large, framed photograph of a pretty blonde schoolgirl. She's starting to become familiar with this image.

Danielle Dixon.

Under the image is a paragraph of text written in Italian. Rows of burnt-out tea lights sit on a metal shelf. Someone has left delicate flowers, the stems poked through a tin vase. Reedy incense sticks from a bronze holder emit curls of fine, smoky fragrance. She coughs and the sound echoes. She silently steps forward to light a candle and pulls her phone out to take a photo of the shrine before her. The click echoes. She forgot to put it on silent.

A male voice comes from behind her. 'Did you know her?'

She gasps. Her heart thrums.

'Sorry, I didn't mean to make you jump.'

Rosie recognises him immediately. His distinctive dark wavy hair. He talks in near-perfect English, a seductive lilt to his words.

'It's fine.' Rosie steps past. The policeman's eyes linger on her.

'I'm Giovanni, by the way.'

She remembers Theo and Luke's reaction to him coming to the house.

'I know.'

He sits at the end of the nearest pew, clasping his tanned

hands. Far enough away to show he's not a threat but close enough so she knows he wants to talk. His broad stature is intimidating but there is something welcoming about his face. Still, she is wary of trusting him.

'My *nonna* told me every day that I had to be good as God was watching me.' Giovanni smiles, seemingly talking to himself. The tanned skin around his brown eyes creases. 'She must have meant watching *over* me, but I took it literally, as young children do, that He was able to see everything I did. I figured He had to sleep so I'd get a break from being observed, but I remembered Jesus, who could step in to take over the role of watching me. Then, when he needed a break, it was the turn of the Holy Ghost.' He pulls a face. 'You can imagine how terrifying that was as a child – to imagine a spirit watching me.'

She thinks of the ghosts that haunt her.

He presses two fingers to his chin, his gaze fixed on Danielle's smile. 'Sometimes I tell myself that one day she'll return and share the incredible adventure she's been on. Maybe then the town can begin to rebuild the reputation we've lost.'

A shuffle of shoes squeaks on the polished floor tiles, followed by a pointed cough from the older couple.

'But how can a girl disappear? Some think she ran away but her bank account has never been touched. She has never made contact with anyone.'

'I should be getting back.' Rosie inches away. She knows first-hand how innocent conversations can quickly spiral with people like him.

'You didn't answer my question . . .' He nods to the shrine. 'Why did you take a photo? Did you know her?'

Rosie swallows. The cool church air has vanished, replaced with a prickling heat under his intense gaze. 'No.'

***

Rosie walks away from the church, and quickly puts on her sunglasses as the glare of the sunshine hits her face.

Giovanni has followed her.

'*Scusa,* I'd like to talk to you,' he persists. His forehead is knitted in a frown. She notices the smattering of freckles flecked across his neat nose. She will not allow herself to be swayed by his good looks.

'I'm sorry, I'm in a rush,' she says.

'Listen, please. Be careful of that family, those men in particular,' Giovanni orders in a low voice.

Be careful.

Despite herself, she stops. 'The Fraser family?'

'*Sì.* Please listen to me. I think—'

The jaunty toot of a car horn cuts off what he's about to say.

'Hello, Rosie,' a man's voice calls.

It's Gerry. He leans a hairy arm out the driver's window, his eyes hidden behind mirrored aviator sunglasses. She steps towards the car and catches her reflection, taking in her perspiring pink face, the wild strands of hair that are coming loose from her hair bobble, and the look of being caught doing something she shouldn't.

'Everything ok, Rosie?' Gerry asks.

'Fine,' she says, self-consciously patting down her hair, hoping the heat leaves her cheeks.

Gerry looks Giovanni up and down. 'Oh, hello, officer.'

'*Buongiorno,*' Giovanni replies. Before he can say anything else, the door to the church opens and the elderly couple come out. They immediately start talking to Giovanni in Italian, turning their backs to the holidaymakers.

'Lovely day, isn't it?' Gerry says to Rosie, with a half smile once they are alone. 'Where's Theo?' He glances around as if his stepson will magically materialise.

'He's sleeping. I fancied a walk . . .' Her heartbeat hasn't returned to normal.

What did Giovanni mean when he'd told her to be careful of the Fraser men?

'Hop in. I can drop you back if you like?' Gerry offers.

She walks to the passenger side and opens the door. He moves the empty food wrappers from the passenger seat and squishes them into the gap in the door. 'Whoops, don't tell Marianne. She'll kill me. The doctor told me off for snacking, not good for the old cholesterol apparently, but I'm on my holiday.'

The clock on the dashboard says it's eleven o'clock. She's been out for two hours. They sit in silence for a few seconds as he performs a three-point turn. The car smells of cheesy crisps.

He speaks first. 'Did Giovanni talk to you?'

She pictures the serious look on the police officer's face. *Be careful.*

She shakes her head.

Gerry sighs. 'I wonder if he's had any updates on Carla. We're completely in the dark. I don't know if we need to advertise her job or if she's going to turn up. It's a real headache.'

They're stuck behind a car that's got its emergency lights on. The rhythmic orange flashing isn't helping her headache. She wants to turn the air-conditioning up. Sweat gathers behind her knees. He offers her a mint. She shakes her head and looks out of the window, coming face to face with Danielle Dixon yet again.

The missing schoolgirl's face is plastered on a lamppost, placed at eye height for those waiting at the lights. The same smiling photo Rosie saw in the church, except this one is bleached by the sun. Danielle's blonde hair is now an even lighter shade.

'The town hasn't been the same since she disappeared.' He sighs.

'August 22nd, 2010 . . .' she reads the date.

'We didn't know anything about it until the next day when we saw the police helicopters. There was a period, before the attention went on the school teacher, when the locals were majorly pissed off with the negative press and they started to take it out on anyone who was an outsider. That was why I rigged the house with CCTV, to protect the family. A way to capture any evidence in case we have the finger pointed at us for anything.'

'It sounds pretty stressful.'

'It was. But nothing like what her family has gone through. They may never discover where her body is and that's heart-breaking. However, they're clutching at straws that something new is going to come up. I guess you have to admire their tenacity. I know Marianne would be the same if something happened to her boys.'

Rosie nods. 'Where do you think she is?'

'Me?' He lets out a loud crunch, breaking his mint in two. 'The lake. She probably thought she was invincible, like teenagers do, and made some bad choices. The biggest one being to trust her teacher. Who knows where he put her.'

'Did the police not check the water?'

He nods. 'Yes, but they've never found any sign of her.'

A shiver dances over Rosie's skin. The pretty girl's eyes may be faded by the sun, but it's like she's looking straight at them.

30

FENNA – DAY 7

With a grunt of effort, Fenna pushes the pushchair up the steep driveway. She needed to get out of the house this morning. What a week it's been. They're halfway through this trip and it feels less like a holiday every day.

Luke is in bed, nursing another hangover. She's only seen Marianne this morning. They had an awkward moment in the kitchen where neither of them mentioned the formula milk incident, which got lost in the drama of Alba going missing. Fenna is still silently seething.

Marianne made polite small talk and tried to hide her embarrassment at not knowing where anything went. *If this was my house I'd be a lot more organised*, Fenna had thought, watching her mother-in-law open and close cupboards at random, blaming the staff for putting things where they weren't meant to be, muttering about how standards were slipping.

It's a relief to be by herself and out in the fresh air. Miraculously, Alba and Raffi are both napping in the double pushchair, so Fenna decides to take a gamble and stop at the small cafe in the town. Hopefully both children will stay asleep long enough for her to have a drink in peace. She orders an iced coffee and a pastry from a young waitress and takes a seat at an outside table.

As she settles back in her chair, something catches her eye over the road.

Rosie is coming out of the church.

Perhaps this is her chance to speak to her about yesterday? The dramatic events churn around her mind. She still doesn't understand how Alba made her way to that lower garden. Or what Rosie was doing down there in the first place. She should call her over and see if she wants to join her. They need to talk.

She starts to lift an arm to wave her over but drops it. Rosie's not alone. Giovanni has followed her out of the church. There's a funny twist in her stomach at the way Rosie is acting. She seems nervous, shifting on her feet as the police officer says something to her.

The waitress returns with her drink, momentarily blocking her view. Ice-cubes clink in her tall glass, the sugar glaze on the pastry glitters in the sunlight. Fenna glances back at the church as the waitress goes to get the card machine.

Rosie has gone.

Fenna twists in her seat. She looks down the street. There's no sign of her. Both Rosie and Giovanni have disappeared.

'*Grazie.*' Fenna taps her card against the screen, distracted by a rush of thoughts. What was she talking to Giovanni about? Why does Rosie seem so nervous all the time? Has he picked up on something too?

'*Scusa, non funziona,*' the waitress apologises, bringing Fenna back to the present.

Her card is declined.

She must be using the wrong bank account. Luke hasn't sent her any information yet. Has she got enough cash on her? She rummages to find her purse in her bag; perhaps she has some loose change in there. Her clammy fingers push nappies and spare clothes out of the way.

'*Solo un minuto,*' Fenna mumbles. She's sure she saw cash in here, didn't she?

'I'll get this,' a reassuring, deep voice says in Italian from behind her.

Giovanni hands over a twenty euro note and orders a double espresso to take away. He tells the blushing waitress to keep the change.

'Are you alone?' he asks Fenna, gesturing to the empty chair opposite her. 'Would you mind if I sit for a moment?'

'Sure. Be my guest.' She brushes hair from her face, aware of how warm it has gone all of a sudden. 'Thank you for paying.'

'My treat. How long are you staying this time?' he asks, smooth, authoritative.

'One more week.' Fenna runs her tongue over her teeth, unsure if she remembered to brush them before she left the house.

His legs touch hers. Neither of them move.

Luke doesn't know that Fenna and Giovanni have met before.

No one does.

It was when they were here on holiday last summer. She was in the hire car, distracted by Alba crying in the back, and drove the wrong way down a one-way street. Two police officers pulled her over. Giovanni was one of them. He could see it was an honest mistake and let her go with a warning, persuading his colleague not to issue a fine. She never told Luke about the embarrassing incident. If she had tried to tell him how kind Giovanni was her husband wouldn't listen. He has some stupid teenage rivalry with this man.

What would Luke say if he saw them together now? She's suddenly grateful that Rosie has vanished. Not that Fenna's doing anything wrong, she's just a woman sitting in a cafe, talking to a friendly police officer. However, her hands are suddenly slick with sweat being so close to him. She forgot how handsome he is.

Her sex drive is non-existent since having Raffi, so this unexpected tingle of desire takes her by surprise. It must be the uniform. *Get a grip.* She brushes the rush of illicit thoughts away, grateful that he can't read her mind.

Fenna picks up her glass, pleased to have something to help her parched mouth. The waitress returns with a coffee for him in a tiny takeout cup. They must know one another as they talk briefly about the state of the church allotment. Giovanni says he has volunteered to help clean it up in a few days' time.

'Did I see you talking to Rosie? She's Theo's girlfriend – I mean, fiancée. I saw you by the church,' Fenna says, when they are alone.

'The English girl? *Sì*, I bumped into her inside.' He leans forward and fixes his dark eyes on her. Her heart beats quicker. 'She was looking at *Signorina* Dixon's memorial. I wasn't sure if she was about to do something like your husband did.'

She remembers him coming to the house to talk to Luke about pulling the appeal poster down the night he went to the bar with Theo and Rosie at the start of the holiday.

'Boys will be boys,' she says, taking another sip, hating

herself for echoing Marianne's words, and for defending her husband when she wasn't there and doesn't know what happened. It doesn't sound like something Luke would do, but then again, he has been acting strange recently.

'Hmm. I remember your husband as a young man. Be careful of him, he still thinks he owns this place.' He sips his coffee, not breaking eye contact.

'Any news on Carla?' she asks, wanting to change the subject and not be dragged into some teenage drama that they should have left in the past.

'Maybe.'

'What do you mean?'

He glances around. 'This is confidential information.'

'You can trust me to keep a secret.'

Is she flirting with him? Is that what's happening right now? She presses her cold glass to her lips, hoping the heat in her face subsides.

He clears his throat. 'Carla's bank card has been used in Pisa so we're trying to track her down there.'

'So she's ok?' Fenna says, remembering the theory that Carla had a row with her boyfriend and went to visit family. 'That's a relief.'

Giovanni gives a half shrug. 'We'll know more soon. But if you do think of anything that might help us find her, here is my number.' He hands her a business card that she tucks into her pocket. 'You had another baby?' he asks, peering at Raffi, his features softening.

'Yes, a little boy.'

Her phone chimes to life with a call from Luke. She jumps and is instantly embarrassed at her reaction. Why does it feel like she's been caught doing something she shouldn't? Giovanni smiles.

She silences her phone – she'll call Luke back when she's alone – and finishes the rest of her coffee, wrapping the pastry in a napkin to have later. She gets to her feet, knocking the table in her haste.

'I should go. Thanks again.'

'Of course. Anytime. Take care, Fenna.' He leans over and kisses her on the cheek. '*Ciao*.'

Her clammy hands grip the pushchair handle as she rushes away in the opposite direction, praying that her heart will stop pounding.

31

ROSIE – DAY 8

The cars will be here soon to take them out for the day at the lake. There is a buzz in the air this morning over breakfast about the trip on Richard and Evelyn's luxury yacht. Rosie's trying to match everyone's enthusiasm but there's something about spending the day on the infamous *Lago Parrocchetto* that fills her with uncertainty. She tries to ignore the butterflies in her stomach as she takes her empty plate to the kitchen. They're leaving in ten minutes.

Julietta glances up from the sink and gives her a polite smile. There is a pan full of bubbling water on the hob. A sweet roasting scent hangs in the air.

'*Grazie*, you didn't need to do that, *cara*,' Julietta says.

'Well, with Carla not around I thought I'd help . . .'

'I appreciate it.'

It's been three days since Giovanni delivered the news that Carla was missing. Not one of the Frasers has mentioned her name since.

A meowing fills the kitchen. It's coming from behind the closed stable-style door. Julietta opens it and a milky white tabby cat, a skinny thing, slinks through the small gap.

'Aww, she's lovely.' Rosie smiles.

'She's a stray. Decided this is her home.'

'Hey, little one.' Rosie bends down, the cat winding through her bare legs, reminding her of the cat she had as a child. Albeit a smaller, scrawnier version.

Julietta gets a saucer and pours out milk, and tears chicken from the fridge into smaller pieces. She presses her fingers to her lips. Rosie smiles and mimes zipping her lips, watching the older woman gently drop the scraps to the stone floor. The cat wastes no time in hoovering up the treats.

'It was Carla who started feeding this thing not long after she started here. It pops by most days now. She loves animals. She would never leave her beloved dog behind. Never.'

'Any news on where she might be?' Rosie asks, stroking the cat.

Julietta shakes her head. 'I wish the police would do more, but they only seem to care about the good girls. Carla is not from the best area and this was supposed to be a fresh start for her. Don't get me wrong, she has her problems, but who doesn't?'

Whilst they've all lazed in the sunshine, doing half-hearted laps in the pool, and celebrating the engagement, Julietta has been nervously waiting to find out where her friend is. She must watch them from the window, silently hating every one of the guests here.

'Do the police think her boyfriend is involved?' Rosie asks.

Julietta gives a half shrug. 'Between us, she has a lot of male friends . . .'

Rosie stands, smiling sadly at the cat who is licking the plate clean.

'Anyway, where are you going today?' Julietta asks, opening the cutlery drawer.

There is a rumbling sound. The water in one of the pans on the hob starts to bubble.

'To the lake.'

Julietta drops a spoon and says something in Italian. The metal clangs as it hits the worn stone tiles. There's a hiss and a spit of boiling water. Rosie bends down to pick up the spoon and passes it to her.

Julietta doesn't let her hand go. Instead of admiring her engagement ring, she unexpectedly leans closer. 'Please be careful. This family, they . . .' She stops herself as a door slams from somewhere in the house. Her eyes widen and the colour drains from her face.

Be careful.

Rosie's heart thumps. 'What?'

A second later, after a furtive check that no one is going to join them, she continues. 'The family say they have no idea what happened to Danielle.' Julietta chews her lip, speaking quickly and quietly. 'That's not true.'

The rumble from the hob grows louder.

Rosie swallows, alarmed at how serious Julietta has become. Gone is the ruddy-cheeked *nonna*, replaced with a scared, middle-aged woman gripping a spoon so hard her knuckles turn white. Boiling water spills over the top of the pan.

'W-w-what? What do you know?' Rosie stutters.

'Listen to me. You can't trust them.'

'Who? I can't trust who?'

Footsteps echo down the corridor. Someone is coming.

'All of them.' Julietta's wild eyes flick from Rosie to the closed kitchen door. 'I have always had my doubts about what they are capable of . . .'

A second later, a looming shadow enters the room. Julietta quickly slides the cat's saucer behind her foot.

'Ah, Rosie, here you are. Everyone is waiting for you outside,' Luke says, stopping short inside the door.

Julietta darts to the hob and turns the heat down. She starts to scrub the countertop, her arm jerking swiftly over an invisible stubborn stain, flashing Luke a polite smile, which he ignores.

The cat is nowhere to be seen.

'I was getting a glass of water,' Rosie replies, hoping he doesn't pick up on the waver in her voice. Is it her imagination or does he glance at them both with suspicion?

'Julietta, any news on Carla?' he asks.

Rosie turns to the sink, the cold water a refreshing relief against her trembling wrists.

'No. Not yet,' Julietta replies.

'Rosie.' Theo calls her name from somewhere.

Rosie wants to slip out of the kitchen. The stifling air is much too tense. She needs to get Julietta on her own and find out what she was about to say, but it will have to wait until they return from the day trip.

'Are you sure everything is ok, Rosie?' Luke asks, one eyebrow raised. He steps and blocks her path.

'Fine. Never better,' she replies, her voice high-pitched and forced.

'Good to hear it. Julietta, do you know if we have any ice-cream?' he asks, opening the freezer doors. 'It feels like a day for ice-cream.'

32

FENNA – DAY 8

There is a pop of a Champagne cork and a whoop of joy. Fenna longs to be holding a chilled flute up on the top deck of the luxury yacht with the others. Instead, she is in a small windowless bathroom holding the baby and telling Alba to wash her hands or they're going home. For some reason, Luke decided to give Alba a syrupy red ice lolly in the car on the way to the lake. Fenna has been having mild heart palpitations every time Alba goes near anything. Everything inside the yacht is pristine cream.

Marianne is sulking, making a point of not coming to help with the kids. Things are still frosty between the two women. Despite Fenna apologising for raising her voice at her mother-in-law for giving Raffi a bottle of formula, she's clearly still cross about the whole thing. Luke said sorry for his part. He promised it was a lapse in judgement and he didn't mean to upset Fenna. For the sake of the rest of the holiday, if nothing else, they need to try and make peace.

Fenna takes a deep breath and mentally counts to ten, wishing Julietta was here to lend a hand. When she asked if she could join the family for the day out, she was told that 'Julietta doesn't like going to the lake'.

It seems a lot of the locals have superstitions about coming here. What started as rumours that Danielle Dixon is somewhere in the waters has since become an urban legend. Nothing has ever been confirmed by the police, but it was enough to drive tourism away and steal livelihoods.

But for Fenna, this opportunity to get onboard *Dolce Vita* was too good to miss. It reminds her of the shoots she did in her early twenties. Except back then she had bad-tempered photographers to manage instead of children with sticky fingerprints to worry about.

Richard gleefully gave everyone the tour when they arrived. Most of what he said went over her head – thirty-two metres long, something about a cruising speed of twenty-six knots – but she did pay attention to where the wine fridge is located. A quick Google search reveals that chartering the yacht for the week costs a cool sixty thousand euros. The opulent boat has touches of luxury Italian design everywhere, from the gold-plated door handles to the sumptuous fabric on the plump sun loungers on the upper deck.

The clang of the bell calls everyone to lunch. The rich scent of barbequed meat and smoked fish skewers hits her as she carefully climbs the steps with the children to the upper deck. The men have congregated at one end of the dinner table and the women at the other. Luke helps strap Alba into the travel highchair beside him. Fenna cradles Raffi in her arms, finding a shaded spot to rock him to sleep.

Richard is pointing out their holiday home to Rosie, waving his arm in the direction of the dense woodland on the other side of the water.

'So, what else has been happening on your holiday?' Evelyn asks, passing over the bread basket. Her many gold bracelets jangle on her wrist. 'Apart from the exciting engagement news, of course.'

'We're all having a wonderful time so far,' Gerry replies.

'Good to hear it.' Richard raises his glass in the air and proposes a toast, 'To loyal friends and precious family.'

'Well . . .' Marianne draws a breath once everyone has clinked their crystal flutes. She's declined the plates of food being passed around. Fenna looks on longingly. If she can get Raffi to have a nap she might be able to eat in peace. 'The slightly worrying news is that one of our members of staff has gone missing.'

Fenna is surprised Marianne has brought this up.

Evelyn tries to frown through her Botox. 'Who? What's happened?'

'Carla hasn't been seen for five days and we've had no news about where she could be. The police are involved,' Marianne explains.

'That's terrible. Carla? Isn't that the one we recommended to you?' Evelyn asks. 'The name rings a bell.'

Luke coughs loudly. 'Sorry, it went down the wrong way.'

The sound startles Raffi from his drowsy slumber. Fenna throws daggers at the back of Luke's head.

'Shhh, it's ok,' she says to her son, patiently, eyeing up the delicious spread that's out of arm's reach. Everything is drenched in sunshine and olive oil. Plump tomatoes sit against generous slices of mozzarella, there's warm figs and rustic slices of bread, and a large bowl of *spaghetti alle vongole*, her favourite. She can practically taste the gleaming strands of pasta and glossy clams garnished with red chillis.

Luke hasn't thought to get her a plate ready.

'Carla worked for you, too?' Rosie asks Evelyn.

'Sort of. She temped for us when one of our regular team was off sick. *Common.*' She mouths the final word. 'If you know what I mean?'

'Do the police think it's serious?' Richard asks.

'No idea. We are completely in the dark with it all,' Gerry sighs.

He sounds nonchalant but the fact the police are involved proves this is more significant than they are letting on to their friends.

'She's been spotted in Pisa,' Fenna cuts in. 'Well, her bank card has. Maybe her phone, too.'

They turn to face her.

'How do you know that?' Luke asks.

Her heart thrums. She shouldn't have shared the information Giovanni told her. She did it without thinking. She quickly swallows. 'Julietta told me . . . Maybe she heard it from one of the locals?'

'She did seem flighty.' Evelyn purses her lips. 'But you'd hope she would have the decency to hand in her notice. I know how hard it is to find the right staff that you can trust.'

'Pisa, huh?' Gerry muses. He dabs a napkin around his mouth, leaving an oily mark on the linen fabric.

'That's all I know.' Fenna shrugs and focuses on the baby.

'Wherever she is, I bet it's brought back a lot of bad memories having a girl go missing during the anniversary week of Danielle Dixon disappearing? How terrible,' Evelyn soothes. 'That was an awful time, wasn't it. Did you hear about this, Rosie? Danielle was a schoolgirl who snuck out in the middle of the night – supposedly to meet someone – and never came home.'

'It sounds like a terrible tragedy,' Rosie says.

Theo draws her attention away and tells her the name of Italian delicacies on the table that she's not tried before. They giggle over her pronunciation of certain words.

'You can say that again. It's been the worst PR for this amazing town,' Evelyn continues.

Fenna glances over at her mother-in-law, bracing waiting for her to shut this conversation down. But Marianne sips her glass of wine and stares over the water. She looks as if she's lost in her own world.

Richard clears his throat. 'I don't know why we're all still talking about this case. The foreign exchange teacher was behind it. He had Danielle's mobile phone on him when the police interviewed him. And he was seen arguing with her.' He starts to tick each piece of evidence off his tanned fingers. A gold signet ring catches the light. 'They were in a secret relationship and Danielle wanted to end it. The guy was married and double her age, don't forget. He had the strength to kill her and move her body . . .' He trails off, his eyes falling to the water.

'Jeez. This chat's gone heavy.' Luke raises his eyebrows. 'Theo, pass the wine.'

His brother looks up from the antipasto platter in front of him. Fenna's stomach grumbles.

'People think she's in the lake because her things were found somewhere on the shore, if I remember rightly,' Evelyn says.

'A Polaroid camera and a denim jacket, covered in blood.' Gerry wafts his fork.

Evelyn shrugs. 'It doesn't make sense to me.'

'When someone disappears, a lot of things don't make sense, darling.' Richard puts the salad bowl on the table with a clatter.

'Well,' Gerry holds up his glass, 'if I'm brutally honest, Danielle's background has had a huge impact on the investigation.'

Fenna frowns. 'What do you mean?'

'If she was middle-class, instead of from a single income working-class family, more people would care that she's still missing. It came out that she was on a bursary at that private school, remember? If anything, I'm pleased the local coppers are still trying to get answers. I know the British police sees it as a closed case because it happened on Italian soil. They've washed their hands of her,' he concludes.

'Maybe it's about class, maybe not. You've got to agree that the police are clutching at straws if they think they'll find something new fifteen years on,' Richard says. 'The money investigating this could be better spent elsewhere.'

'Hmm. Well, someone knows. Someone has this on their conscience.' Evelyn picks up the vinaigrette and offers it to Luke. 'Would you like some, darling?'

He shakes his head.

'Anyway, I'm sure Carla will show up. At least that pervert teacher isn't a problem anymore,' Gerry adds. Richard nods in agreement.

Rosie clears her throat. 'But what if—'

'Can we change the subject, please?' Theo snaps.

Rosie flinches. Fenna's never heard Theo raise his voice before. To anyone.

'Theo?' Richard says, frowning.

There's an awkward pause. Rosie narrows her eyes, clearly irritated at the way Theo spoke to her in front of everyone.

'We're only making conversation,' Evelyn says, with a light laugh.

'Sorry.' Theo dips his eyes. 'Luke's right, it's a bit heavy.'

Marianne shifts in her seat. The leather crackles as she moves. 'Carla will turn up, everything is fine. Now, let's have a nice day.' She lifts her half-empty glass to her lips. Fenna is sure she sees her hand trembling.

33

FENNA – DAY 8

After a hurried one-handed lunch, as Raffi refused to nap, she decided to bring him somewhere less stimulating. Luke didn't look up when she walked past, too busy pouring himself another glass of wine to notice. At least Alba is enjoying having lots of attention. There are safety nets and childproof features, plus a helpful member of the crew who is delighted to play with her.

The master bedroom is the furthest room away from the noise of the upper deck. She stepped inside and looked around in awe. It looks like it's never been slept in. A deep window seat offers views of the calm water. There are two walnut-brown built-in wardrobes, a plush ottoman and recessed shelves full of polished antique ornaments. The spacious marble wet room ensuite has neatly folded fluffy white towels folded over a rail, embroidered anchors all facing the same way.

She's tempted to take something as a memento. If it wasn't for the rocking motion and the occasional creak from the hull, you could be mistaken for thinking you were in a five-star hotel. The gentle movement calmed Raffi, who has been asleep for the past hour.

Fenna picked up her phone to take a photo of the incredible room but ended up flicking through her photo album, landing on the shot she took of Rosie's notebook.

Those strange, scribbled pages.

She brings it closer to her eyes, trying to decipher the crossed-out text. The word '*Fraser?*' and the local address are the only things legible. The address that Luke told her was the site of the old shoe shop. Rosie could have been hunting for a pair of authentic Italian leather sandals, but she doubts it.

Mario's Shoes.

Fenna taps open Google and sees what comes up.

Mario's Shoes, Laprezia. Permanently closed.

She frowns.

Why is Rosie interested in a shoe shop that doesn't exist anymore? In amongst the search results is a chatroom-style thread all about the town.

Anyone know what happened to Mario's Shoes? I remember walking past and smelling the sun-warmed leather when we used to go there on holiday many moons ago. (Pauline_73)

I've never seen it open. (MirelleL)

It shut down years ago. That building is cursed. (ManUDad)

A user has added a wide eye emoji.

What do you mean 'cursed'? (Pauline_73)

It belonged to the Bernardi family. They tried to keep it going for as long as they could but sales pretty much died overnight. They moved away a few years later. It's lay empty since. No one knows what to do with the building. No one wants to buy it because of the connection to DD (ManUDad)

A rush of heat breaks across her chest.

DD? I don't understand?? (Pauline_73)

The Bernardis were Danielle Dixon's host family (ManUDad)

Fenna sits up.

It can't be a coincidence that Rosie wrote down this particular address, the last place Danielle was seen alive. Rosie made out that she'd never heard of Danielle before she arrived here. The Frasers were the ones to tell her all about the missing schoolgirl. Weren't they? There's a cheer from the deck above.

Fenna blocks out the fun that everyone is having and opens Rosie's Instagram profile. There must be something she's missed. She scrolls quickly but there's nothing on Rosie's neatly curated feed. It's unexciting and bland. What was her friend called? Lucy? Lydia! Perhaps there's something on her page?

Right down Lydia's feed is a throwback post, a compilation of school photos that were taken a few years ago, including a full class line-up of gangly teenage girls with matching plucked eyebrows and sharp orange tide marks of foundation. An unsmiling Rosie is tagged sitting beside Lydia in the front row. The image is timestamped 'Year 10. June 2010.' Rosie and Lydia would have been fourteen or fifteen. Fenna pulls the phone closer to her eye, swallowing the sudden sour taste in her mouth.

She's seen this navy uniform before. The identical school crest is on the many missing posters around Laprezia.

Rosie went to the same school as Danielle Dixon.

Fenna frowns, trying to work out the dates. She would have been in the year below. Did she know her? This is starting to feel like too much of a coincidence. First, the address where Danielle was last seen, and now the school connection. What the hell is going on? A shiver rolls over her. Alba calls for her from somewhere in the yacht, but she's glued to her seat.

Her eyes drop back to the image. Amongst the blazers, straightened hair, and pleated slate grey skirts is a curly haired male teacher in his early forties who stands proudly at the end of the row.

She reads the comments under the images. There are angel wings and white dove emojis.

RIP Jonathan M. Queen Mary's Legend. Heart of gold, f**k the haters.

Paedophile Mills you mean? 😠

😮

They must be referring to the teacher accused of having something to do with Danielle's disappearance. Is Jonathan Mills the same man in the group photo? Did he teach Rosie, too?

Why has she kept this quiet?

Fenna types his name into the search engine. A list of sites flash up. The top one is for an English tabloid newspaper with a story from December 2010. She clicks the link.

TEACHER 'TOOK OWN LIFE' FOLLOWING FATEFUL SCHOOL EXCHANGE

A teacher questioned by police over the disappearance of a British schoolgirl took his own life, a coroner has ruled.

The body of Jonathan Mills, 45, Head of Italian at Queen Mary's Girls' School in Guildford, Surrey, was discovered by a train line in the town in September. The father-of-one had led students on a foreign exchange in Tuscany the previous month in which he was linked, and then cleared, over the missing schoolgirl Danielle Dixon, 15.

An inquest heard that Mr Mills had 'struggled to come to terms' with being wrongly implicated over Ms Dixon's disappearance. Recording a conclusion of suicide, coroner Alan Stevenson said: 'Mr Mills had nothing to do with the missing persons case, but events took a tragic toll.'

After the hearing, Mr Mills' wife told waiting reporters her husband had endured relentless press speculation.

Bethany Mills, 46, said: 'Jonathan felt responsible for what happened during the exchange even though he was blameless. The Italian police and British press have blood on their hands. One day the truth will come out.'

Italian police believe Ms Dixon ignored her curfew and went out to meet an unnamed person on August 22 2010. The search

> for her, which began when she failed to return to her host family's home, continues.
>
> Detectives discounted Mr Mills from their investigations as witnesses confirmed his alibi, Italian media reported. However, the inquest heard that despite being cleared, Mr Mills 'endured continuing local gossip and rumours', Mrs Mills said.
>
> Items of bloodied clothing and a camera belonging to Ms Dixon were found by Lake Parachetto, Laprezia. Despite numerous public pleas and vast searches of the local area, Ms Dixon has not been traced.

She stares at the photo of Jonathan Mills on the news website, his official headshot. He has a recognisable birthmark under his left eye. It is the same curly haired man in the school photo. Fenna chews her lip, willing her exhausted, sleep-deprived brain to think faster. There's something about Mr Mills that claws at her.

She goes back to Rosie's Instagram and zooms in to the nostalgic Christmas morning shot buried at the bottom of her page. The air leaves her lungs. Rosie's dad has curly brown hair and a birthmark under his left eye.

A shiver rolls over her. She tears off the lid of a nearby bottle of mineral water and gulps it down.

Jonathan Mills – the man accused of killing Danielle Dixon – was not only Rosie's teacher, he was her father.

34

ROSIE – DAY 8

Rosie leans against the polished handrail that runs the length of the yacht and looks over the lake. *Lago Parrocchetto* is much bigger than she expected.

She remembers the faded postcards in the town's dusty shop window. The sun-bleached tones don't do justice to the bright colours around her now. Fifteen years ago, this place was thriving with holidaymakers, locals, and tourists rushing here to swim in the glittering water. Now it's pretty much empty, bar a few other smaller boats in the distance.

Further down the bay is a boarded-up beach shop and cafe. The weathered sign and flaking wooden slats reveal how long it's been abandoned. The next door brick building once advertised water sports, but nature has reclaimed the land. Thick, mossy green leaves shroud the doorway. The broken picnic tables sit empty. All because of what may have happened to Danielle here.

She can't help but picture Danielle's bloodied denim jacket that Evelyn said the police found near the water's edge. Was it this side or the opposite? A rush of nausea hits her as the boat rocks.

Theo comes up beside her, threading his arm through hers, drawing her attention from the view. He looks at home in his deck shoes, khaki green shirt, and shorts, his blonde hair peeking from under a baseball cap.

'Evelyn told me to tell you that it's cocktail time,' he says, kissing her cheek.

Rosie can't stomach anything else right now. Getting through the decadent lunch was bad enough. Julietta's ashen face zooms to her mind. Scared at the thought of them going to the lake.

Whatever she was going to tell her before Luke interrupted them has been on Rosie's mind since they left the house.

'Rosie!' Evelyn calls. 'You must try my limoncello spritz. It's to die for.' She waves a full martini glass in the air.

'You've got a new best friend.' Theo nudges her.

'Thanks, Evelyn. I'll have one in a minute,' Rosie replies, as politely as she can and excuses herself to go to the bathroom.

She carefully steps down to the lower deck, relieved to be out of the sun for a moment. The icy air-conditioned corridor is lined with closed doors. Before she can find out which one might be the bathroom she bumps into Fenna. Her face is like thunder.

A door opens and Rosie is jerked backwards into a room. It's an empty lounge, bigger than her flat back at home.

'I knew something was going on,' Fenna hisses, checking they are all alone.

'What do you mean?' Rosie asks, keeping her voice as light as she can muster. Her heart thumps in her chest.

'It's time you stopped lying.'

'Wha—'

Fenna jabs her phone and thrusts the screen at her. 'Do you want to explain this, Rosie *Mills*?'

The photograph of her dad on Christmas morning when she was eight years old. Happier times. A rush of saliva floods her mouth. Rosie doesn't trust herself to speak.

Fenna's figured it out.

Anger and confusion flash in Fenna's eyes. 'I don't know what game you're playing here, but you'd better start talking.'

Rosie swallows the bitter taste in her mouth. She could carry on the lie but what's the point? Fenna doesn't want to hear her excuses.

This is killing her. She desperately needs an ally. But can she trust Fenna with the truth? Trust her to keep this to herself? She glances at the closed door, praying no one is within earshot, and drops her voice, hoping Fenna will do the same.

'My dad was Dani's teacher, yes, but he doesn't have anything to do with her disappearance.'

'How do you know?'

The boat rocks.

'Because someone else knows what happened to her.' Rosie takes a deep breath. 'Someone onboard.'

35

ROSIE – DAY 8

Rosie only got a place at Queen Mary's because her dad worked there. They could never have afforded the fees otherwise. She wishes she could go back in time and change so many things. She would never have let him take that Italian teaching job if she knew what was going to happen.

Danielle Dixon. The girl that would ruin her life.

Rosie was transfixed with Dani throughout high school. The cool girl in the year above. Both were bursary students. Both had to find ways to fit in. Dani was granted a place due to her intelligence, spotted by a police officer when she was arrested for shoplifting, or so the story goes. She came from a rough council estate and had been in and out of care. However, her intelligence was a double-edged sword; she grew bored easily and acted up. She also had a temper. She was headstrong and feisty and opinionated, and Rosie loved that. Dani was all the things she was not.

Once she overheard the PE teacher say how 'Dani's mouth would be the death of her'. The same PE teacher gave a heartfelt interview with a local radio station telling the world how

Dani was an angel and how she had always thought there was something 'off' about Mr Mills.

Everyone's opinion of her dad changed overnight. He went from being a much-loved teacher to the most hated man in Britain.

Rosie foolishly went back to school for the new term, hoping that being with her friends would provide a distraction from the car crash of her life. She lasted one day. The rumours of his involvement had started and cruel whispers trailed down the school corridors after her. Horrific graffiti was scrawled in the girls' bathroom. She remembers the splintered wood on her dad's classroom door – his brass nameplate prised off as if doing so could erase the past.

After her dad's death, her mum suggested moving up to North Yorkshire. It would help them both as they tried to heal. A new area. A fresh start. She used her mother's maiden name, despite it feeling like losing her dad again. The only friend she kept was Lydia. Her singular link to the past.

Rosie doesn't know how she scraped through her exams at her new school. She thought things would get easier over time but with every anniversary of the disappearance there would be an appeal in the news for information. Danielle's family were desperate to know where her body might be so they could have a proper goodbye. The hate-filled, hurtful comments resurfaced. Her dad's assumed guilt was shared as if it was fact. People still thought he did it, taking the secret of where he'd put the girl's body to his grave.

Six months ago, her mum discovered a box of Rosie's dad's belongings that was mislabelled and stored in her grandma's loft. That's when her world split in two again.

Inside was a notebook. His notebook. The years slipped away as she turned the pages. He had started an investigation into Dani's disappearance, and it was all in there. Documented. Labelled. Scribbled pages full of his thoughts. Some legible, some not. One name stood out. A thick question mark beside it.

Fraser?

In the box, beside the notebook, was a dictaphone. As soon as she pressed play and his voice filled her bedroom, she realised there was no going back. He'd left himself audio notes in a breathless panic.

August 22nd 2010

12.05. Text received from Fraser. It reads:
You still up for hanging out later?

23.59. Text received from Fraser. It reads:
You made me do it. You gave me no choice. Sorry—

Who is Fraser? DD only added this number into her contacts the day she went missing. No other text messages between these two people. This person is key. Will tell police to investigate. It must be significant. The last person to see her alive?

This evidence had never publicly come to light.

At first Rosie thought Fraser was a boy's name, but as soon as she realised it could be a surname, her investigation picked up. She discovered the retired artist Marianne Fraser who owned a holiday home in the same small Italian village of Laprezia. She was there with her family when Danielle disappeared.

One of the Frasers *had* to be the contact in Dani's phone, the person who messaged her on the night she vanished. Rosie was certain that it was one of Marianne's sons – Luke or Theo – but she couldn't jump to conclusions. She needed to find a way into the family. As soon as she had concrete evidence she could go to the police and clear her dad's name.

Internet digging revealed Marianne Fraser would be at the Dursak Gallery in Soho the following month for a prestigious award. The Frasers' lives were so charmed compared to the hell Rosie had endured. She bribed a bored doorman to let her into the London event. She hid in the shadows of the packed room, listening to Marianne give an impassioned speech on authenticity in art. There was an after-party at the bar next door. Rosie had a backstory ready. She positioned herself near the door of the pub, a vulnerable woman recovering from a terrible fictional Tinder date, a damsel in distress. Theo was her knight in shining armour.

All she needed was answers to her dad's questions, but she couldn't come out and grill him. Patience was needed to buy his trust.

It wasn't long before she shared a fabricated version of her life with him. It was exhausting coming up with excuses as to why he couldn't meet her mum, not even on FaceTime, or why there were no photos of her father. He has no idea she has a connection to the tragedy that happened in the small Italian village that he knows so well.

She learnt that he had aspirations to be a professional footballer when he was younger and had competed for scholarships all around Europe. The dates he was in Croatia at a training camp meant that he couldn't have been in Laprezia. So that left Luke as the prime suspect. Unless Gerry or Marianne texted Dani on the night she went missing – but why would they have her phone number? Rosie couldn't leap to assumptions. She needed to investigate more.

However, the more time spent together, the more Rosie grew to like Theo. Feelings got involved. No one had treated her so nicely. As they grew closer, she started to feel anxious thinking about life *without* him.

For months she's wrestled with the fact that she is trapped in a lie. She had to make a decision to come clean or not. She couldn't live like this forever.

Then Theo's mum invited them on holiday to *Villa Speranza*.

It was her ticket in.

She instantly knew something was off when she arrived and saw all the security cameras around the enormous estate. Who needs that much security in a quiet little town? The taxi driver telling her to *be careful* cemented the risk she was taking. If her dad's investigation was right, she could potentially be on holiday with a murderer.

She set out to discover the truth but knew that doing so will ruin the best relationship she's ever had. This love story has played out on borrowed time. She doesn't belong in this family. And never will. Yet she still tricked herself that it could be different.

Since arriving, she's been bathed in luxury and welcomed by a kind and generous family. Everything she's always wanted. When Theo unexpectedly proposed, part of her was desperate for this lie to carry on a little longer. That's why she said yes. Why shouldn't she have some happiness after all the trauma in her life?

But none of this is real.

The truth had to come out one day.

And now Fenna knows. It's going to come crashing down. All she can do is beg her to help.

36

ROSIE – DAY 8

Rosie swallows. 'I had a plan. I thought it would be simple. I needed to get in with the family, come to Laprezia, look in their holiday home—'

'Look for what?' Fenna interrupts.

'Clues. Signs that Dani had been there. I don't know.' She drops to the sofa. Her legs are unable to hold her upright any longer. 'My dad was looking into who could have killed her before he died. I had no idea about this research until six months ago. I found his notes and decided to finish what he started.'

Fenna paces in front of her. She wishes she'd sit down too.

'Go on . . .'

'There was an incident with another student who broke the hair straighteners that Dani had lent her. It got violent. My dad had to step in and told Dani's host family she should be grounded for the night. He also confiscated her phone. At some point in the night, she breaks curfew. Her host family don't realise she's missing until eleven o'clock the next morning because no one had checked her room. They thought she was being a lazy teenager and missed breakfast. That's when the alarm is raised.

Rumours were that she went to meet my dad. But that's not true. She went to meet someone called "Fraser".'

Fenna scrunches up her nose as if a bad smell has wafted across the lounge. 'Fraser? How do you know this?'

'Because there was a text sent around midnight from "Fraser" apologising for something, saying she'd left them no choice. They clearly met and the night didn't go to plan. This person knows where Dani is.' Her breathing is coming out too fast.

Rosie tries to analyse Fenna's reaction. She never imagined saying all of this out loud, especially not today, with the rest of the family on the deck above. Who knows who is in earshot?

Fenna frowns. 'This was never reported in the news.'

'I know. The Italian police *lost* Dani's phone. There's no evidence of texts from "Fraser", apart from in my dad's notes . . .'

'Wait. So why the hell are you here? What are you planning to do? Avenge your dad's death? You've lied to everyone, created a fake relationship with Theo—' Fenna snaps.

'It's not fake.' Her voice wavers. She loves him, more than she ever thought she could. But she can't forget that he's a Fraser, too. 'I want to find the truth.'

'What truth? The truth is your dad had Danielle's phone. He abducted and murdered a schoolgirl and made up this stuff, trying to pin the blame on someone else. Everyone thinks the same – your dad was a paedo.'

'He's not a paedo. He was stitched up.' The vein in her head is going to explode. 'He'd *confiscated* Dani's phone, hours before she went missing. The papers reported it wrong.' She tries to calm her breathing. 'And on this phone was evidence that he told the police, but they ignored him. His DNA was never found on her clothing by the lake. He had an alibi. But lies were spread. Mud sticks. He killed himself because he couldn't live with the guilt of letting her down, not because he killed her!' Rosie tries to keep her voice down but she's shaking with anger. 'I will tell you everything I know but you can't tell Theo.'

'You accepted his proposal,' Fenna hisses. 'I can't believe what I'm hearing—'

'Can you help me or not?' She swipes the tears streaming down her face. Her make-up will have run. How will she explain the state she's in to Theo?

Theo.

'No.' Fenna turns to leave.

The boat rocks suddenly. Rosie grabs on to the shelving unit and as she does she knocks a vase to the ground. Her stomach lurches at the sound of it smashing.

'Please,' she begs.

Someone calls their names. Rosie can't let Fenna walk out. She presses her fingernails into her palm.

'I think Luke has something to do with it.' The words are out of her mouth before she can stop them.

Fenna stops still. The muscles in her back tense. It is an eternity before she turns to face her. The colour has drained from her face. She looks deathly ill.

'. . . What did you say?'

Rosie swallows.

'Someone in his family knows more than they're letting on. I think he has been lying to you. Do you trust him? One hundred percent trust him?'

'Are you threatening my family?' Fenna's eyes blaze with anger.

The door handle turns.

'No, I'm not. I promise. I . . .' She releases the breath trapped in her lungs. 'I really need your help. I know this is a lot to take in, but I need you to listen to me. Appearances can be deceptive. Give me twenty-four hours. Watch him and tell me that I'm wrong. Please.'

37

FENNA – DAY 8

Fenna grips the sideboard as the door bursts open and Evelyn and Marianne rush into the lounge. Their eyes widen at the sight of the smashed vase and Rosie's tear-stained face.

'It was my fault. I felt faint and tripped. I've had too much sun. Luckily Fenna came to help me. I can't believe it . . . I'm so sorry, I'll pay you to repair it,' Rosie manages to say in between sobs. She lifts a trembling hand to push back a strand of hair that's come loose. Her forehead is speckled with beads of sweat.

Fenna tries to speak but words don't come out.

'You poor thing.' Evelyn and Marianne cluck, telling her it was an accident, the vase can be repaired, no harm was done. They usher her to the upper deck, leaving Fenna alone. She overhears them telling the captain to turn around. They need to get Rosie home.

Yacht trip over.

A crew member calmly sweeps up the ceramic shards and asks Fenna if she's ok. She can barely nod. Her legs shake with adrenaline. Rosie's secrets suffocate her.

She emerges from the lower deck in a daze, blinking in the sunlight. Blood rushes in her ears. The briny lake water turns her stomach.

'You alright, Fen?' Luke slings a sunburnt arm around her. His whisky-laced breath hits her face. 'You were gone ages.'

Fenna can't think straight.

'Fine.' She shrugs him away. She can't bear to be near him. He told her he did a background check on this girl.

He lied to her.

***

She gets back to the house and puts the children to bed. Luke stumbles over one of Alba's books left on the floor and flops to the armchair opposite their bed.

'You ok?' Luke asks. 'You've acted weird all afternoon.'

She doesn't want to talk about it. About anything. Rosie's confession plays on a loop. Her brain is in overdrive since getting off the yacht.

'I'm fine,' she mumbles, struggling to look at him.

Rosie told her to observe Luke for twenty-four hours.

She thinks of his white lies – the damage he and Jonno got up to when they last visited Laprezia, moving their money without asking her, and the fact he's drinking more than she's ever known him to drink. Sometimes when he says things that don't sit right, she puts it down to her hormones and exhaustion. But what if there's more to it?

She remembers when Giovanni came to the house. He said Luke tore down Danielle Dixon's missing poster on purpose. Why would he do such a thing? What if being back here is bringing something out in him? Theo was away when the schoolgirl vanished. So if Rosie's dad's theory is right that it was someone from the Fraser family meeting her on the night she died, then it must be Luke . . .

She catches herself. *No. This is ridiculous.*

Her husband is not involved in the disappearance of Danielle Dixon. This is the desperate act of a woman unable to believe her father could do something horrific. Unthinkable. Even though it was never proved that Jonathan Mills harmed Danielle, he was tried by public jury. There has never been suspicion around anyone else. No one else is linked to the case.

Yet, something niggles.

Rosie didn't come across as deluded. There was a steeliness in her eyes. A desire for Fenna to help her discover the truth. She has evidence that has never come to light, which begs the question – what if this is a miscarriage of justice? What if the real killer is still out there?

'Is it my mum again? Has she said something?' Luke waves a hand in front of her face. The action breaks her spiralling thoughts.

'Hmm? Oh, no.' All she wants is to get into bed and try to go to sleep. She makes a fist and thumps her pillow, certain that Luke keeps taking the plump ones for himself.

She realises he is still talking. '. . . especially as they're planning on selling this place.'

Fenna darts upright. 'What? They're selling *Villa Speranza*? When? Why?'

'Weren't you there? I overheard Mum say to Richard that she'd be in touch. The paperwork would be with him soon.'

She swallows. 'That could be about anything. How do you know they're selling?'

'Why else would Richard be involved? He used to be a solicitor.'

She doesn't have an answer for that. The thought of this house not being in the family makes her feel sick. She can't imagine strangers living here. What happened to Marianne promising them mates' rates to stay here? No. She can't lose this house. She had hoped that one day they would inherit this place and raise the children here. Marianne once said she would be carried out of *Villa Speranza* in a box. There's no way she'd sell. He must have misheard, he was drunk for most of the afternoon after all.

Luke continues, unaware of the thoughts in his wife's head. 'Still, it's odd. Like, what's the rush? I guess you never know with Mum what she's thinking.'

'That's one way of putting it,' she mutters.

'You're not annoyed at me, are you?' He yawns. 'I know I should have helped more with the kids today. Sorry.'

She turns to finally look at him, slumped in the chair. There is a drunken sheen to his pink, sunburnt cheeks.

'Do you know what? Yeah, I am pissed off about that. Why do you have to drink so much?' She knows this isn't the right time but she can't help herself.

'We're on holiday!'

'That's not an excuse; you can't keep thinking about yourself. No one else is drinking as much as you.'

'You don't know what I'm dealing with.' He gets to his feet.

'What?'

'Nothing. Forget it.' He storms to the ensuite. It's like he can't get away quick enough.

38

ROSIE – DAY 8

Theo has pandered to Rosie's every need since returning from the lake. He said he was worried that she might need to go to the hospital to rule out sun stroke, but thankfully she managed to persuade him that was unnecessary. He took her straight to their bedroom and laid her on the cool sheets. A fan aimed in her direction. She didn't have to try hard to act ill, she feels sick at the thought of Fenna knowing her secret. He kept commenting on how poorly she looked and how she needs to get better for the engagement party. She promised him she would be fine. It's three days away.

But who knows what will happen by then?

Rosie ate a light supper in bed, brought to her on a tray. Would he still want to marry her if he knows how she manipulated her way into their family? That she's here because she needs to discover the truth? That she believes one of them is capable of killing a schoolgirl?

Theo stayed by her side all evening so she couldn't slip out of the bedroom and speak to Julietta to see what she'd meant earlier. She still needs to ask her more questions. She's not forgotten the comment she made before they left for the yacht trip.

'The family say they have no idea what happened to Danielle. That's not true. Listen to me. You can't trust them.'

It's almost three o'clock in the morning. Rosie has been pretending to sleep for hours. Her mind won't stop whirring. She's furious at herself. She came here to find answers but she's no further along in the investigation and time is ticking now that Fenna knows who she is.

If Fenna tells Luke it will all be over. All of this will have been for nothing. She refused to look at Rosie when they disembarked the yacht and she hasn't seen her since. Will she tell her husband, or will she do as Rosie begged and observe him? See if he reveals something that could help the investigation. Her stomach clenches with a wave of nausea. She doesn't have time to waste.

Once she's certain that Theo is in a deep sleep she uses the light of her phone to guide her way out of the bedroom.

Her dad didn't have anything to do with Dani's disappearance. He wrote the name Fraser down for a reason. He didn't make up the text details. There is no doubt about that – they were real. They existed. Whoever 'Fraser' is was the last person to see Dani alive. Her gut screams that she's on the right track. Gerry, Marianne, or Luke – the Frasers who were here that summer – are key to discovering the truth.

Speaking of keys . . . Her hand curls around the antique key she found in the wildflower garden a few days ago. It didn't fit the lock in the outhouse. So where does it belong?

The basement.

The only place she's not yet looked. With a deep breath she

moves towards the kitchen. It's now or never. The ghostly glow from a full moon offers her the light she needs. Her heartbeat rushes in her ears over the occasional unnerving creak from the wooden floorboards. There's a chill underfoot as she hurries across the hallway and dashes to the locked basement door.

What are they hiding down here? She doesn't buy Gerry's overly cautious approach to keeping the children out of harm's way. Raffi is a baby and Alba is too short to push the handle. She presses a hand against the wood and runs her fingers over the padlock. The thick rubberised cover looks brand new. She pulls the small key from her pocket. Her shoulders drop.

It's much too small.

Where would they put the actual key? Didn't Gerry say the laundry room was downstairs? If so, Julietta would have a key. Rosie needs to find it. She pushes open the kitchen door. A rush of bright light makes her blink. There's someone in the room.

She leaps in fright.

'Jesus. You made me jump,' she gasps, clutching her chest.

'Oh, sorry, darling,' Marianne could be a ghost standing there in her ethereal white nightdress. Her eyes are ringed with red and her pale face is blotchy. She looks much older without any make-up on. 'Can't sleep?'

'No. I mean, no, I came down for a paracetamol . . . Are you ok?' She's impressed at how quick the lie flew from her lips.

Marianne moves her hand to hide whatever she was doing. There's a flash of silver. A puckered pill packet. 'Godawful hay fever. I've tried every tablet and spray but nothing seems to work.' Her voice is light and chirpy, but her bloodshot eyes tell a different story.

'Sorry if I disturbed you,' Rosie says, relieved that at least

Marianne didn't catch her rummaging in drawers looking for a key to the basement. How would she explain that?

'It's fine. I was hoping to find an antihistamine. I swore I saw a packet in here but Julietta must have tidied them away.' She frowns at a cupboard crammed full of herbs. 'Let me see if I can find any paracetamol for you.'

Rosie hovers on one foot. She wished she'd picked up her robe. She rubs her bare arms, feeling exposed in her t-shirt and shorts pyjamas. Marianne's determined hands rifle through the contents of a drawer. There's a frenetic energy coming from her.

'Nope. Not here.' She brushes her hair from her eyes and straightens. 'I need to speak to Julietta about a better system. She complained to me that food was going missing. It's probably because she's got such a haphazard way of keeping track of things. It never used to be like this. There used to be order here.' Her words tumble over themselves.

'Don't worry. I should head back to bed . . .' Rosie places a hand on the door frame and tries to summon a convincing yawn. 'Are you sure you're ok?'

'I'm fine.' She reaches across for a piece of kitchen roll and dabs her eyes. 'God, what am I like. I'd blame the menopause but . . .' She loudly blows her nose into the tissue. 'Never mind.'

'Has something happened?'

Marianne turns and attempts to rearrange the mugs hanging on the hooks, taking each one off to face the opposite direction. 'Let's just say I'm so grateful for your wonderful news. It is the tonic we all need. I pray that you will swiftly plan the wedding. Some people have such long engagements, but I don't understand why they think they have time . . .'

Suddenly a cup falls from her grip. It shatters on the stone floor. Rosie leaps at the sudden sound. It echoes in the silence of the sleeping house. It takes her back to the smashed vase on the yacht. Fenna's furious expression looms at the front of her mind.

'Oh dear.' Marianne's face crumples. She moves to pick up the broken pieces.

'Careful,' Rosie says.

A trickle of blood trails down Marianne's wrist.

'I don't know where the dustpan and brush are.' She sniffs. 'How ridiculous is that? You must think terribly of me, not knowing where we keep things. But Julietta takes care of all of this for us. We have to get all these pieces. People could walk in with bare feet. Alba might toddle in and . . .' Marianne lets out a gasp of breath and starts to cry. Her shoulders heave with every sob.

Rosie crouches down beside her, tentatively placing an arm over her slender, juddering back.

'It's fine, it's a mug,' she soothes, taken aback by such raw emotion. 'You should clean your wrist. Why don't you sit down? I can clear it up. Let me get a piece of kitchen roll for you.'

Rosie starts to move away but Marianne grips her hands. Her eyes are wild and huge.

'You can still get sunshine in October you know. An autumnal wedding would be beautiful here.'

'This October?' Rosie asks slowly, trying not to wince at the surprising strength of Marianne's grip.

It's August.

'Yes. Or November. Have you thought about a winter wedding? You won't be guaranteed snow here, but it is still a magical place to come. We can light the fire and . . .' She lets go of Rosie's hands and stops abruptly.

A slow dawning washes over her.

'Everything's not ok, is it?' Rosie drops her voice.

'I'm sorry. I just want to see my baby get married.' Marianne closes her eyes. 'The doctors don't know how long I've got left.'

Things suddenly make sense. The last-minute holiday. Crying in the wild garden. The family heirloom engagement ring. The desperation for everyone to get along. A lump of emotion leaps to the back of Rosie's throat. She tugs a few sheets of kitchen roll and wraps them gently over the cut as a makeshift bandage.

Marianne winces. 'The boys don't know. Please promise me you won't say a word to Theo. His dad's death hit him hard.' Her voice wobbles. 'I'm trying to keep it together but it's impossible. This holiday will be the last one I ever have.'

'I'm so sorry.' Rosie blinks.

Marianne juts her chin out. 'Don't be. Please. I've had a longer life than many.'

Rosie carefully collects all the pieces of the broken cup and tips them into the bin.

Marianne stands and takes Rosie's hand once more. Her grip is just as intense. 'Promise me you won't tell a soul, Rosie.'

She's keeping enough secrets; one more won't hurt.

'I promise.'

39

FENNA – DAY 9

'Why is your mum here?' Fenna asks Luke through gritted teeth.

Marianne insisted on pushing Raffi's pushchair through the crowds of tourists huddling around the 'finest olive oil in Tuscany' stall, keen to try a free sample.

'She wants to hang out. What? Don't give me that look. I could hardly say no,' Luke scoops Alba up from nearly being run over by a teenager on a scooter.

It's unbearably hot and the temperature is set to rise. The narrow mediaeval streets of Monterchi are filled with bargain-hunters clogging up the cobbled pavements for the weekly farmers market. Fenna didn't want to come and not because Rosie's confession plays on a loop in her mind from yesterday. It's crowded and noisy. The air smells of deet, suncream, and boiling oil from a food stall on the corner selling *coccoli,* fried salty doughballs. Normally one of her favourite snacks, but she has lost her appetite.

Alba is clearly not in the mood either and keeps screaming to be put down. Luke is oblivious to the chaos and has stopped at a stall selling artisan leather belts. He holds up two tan-coloured ones with silver buckles and black stitching.

'Which do you prefer?' he asks.

'They look identical to me.' She holds on to Alba's clammy, wriggling hand, whilst keeping an eye on Marianne at the next stall with Raffi.

'Hmm. This one's nicer.' He pulls out his wallet. The stall holder quickly appears with a card reader.

'My card wasn't working the other day,' Fenna remembers.

'I'll speak to my accountant to see if he's moved the money from that high interest savings account yet.' Luke frowns at the belts. 'On second thought, I'll leave it.'

The stall holder mutters something and snatches the merchandise off Luke.

'Are we ok, Luke? Financially I mean?' she asks, unable to hide the worry in her voice.

He lied about checking Rosie out – is he lying about this?

'Course. Why?' He puts his wallet away.

'I know we said we'd not live beyond our means whilst I'm on maternity leave, but we are ok?' She knows she should take more ownership of the family finances but there's not enough space in her baby-fied brain to fit it in.

'Everything's fine.' He moves to the side to let a heavy-set woman barge past holding a watermelon.

She nods, believing him. He is obsessed with money, there's no way he would take a gamble with their funds.

'Oh, I forgot to tell you.' He breaks her thoughts. 'Theo said he wanted to take me out tomorrow. There's something he wants to talk about. I bet he's going to ask me to be his best man. Mum would bloody love that. Maybe you and Rosie could hang out? Get to know each other before she becomes part of the family.'

Fenna's body must react before her brain. She freezes. What the hell is she going to do about Rosie?

'What? You still don't trust her?' he asks, misreading her silence.

If only he knew.

For a split second she thinks about telling him what she discovered about Rosie, but an Italian man selling hand-painted clay figurines loudly yells from the stall beside them, making her jump. This is not the time or place for that conversation.

'Are you ok, Fen?' Luke frowns.

'My feet are killing me. Let's see where we can get an ice-cream,' Fenna says. Alba stops protesting at this suggestion. 'Somewhere with air-con.' She waves a sweaty arm in the air to get Marianne's attention.

***

They have to cut the trip short. Alba is sick from eating her tutti-frutti ice-cream too quickly, Raffi has two nappy explosions, and they've run out of changes of clothes for them both. Luke grumbles that the changing bag hasn't been replenished. She argues that it wasn't her responsibility to keep on top of it, not when he used the last spare babygrow the other day and didn't tell her.

Marianne strides ahead, away from them bickering. 'I'm not taking sides.'

She stops suddenly.

'Mum?' Luke calls.

Something has caught Marianne's attention. She thrusts a

trembling arm out for support, clamping a hand onto a stone pillar and muttering to herself.

Luke and Fenna exchange confused looks.

'Mum, are you ok?' Luke asks.

He gets no answer. He jogs further up the street to check on her. Alba complains about something in her shoe that's hurting her. Fenna bends down to pick out a small stone that's wedged in her tiny open-toed sandals and misses what Marianne says.

When she looks up she sees Carla peering down on her.

She gasps. Carla's face is on a poster in a shop window. An appeal for information. *Mancante.* Missing.

Luke guides his mum to sit on a bench in the shade beside two colourful planters. He runs back to Fenna and the children, still walking at Alba's snail's pace, and pulls the changing bag from the handles of the pushchair.

'Where's that bottle of water?' he asks, rummaging in the bag.

'Is your mum ok?' Fenna asks. She's never seen her like this.

Marianne has her head in her hands. She suddenly looks very frail. The noise of the market carries on around them. A woman selling lace tablecloths glances over from her stall, clearly wondering what's going on.

Luke swears, pulling out spare dummies and soiled baby clothes with wild abandon. 'It's shock.'

He knocks something onto the floor. Alba cries that her toy is rolling away.

'I didn't know they were putting out posters . . .' She trails off. It makes it feel real that Carla's missing. What about the theory that she's visiting friends in Pisa? Her stomach clenches. This is serious.

'Me neither. Where the hell is the bottle of water? Did you finish it?' Luke snaps.

She takes the bag from him and opens the side pocket. 'It's here.'

He takes it and strides over to Marianne.

Fenna takes one last look at Carla and shivers.

40

ROSIE – DAY 9

Rosie needs time alone to process things. It's like she's on a train that won't slow down. Marianne's confession about her health plays on a loop. Another thing she has to keep from Theo. All the secrets are adding up and she's struggling to cope. She's still not had a chance to speak to Fenna to see if she's going to help her or not.

She watches from the side of the dining room as Luke shows Gerry all the things they bought at the market that morning, laying items out on the table. How can they be shopping right now? Acting like everything is fine?

'This smells amazing, doesn't it?' Marianne wafts a scented candle under Rosie's nose. A strong burst of lemongrass and herbal plants makes her want to sneeze. She is like a different woman from the one crying in the kitchen last night. 'I couldn't resist.'

Rosie looks around the room. It's the picture-perfect image of a happy family holiday. Alba whizzes around, pulling a hand-painted wooden car by a red ribbon, the others share crunchy biscotti fingers and thinly sliced pecorino Toscano cheese. She can't stand here and watch them act like everything is fine.

'Just going to get a glass of water,' she says to no one in particular.

Rosie plods to the kitchen, surprised to see Julietta in there, washing up. Her spirits lift.

'I've been trying to find you,' Rosie says, keeping her voice low.

'*Signora* Fraser says I'm not organised enough, but I know this kitchen. I know this house. She forgets I've worked here for twenty years.' She slams a soapy saucepan on the drying rack and says something in Italian that sounds like a swear word. 'I know when things go missing.'

This is the first time she's seen Julietta without a cheery smile.

'Missing? What's missing?'

'Food. Tins, fruit, and some snacks that I had put aside. I know they're not being eaten because there is no rubbish.' She mutters something unintelligible.

Rosie stands still, clasping her hands. Clearly now is not a good time for a chat.

Julietta lets out a breath. Her plump cheeks are pink and her eyes look watery. 'Sorry, Rosie. You caught me at a bad time.' She glances at the closed kitchen door. 'Please do not say anything to the family. I am not complaining, I am frustrated. I shouldn't have said anything.'

'I won't. It's fine to have a moan now and again. I'm sure it will all turn up.' Rosie flashes a smile. She thinks of Gerry's clandestine snacking in the car; he must be the culprit. Another secret she's been bound to keep. 'Listen, I need to talk to you about Danielle Dixon. You said to me that—'

Julietta roughly wipes her red-rimmed eyes. 'It is a good idea that you don't say that name.'

'What? But—'

'Please, *Signorina*. Enjoy your holiday and then go home.' There is a sternness to Julietta's voice that wasn't there before.

Rosie's skin prickles. 'But . . .'

'Promise me.'

Why does she look so scared?

Rosie stutters. 'I don't understand. You told me someone was lying. You said I should stay away from the Frasers. What's going on, Julietta? If I'm in danger, you need to tell me.'

'The Frasers are very kind people,' Julietta replies, avoiding her eyes. Her voice robotic.

A trickle of panic runs across Rosie. Who is this woman? It's like she's been drugged or something. Julietta closes her mouth and smiles again. It doesn't reach her darting eyes.

The doorbell rings. The sound of it makes them both jump.

'Please, I don't understand . . .' Rosie shakes her head, needing to gather her thoughts. 'You were working here when Dani – I mean, Danielle – went missing, now Carla has vanished, too, so if there's something you know then you need to tell the police.'

Julietta's name is called. She wipes her soapy hands on her apron. '*Scusa*. I need to get to work.'

'Wait, please,' Rosie begs.

The chime of the bell rings once more. A door slams.

Gerry yells down the stairs. 'Can someone answer that? It's the bloody police.'

The police?

Julietta steps away.

Rosie reaches an arm out to stop her from leaving. 'I know you know more than you're telling me.'

Julietta flinches. She opens and closes her mouth. Uncertainty and fear are etched on her flushed face. After a second's hesitation she flies out of the kitchen before Rosie can say another word.

***

Rosie gets herself a glass of water, needing to calm down and bring her heart rate back to normal. She rinses out the empty glass, takes a deep breath, and hurries to join the others in the dining room as Giovanni walks in. The mood immediately shifts.

Marianne asks Julietta to take the children outside.

'*Buonasera*,' he says without smiling. His intense brown eyes scrutinise their faces.

Theo pulls a chair out for Rosie. Everyone else takes a seat around the table. The produce from the market sits in the centre. Smells of nutty, salty cheese and the herbal scented candle hang in the stuffy air.

'What's going on?' Luke asks. The vein in his forehead is prominent.

Giovanni explains that a known thief in Pisa was caught using Carla's bank cards. It had been one of their leads. The man alleged that he'd found her purse tossed near a bin in Laprezia when he was travelling through and took the opportunity. 'We now believe that Carla never left the town. Her bag was discovered in a farmer's field down the road. At first we thought she may have been sleeping rough.'

Rosie sits forward, her heart racing once more. She steals a look at Luke. He has a poker face, listening intently to Giovanni. Is she imagining it or are his knuckles turning whiter as he grips the back of Fenna's chair? She darts her eyes away when he catches her staring.

'Is she ok?' Marianne asks.

He shakes his head. 'We don't know. There were signs of a struggle.' Giovanni lowers his voice to add, 'And a lot of blood.'

There is a collective gasp from the women.

'We will be conducting more thorough searches in the area,' he adds.

'She's not here if that's what you think,' Luke snaps.

'Now, now, Luke,' Gerry warns. 'He's only doing his job. It's nothing personal.'

'Really?' Luke folds his arms, glaring at Giovanni.

'Do you have something to say, *Signore* Fraser?' Giovanni's nostrils flare.

The air crackles with tension. Rosie frowns. Surely Fenna can see how obstructive her husband is being? The question is why.

'Luke.' Marianne reaches out an arm to her eldest son. 'Sorry, officer. We all want Carla home safe and sound, so if there is anything we can do to help we will. Won't we, Luke?'

Luke pulls away and says nothing.

Rosie tries to catch Fenna's eye. Surely this reaction is causing alarm bells?

'What about the boyfriend? Julietta mentioned Carla had one. Have you searched her boyfriend's place?' Gerry suggests. 'It might be worth looking at those closest to her.'

'Oh yes, good idea,' Marianne enthuses. 'Surely, he needs to be investigated fully. I thought he was your main suspect?'

'At this stage, we're not ruling anything out.' Giovanni notes something down on his pad. 'We will be making sure to look everywhere.' He takes a breath. 'Time is not on our side.'

'What do you mean?' Theo asks.

Dread lurches in the pit of Rosie's stomach at the look on the police officer's face. The only sound is the slow tick-tock of the antique clock on the wall.

'Officer?' Gerry pushes.

Giovanni takes a deep breath. 'Did Carla tell you about the medication she takes for a heart condition?'

'What? No. I didn't know she was ill,' Marianne says, blinking. 'She didn't tell us this, did she, Gerry?'

'No,' Gerry says as the colour drains from his face. 'Julietta didn't mention it either.'

'Julietta may not have known about it. Carla's parents say she was embarrassed and didn't tell many people. However, due to the urgent situation, we will be making this news public. The longer she goes without taking it, the more chance there is that her heart could fail.'

Rosie and Fenna lock eyes.

Another girl is missing and in grave danger.

Surely, Fenna will help her now?

41

ROSIE – DAY 9

They've come out for dinner as it's Julietta's night off. Marianne suggested a change of scene would do them all good. The restaurant may be simple with its décor of earthy tones and distressed wood, but it's the view over the lantern-lit olive groves through the floor-to-ceiling window that takes Rosie's breath away. However, being here is a sombre affair. It's as if the children picked up on the strained mood, as they went to sleep in the double pushchair with minimal fuss.

Gerry insisted they had a table inside away from the mosquitoes. The air-con makes Rosie shiver. She's still waiting to have a conversation with Fenna; every time she tries to catch her eye she glances away.

'This is delicious,' Marianne says, cutting her pasta into tiny strands.

Since Marianne shared her health secret with her, Rosie can't help but think how frail she looks. It's as if she's half the size of the woman who welcomed her to Tuscany over a week ago.

Gerry takes a deep breath. 'I had a call from a journalist earlier. They're running the news about Carla. I said we wouldn't be commenting.' His face is drawn and pale. 'None of us. I've told Julietta not to speak to any media either.'

'Do you think her family will appeal for her to come home?' Fenna asks, scraping butter across a rustic slice of sourdough.

'I don't know. Let's leave the police to do their job. It's not our place to get involved. Anyone want red?' he asks, lifting up the bottle.

'Keep on pouring it,' Marianne says slowly. Her hand wobbles as she places her wine glass back on the table. 'Now more than ever we need to put on a united front.'

Rosie pushes her pasta around her plate. She can't stomach anything. The few mouthfuls of spaghetti dressed in vibrant basil leaves and lashings of olive oil slosh around her stomach.

'Anyone else feel like people are staring at us?' Luke mutters.

'It's in your head.' Marianne clears her throat. Her eyes dart around the table. 'Please tell me you're going to stay? All of you?'

Fenna's knife scrapes the ceramic.

'Of course, Mum,' Theo says.

'We're not going anywhere.' Luke nods decisively.

Rosie lets out a sigh of relief. She's not leaving until she's got answers.

Gerry places a protective arm around Marianne's shoulders. 'I told you they wouldn't leave early.'

'Thank goodness. I was so worried you'd all want to go.' Marianne sniffs. 'The only way for us to get through this is as a family.'

***

Rosie excuses herself. She bumps into Theo outside the bathroom. He fumbles with his phone camera, wanting to take a selfie of them beside an amusing framed print of a dog driving a car.

'On second thought, I think we should go,' Theo says, holding his phone up.

'Go? But we've not had dessert,' Rosie says.

'No, I mean we should go back to England. Change our flights and leave earlier than we planned.'

Her stomach flips. She can't leave now.

'What? Why? No. We need to stay!' She quickly rearranges her face into a bright smile for the photo.

'Have you not had enough time with my family?' He smiles at the shot.

'No. I mean I know it's full on at times but I'm having a lovely time.' She rubs his arm. 'Plus, your mum's organising an engagement party; we can't leave before that.'

He rolls his eyes and tucks his phone in his back pocket. 'It's not for us. It's another excuse to spend time showing off with Richard and Evelyn.'

'I thought you got on with them?' She's confused. He seemed to be enjoying himself on their yacht. What's changed?

He rubs his face. She realises he looks exhausted. There are deep bags under his eyes that don't normally belong there. 'I've reached my limit with my family. Luke in particular is getting under my skin. He's so obstructive. Rubbing people up the wrong way, thinking the world revolves around him. Mum'll get over it. There's always next year.'

'No. I mean, I want to stay.' Rosie coughs. 'Please.'

I need more time, she wants to scream. *We can't go. Not yet.* For too long, she's been distracted and now he wants to leave? Her hands grow clammy.

Theo hesitates then sighs. 'I'll tell Mum to tone the party down. Not go all out like she wants to.'

'That's a good compromise,' Rosie says and kisses him. Allowing herself to breathe a sigh of relief.

As they join the others at the table, the door to the restaurant opens and three young Italian men walk in. One of them spots the family and starts nudging his friends. Immediately their expressions darken and the whispers grow. A prickle of unease sends the fine hairs on her arms on end.

'Is there a problem?' Gerry boldly asks, catching one of their eyes.

The youngest-looking man, in a tight navy t-shirt and ripped jeans, replies in Italian. He leans forward aggressively. His friend has to fling a meaty arm out to hold him back.

'*Le bugie hanno le gambe corte*,' one spits as they move past.

An apologetic member of staff dashes over and leads the glaring men to the back of the restaurant to pick up a takeaway pizza.

Their arrival has caused a commotion amongst the other diners. Everyone in the restaurant is now staring at the English family.

'What did they say?' Marianne asks Fenna, nervously glancing at the men who look like they're now having a row with the manager. Voices are being raised and fingers are pointed in their direction.

Fenna gulps her wine. 'He wants to know why we're here when we should be out looking for Carla . . .'

Rosie tries to catch her eye. Is this making her as nervous and on edge as she feels?

Gerry swears. 'What do they expect us to do that the police

can't? I'm sorry but I'm sick of it. This is supposed to be our holiday!'

Marianne rubs a reassuring hand over his tense arm. Her eyes fill with tears. 'Let's get the bill, darling.'

'No. We are having dessert,' Gerry says firmly. Rosie has never seen him so assertive. Even Theo is taken aback at the change in his stepdad. Gone is his usually placid demeanour, replaced with anger. 'What? Don't look at me like that. We're not letting others intimidate us. We've done nothing wrong. Remember that.'

42

FENNA – DAY 10

Fenna can't stop thinking about those furious Italian men in the restaurant last night. Her appetite vanished immediately when she overheard their conversation. It was obvious from the way they glared at the family that they had links to Carla. One was the spitting image of her – family, perhaps? She only told Marianne some of what they'd said.

The shorter one, with the more menacing eyes, had said in pointed Italian, 'Another girl that's vanished whilst *they're* on holiday.'

Every word was laced with suspicion. She didn't tell her mother-in-law that the phrase he used isn't common. But she understood the meaning. *'Lies have short legs.'* The lies won't last long, the truth will come out eventually.

Their reaction ignited something. She's never seen such disgust on a stranger's face. Has she been ignorant to how the locals view the Frasers for all these years? She thinks about what Giovanni said about Luke in the cafe. *Be careful of him.* She thought it was because he has this weird grudge with her husband but what if there's more to it?

What if Rosie is onto something? What if there are secrets to uncover? Could one of the family know more than they're letting on about Danielle? About Carla?

She needs to speak to Rosie.

The following morning, Luke and Theo go out early. She hopes he won't be asked to be the best man. Surely it won't get that far? Luke practically pushed her and Rosie together and told them to have fun.

He has no idea.

They stroll away from the house, down the garden path that leads in the opposite direction to the swimming pool. Rosie looks nervous. They silently walk through a stone arch, past a well-trimmed bush covered in speckled purple flowers. A pleasing perfume scent fills her nose as they go. Alba plods ahead, picking up fallen petals and singing to herself.

'You need to start with what you know . . .' Fenna breaks the silence first. Her hands grip the pushchair.

'So you believe me?' Rosie asks, avoiding her eyes.

Fenna's insides twist. After a moment's hesitation she slowly nods her head. 'I'm ready to listen to what you have to say.'

Rosie checks they are alone. She takes a deep breath and starts to talk.

43

ROSIE – DAY 10

Rosie can't believe she's able to say everything out loud. For so long, she's kept this to herself. It almost feels like a trap.

She makes sure Alba is out of earshot and lowers her voice, 'Dani went missing on August 22nd 2010. A few days later, her Polaroid camera and her denim jacket, which was covered in blood, were found near the lake by a dog walker. This became the main theory – that she was killed and her body thrown in the water—'

'By your dad.' Fenna swats a mosquito away. 'He had Danielle's phone. He was seen rowing with her earlier that day. No wonder everyone assumed he killed her.'

She clenches her jaw. Her heart aches every time she thinks of her dad and all he put up with. It must have been terrifying. The witch hunt. No one in his corner. 'He didn't kill her. It wasn't until the next day that he remembered he'd *confiscated* her phone. He had an alibi – his host family said he was in all night. None of his DNA was found on Dani's things by the lake. Yet mud sticks.'

With no body but bloodied, abandoned clothes the

speculation was rife. The town was overrun with journalists, which frightened the tourists away. Fingers were naturally pointed at the only man in the country who was supposed to be taking care of Dani.

Fenna folds her arms. 'Anyway, you said there was a message on her phone from someone called Fraser?'

Rosie explains how she discovered that *Fraser* must mean *The Frasers*. 'When I found out the Frasers own a holiday home in the same town where she vanished I knew this was who my dad meant. It has to be one of them. Theo wasn't here that summer. So it's got to be Marianne, Gerry, or Luke Fraser. One of them messaged Dani and—'

'And you're *sure* Theo was away?' Fenna cuts in.

Rosie nods. 'He was at a football camp in Croatia when Dani went missing.' She remembers the framed certificate in his room. The photos with the famous footballer. 'I also went through the family photo albums. Everything happened at a time when digital cameras were everywhere, so there's plenty of evidence that Theo is telling the truth. It's all Luke, Marianne, and Gerry in the snaps from that summer.'

Rosie doesn't know if the penny has dropped about what this means for Fenna's marriage.

'Wait. So if you – and your dad – believe this mysterious phone contact is such a key part to discovering the truth, then why has that name never come out in the press?' Fenna continues.

'Because the police went and *lost* her phone when it was in storage. All the evidence they had to go off was that at one point my dad had her phone – and his prints were all over it. They put two and two together and got five. Or the media did.'

'So what did this text message say?'

'It was written in English and sent by Fraser at midnight. It said, "*You made me do it. You gave me no choice. Sorry—*" '

Fenna's eyes widen.

Rosie had the same reaction. She can still hear her dad's breathy, panicked voice, the rustling of his trousers as he paced, his thoughts tumbling out, speaking as fast as he could. The panic in his voice scared her.

Fenna frowns. 'It could have been sent about something totally unconnected and innocent. It doesn't mean anything ominous.'

Rosie gawps at her. '*You made me do it. You gave me no choice. Sorry—!*' she repeats, dropping her voice when she realises she's drawn Alba's attention. 'What else could it be referring to?'

Fenna's mouth draws into a tight line. 'Was there any other evidence?'

'According to my dad's information, there was one sighting of her on CCTV at half past ten when she left her host family's house—'

'Mario's Shoes . . .' Fenna interrupts.

'Sorry?'

'Nothing. Go on.'

'She turns down the main road, the one leading from the church, and vanishes. Somehow her Polaroid camera and bloodied denim jacket end up near the lake. In my dad's journal he'd drawn maps based on the newspaper reports of the routes she could have taken to get there. *Villa Speranza* is on every possible route from where she was staying.'

'Why didn't you take this evidence to the police?' Fenna asks, after a pause.

Rosie looks away.

His journal looks like the scribbles of a madman. Things crossed out. Angry lines underlining words. Circles and arrows linking possible thoughts. It's taken her months to work out what he was trying to say. The dictaphone tapes don't help either. He sounds as if he's having a psychotic episode.

'I don't trust the police,' she says firmly. 'All they would do is lose it like they suspiciously lost Dani's phone. They treated my dad like a criminal from the very start. The Italian police didn't once reveal he had an alibi or that his DNA wasn't on her belongings by the lake. Instead, they openly disclosed it was suspicious that he had her phone. They let the media and the public tear him to shreds. Journalists hounded him.' Her voice crackles. 'They hoped that by having a "bad English guy" linked to the case, tourists would come back to the region once more since the locals were trustworthy. It was political.'

As well as the many police interviews, he was dragged in front of the board of school governors, and the media wanted a pound of flesh. Journalists huddled in a cloud of cigarette smoke outside their house. Paparazzi snapped pictures of him with his coat over his head as he leapt into his car. They made him look guilty. It was relentless.

'My dad was a proud man who was let down by everyone. He was humiliated, publicly. This was fifteen years ago, remember, the world was different. His reputation, built up over a lifetime, was irreparably tarnished and he could do nothing to stop it.'

They sit in silence. Fenna is the first to speak.

'But you came here, despite all this.'

'I had to.' She accepts the tissue Fenna pulls from the packet tucked in the hood of the pushchair.

Alba presents her with a bunch of colourful weeds, crushed in her sticky palm. Rosie smiles and dabs her eyes.

'I know my dad didn't have anything to do with Dani's disappearance. I just don't know who does.' Rosie sniffs, staring up at the imposing Tuscan farmhouse. 'I wanted to be proven wrong. I wanted to discover the Frasers have nothing to hide, but then Carla went missing.'

44

FENNA – DAY 10

Fenna can't believe what Rosie is saying. 'You think the Frasers have something to do with Carla disappearing, too?'

'I don't know. It's too much of a coincidence for it to happen again, whilst the same family are here on their summer holiday.'

Fenna tries to keep her voice steady. 'Danielle vanished fifteen years ago. No one else has gone missing since then.'

The men in the restaurant who accused the Frasers of being involved in Carla's disappearance leaps to the front of her mind. She pushes the thought away.

Fenna nods at the giant rock on Rosie's finger. The inherited heirloom that she had no qualms accepting. 'Have you been looking for clues or are you too caught up playing the role of Theo's sweetheart?'

'I had no idea he was going to propose. It's as much of a shock to me as it is to you.'

'You still said yes. You've played everyone.'

'I haven't. I promise.' Rosie fidgets with the mosquito repellent band on her wrist.

Fenna clenches her jaw. 'So what *have* you done to find out who this "Fraser" is?'

'It's been harder than I'd imagined.' Rosie gazes at Alba who giggles and chases a white butterfly. 'They've *all* made me suspicious at certain times.'

'The Frasers have been nothing but kind to you,' Fenna mutters. She doesn't know why she's still listening to her.

But something is keeping her here.

'This is a family I never had, especially Marianne. She . . .' Rosie stops talking and clears her throat. Swallowing emotion that's emerged from somewhere.

'What about Marianne?'

She shakes her head. 'Nothing, it doesn't matter. All I wanted to say was how hard it's been to keep this lie going. I've watched and observed. Waiting for someone to slip up. I'm not alone in my doubts. I spoke to Julietta who told me the family are covering up what happened to Dani.'

'Julietta said that? Are you sure?'

A dart of hurt flickers in Fenna's chest. She has known Julietta for years. Trusted her. Why would she say something so explosive? Let alone to the new girl?

'Yes, that's what she said.' Rosie brushes her hair from her face. 'She looked scared.'

'Julietta? Scared? Pfft.'

This is nonsense. She's the toughest woman Fenna knows.

Rosie clears her throat. 'The taxi driver who brought us from the airport also told me to be careful. He said it in Italian and I only understood his message when I heard you say it to Alba by the pool.'

So that was why she'd reacted so strangely. Giovanni's equally ominous command zooms to the front of her mind. She brushes it away and calls Alba to come and top up her suncream. The coconut holiday scent fills her nose as she squeezes a thick blob on her daughter's wriggling arms.

'Danielle's case is fifteen years old. How are you going to discover anything that the police haven't?' she asks, rubbing the cream in. Alba's protests cut over Rosie.

'I know it's a lot to take in but there *must* be something they overlooked, something that someone isn't saying, which will lead us to the truth.'

Us. Fenna could laugh at the absurdity of the situation. She's on a family holiday; she's not here to solve crimes. Especially one that might implicate her in-laws.

'. . . I've looked around the house every day. I nearly got caught once or twice. I'm sure Gerry suspects that I'm up to something,' Rosie continues. 'I was planning on speaking to everyone who was here at the time, but trying to figure out how to bring it up in conversation without making them suspicious has been tough. And then Theo proposed, which made it even harder.'

Fenna drops to sit on an old sleeper tucked in the shade of a fig tree. The wood is rough against her bare legs. Alba brings her a stringy bunch of flowers she's plucked from the ground. Fenna pretends to hold them to her nose and sniff them. Her head is spinning.

If what Rosie is saying is correct, and one of the Fraser family knows what's happened to Danielle Dixon, then Gerry, Marianne or Luke could potentially be complicit.

Rosie is basically accusing Fenna's husband of murder.

Luke was not that much older than Danielle.

And he was here when she vanished.

As if reading her mind, Rosie tentatively perches beside her, hitching up her denim sundress. 'Do you have any doubts about Luke? About what happened that summer?'

'Is this to do with him pulling down that appeal poster? You know that was stupid, childish behaviour. Showing off. It doesn't mean anything. You're getting carried away with this detective role you're playing.' She folds her arms and inches away from her. 'My husband is not involved.'

This is unreal. She's known the Frasers for six years, yet some woman who's been here for five minutes is alleging that one of them is behind the greatest tragedy of this town.

A bird takes flight from a bush nearby, making her jump.

Rosie wrings her hands. 'You know this family better than me. I need you to help me.'

'Then what?' Fenna asks.

'What do you mean?'

'I mean . . . If we prove your dad's innocence and find out what really happened to Danielle, then what? You can't stay in this family. You have to make a choice. This life with Theo or clearing your dad's name.'

Rosie throws a longing glance at the house. The wooden shutters are all open. There is a faint clanging of crockery and Italian music playing on a radio from one of the open kitchen windows. A lizard the size of her palm skitters over the sun-scorched bricks. Julietta has pegged bright white sheets on the washing line that barely move in the still, muggy air.

A lengthy silence follows Fenna's ultimatum.

'If we find out the truth and that the Fraser family are innocent and my dad was wrong, I'll break it off with Theo,' she says resolutely. 'I'll tell him I've got cold feet. He'll never need to know my connection to Dani. I'll leave it to the police to discover what's happened to her.'

Fenna allows herself to breathe. Of course the family are innocent, she doesn't need to hear the alternative. All she has to do is play Miss Marple for a few days and this woman will leave their lives forever.

'So, what's the plan?' She sits taller.

'I don't know. If Carla hadn't gone missing, maybe I would have given up.' Rosie swats a mosquito. 'Don't you find it weird how they reacted to the news? Her name is barely mentioned. No one seems concerned with trying to find her. What are they *not* saying?'

Fenna is growing frustrated. 'They're in shock. It doesn't mean they have something to do with it.'

Rosie stays silent.

'. . . Unless there's something you know that I don't?'

Rosie refuses to meet her eye. 'Maybe you should talk to Luke about Carla?'

'Why?'

'How well does he know her?'

'Luke? He doesn't know her at all.'

'Doesn't he? Maybe ask him about that . . .' Rosie brushes her hair from her face. Her forehead is dotted with beads of sweat.

Fenna gets to her feet. This conversation is over. She's heard enough.

'Wait. Please. Julietta knows more than she would tell me. Perhaps if you spoke to her in Italian she will open up?' Rosie chews her lip. 'And one final thing, do you know where the key to the basement is?'

45

ROSIE – DAY 10

This holiday has been full of glimmers of a life Rosie will never have. The incredible holiday home, the warm welcome, and the taste of luxury . . . Those things don't exist, not for her.

Tears push at the back of her eyes. Saying it all out loud was tough. Rosie is amazed that Fenna sat and listened to her for as long as she did.

She had two jobs – to find out what happened to Dani and to clear her dad's name – but she got in too deep and has genuinely fallen for Theo. She doesn't know if she can keep this charade going. Every moment she's terrified he will find out who she is and why she's really here.

But there's no way she can come clean to him after all this time. He wouldn't trust anything she said again. It's a lose-lose situation. She's in too deep to go back now.

She was certain that Theo suspected something was up when he came back from his walk with Luke earlier. He kept asking her how her morning with Fenna was. His questions seemed innocent, but it was as though he was trying to trip her up to reveal how she *really* spent it. Not that she could tell him. 'Oh, plotting with your sister-in-law to investigate the disappearance of two women that I believe your family is somehow involved with, darling . . .'

Fenna passed her a crumpled note as they were waiting for the nightly aperitivo on the terrace. She took the folded paper with clammy hands and thrust it into her pocket. Her Negroni tasted bitter as she casually tried to join in with the conversation. She wondered if anyone looking into this relaxed pre-dinner drink from the outside could spot the acting.

Rosie managed to sneak to the bathroom, lightheaded with expectation, as the first course was being cleared away.

I found a key. Meet me in the kitchen at 3 am.

***

Theo rolls over and murmurs something incomprehensible as she creeps out of the bedroom. Rosie freezes, her hand gripping the door. A draught blows from the open window down the landing. Goosebumps erupt on her skin. She hasn't slept. She couldn't risk setting a phone alarm and explain to Theo why it went off at three in the morning. She pretended to nod off, laying with her eyes closed, running through the things that may be down there. Why all the extra security? What are they hiding?

She swiftly darts down the corridor, holding her breath until she's downstairs. What if Theo wakes up to find she's missing and comes looking for her? How is she going to explain this?

Fenna waits at the kitchen island. She reaches into the pocket of her floral cotton robe, worn over matching shorts pyjamas, and pulls out an ordinary-looking brass key on a leather key fob with a silver reflective strip down the middle.

'Where did you find the key?' Rosie whispers.

'It was in the drawer beside the coffee machine. I saw Paulo put it in there. Come on, let's get this over with.' Fenna walks towards the basement door. 'Who knows how long we've got.'

She puts the key in the lock and turns it. The door creeps slowly back. Rosie goes first. A sudden breeze wafts Fenna's robe as she follows.

The door shuts behind them.

'Wait,' Rosie screeches as the chink of light is swallowed up.

'I can't get the light to work,' Fenna hisses. 'And I can't see where the door handle is.'

'What?' Rosie turns so fast she almost loses her footing. Her heart thumps in her chest. It is pitch black. She presses herself against the wall and blindly fumbles a hand to find the door handle or the light switch. The rough concrete walls press around her. There is clicking as Fenna flicks the light switch multiple times to prove it's not working.

'Use the torch on your phone,' Fenna says.

'I can't. I left it charging by my bed.' Rosie swallows. Her heart thrums.

Where the hell is the door handle? She worries they are making too much noise.

She was the one who wanted to come down here. She can't have a panic attack, not now.

'Hold on.' There is the sound of fabric rustling before Fenna taps the screen of her phone a few times and a beam of white light illuminates the deep stone steps before them.

The only sound is Rosie's laboured breaths. The light bounces down the gloomy steps as they descend. She tries to calm her racing heart.

The basement isn't as big as she was expecting; it doesn't run the full length of the house. Instead, it looks as if it was previously used as stables. Curved brick archways lead to individual 'rooms', but no doors separate the spaces. One has an industrial-sized washing machine and airers full of linen. Another has brown cardboard boxes neatly stacked. One of the boxes is open to reveal glassware and bubblewrap. They quickly move around the space, huddled together, away from the shadows.

Once they've searched all of the 'rooms', Fenna hugs her arms to her chest. 'We've looked everywhere. There's nothing out of the ordinary.'

Gerry was right. The only things down here are Paulo's tools and the laundry area.

Fenna mutters something unintelligible. She looks deathly pale in the torch light.

Rosie panics she's going to tell Theo that his fiancée has lost her mind, making her go on wild goose chases at three in the morning to look for clues that don't exist.

Rosie was certain there would be something – *anything* – locked away down here that would help her investigation. She dejectedly follows Fenna as they move towards the stone staircase to head back upstairs. Something catches her eye. They didn't see it when they came down, too focused on the space ahead of them. On the right of the stairs is a narrow door with an arched top. She tugs the handle, but it's locked.

Fenna yawns. 'It's probably a broom cupboard. Come on.'

Rosie pulls the door handle again, but it's firmly shut. 'Are there any other keys on the fob?'

Fenna shakes her head.

She remembers the key she found on the bench in the wild garden. Could it fit here?

'What are you do—' Fenna questions as Rosie pulls a key from her pyjama pocket.

'I found this in the garden the other day and . . .' Rosie's breath catches in her throat.

It fits in the lock perfectly. She pulls the door open.

Her knees buckle.

The narrow door is deceiving. It opens to a room much bigger than a broom cupboard. A semi-circular window lets in light. It looks like a space previously used to store meat. Threatening hooks hang from the concrete ceiling. But that's not what's alarmed her. Propped on the floor are A3-sized canvas paintings. One in front of another. Row after row. The subject is the same in all of them: Danielle Dixon.

46

ROSIE – DAY 11

'What . . . the . . . hell?' Fenna gasps.

Rosie blinks at the cache of artwork before them. There must be an oil painting for every year Danielle has disappeared. In some of them, she has aged – an artist's impression of what the young schoolgirl might look like now. In others, she is a smiling fifteen-year-old in front of the lake.

Fenna swings her torchlight across the canvases, it picks up the brush strokes, the way the light falls on the water and the green parakeets that watch over her.

Rosie's skin prickles.

It is the creepiest thing she has ever seen.

Fenna points at a white squiggle on the bottom right-hand corner of each piece of art.

Marianne's distinctive signature.

'Marianne painted these?' Fenna says slowly. 'But Marianne stopped painting.'

'Clearly not . . .' Rosie breathes.

A bolt of energy passes through her. She carefully pries apart each painting, counting. The sound echoes.

Fenna opens her mouth to say something when there is a bang from above their heads. 'Come on, we need to go.'

They lock up the creepy, art-filled cupboard and scan the torchlight over the silent basement once more. Why has Marianne painted fifteen portraits of the missing schoolgirl? Is she an innocent muse or is there more here?

'What's that?' Fenna hisses.

Rosie's gaze follows where she's looking. A small, white, rectangular box has been wedged under the gap at the bottom of the door.

She steps forward and tugs it from its space.

'It's heart medication,' Fenna reads. 'It's . . . Carla's,' she whispers.

Rosie gasps. 'What? Are you sure?'

Fenna passes the misshaped box to Rosie. The label is written in Italian, but she can work out that it's medication prescribed for Carla Conti.

'They could have fallen out of her bag,' Fenna sounds calm, but her wide eyes give away how she really feels.

Rosie shivers. 'No. Someone hid them on purpose.'

'We need to go to the police.'

'No. I . . . The police?' Rosie shakes her head. 'The Italian police ruined my family. No way. I . . . I can't trust them.' She thrusts an arm against the cold brick wall to support herself.

Fenna lowers her voice. 'You can trust Giovanni, he's a good guy.'

'How do you know?'

'I know, ok? He's dedicated to this case. Everyone else has given up on Danielle. He will help, I know it.'

Rosie looks up from the crumpled box of Carla's medication and swallows. What choice does she have?

47

FENNA – DAY 11

Giovanni pulls off his hard-wearing leather utility gloves and drops them on the top of an upturned terracotta pot, pushing his dark wavy fringe out of his face. Fenna takes in his camel workman boots, the mud-splattered, dusty, knee-length cargo shorts, and the tight khaki t-shirt. Her stomach flips.

'Are you sure we can trust him?' Rosie whispers as they near him, clutching a bottle of mineral water.

Fenna ignores her question and waves to Giovanni from the other side of the church allotment plot. She is tired from another night of broken sleep, tired of Rosie's panicked questions, and tired of coming up with a plausible excuse why the two of them needed to nip out leaving the children with Luke for an hour.

Giovanni leans across to kiss Fenna on the cheek. She blinks away the sensation that they are doing something illicit by being here. She feels like she's deceiving her husband entertaining Rosie's accusations, then she remembers the deep stack of original Marianne Fraser paintings locked away in the creepy basement, and shudders.

Marianne clearly has an unhealthy obsession with Danielle Dixon, but surely it doesn't mean anything more – like Rosie is insinuating. But then again, why keep these priceless pieces of art hidden? She was adamant she had stopped painting for good. Her mind swings between rational and irrational theories as to why they exist.

Her mother-in-law might be many things, but Fenna would know if she was capable of being involved in the missing schoolgirl. Wouldn't she?

Rosie is convinced that finding Carla's crumpled box of medication is evidence that a crime has taken place. Fenna, on the other hand, tells herself it's perfectly reasonable to believe Carla simply dropped her box of pills by accident when she was last in the basement helping Julietta with the laundry, and they got kicked to the side and squashed into the gap of the door. There's nothing to suggest foul play. And yet, when she called Giovanni, using the number on the business card he'd given her, telling him they'd found something belonging to Carla at the house, he was keen to meet.

'Giovanni, this is Rosie Riley,' Fenna says, stepping back. 'Theo's fiancée.'

'*Ciao*.' He smiles as he holds a large, dusty hand out to Rosie.

She shakes his hand for a micro-second and mumbles hello.

'Thank you for meeting us on your day off,' Fenna says. She tries to subtly wipe her upper lip, which is beading with sweat. *Get a grip*. 'It's best if Rosie starts . . .'

Fenna knows Rosie's reluctant to share things with the police, but if she's serious about avenging her father's death she needs to try and trust Giovanni.

They move to the shade of the church. Out of sight from any

passing cars. After double-checking the coast is clear, Rosie takes a deep breath and explains everything.

She tells him about why she's really come to Laprezia, about her dad's 'investigation' to discover who 'Fraser?' is. She explains the text, the unusual behaviour of certain family members, Julietta being scared, the taxi driver telling her to be careful, the CCTV, the locked rooms, the paintings of Danielle in the basement, and Carla's hidden heart medication.

'. . . I'm convinced someone in the family is hiding a terrible secret,' Rosie says, tucking a strand of hair behind her ear.

A flutter of panic rises in her chest. She looks at Giovanni for reassurance.

He's not smiling now.

'This is all confidential,' Rosie adds. Her voice is dry and scratchy by the time she finishes.

Giovanni nods. 'I wasn't working on the case at the beginning. I don't know about this "lost" phone.'

'One of your colleagues hid it on purpose. That text, reads to me like a confession. Who knows what else was on her phone,' Rosie says, unscrewing the lid on her bottle of water. 'I'm certain that if we can find Carla it will help us discover what happened to Dani.'

'There's no evidence that the two disappearances are connected,' Fenna chips in.

'Not yet. It could be a huge coincidence, but . . .' Rosie takes a few gulps of her water and turns to Fenna. 'Did you speak to Luke about Carla? Did you ask him how well he knows her?'

'No. I don't need to.' Fenna can't keep her cool much longer. 'My husband has nothing to do with her.'

Giovanni presses his fingers to the bridge of his nose. 'At the moment there's not enough physical evidence of the family being involved with either missing girl. If you want to write a statement explaining everything you've told me, we can at least keep this on record. You'll need to go to the station. It's in Monterchi and—'

Rosie cuts him off. 'We can't go. Don't you understand? It's risky enough us coming to talk to you here.'

Giovanni's lips form a sad smile. 'Trust me, I want to help, you know I do, but you need more.'

He's right. Mysterious texts that may or may not exist, medication in the basement, and creepy paintings are not enough. Fenna wishes she'd not betrayed her in-laws and set this pointless meeting up.

'What happened with the CCTV cameras at the house?' Rosie asks.

'There was nothing of interest there. It's as though Carla simply vanishes.' He sighs. A noisy motorbike splutters past the church garden. 'Do you have anything else?'

Neither of the women say anything.

'Come on, we should go,' Fenna says, checking the time.

'Wait.' Rosie holds up a trembling hand to Fenna. She steps closer to Giovanni. 'There's going to be a party for our engagement tonight. It's the perfect opportunity. Everyone will be out so you can sneak in and look around for hours, as long as you've gone before we come back.'

Fenna splutters. Is she hearing her correctly?

'*Che cazzo*. You want me to break into the Frasers' house?' Giovanni pulls himself tall.

'No, not break in . . .' Rosie backtracks.

Fenna stares at her. The woman has lost the plot. Has she

forgotten she's talking to a police officer? 'We need to make a move,' she says, bringing this absurd conversation to a close. They've wasted enough of his time.

Giovanni rubs the back of his neck. 'I'm sorry. Unless you can find anything we can use to make an arrest, there is nothing I can do to help.'

Rosie looks as if she might say something but stops. She thanks him for his time and walks away, mumbling to herself.

Giovanni reaches out and lightly presses his fingers against Fenna's arm, pulling her out of earshot. He talks to her in Italian. 'You believe what she says?'

'I don't know. She seemed convincing but perhaps I've misjudged her.'

She's embarrassed that she's fallen for Rosie's ridiculous rumours. How could she suggest he breaks in? The woman is clearly clutching at straws.

Fenna holds his gaze. 'The Frasers aren't involved. They can't be, because if they were then . . .' She can't bring herself to finish that sentence. 'No. She's wrong.'

Giovanni's breath brushes her cheek. There is a flicker of something that crosses his tanned face. 'But what if she's right?'

48

ROSIE – DAY 11

Rosie dabs the mascara smudges under her eyes with a damp tissue. She's too nervous to sit in the stuffy bedroom and do her make-up, but she needs to act like everything is ok. She is supposed to be an excited, blushing bride-to-be.

Get it together . . .

She finishes her make-up and gets up to close the shutters in the bedroom, catching sight of the wild garden. Something niggles at the back of her mind. She's risked everything to be here and she is no further on than when she first arrived. Giovanni was uninterested. And, as much as it pains her to admit, he's right. She needs to discover a solid piece of evidence that a crime has taken place. All she's got is a series of suspicions and a gut feeling. Fenna didn't speak to her the whole way home. She's ignored her ever since.

A beeping sound from across the room pulls her attention. She picks up her phone. A flurry of messages and a couple of missed calls are waiting for her. All from her mum. She must have connected to the internet again and picked up Rosie's voice note. Rosie takes a deep breath, scrolling a finger down the screen to read them.

Mum: *Have you lost your mind? Can you call me, please? I'm seriously worried about you now.*
Mum: *Rosie? Please let me know that everything is ok.*
Mum: *Call me back. Please.*

Rosie lets out a slow and steady exhale and turns her phone off. She doesn't have the time to explain it all now. She hurries downstairs. Everyone has congregated in the hallway. The men are in muted smart shirts and chinos, and Marianne looks elegant in a long floaty cream skirt and chic, one-shouldered top the colour of nectarines.

'You look lovely, dear,' Marianne smiles at Rosie.

She tugs at her knee-length, chiffon dress that she's owned for years. Pale yellow with all-important pockets. Luckily, she had packed something elegant in her suitcase. She never imagined that she would be wearing it to her engagement party.

'Thank you. You, too.' Rosie clenches her jaw. It takes all her effort to smile and return the compliment.

Despite what Fenna and Giovanni think, Rosie believes Marianne is up to something. Could she be the one who texted Dani the night she went missing? The many hidden paintings reveal a secret side to Marianne. Who knows what else she's hiding.

Theo steps forward and kisses her softly on the cheek. He has no idea. 'You look amazing. The taxi will be here any minute now.'

'Is everyone ready? Where's Fenna?' She tries to sound natural but her heart gallops in her chest trying to remain calm.

'She's changing the baby. Why?' Theo asks.

'No reason. She said she'd lend me a lipstick. Let me see if I can find her.'

'We don't want to be late for our own party,' Theo calls after her.

She walks as fast as she can in her uncomfortable heels down the tiled corridor. The house is unnervingly quiet. She needs to do one final check, and she knows exactly where to go. She glances over her shoulder to make sure no one is watching. They have gone to wait for her outside. She dashes to the library. She needs to look at the photo albums again. There must be something she's missed.

She examines the floor-to-ceiling shelves, running her clammy finger across the spines. A lot of photography and art books, a couple of romance novels, a selection of Tuscan and Umbrian guidebooks, and the odd Richard Osman.

Where are they?

There is a fireplace on the opposite wall. She wanders over to the large mahogany desk in the corner, tucked in an alcove. More books are stacked on their sides, next to an Italian newspaper and junk leaflets. Her eyes roam around the room before they land on what she's searching for. The photo albums that Marianne left out for her are neatly placed on a shelf. She pulls them out and flicks through the plastic pages past gappy smiles, action shots of the boys leaping into the swimming pool, eating dripping gelato, and enjoying candle-lit meals on the terrace. A normal family holiday. She goes faster, pulling out the other albums to see what she might have missed.

There's nothing out of the ordinary.

'Rosie,' someone shouts her name. 'Taxi's here.'

There is a beep of a horn. It won't be long until they come looking for her.

She sits on a padded pouffe in the centre of the room, needing to think. Her pulse races. Another book catches her eye. She hadn't spotted it before.

The Light Within.

The book that was mentioned on the first night of the holiday about the Soho set that Marianne and Gerry were once part of. Rosie picks up the heavy coffee table hardback from the bottom shelf. The front cover is an arty black-and-white shot of a dimly lit doorway. Two men in a suggestive embrace are pressed against the brick, their silhouettes lit by a streetlamp. She flicks to the page where the book naturally falls, prised open by many hands over the years.

It's a black-and-white shot of Theo's mother lying on a picnic blanket, laid out on the sand, surrounded by sharp bull reeds and spikey shoots of seagrass at odds with her soft, stretched-out form. She is completely naked. The tuft of hair between her legs is a shadow. Marianne has her arms over her head and her eyes shut as if sleeping. No wonder Theo didn't rush to show her this. It must have been mortifying as a teenage boy to imagine your mother naked, let alone see her displayed in an exhibition put together by your stepdad.

Rosie goes to close the book but there is something stuck in the back pages. A Polaroid picture. She pulls it out. Her breath catches in her throat.

The smiling face of Danielle Dixon beams up at her.

'Rosie!' Her name is called yet again. She ignores them, her heart hammering in her chest as she stares at the Polaroid.

Dani is sitting on the ground with her back against a white-washed wall, a trailing pink flower hanging overhead from a trellis. She is doing the peace sign with a lopsided grin. The photo was taken at night. An outdoor light has lit up an ornate window above her head. Inside the circular mahogany frame is a stained-glass pane depicting a sailing boat.

Where was this taken? Rosie's certain she's not seen this distinct backdrop anywhere in the house. Dani is wearing a yellow daisy print top and a denim jacket. The same jacket was found covered in blood by the lake, along with her Polaroid camera. This shot was taken on the night she disappeared.

How the hell has it ended up here? In Marianne's art book?

There is a shadow in the corner of the shot. Rosie holds it closer to her eyes, her hand trembling. It's impossible to make out who it might be. A blur of a body.

There is the sound of approaching footsteps.

'Rosie? Are you ok?' Marianne's concerned voice drifts down the corridor.

She shoves the photo in the pocket of her dress as Marianne walks into the library.

'Is everything ok . . .?' She trails off, her eyes widening. 'What happened?'

'I heard a noise. Something must have fallen and I was trying to tidy everything up.' Rosie quickly attempts to organise the mess around her feet, refusing to meet Marianne's eye.

The hidden racks of paintings in the basement leap to the front of her mind. Danielle Dixon as Marianne's muse. Nausea churns in her stomach. She needs to call Giovanni and tell him what she's found. This is the piece of the puzzle they need.

There is another toot of a horn.

'Leave it. Julietta will tidy it up.' Marianne tugs her arm. 'Come on. They'll kill us if we're late.'

49

FENNA – DAY 11

Luke is busy strapping the children in the hire car. Fenna keeps her eye on Rosie who is awkwardly posing for a photo with Theo under the shade of a fig tree. Gerry has his professional camera in the air, instructing them both to smile. Fenna can see that it's forced. Rosie's eyes dart around the driveway, her body tense. A gnawing sensation spirals in her gut. She tries to ignore the voice at the back of her confused mind, the one that warns her not to trust this woman.

'Daddy will get it in a minute, petal, sit back for me, please.' Luke is growing frustrated with Alba squirming in her car seat. 'Maybe Mummy will get your dolly?'

'Give him a kiss on the cheek.' Another click of Gerry's camera before Marianne tells him he can take more photos when they get there. They don't want to be late.

'Fenna? Can you reach her doll? She's thrown it in the front seat? Fenna?' Luke grumbles.

'Sure, sorry.'

'You ok?' Luke asks as she climbs into the stuffy car a moment later.

'Fine.'

'Is Rosie ok?'

'Hmm?' Fenna says, fumbling with her seatbelt.

'She looks ill. Don't you think?'

'Ill?'

'Yeah.' He frowns, turning the air-conditioning to full max. 'Something's going on. She's acting weird. Maybe she's pregnant . . . That would explain the rushed proposal. Has she not told you anything?'

'Me? No.'

She remembers what she saw on the TV earlier. The local news was on whilst she was changing Raffi's nappy. Carla's worried father sobbed at a press conference, her mother mute with pain, clutching a teddy bear. Eight days without her medication. A dour-faced reporter showed a clip of police searching in undergrowth. There's going to be a vigil tonight in the centre of town. The Frasers mustn't know about this, otherwise they would cancel the engagement party. Wouldn't they?

Luke puts the car into reverse. As the house grows smaller in the distance, a sinking feeling sloshes around the pit of her stomach. The air is charged as if secrets are going to explode.

Alba insists they play her nursery rhymes playlist, Fenna hasn't got the energy to argue. A high-pitched rendition of 'The Wheels On The Bus' fills the car.

She had hoped Luke would compliment her outfit. Her sage-green wrap dress, with a flowing tiered hem and easy nursing access, may not be the sexiest thing she owns but she thought he might pick up on the effort she's made. Instead, he's distracted. Lost in his own thoughts. He gestures in annoyance as a motorbike cuts him up.

A mosquito buzzes around her head. She slams a hand on the dash and kills it.

A few minutes into their journey she clears her throat. Time to bite the bullet. 'Where were you when Danielle Dixon went missing?'

He takes his eyes off the road and gives her a confused look. 'Why?'

'I want to know.'

The playlist moves on to 'Baa Baa Black Sheep' and Alba starts to sing along. Her phone rings with a number she doesn't recognise. She lets it go to voicemail.

'So?' She waits for his reply.

'Why do you want to know?' he asks again.

'Why are you being defensive?'

'I'm not! I can tell you exactly where I was that night. Stuck watching football with Gerry.'

'Gerry hates football.'

'I know, but Mum forced him to spend time with me. Bonding or some bollocks.'

'So you didn't meet up with Danielle?'

He stiffens. 'What? No. Where has this come from?'

'Nowhere. I never asked you before.' Is it her imagination or is the vein in his neck more pronounced?

Alba carries on singing out of tune.

She remembers Giovanni saying Luke was seen talking to Carla at the bar on the night he went for drinks with Theo and Rosie. Rosie's cryptic comments rush back. *'Maybe ask him about Carla . . .'*

'And what about Carla?'

'What about her?'

The synthetic smell of limes from the air freshener dangling down from the rearview mirror doesn't help with the rush of nausea.

'Do you know her?'

'Only as much as you do.' He forcefully changes gear. 'Babe, I don't know where this interrogation has come from, but I don't have any secrets from you.'

Is he sweating? A ripple of panic washes over her. Her phone chimes with a voicemail. The sound pulls her from her spiralling thoughts and she plays the message. She's half listening as she keeps an eye on Luke. He fumbles with the dials so a rush of cold air whirs from the vent.

The polite woman on the other end of the line introduces herself as the voicemail plays.

'It's PC Woods here. I'm investigating your home invasion, case number 0382. We've reviewed the footage from your neighbour's security doorbell and there are some discrepancies . . .'

Fenna frowns.

'That's weird . . . The police want me to call them. Something to do with the burglary,' Fenna says, replaying the message on loudspeaker. 'God knows what that means.'

She hovers her finger over the button to return the call when Luke yells, 'Wait.'

She jumps in her seat and her phone tumbles to the footwell. Raffi bursts into tears at the unexpected noise. Alba carries on singing, hitting the chorus with gusto.

'What the hell, Luke? What's wrong with you?' Her seatbelt digs into her as she turns and leans into the rear of the car to stroke Raffi's head. She gently shushes him. 'It's alright, darling. Daddy was being silly.'

'I'm so sorry, Fenna.' Luke's voice crackles with emotion. 'I've let you down.'

'What do you mean?' she asks turning back slowly.

He grips the steering wheel so tight she can see the whites of his knuckles. 'I took a gamble and it didn't pay off.'

'What sort of a gamble?' Her heart pounds.

His jaw flickers. 'Jonno had a tip-off about this business scheme. All I had to do was invest into this new startup portfolio and I'd double my return.'

'What?' She tries to keep up. 'What does this have to do with the burglary?'

There's a moment of silence filled by the next track on Alba's nursery rhyme playlist.

'The company wasn't legit. They were never going to pay me back. I got into a situation where I had to pay creditors but I was out of pocket myself. I needed to get inventive.' Luke drops his voice. 'But Jonno took it too far.'

'What do you mean?'

The car bumps over a pothole.

'We had a deal, a way to get some money, but I didn't know he would come in whilst we were asleep—'

'Jonno was in our house? You faked a break-in?'

'I told you I was desperate . . .' He trails off. He looks like he's about to cry. 'I thought I could buy myself time with the insurance claim. Tide us over for a bit.'

She presses her lips together and squeezes her hands against the seatbelt, trying to control her breathing. 'Luke . . . That's fraud. What if you got caught?' She can't believe this. His oafish best friend was behind it all?

'I was desperate, Fen. We could have lost the house.' A single tear falls down his flushed cheek.

She mutes the jazzy version of 'Twinkle, Twinkle, Little Star' that's playing. She can't take any more.

'Why didn't you tell me you needed money? We have savings and—'

Alba cries at the interruption to her music. 'Mama!'

Fenna rummages in the glove compartment for her tablet, trapping a finger, wincing at the pain shooting down her nailbed.

'It's all gone. I've used our savings to try and patch up the gaps but that wasn't enough. So, I had to find another way.' Luke wipes his eyes with the heel of his hand.

'Our savings?' She sucks her throbbing finger, desperately fighting everything not to raise her voice in front of the kids. Furious that she's trapped in this confined space with him.

'Gone . . .'

This must be a prank? He can't be serious right now.

'Fenna, I—'

'Rosie was right . . . She told me not to trust you.' Her voice is low. She picks up her phone, her hand trembling.

'What? Wait. Please don't call the police back. I'll fix it,' he begs.

'How? They've said there are discrepancies. They must be onto us.'

'I'll fix it. I promise,' he vows.

How has he kept this to himself? She presses her fingers to her temples and tries not to unleash the fury coursing through her. Her eyes dart to the children in the back of the car.

Thankfully, Alba is glued to her tablet, she isn't paying any attention to this catastrophic confession.

'Your family is loaded . . .' Fenna forces a juddering breath through her lips. 'If you were so desperate for money why didn't you ask them?'

'They won't help. I asked Mum for a loan but she told me to use Dad's trust fund. I couldn't tell her it was gone, that we spent most of that on the renovation work. I asked Theo. We didn't meet to talk about me being his best man, I needed to get him alone to persuade him to help us. But he refused. I literally begged him for a loan, and he turned me down.' His tone changes. Gone is the sadness, replaced with a flare of anger. 'All I've done for him, and this is how he treats me.'

'I can't believe this,' she mutters, fanning her face. 'Why did he say no?'

'He thinks I'm irresponsible.' He clicks his teeth. 'I know it's a lot to take in but listen, I've got a new plan. I'm going to speak to Richard at the party tonight.'

Richard's luxury yacht springs to mind. He's got plenty of money. She allows herself a moment to exhale.

'And if he doesn't help?'

He takes a breath. 'The company will fold.'

She spins so fast that her neck twinges. 'How are we going to pay the mortgage? The bills? My work won't cover everything.'

'I don't know.'

She stares out of the window, unable to look at him for a second longer. Anger fizzes through her veins. She fantasised about how they could move to Italy with the proceeds of their house sale. They would live in the space and peace of *Villa*

Speranza and enjoy the simple pleasures, buffered by their nest egg. Her dream has been shattered.

All their money has gone.

Her idiotic husband has lost them their savings and is at risk of a police investigation. She clenches her fists. She could literally kill him.

50

ROSIE – DAY 11

The taxi journey is hell. Rosie's heart beats against the glossy Polaroid tucked in her dress pocket. Until she's spoken to Fenna about what the hell they are going to do, she needs to act like everything is fine.

'Don't be nervous.' Theo squeezes her hand tightly.

He has no idea what his mum is hiding. Whenever she looks at Marianne she pictures her hunched over those canvases, paintbrush in hand, trying to capture Dani's youth. Of course the famous artist never stopped painting. She just found a muse she couldn't admit to publicly. It's clear that Marianne will do anything for her family – did Dani fall victim to that?

Rosie forces herself to smile.

'Hang on . . .' Theo frowns. 'I thought we were going to *Luigi's*? That's on the other side of the lake.'

'Surprise!' Marianne grins. 'Evelyn and I have planned a little something at theirs instead. It's easier for Fenna if Alba has got space to run around instead of being constrained in a highchair in a busy restaurant. You're going to love their place, Rosie.'

'*Per favore prendi la prossima a sinistra*,' Gerry says to the driver, elongating every word.

The indicators click-click-click.

'The caterers should be there. We've not had enough *frutti di mare* this holiday, so I've gone for a selection of squid and calamari and steamed crab and . . .' Marianne continues to list seafood items on her fingers.

Rosie's stomach turns.

Who knows if she's got a terrible illness? Is that a lie, too? A way to get Rosie to feel sorry for her?

The taxi slows. Two black metal gates automatically open, leading to a wide driveway full of expensive-looking cars. Richard and Evelyn's house is a similar enormous size to the Frasers' farmhouse, but strikingly modern. Tall sheets of polished glass sit against rendered bricks and double-height windows, all lit with uplighters that cast ominous shadows.

'Wait until you see their garden. The terrace is so high it's like you're in the trees.' Marianne winks, opening her door and letting in the sound of a lively jazz band.

Gerry settles up the fare, jangling his change in his pocket. 'You can't see it from here but the lake is through the trees, at the far end of their garden. Sorry, grounds.'

Marianne takes Rosie by the arm and whisks her away. She has to fight every urge to shake off her grip. She is led up a flight of stairs to the gigantic terrace. A crowd of around fifty or sixty people are chatting and drinking without a care in the world. They must be Richard and Evelyn's friends.

The whole place twinkles with fairy lights and flaming torches. A banner saying 'Theo and Rosie' with a big love heart hangs between wooden pergola beams. A quartet of musicians plays soulful Italian love songs. The sun is setting. A band of hazy orange dips around the line of trees. A sudden rush of tears prick the back of her eyes. It's perfect. She swallows the unwanted emotion that this is all for her and Theo. From the expensive ring on her finger to the smiling friends congratulating, welcoming her, it's all she's ever wanted . . . yet none of it is real.

Where have all these people come from? Clearly Richard is connected around here. Evelyn flits about the terrace air kissing her guests. Theo was right. This party is an excuse to show off.

'Richard, you're spoiling us,' Gerry laughs, slapping his friend on the back.

'Evelyn organised it all.' Richard dabs a napkin against the sheen on his bald head. The evening air is still heavy with the day's heat. It needs a thunderstorm to bring some relief.

Rosie cranes her neck to spot Fenna in the crowd but she can't see her.

Keep acting like everything is fine.

She finds her voice. 'It's very kind of you, thank you.'

'Like I said, this was not up to me,' Richard replies curtly then walks off.

'Ignore him, he's probably working out how much this is going to cost him.' Gerry gives her a friendly nudge.

'Maybe,' Rosie replies, shaking her head as a tray of intricately decorated canapés is offered to her. A waft of fish turns her stomach.

She catches Marianne on the other side of the terrace, smiling for a photo with a woman in a chic, colourful headband, she drags Richard into the selfie. He doesn't smile. There is something different about him tonight. Marianne throws her head back and laughs at a joke the woman said. Not a care in the world. She tries to raise a smile on Richard's lips.

Rosie itches to get the snapshot out and look at the unusual stained-glass window in the background of the Polaroid. She definitely hasn't seen one anywhere at *Villa Speranza*. Where was it taken?

Luke is standing at a make shift bar further away, with his back to them. He tips a shot glass of clear liquid into his mouth and pours another. Fenna is still nowhere to be seen. Rosie doesn't know how much longer she can act like everything is ok. Her heart clenches. What will Theo say when it all comes out? How will she begin to explain what was happening when he was away playing football?

'I'm sorry I've not brought my drone here.' Gerry's voice cuts into her thoughts. 'I could have taken some cracking shots. The skyline is something else.' He glances over the canopy of trees. 'There were reports of a resurgence in the numbers of moths to the area . . .'

Rosie takes a mouthful of her drink. The wine is bitter and she struggles to swallow it. She needs to extract herself from this tedious conversation and properly examine the photograph. Could that be Marianne's shadow in the corner of the image? Rosie surreptitiously pats her pocket as Gerry is talking.

A bolt of unease hits her.

It's empty.

She asks Gerry to hold her drink whilst she checks her other pocket.

'Everything ok, Rosie?' he asks, breathing smoked salmon breath on her.

Her stomach lurches. The photo's gone. Where the hell is it?

It was definitely in her pocket when she left the house. Did she leave it in the taxi? Has it dropped out somewhere? She darts her eyes across the floor.

'Have you lost something?' Gerry asks.

She mumbles a response. 'I think I left something in the taxi.' A pounding thrum grows at the back of her head.

'Do you want me to call the taxi company? They're coming back at midnight to take us home . . .' He pulls out his phone and scrolls through his contacts. 'What is it you've lost?'

'A speech I wrote for tonight,' she thinks quickly.

He talks to someone at the taxi firm in slow, stilted Italian. She wrings her hands together with every second it takes.

'Nothing's been handed in,' Gerry says as he hangs up.

That means someone here must have picked it up. Suddenly an arm tugs her to the side.

'What haven't you told me?' Theo's voice whispers in her ear.

It's as if she's been electrocuted.

'You didn't tell me how hot you look in yellow.' He winks, pressing himself against her. His aftershave settles on her skin.

'Oh, this. Thanks.' She flattens her dress under his appreciative gaze. Can he feel her heart pounding?

There's a tinkle of metal against glass.

'Speech.' Someone cries from the crowd. The music is turned down and Rosie is handed a flute of bubbles.

Pairs of eyes stare at her expectantly.

'And you lost your speech.' Gerry shakes his head at the unfortunate timing.

'You wrote a speech?' Theo asks.

She mumbles about being prepared, willing the heat to subside from her cheeks. Richard and Evelyn step closer. Phones are raised in the air, ready to record the moment. Luke hovers at the back of the haphazard semi-circle of partygoers, necking another shot of liquid. She can't see Fenna amongst the crowd.

Theo clears his throat. 'I'd like to say a few words on behalf of me and my fiancée . . .' The guests whoop.

Rosie is getting sweatier by the minute. She needs to find that photograph. She presses her glass against her wrist to try and cool down, praying this will be over soon.

'From the moment I met Rosie, I knew that she was the one. She's kind, caring and honest—'

'When are you going to share this secret you've been keeping?' Luke cries from across the terrace. There's a stain on his shirt. It looks like red wine.

Rosie's heart leaps into her throat. What has Fenna told him? She lets out a nervous laugh and tries to remember to breathe. Is this the moment it all comes crashing down?

Theo stiffens beside her. 'What is he talking about?'

'I have no idea. He's drunk,' she whispers.

'What, mate?' Theo calls back. 'Did you want to say something?'

Luke waves an arm at them. He's unsteady on his feet. 'Get to the point. Announce you're having a baby or whatever—'

'Is this true?' Marianne gasps. Tears fill her eyes. 'That is wonderful news.'

Evelyn squeals with joy and orders the hired photographer to capture the moment.

'What? No. That's not true.' Rosie blusters, blinded by a bright flash.

Hushed whispers break out in the crowd.

Luke frowns. He sways to the side slightly. 'Sorry, everyone. My bad. Something's going on though . . .'

Theo groans. 'You can't be happy for me, can you?'

'Me? What about you? Don't play the caring brother card now. You've never been there for me.' Luke lurches forward and knocks into a table.

'What? Because I wouldn't loan you money? It's not my fault you spent all of Dad's trust.' Theo scoffs.

'That was private, you little shit,' Luke growls.

'What? Luke? Is this true?' Marianne stutters.

Luke stays silent, but he continues to eyeball his little brother as if he wants to punch him.

'Answer your mother, Luke,' Gerry demands.

'Or what?' Luke says, squaring up to his stepdad.

'Stop it.' Marianne screams. 'There are bigger things to worry about than money. Life is too precious to waste arguing. You need to start looking out for one another. I'm sick of this squabbling. I'm not going to be here to play referee forever, you know.'

Rosie's never heard her raise her voice like this before. Her face has flushed puce-like in colour. A vein at her temple throbs as she yells.

Luke makes a pfft sound. 'He started it.'

'Grow up,' Theo snaps.

'Stop. Please stop.' Marianne shouts. 'You're ruining my last ever holiday.'

'Alright, no need to be dramatic.' Luke rolls his eyes. 'You don't know that it's your *last* holiday'

Marianne cries. 'Yes, I do!'

51

ROSIE – DAY 11

'I've got cancer. It's terminal.' Marianne sobs. 'I'm sorry, this is not how I wanted to tell you.'

'What?' Theo spins to face her. 'Mum?'

Both the boys wear the same expression of disbelief. Conversations cease and the music halts. All Rosie can hear is the pounding of her heart and the strangled cries of Marianne.

Luke necks the rest of his drink in one. 'But you look fine.'

'I'm on a lot of medication. I had treatment for a while, but it's not shrunk the tumour and there's little more they can do. This is my last holiday.' Marianne's voice breaks. She looks as if she's diminished in size. 'This trip was the chance to do something different. For all of us to get along. No arguments, no disagreements, just a wonderful time with my precious boys – and their girls of course. The grandchildren are growing up so fast and, well,' her voice crackles, 'I want to savour each moment.'

No one moves.

'Surely they can do something? Go private?' Luke questions.

'I've seen every specialist under the sun. It's been hard, really hard. You know I hate hospitals—' She stops suddenly and pulls a tissue from the deep pockets of her flowy skirt.

'Darling, I think you should sit down,' Gerry says, coming to stand beside her. 'The doctor's told you to try and avoid excess stress.'

'Wait. He knows but you didn't tell us?' Luke directs his anger towards his stepdad.

'I made him promise not to say a thing.' Marianne's red-ringed eyes meet Rosie's gaze. 'I didn't want to ruin this trip but so much has gone on and . . .'

Theo turns to Rosie, slowly working out why she's staying so quiet, filling in the blanks. 'You knew?'

'Your mum told me a few days ago . . .' She trails off.

'How could you not tell me?' He looks at her, distraught. 'Luke was right about you keeping secrets.'

'Wait. Please.' Rosie tries to stop him but he moves too quickly, heading for the other side of the terrace, to the stone staircase, and down the long stretch of manicured lawn away from the guests and the pitying looks of sympathy.

'Theo,' she calls after him. 'Theo. Wait!'

A thick arm holds her back from chasing after him.

'*You* knew our mum was dying? How the fuck did *you* know but not *us*?' Luke steps in her path. A blast of booze hits her nostrils. His eyes are glazed with drink. He casts a domineering shadow over her.

'I . . . I . . .' Rosie stutters. Her cheeks flame under his angry gaze.

'Fenna was right about you. You've charmed your way into this family but none of us know who the hell you are. Everything was perfect before you came along. What have you been saying to my wife? Telling her not to trust me. I don't know what your game is. Stirring the pot? Was this your plan? Turn us all against each other?'

Rosie can't catch her breath. His face is scrunched in fury. Her eyes roam the party guests trying to find Fenna in the crowd. Where is she? She could surely talk sense into Luke. Everyone is staring.

'Luke. Stop. I made her promise not to say a thing,' Marianne says firmly, placing a hand on her eldest son's arm.

Luke steps away from Rosie, muttering to himself.

She races to find Theo.

52

ROSIE – DAY 11

The grounds of Richard and Evelyn's property feel never-ending. Rosie eventually manages to catch up with Theo at the edge of the lake. She can barely hear the sound of the party from down here. He's not moving an inch, staring at the dark water lapping the shingle. The moon casts him in an ominous shadow. It's much more eerie at night compared to when they were sailing in the day. The yacht was moored on the other side, near those abandoned beach huts. She remembers seeing the dense woodland from a distance but couldn't pick out the small, concealed paths that led to the super-rich properties.

'Are you ok?' she asks, tentatively placing a hand on his back. His shirt is damp with sweat.

'Do you think I'm ok? After that?' He pulls away.

'This is a huge shock for all of you.'

His puffy eyes glisten with tears. 'But not for you, apparently,' he says bitterly.

'I'm so sorry I didn't tell you about your mum's illness. I . . .' She swallows. She needs to come clean and tell him about all the lies. This is the tip of the iceberg but where is she supposed to start?

She takes a breath but he gets there first. 'Let's go for a walk. I need to clear my head.'

He strides ahead without waiting for her answer. What should she do? She doesn't have time for this.

'Are you coming?' He spins, arms outstretched, confused as to why she's not following him.

She needs to find the Polaroid and tell Fenna about Marianne hiding the evidence in her art book. But Theo needs her more right now. She jogs to catch up with him. Their footsteps fall in line with one another as they follow a gravel path that takes them deeper into Richard and Evelyn's garden. It winds through the trees, the moonlight fading the further they go.

'I can't believe it.' His voice is low and subdued. 'After all our summers spent here, this might be her last holiday . . .'

'You can't think like that,' she says, rubbing his arm. This time he doesn't pull back.

'When did Mum tell you?'

'A few days ago. She made me promise not to say anything.'

'Mum can be persuasive when she wants to be.' He clears his throat. 'Sorry for losing my cool, it's a shock. I thought I'd be able to tell if you were keeping something from me.' He doesn't catch how she flinches at that. 'Come on. I need a drink.'

She expects him to turn the other way, retrace their steps and return to the party, but he heads further into the woodland that skirts the edge of the lake. She can hear the lapping of the water but can't see it.

'Where are we going?' she asks, chewing her lip.

'I need five minutes alone from everyone.'

It's too dark to see much further. He pulls out his phone and turns on the torch. It illuminates a narrow path towards a hidden stone-clad cottage. Murky shadows from the tall, spiky bushes loom over them. There is a snap of twigs. A cry from a gull overhead. She presses herself closer to him.

'Luke and I used to come to Richard and Evelyn's lake house when we were teenagers. They didn't care that we smoked weed or drank when Mum told us we couldn't. I ended up crashing here most nights. If I'm right, it's also where they still store their best bottles of wine.'

Clearly he is on a mission to get drunk, and she can't blame him. She wishes it wasn't tonight. She is so close to uncovering this family's secrets. But being down here, away from everyone, unable to keep an eye on Marianne, is killing her.

'Ok, but let's not be gone too long . . .' She hopes her tone sounds as neutral as she's trying to make it.

'Did you see how many guests they had? No one will even notice we're missing.'

He lifts up a lumpy rock to reveal a silver key hiding underneath. 'Aha. Let's hope it still fits . . .'

He pushes open the front door. A groaning sound from the rusty hinges travels through her. Theo doesn't seem fazed by the creepy noise. Stuffy, trapped air catches at the back of her throat. Stale. No windows have been open in a while.

He reaches forward into the dark space and flicks a light switch. Nothing happens.

Theo mutters, 'They must have turned the electricity off.'

'Let's head back and get a drink at the party. Your mum will be worried about you, and no doubt she'll want to speak to you.'

'What's the rush? Hang on, I think I remember where the fuse box is.' He kicks his shoes off and leaves them by the door before stepping inside, using the torch on his phone to guide his way.

Reluctantly, she does the same. She kicks her heels to the side and pulls her phone out the second she is alone. She turns it back on, expecting to have more worried messages from her mum but there's no signal. Theo rummages in the room next door. Before she can tap her torch app, the overhead light pings on and she can see the room more clearly. It's bigger than it looks from the outside. She's standing in an open-plan lounge.

There's a two-seater tan leather sofa pushed against one wall and a sleek flatscreen television on the other, a nest of walnut brown tables at the side and an Aztec print rug under her bare feet. A compact kitchen sits at the back, separated behind a tall breakfast bar.

'Has that worked?' he calls from behind a closed door, off a compact square corridor.

'Yes.'

'Great. I'm going to use the bathroom. Try and find where they've hidden the wine,' he shouts.

Cream-coloured expensive pans in different sizes hang from the wall over a fancy oven. She moves past an enormous coffee machine and sleek silver fridge. The sooner he has a drink, the sooner they can rejoin the party. She spins her engagement ring around and around, trying to stay calm. She understands he's upset, but she needs to go back to the house and retrace her steps to find the Polaroid. And keep an eye on Marianne.

A toilet flushes.

She spins her ring too much and it pings off. There is the ting of metal as it hits the floor. She swears. *Where did it go?* She can't see it anywhere.

'I found their stash. Any luck on the wine glasses?' Theo says, plodding into the room, holding a bottle of red wine. 'Perhaps the signs were there all along. On the yacht Evelyn let slip that Mum mentioned she was writing a memoir. I have no idea who she expects to read it, but I guess you get delusional when you're dying, and you write everything down in order to start trying to make sense of things?'

He puts the bottle on the counter and pulls out a corkscrew. He's too focused on getting himself a drink to notice Rosie frantically checking the kitchen floor.

'Mmm.' She casts her eyes to the marble tiles. *Where is it?*

'I thought things were finally coming together and now this.' He struggles to get the cork out, cursing as it fights against him.

'Can I help? You're in shock,' she offers.

Theo shakes his head. His eyes are watery and his cheeks are flushed. 'I can do it.'

There is a moment of silence. *Where has her ring gone?*

'You do want to marry me, don't you?' he asks.

Oh God. Her stomach flips. Locating her ring will have to wait. She leans across and takes his clammy hand.

'Of course. Why are you saying that?'

'Just checking . . .' The cork finally comes out with a cheerful pop. 'I love you, you know. I'm so lucky to have you, especially now. I can't bear the thought of losing Mum and losing you, too.' His voice cracks. He clears his throat, concentrating on pouring the wine into two crystal glasses. He picks the fullest one to gulp.

Is this a reaction to his mum's terrible news, or is there

something else going on? Why is he talking about losing her? She watches him pour himself more wine; it almost reaches the rim of his glass. His hands tremble.

'I know you're in shock but getting wasted isn't going to help. What about your training? The marathon,' she says, as gently as she can.

'There is no marathon.' He refuses to meet her eye. 'I lied.'

Her heart thrums. 'What? But every day you've gone out running . . .'

The room is too hot. The dusty, stale air starts to choke her.

He finishes his glass and says nothing.

'Theo? If you haven't been training, what have you been doing?' Her voice wobbles with uncertainty.

She thinks of the pattern of his 'daily runs', the scratches on his body. The running route where he went back to look for his lost AirPods. A rush of nausea ripples across her.

He presses the heel of his hands to his tear-stained eyes. 'You don't want to know.'

53

ROSIE – DAY 11

'What do you mean? What have you been doing?' Rosie demands.

Theo's phone rings from the kitchen counter. The sound goes through her. The screen lights up as it buzzes across the surface. Richard's name appears. Theo doesn't make any move to pick it up.

'Forget it. It doesn't matter,' he says.

'But—'

It rings again. Why isn't he silencing it? He gulps his wine and mutters something but doesn't answer the call. She's never seen him like this. It scares her.

'People will be wondering where we are, Theo.' She can hear the panic in her voice. 'What's going on?'

'I've gone running, that's true. But it's not in preparation for a marathon.' He takes a deep, shaky breath. 'I've run every day to try to find the missing schoolgirl. It's ridiculous. I didn't want to tell you as you'd think I was crazy. I do it whenever I come here, I try to search for her. It's stupid but I feel that I owe it to her.' He stops abruptly.

'What do you mean you "owe it to her"?'

He doesn't say a word.

'Theo?' She steps to the side. There's a prism of cornflower blue light illuminated by the porch light that's reflected on the wall.

A sickening sensation swirls at the base of her stomach. The light has picked up the different shades of blue and what looks like a tiny boat. The stained-glass window. The Polaroid. Dani laughing with her back against a white stone wall, head tilted upwards, pink flowers dangling over her like a crown.

She can't breathe. It's like someone is wrapping their hands around her throat. *No. This can't be right.* There's a clicking noise coming from somewhere. It takes her a second to realise it's the sound of her bracelets as she wrings her clammy hands.

Dani was here.

The reason she's found no trace of her at *Villa Speranza* is because she was never in the Frasers' house. She was here. The Fraser boys' summer hideout. She's been searching the wrong place all along. Suddenly everything shifts.

Theo steps in front of her. She hadn't realised before now how broad his shoulders are, how imposing he can be.

'When were you going to tell me why you're really here?' he asks. His voice low.

It's as if the air is sucked from the room.

'Has Fenna said something to you?' she croaks.

He frowns. 'Fenna? No, Fenna hasn't told me anything. It was Richard. He worked out where he knew you from. On their yacht, Evelyn insisted she had met you before. She was right. Richard showed me the photos from Mum's event, the one at the gallery, that he'd taken on his phone, and there you are. You're in the background . . .'

Rosie's breath gets trapped in her lungs. That's why Richard was being off with her when she arrived tonight.

'. . . It had to be a mistake. You weren't at Mum's event. You had the whole Tinder date disaster and we met after. But you lied, didn't you? I told myself there must be a reason you never admitted to being at her party, but other things haven't added up.'

'Theo, look. I—'

He speaks over her. 'Like, why did you take such an interest in my mum's holiday home? All those questions you were asking Gerry when we first arrived. The eagerness to go through old photo albums. I should have realised you had an ulterior motive.'

Saliva rushes to Rosie's mouth.

'Are you going to tell me who you really are?' Theo pushes.

Tears fill her eyes. She forces herself to act calm despite her racing heart. 'Let's go back to the house and I'll explain . . .'

His phone rings again.

'Theo—'

He slowly pulls something from his trouser pocket and places it on the counter next to the empty bottle of wine. A piece of glossy paper.

The Polaroid.

She glances up at him. The incessant ringing stops. There's a moment of eerie silence.

'Why did you have this on you tonight?' His voice wavers.

'I found it in your mum's things. Theo, she knows what happened to Danielle.' She stops suddenly as something he said earlier zooms to the front of her mind. 'What did you mean when you said you *owed it to her* to search for her?' she croaks.

'Forget about that. Who the hell are you?' His voice rises.

'You know who I am. The only thing I haven't told you is that my dad was the school teacher on the foreign exchange trip. The one that people believe killed Dani. I know he didn't.' She takes a shaky breath. 'But I think your mum did.'

Your dad?! What? . . . Wait.

'No. She didn't.' The emotion vanishes from his voice.

In an instant her adoring fiancé is replaced with a stranger.

'You weren't here, you don't know . . .' She swallows and picks up the Polaroid. 'This was taken on the night Dani disappeared.'

There's a pause.

'I know. I took the photo.'

A shiver tears through her as if an icy hand has gripped the back of her neck. 'Please, Theo. You're scaring me . . .' Her heartbeat quickens.

His phone buzzes again. He snatches it and thrusts it in his pocket. She can still hear the muffled vibrating.

The texts on Dani's phone. *You made me do it. You gave me no choice. Sorry—*

'You need to tell me what you know, Theo.' Her heart hammers in her chest. 'Did *you* kill Danielle Dixon?' Her voice is barely more than a whisper.

His eyes widen. 'No. She was alive when I last saw her.'

She grips onto the breakfast bar and remembers to breathe. 'You told me you were away . . . The football camp in Croatia.'

'I lied.'

'What? But the certificate . . .'

'Forged. I needed it to look like I was still there when she went missing. No one could know I'd come back early.' He runs his hands through his hair. It sticks out in wild clumps. 'I got kicked out for smoking weed so I decided to surprise Mum and come here. I happened to meet Danielle at the bus stop when I arrived. I thought she was cute, we got chatting, and we arranged to meet here later that night.'

Rosie's head spins. She pictures her dad's notes, the contact in Dani's phone: '*Fraser?*'. Theo Fraser . . . Frantic thoughts zip over one another. How has she got this so wrong?

'We came and hung out on the deck.' He nods to the patio doors leading from the kitchen. 'The night wasn't meant to end like it did. I wasn't expecting her to turn up with class A drugs. She told me she'd done coke loads of times before. I was trying to show off so I acted like I had too. I lied.'

'You took drugs? Here?'

'It soon became clear that it wasn't coke, or if it was it had been cut with something else. Poison. She started spinning out, not making any sense. Her eyes were fucking massive. Her nose started to bleed. It wouldn't stop. Like, it kept gushing out. I've never seen anything like it.'

The blood-stained denim jacket.

'What happened to her?'

'I don't know. She ran off. Honestly, so much of the night is a blur. I woke up alone in the bedroom the next morning.' He nods his head to the square corridor with the closed doors. 'I had the mother of all comedowns and convinced myself that it was some horrible, drug-fuelled trip. The next thing I hear she's missing. The nightmare was real.'

She doesn't know whether to believe him. He looks distraught but he's managed to keep this a secret for fifteen years, a voice reminds her. It feels too neat that he happened to 'forget' facts because he was on drugs.

'I thought she'd turn up, that she was sleeping it off somewhere. But the days went on. When I heard about her teacher and the rumours that he had something to do with it I convinced myself that was true. But deep down I've always doubted that narrative.' He wipes his face. 'I've waited years for someone to realise I was the last person to see her alive. You have to believe me that I did nothing wrong. I was young, I was stupid.'

Rosie's mouth has gone dry. 'What about her things?'

The Polaroid camera and her jacket.

'I have no idea. I was too spaced out to notice what she'd brought with her. There was definitely nothing of hers here when I woke up the next morning. In fact, it looked as if there had been no party at all. I must have cleaned up before I passed out, worried that someone might find the empty drug bags.'

'You can't have been that spaced out! You were sober enough to text her. "*You made me do it. You gave me no choice. Sorry—*" '

'H-h-how do you know that?'

'My dad confiscated her phone. He made a note of the message as he thought it was suspicious. Thank God he did as the police lost her phone once he handed it over. How did you get them to "lose" the evidence?'

'What? I didn't . . .' He blinks. 'I don't know what you're saying.' His eyes fly to the closed door down the corridor. 'Did you hear that?'

'Hear what?' She can't hear anything other than the blood rushing in her ears.

'Nothing.' He picks up the Polaroid. Fingers trembling.

'Danielle asked me to take this. I'd forgotten all about it until I saw you drop it tonight. Where did you find it?'

'It was in your mum's things.'

'Mum?' he says, slowly as if coming to a realisation. His eyes widen. 'Mum had this? No. That's not right . . .'

'Don't pretend you two aren't in on this together.'

She stumbles backwards. Her gut orders her to leave. He's not telling her the whole truth, she's sure of it. Him and his mum know what happened to Dani.

'I swear.' Tears streak down his pale cheeks. 'Mum has no idea I was here. No one does.'

'Clearly that's not the case.' She shivers at the memory of the creepy paintings in the basement. Dani was her secret muse.

She can't work out what he's saying. It's like he's arguing with himself. 'Impossible . . . who cleaned the blood . . .'

Blood.

He pulls open a drawer and with a shaking hand takes out a long, slender lighter. His breathing speeds up. 'I never knew how it all went away . . .'

'No! You can't burn it.' Rosie yells.

Flames lick the glossy paper in seconds. He steps to the sink and throws the rest in, leaving a trail of black smoke as it chars away to nothing. She needs to get out of here. If he's willing to burn evidence and protect his mum, what other lengths will he go to, to keep their secret? Why did he really bring her down here?

She turns and her legs hit a bookcase. The contents wobble and a photo frame drops to the floor. Something skitters to her bare feet. It's a white box.

'Please, Rosie, sit down . . . We need to talk. You've lied to me and I've lied to you. Come on, we can fix this. Start again . . .'

His words are drowned out by the roar of panic in her skull. She bends down. It's another box of Carla's medication. Rosie gasps. Theo went for a run that morning and came back with bloodied knees and mud on his shorts, panting and out of breath. Those scratches she saw on his back. His torn t-shirt. He told her he fell into a spiky bush, that he wasn't concentrating and tumbled. That was the day Carla disappeared.

'Where's Carla?' she asks, her voice wavering.

'What? Why are you looking at me like that?'

'You know where Carla is . . .'

'No I don't. Can you stop a second? I need time to think!'

There's a sound from behind one of the closed doors. A thump-thump-thump.

He suddenly turns to pull open a kitchen drawer, revealing a row of knives; the sharp silver edges glint under the spotlights. This is her chance. She throws her glass of wine over his back and prepares to escape.

54

FENNA – DAY 11

Fenna glances across the serene lake. Raffi didn't need a feed but she used him as an excuse to sit somewhere quiet. She leans her aching back against the wooden bench near the water's edge. The night air smells of pine and the last of the day's heat. There is the faint sound of helicopters in the distance. Perhaps searching for Carla? Clearly the Frasers didn't care to cancel tonight's celebrations as a sign of respect to Carla's family.

She went into the party to get herself a drink and slipped out before anyone noticed, but in that brief moment she was taken aback by the number of guests. Faces she's not seen before. Names she won't remember. Such a lot of effort for a sham engagement party. She doesn't want to be here, surrounded by people she doesn't know, to celebrate this bullshit union.

Marriage is a mistake.

Luke's confession plays on repeat in her head. He's spent all their savings without telling her and thought it was a clever idea to stage a home break-in. What the hell is wrong with him?

A faint commotion comes from the house. Whatever drama is going on over there, she doesn't want to be part of it.

A gull swoops near the surface of the dark water. She inhales Raffi's newborn smell. The sweet biscuit scent instantly calms her. She nestles him against her and kisses his velvety soft cheeks. Luke has no idea of the pain he's put her through. The nightmares she's endured because of that burglary have plagued her. She's tortured herself with the many 'what if's' from that night.

What is she going to do? The police haven't called her again. She replays the voicemail, trying to decipher the police officer's tone. It sounds friendly. Perhaps it's a courtesy call? Maybe they don't have any suspicions? Whatever the reason, this is Luke's mess. He needs to fix it.

She tries to focus on being in the moment, reminding herself of the hypnobirthing breathing techniques she learnt when she was pregnant. But she's never been any good at meditating. Her mind is always too full. She gently places Raffi back in his pushchair, silently doing the clasps so he's nice and snug. Earlier, a blur of colour caught her eye.

Theo tore down the garden, heading towards the lake. Rosie followed him not long after. She was too fast and too far away to call her name. Neither of them saw her.

Has she told him the truth about who she is?

He must have broken off the engagement. *Good.* Fenna glances at the time on her phone, it's gone ten o'clock. Hopefully they can all go home soon. A faint beat of music starts from the house. Voices fill the air once more. Whatever drama happened at the party has been forgotten.

Where have Rosie and Theo gone? It looked like they headed into the woodland. Richard and Evelyn own so much land it's easy to get lost. Wherever they are, they've not reappeared. God knows what Marianne will say about her golden boy and his precious Rosie breaking up.

She heaves herself to her feet and unlocks the brakes on Raffi's pushchair, deciding to follow the shingle path that edges this part of the lake whilst he's asleep. She's relieved not to be making small talk with anyone. Luke will no doubt be getting wasted on Richard's hospitality. She prays that he's convinced him to financially bail them out.

But what if Richard says no?

Her phone trills to life. Her husband's name flashes up. She rejects the call, too angry to speak to him. Right now, she could kill him.

She stomps down a path flanked by sharp, spiky, thorn bushes. Too distracted by her furious thoughts, to focus on where she's going.

Darkness suddenly wraps around her.

Luke told her that he'd acted out of desperation and that he would do anything to protect his family. She remembers what Marianne said at the gallery about the lengths you go to for the ones you love. How dare her mother-in-law and Theo not help them when they need it? Families should look out for one another. If they were in the position to offer a financial handout to a relative, they would in an instant. So why wouldn't Theo lend his brother the money? Luke had told him how desperate he was.

Further ahead, is a small stone cottage, hidden behind spindly trees and unkempt foliage. A solitary porch light casts an ominous glow on the water's edge. Is this where Rosie and Theo went when they raced past earlier?

Fenna steps closer. What is this place? It looks like a

groundskeeper's lodge, a little lake house, or perhaps a bolthole for Richard's fishing trips. Judging by the thick layer of dust on the windows and the neglected planters on either side of the weather-damaged front door, it's not been used in a while.

A rush of balmy evening air rustles the branches of the trees. Is someone watching her? There is a crunch of a twig and she spins, her heart leaping to her throat before seeing a tiny brown bird in the undergrowth. *It's your mind playing tricks on you.*

Fenna knocks on the front door. She needs to talk to Theo and see if she can persuade him to help them. She needs to clean up her husband's mess for the sake of her family.

No one answers. She tries the rusting metal door handle. It opens with a sinister creak. The sound shoots under her skin.

'Rosie? Theo?'

She holds her breath to see if she can hear anyone talking but the only sound is crickets in the long grass and the faint hum of music from the party back at the main house. She spots Rosie's heels kicked off beside the front door. She won't have gone anywhere without them on.

'Hello?' she calls into the silence.

There's no answer. She walks inside, keeping an eye on Raffi sleeping in his pushchair with every step she takes away from him. A full-length window in the lounge reveals her reflection, making her jump. She can smell coffee, red wine, and something else. Something unpleasant and metallic.

'Theo? Are you here? I need to talk to you,' she calls. She glances around the tidy lounge. What is that smell? She walks towards the kitchen at the back of the room. 'It's out of order that . . . Oh God.'

She sees a foot on the floor, poking out from behind the tall breakfast bar. As she gets closer she is confronted with a scene from a nightmare.

Cream-coloured Le Creuset pans are splattered with an arc of blood that climbs the kitchen walls. Glittering shards of glass and coffee granules are scattered on the floor tiles.

Fenna shoots a trembling hand out to steady herself against the kitchen counter and clenches her eyes shut praying this is a nightmare. A bubble of bile rises from the base of her stomach.

A body is lying face down. There's a deep, purposeful crack in their skull. No one can survive an oozing, gaping wound that big.

She throws her head back and screams.

55

ROSIE – DAY 11

Long grass painfully whips Rosie's legs as she sprints away from the lake house, clueless as to where she's going. Sharp, brittle rocks slice the soles of her bare feet. Her lungs are on fire. Every muscle protests at this sudden burst of energy.

She's taken a wrong turn somewhere. She finds herself deep in the woods. A bird calls from high in the dense trees. She tries to listen out for footsteps over the roar of blood in her ears. She's sweating so much she might pass out.

How long has she been running? A minute? Five? She dropped her phone so has no idea what time it is. She knows she can't stop.

Eventually, she sees signs of life. A streetlamp, a paved road. She is certain she can hear the hum of an engine. A blur of headlights blind her. She must have made it to the main road. Where the hell is the house? She's completely lost her bearings.

'Stop. Please!' she yells.

The blue estate car slows down. For once, she's not concerned for her own personal safety. All she can concentrate on is getting to the police station and telling them what's happened.

'Wait. I know you,' she gasps.

It's the same taxi driver who picked her and Theo up from the airport.

'*Stai attento!* Be careful. You told me that. Remember?' she wheezes, glancing back the way she came.

The terrified driver says something in Italian.

She catches sight of her reflection in the rearview mirror. Her hair is wild, her eyes blazing. Black tears of mascara drip down her flushed cheeks. He won't remember her as the woman he dropped off at *Villa Speranza* eleven days ago. She looks like a completely different person. She *is* a completely different person.

Her heart hammers in her chest. She needs him to help her. She presses her hands together in prayer.

'Please, help me. I mean, *grazie*. I need to go to the police.'

'*Polizia*?' His wide eyes move across her, landing at her bare, bloodied feet, now caked in mud and dirt. He swears loudly in Italian.

'Yes. *Sí! Polizia*!'

He nods for her to get in.

Relief washes over her as she drops into the back seat. He taps at the map app on his phone and crunches the gear stick and accelerates. She takes one look back at the forbidding forest as he drives away. Only then does she allow herself to breathe.

56

ROSIE – DAY 11

'*Stazione di Polizia*,' the driver says, nodding his shaved head at a set of imposing metal gates. A rectangle of mud-brown concrete and a limp Italian flag welcomes them. It's the first time he's spoken since picking her up.

For most of the journey he struggled to keep his eyes on the road. They kept flitting to her in the rear view mirror. She was hyperventilating the entire time. What the hell was Theo planning to do to her? He turned into a stranger before her terrified eyes. The flash of knives will haunt her for a long time.

The driver leads her to the doors of the building. Adrenaline courses through her. She can't feel the pain in her bare feet. He talks in Italian with the officer behind the desk. Kept separate by a piece of scuffed plastic. The stark room smells of floor polish and lies. A broken blind hangs on a wide window and a strip light flickers over a table full of dog-eared magazines.

She was so wrong about Theo. How could she have been so stupid? She can't catch her breath. The moment he casually burnt the Polaroid plays over in her terrified mind.

'*Signorina*?' The officer calls her to come forward.

The door slams and she realises the taxi driver has left. She didn't get to say thank you or apologise for not paying him. What did he say to the man behind the desk? Are they sending someone to the lake house? Is that what the taxi driver instructed?

The officer talks to her in rapid Italian.

'I don't understand. Do you speak English?' Tears fall down her flushed cheeks. 'You need to speak to my fiancé. Theo Fraser. He knows where Carla Conti is.' Her breath judders. 'Find his mum, too; Marianne Fraser. Together they're hiding what happened to Danielle Dixon!'

The officer frowns and replies in Italian. She clenches her fists in frustration that he can't understand the severity of what she's telling him.

'Carla Conti. Danielle Dixon,' she says, slower, elongating the syllables.

His stern frown softens as those names appear to ring a bell, but he still doesn't rush and call for back-up like she needs him to. How is she going to get him to understand?

'Help me, please.' Rosie wipes her cheeks. 'I need to talk to the police officer, Giovanni . . . I don't know his surname. He knows me. He knows the Fraser family.'

'Giovanni?' the officer repeats. He points to a framed team photograph on the wall behind him, tapping Giovanni's headshot.

'That's him. Giovanni!'

Her spirits lift. He leans across and picks up a phone, still going too slow for Rosie's liking. After a brief conversation with someone on the other end, he gestures for her to take a seat and wait.

She prays Giovanni is on his way. She slumps onto a cold,

plastic chair, her legs unable to hold her upright any longer. How has the night ended like this? Her dress is torn and her arms have painful scratches criss-crossing her sunburnt skin.

She closes her eyes and replays everything Theo told her. Something gnaws at her. It was the shocked expression on his face when she told him where she'd found the Polaroid. He insisted his mum had nothing to do with Dani's disappearance but how else to explain that photo turning up in Marianne's art book? He said he had no idea where she went or where her body might be, but how can she believe him? He'd made sure there was no evidence that he was here that summer. You don't do that if you're innocent.

Her legs jig impatiently. She's not sure how long she's sat there for; the clock on the wall isn't working. No one is in a rush to help her. Her stomach growls with hunger and she wants a glass of water, but everyone looks too busy to interrupt. The phones have been ringing non-stop since she arrived. The sound of sirens filters through every time the door opens.

An officer leads in two men in handcuffs. One of them she recognises from the restaurant the other night. He has a nasty cut running across his left eye, and blood trickles down his scowling face. Although she can't undertand, she takes a wild guess that it's vulgar obscenities flowing from his split lip. She turns away and tries to make herself invisible, praying for news soon.

Finally, Giovanni rushes in. Tears fill her eyes at seeing someone she recognises. Fenna told her she can trust him. He speaks to the man behind the desk and turns to her, doing a double take at her appearance.

'Giovanni, Theo—' she starts.

He speaks over her. 'Rosie? It's a busy night.' She's never seen him so harassed. His face is drawn of colour and deep bags ring his bloodshot eyes. 'There was a vigil for Carla that turned nasty. A lot of people were there for a fight.'

His gaze flicks to the man with the bleeding head who is yelling and kicking the metal leg of the chair beside him, two other officers dart over to deal with him.

'Giovanni, I need to talk to you,' she pleads over the commotion.

His name is called from the front desk. A piece of paper is handed to him. She can't get his full attention.

He looks up from the note in his hand. 'Theo? Theo Fraser?' He frowns.

Rosie leaps up. 'Yes. That's why I'm here. I tried to tell your colleague but he doesn't speak English—'

A wailing siren drowns her out. The injured man yells in pain as he's pinned to the ground. The pounding in her head increases. A phone rings. She can't think straight. The officer behind the desk passes Giovanni the receiver, and shouts at the man who quickly shuts up. Her heart thrums.

The waiting room is suddenly quiet and Rosie's not sure what is worse – the rowdy noise or the silence. Her grubby, bloodied feet tap the lino, waiting for Giovanni to get off the phone and speak to her.

Come on, come on.

Eventually, Giovanni hangs up. He races through the door without giving her a backward glance.

***

The hours tick by and still no one has come to see her. Giovanni hasn't returned. There is a steady stream of men with injuries from the vigil. The other officers refuse to speak to her when she asks for an update, instead she is given a plastic cup of room-temperature tap water, and shooed away. She wants to scream for attention.

She glances out of the window at the sudden commotion. Police cars zoom into the parking area. A car door slams and Fenna steps out. Rosie blinks. *Fenna? What is she doing here?* Her stomach lurches at how pale and fragile she looks, guided by a police officer who assists her up the steps. There's blood on her pretty green wrap dress.

Fenna's eyes meet Rosie's through the window. She looks terrified.

Two police officers appear. 'Rosie Riley, you need to come with me.'

'W-What's happening?' she stutters.

She is led into a small room down a dingy corridor. Her heart thuds wildly. She prays one of them will tell her what's going on but they both remain silent.

There is a beat-up black plastic chair behind a small graffiti-covered desk. She drops to the seat and swallows the bile at the back of her throat.

The police officer's gun is aimed at her chest. Her eyes dart between the weapon and the deep frown sliced in his brow.

She can't breathe.

The interrogation room is too hot. Too cramped. Filled with fear. Her legs shake as adrenaline zips across every tense muscle.

Another officer fires rapid Italian words in her direction. She squeezes her clammy hands. Again and again. Needing to feel something real to prove this is happening. The movement brings a faint waft of the coconut aftersun she rubbed over her skin before she got dressed, reminding her how differently this day had started.

The holiday was never supposed to end like this.

Her eyes fall to the blood stains on her dress. The many rips in the delicate silk material. Once the colour of early-morning sunshine, now smeared with mud and splatters of deep crimson. If she tried to explain the past twenty-four hours, would they believe her? Where would she begin?

The officer's unarmed colleague steps closer. He looms over her. His eyes are dark and expressionless. She needs to tell them what she knows, but her words escape her. Shock steals her sentences.

He clears his throat and begins again in English. 'You are under arrest . . .'

A rush of nausea leaps in her stomach. She shakes her head, blinking rapidly.

'Under arrest? For what?'

Her heart pounds with every second it takes for him to answer. When he speaks again, the world stops turning.

'Murder.'

57

FENNA – DAY 11

Fenna perches on the edge of an uncomfortable leather sofa. It's the only item of furniture in the small room. She's never been in a police station before. She can't stop shaking. Everything happened so quickly after she raised the alarm. It's as if she is out of her body. Floating above the chaos and confusion.

She spotted Rosie through the window, waiting in the reception area, when she arrived. But how is that possible?

A female officer sits opposite and explains they need to take some details. A box of tissues is handed to her; she didn't realise she'd started crying again. The past hour or so replays on a loop in her mind. Fenna takes a shaky breath and explains how she went looking for Theo in the lake house and found him on the kitchen floor.

Murdered.

The nightmare she's experienced comes in fragments as she tries to recount it. There was so much blood. She clenches her eyes shut to wash away the image of the inside of her brother-in-law's skull.

She doesn't remember staggering outside but she must have

done. She fell on a bench, Raffi's pushchair beside her, waiting for the nausea to pass. She's not sure how long she sat there before someone called her name, followed by the jingle of change in Gerry's pocket that clanged with every bouncy step he took.

'Fenna? Have you seen Theo and Rosie? Marianne is desperate to talk with him.'

Hearing Theo's name made her throw up into a bush. She quickly wiped her face with one of Raffi's muslins.

Gerry's eyes widened. 'Fenna? Are you ok? I hope it wasn't the seafood canapés. Wait . . . what's happened?' He stared at the blood on her hands. 'Are you hurt?'

Whilst waiting for her to answer, Marianne appeared.

'Why is there blood all over your arms, Fenna?' Marianne gasped, looking at Gerry for answers.

Fenna managed to point at the cottage. The front door left wide open. 'I took his pulse. I had to check if he was alive.'

Moments later, her mother-in-law let out an animalistic roar. The sound will haunt her forever. Marianne collapsed at the sight of her son murdered in the kitchen.

The police arrived and Theo was taken away in an unmarked ambulance, a white sheet covering his bloodied body. Marianne was being given oxygen in another. Gerry went with his wife to the nearest hospital. The lake house was quickly sealed off as a crime scene. Fenna, as a key witness, was brought to the police station. Luke will go home with the children, once the police have spoken to him and all the guests.

'*Respirare.*' The officer hands her another tissue once she's recounted everything. *Breathe.*

Fenna wipes her eyes, catching sight of the dried blood that's transferred onto her trembling hand. They've taken samples as evidence. This isn't some exhausted, out-of-body experience she is having, a sort of psychosis brought on by lack of sleep. The door to the sweltering interview room opens and Giovanni appears. Gone is his usual relaxed demeanour.

'Any news?' Fenna asks, leaping to her feet at the sombre look on his handsome face.

'I've heard from the hospital. I'm afraid Marianne Fraser is not in a great way. They think she's had a heart attack. She has been rushed into surgery, I've asked that we're kept updated on her condition but it's not sounding great.'

Fenna's stomach swoops. This is all too much to take in. Theo is dead. Marianne could die from the shock.

'We need to get to the bottom of what's happened tonight.'

'I told your colleagues all I know,' Fenna explains. 'I saw Theo run down the garden, and Rosie followed him soon after. I didn't see where they went. It must have been around twenty minutes later when I made my way to the lake house. I was hoping to talk to Theo about something.'

She was furious that Theo could ignore his big brother's pleas for help. It all feels pointless now, getting fired up about him not lending them money.

'Rosie's shoes were by the door but I didn't see her. Then I found his body . . .' She swallows.

The officers at the scene spoke animatedly about something they'd found in one of the bedrooms, but quickly stopped talking when they realised Fenna understood Italian. There was no sign of Rosie at the lake house.

'Have you arrested her?' she asks. 'Is that why she's here?'

'I can't tell you that,' Giovanni says apologetically.

'Is there anything that's happened on your holiday that we need to know about?' the female officer asks. 'Anything that might give us a clue as to why your brother-in-law was killed?'

Fenna picks up the room-temperature glass of water. Her hand is still trembling. 'Rosie told me a few days ago that her father was the school teacher in charge of the trip when Danielle Dixon went missing. Her dad thought one of the Frasers knew what happened. She came here to try to hunt for clues that her dad's theory was right.'

Giovanni stays silent. He's heard all of this before.

'So Rosie discovered Theo was involved and killed him?' the female officer suggests, flicking her gaze at Giovanni. He gives nothing away.

Fenna wraps her arms around herself. Has Rosie played them all? Was her intention all along to commit murder?

'Theo wasn't in Laprezia that summer.' Fenna blinks. 'None of this makes sense.'

'She has means, a motive, and an opportunity,' the female officer says, putting her pen down on the table. Case closed. 'There is one suspect in my mind. His fiancée looks guilty as hell.'

'Could someone else have gone into the lake house and killed Theo?' Giovanni asks Fenna, ignoring his colleague. 'There were plenty of people at the party.'

She remembers the feeling of being watched. Was someone else lurking nearby? Someone capable of murder?

'It's possible . . .' Her voice is barely more than a painful croak. 'But who would want Theo dead?'

58

ROSIE – DAY 11

'Did you kill *Signore* Theo Fraser?' The heavily accented police officer's voice sounds robotic.

The room tilts. Rosie blinks, waiting for his words to make sense.

'Theo? Theo is dead?'

No, no, no. They must be wrong. Theo can't be dead.

'Don't lie to us.'

She starts to hyperventilate. Her stomach twists in painful knots. She grips the table, desperate to anchor herself, and tries to regain control of her breathing.

'Why did you kill him?' The police officer's hot breath brushes her cheek. He's purposefully too close, a tactic designed to cause stress and intimidate. It's working.

Where's Giovanni? Why isn't he here to help her?

The stark strip lighting makes the police officer appear ghoulish. The walls and ceiling are painted pistachio green, and scuff marks and dents in the plaster suggest they've seen many a raised fist or desperate lashing out.

'I'm innocent,' she sobs.

They don't seem to understand her. Or, if they do, no one is taking any notice of her pleas. What's 'innocent' in Italian?

Her hands itch to find her phone, to rummage in the pockets of her dress. The same dress Theo complimented a few hours ago. But she knows there's nothing there. Her phone is still at the lake house, dropped as she fled.

'Mr Fraser. You killed Mr Fraser,' he repeats.

'You've got the wrong person. I haven't killed anyone.'

The officer starts shouting in brittle Italian at her.

'I don't know what you're saying. I don't understand you.' Her voice is hoarse.

He slams a fist on the table. His other hand flies past to the wall behind her head, narrowly skimming her left ear. The explosion makes her leap out of her skin. His dark features are menacing and his thick brow is knotted in rage. She quickly looks away.

Now she knows where all those dents in the plaster have come from. Fear courses through her. She wants to scream in frustration but knows she needs to keep her cool, to try and remain in control, as once she's lost it she won't get it back.

'Please. I need a translator. Where is Giovanni?'

The room is stifling. She can smell her own sweat and fear. A tiny rectangular window, almost touching the ceiling, is the only ventilation. It lets in a warm breath of night time air. There's a piece of paper on the table. A biro is handed to her. She takes it before she realises what they want her to do. The paper looks like an official document filled with printed Italian words. What tricks are they playing here?

'I'm not signing anything. I need to speak to Giovanni.'

No translators will be there until the morning. Well, that's what she thinks they say, based on their gesturing and the broken English they use.

Rosie is moved to another room and forced to change into a pile of grey cotton. A top and trousers, two sizes too big, no belt. Her bloodied sunshine-coloured dress is put into a plastic evidence bag. Every movement is monitored by two female officers. They talk to one another in Italian. Neither smile. Rosie's breath hasn't returned to normal. Her chest vibrates with every sob. No one offers her a tissue.

She's led to a cell and told to wait. The deafening clunk of the lock in the metal door pierces through her. She's never felt so alone. What would her dad say to her right now? Her eyes fall on the metal bars over the narrow window. Shells of dead woodlice are curled in balls on the windowsill. She places her head in her hands and sobs.

***

She doesn't know how long she's left alone. The light through the high window has changed. It's gone from navy ink to a smear of bruised purple. Dawn is breaking. The start of a new day. Giovanni knocks on Rosie's cell door.

'Is Theo really dead?' she gasps when she sees him.

Giovanni rubs his unshaven cheeks. 'I'm afraid so.'

The room tilts. This can't be real.

She tugs at her hair. 'I don't know what's happening. They think that I killed him. I promise you he was alive when I left.' Her frantic words tumble over one another.

She's turned their accusation over and over. Someone must have gone into the lake house after she ran out and killed Theo. But who? And why?

'You have to listen to me, please, Giovanni. I didn't kill him!

I couldn't, I wouldn't.' She chokes on a sob that erupts in her throat.

This must be how her dad felt. Accused of a crime he didn't commit. She's being stitched up like her dad was. She refuses to let history repeat itself. There must be a way to prove her innocence. She needs Giovanni to listen to her. He's her only hope.

'We're trying to get you a solicitor.' He hands her a limp, plastic-wrapped ham ciabatta but her stomach lurches at the sight of it. 'Try to eat something.'

She blinks, not taking the unappealing sandwich.

'Please can you tell me what's going on?' she begs.

He glances uncertainly down the corridor. 'I shouldn't be telling you this, but it looks like an argument that got out of hand. They're clamping down on domestic incidents—'

'I didn't hurt him. I ran away after he confessed to being with Dani on the night she disappeared. He and Marianne know what happened to her.'

Giovanni stiffens. 'What did you say?'

She scrunches up her eyes. She needs to remember every word. 'He told me that he randomly met Dani by a bus stop. He was the "Fraser" who texted her. The contact in her phone, that I told you about. Remember? They hung out at the lake house and took drugs, and she had a bad reaction and ran off . . .'

Giovanni nods. Fingers pressed to his chin. He's giving nothing away.

'Theo swore he never saw her again, but he lied about everything else. His mum had a Polaroid photo of Dani tucked into her art book. She was there that night too!'

'*Signora* Fraser?'

'Yes, but—'

Giovanni flicks his eyes down the corridor and leans a little closer. 'You should wait for your solicitor. He will be here soon and a formal interview will take place.'

'Please, Giovanni.' She clenches her hands in prayer. 'You've got the wrong person.'

He walks away and doesn't look back.

59

ROSIE – DAY 12

The door to the interview room flies open and a harassed-looking middle-aged man tumbles in, followed by Giovanni. The stranger, who comes to Giovanni's shoulders and smells of heavy cologne, says something in Italian to the scowling police officer who hasn't taken his eyes off Rosie.

The officer dips his head as if he's been told off.

'Hello, hi, I'm Lucian Silvestri, your solicitor,' he introduces himself to Rosie in perfect English and flashes a crooked smile. He has round, wire glasses that magnify the wrinkles around his brown eyes. He has the look of a man who has been woken from a deep sleep. There's a white tide of toothpaste on his left cheek.

He makes sure she's ok before he begins, nodding to the officer to explain what evidence they have against Rosie. Her stomach is tied in knots. The police officer launches into fast Italian as Giovanni silently observes.

Her solicitor translates, 'Theo Fraser died because of blunt force trauma to the back of his head. The injury is specific and unusual. They believe you hit him with this portafilter.'

She is shown a coloured printout of a kitchen item. The

murder weapon is the deep and heavy silver arm of a coffee machine, one used to filter ground coffee. Made of solid steel.

This is how Theo died? She swallows the burn of bile in her throat.

'They think I hit him with this?' She gasps. 'No. No, I wouldn't. I couldn't . . .' Black splodges creep in at the corner of her eyes. *Stay focused.*

'You have no alibi and an eyewitness saw you headed towards the lake house after him. You have a motive,' Giovanni says in English.

She blinks. She thought he was on her side. As if reading her mind, he breaks eye contact.

'What motive?' she yells, slamming her hands on the table.

Immediately she wishes she hadn't. She can't come across as unpredictable. Quick-tempered. Of course, she's angry; in the past few hours her loving fiancé admitted to being involved in the disappearance that ruined her father's life. Now that same man is dead. But she can't let them see her emotion.

'We know that Jonathan Mills is your father. You came to Laprezia for revenge,' Lucian translates what the police officer is saying.

'Revenge? What? No. I came to find out the truth. My fiancé, Theo Fraser, knows what happened to Danielle Dixon. He confessed to me in the lake house.'

'And then you killed him,' Lucian says matter-of-factly, with an alarming level of calm in his voice, translating the police officer's exact words.

She's trapped in a nightmare. Before she can deny this accusation another photo printout is shown to her. It's her engagement ring, covered in blood.

'This was discovered at the scene, along with your mobile phone, your shoes, and two glasses of red wine. One smashed near the body,' Lucian explains.

'I took my ring off and it rolled away. I threw my glass at him because he was scaring me.' Rosie gasps for breath. 'I found a box of medicine that belongs to Carla.' She stares at Giovanni. 'How the hell would that end up there? He's been going on these daily runs . . . He knows where she is.' She's talking about him in the present tense. It's not lost on her. 'Knew,' she corrects herself.

Lucian leans over. 'I advise you to stay calm.'

She shuts her eyes and tries to get her breathing under control.

Giovanni asks her to recount what happened last night.

'There was a party to celebrate our engagement. Marianne Fraser, Theo's mum, broke some terrible news to the family about her health. Theo was upset. He went for a walk to clear his head, and I followed him to see if he was ok.' She sucks in air, still in disbelief at how everything uncurled from that moment on. 'When we got to the lake house I realised Danielle Dixon had been there on the night she vanished. There was a photograph that proved it. I found it at the Frasers' house, in Marianne's belongings.'

She waits as Lucian translates for the other officer's benefit. He makes scribbled notes.

'And where is this photo now?' Giovanni asks.

Her stomach swoops at the memory. 'Theo burnt it in front of me.' She realises how convenient this sounds. 'I'm not lying.'

The officer purses his lips and says something to Giovanni.

'They want you to talk about drugs found in the bedroom . . . And the signs of a struggle,' Lucian says.

'A struggle? What? We never went into the bedroom.'

The officers speak to one another in Italian. She watches their expressions to see if she can glean what they're talking about. They are giving nothing away.

'What are they saying?' she asks her solicitor.

Lucian takes his glasses off and wearily rubs his eyes. 'It doesn't look good for you, Rosie,' he says. 'We have eyewitnesses who place you there. We have your shoes and phone recovered from the scene, and your engagement ring covered in Mr Fraser's blood.'

'I didn't kill Theo.' She racks her exhausted brain. Who at the party has a reason to murder her fiancé?

'Every guest has an alibi.'

'Then one of them is lying.'

A shiver tears through her. Someone at the party knows the truth and it might cost her her freedom. What if she's being stitched up? Like her dad was? *Is someone framing me?*

'They're going to keep you here for another night,' Lucian explains.

'No.' She goes dizzy at the thought.

'It's standard procedure in a murder investigation. They've got ninety-six hours to discover and present enough evidence to a judge that you committed the crime.'

That word again: *murder.*

Her breath catches in her chest. They can keep her here for *four* days?

'Is there anyone you want to call?' he asks, filling her shocked silence.

Her mum is thousands of miles away and almost always uncontactable. And even if she could reach her, how will she begin to explain the situation she's in? She shakes her head.

'I didn't kill Theo.' She rubs her eyes roughly, stemming the tears that threaten to arrive. 'I loved him.'

Theo can't be dead. He can't be.

'My client needs a moment,' Lucian says.

The police officers grudgingly push their chairs back and file out of the room. Giovanni throws her a confused glance but says nothing.

She is grateful for a moment of peace. The adrenaline that has been coursing through her wears off. She could lay her head on this grubby tabletop and sleep for a week.

Once they are alone, Lucian turns to face her.

'Miss Riley,' he says, pulling her back from the edge of exhaustion, 'if you didn't kill him, who did?'

She chokes on a sob. 'I honestly don't know.'

60

FENNA – DAY 12

The first thing Fenna did when she got back from the police station was check on the children, thankfully Julietta had got them both to sleep. She watched their peaceful bodies, the rise and fall of their tiny chests, unaware of the tragic events that have happened around them tonight. She doesn't know if she'll ever be able to sleep soundly again.

Her brain won't switch off. The police said they weren't looking at anyone else in connection with Theo's murder. Rosie is their prime suspect. But things don't make sense. Rosie had plenty of opportunity to hurt Theo, so why attack him last night? And why would she willingly go to the police station immediately after?

She keeps churning things over and over as she takes a much-needed hot shower, but none of it makes sense. Once the smell of sweat, blood, and grime has disappeared, she changes into clean, comfortable pyjamas and wraps herself in Luke's oversized hoodie. Cold and numb with shock. She can't be alone with her thoughts any longer so she heads to the terrace to find her husband.

He's sitting on the outdoor sofas with Richard and Evelyn. Their matching pale faces and wide eyes hint at how terrible they must feel. Their lake house has been cordoned off as a crime scene so they've come to the villa to wait for news about Marianne from Gerry, who is still at the hospital. No one is mentioning the possibility that she might not come home.

Dawn is breaking. A new day. A new world without Theo. It's unimaginable that they will return to England without him. Her head pounds with exhaustion. Her chest is tight from crying. She tries to follow their morbid conversation. They're talking about sorting out paperwork and speaking with the British consulate, trying to understand the practical procedures they need to undertake following a death abroad. Clearly, needing to keep busy, as if able to outrun the reality of this tragedy.

They have time. The police asked them all to stay in the country for now. They believe Theo was struck with the heavy silver arm of the lake house coffee machine. He had been drinking so it would have been easier to surprise him from behind. He wouldn't have seen it coming. Rosie attacked him and fled. He didn't stand a chance.

'I can't believe it,' Luke says, over and over again, holding out his glass for Richard to top up with whisky. A half-empty crystal decanter sits on the coffee table, which is littered with scrunched-up tissues.

Fenna perches beside her husband, stroking his arm. Their argument in the car is insignificant now. Who cares about money when something like this can happen? He and Theo might not have been best friends, but they were brothers.

Evelyn drapes a soft woollen blanket over Fenna's knees. She hadn't realised she was shaking so much. 'Fenna, you poor thing. I can't imagine what you saw. How are you holding up?'

'Not great.' Her voice cracks.

'If only we hadn't had the party,' Evelyn cries.

'I don't understand why they were down there.' Richard fumbles with a packet of cigarettes. Fenna's never seen him smoke before. All the rules are out the window. It's no surprise. The poor man sees the Fraser boys as his surrogate sons. He must be distraught that something so horrific happened on his property.

'We never use the lake house.' Evelyn wrings her hands. 'We used to let it out for holiday guests but there was a leak in the roof so it's sat empty for weeks. We were waiting for someone to come look at it, but it fell to the bottom of the list.'

'They must have found a spare key. I don't remember one being there.' Richard coughs.

'You can't blame yourselves,' Fenna says.

'She's right. The only person to blame is that bitch, Rosie,' Luke slurs.

'I knew she looked familiar. I should have trusted my gut that she was lying about something.' Evelyn dabs her eyes. 'Richard spotted her in the background of one of his photos. She was at your mum's event in Soho in March.'

'I showed Theo at the party.' Richard clicks his lighter and takes a shaky drag. As soon as he puts one out, he lights another. The smell turns Fenna's stomach. 'That was the last conversation we had.'

Guilt courses through her. What if she had raised the alarm earlier? What if she'd told someone who Rosie was and why she was here in Laprezia? The woman was intent on avenging her dad's death. But why kill Theo? What did Rosie discover that Fenna doesn't know?

'I said she was acting strange tonight, didn't I, Fen?' Luke adds.

Fenna nods, not daring to say a word. Uncertainty claws at her gut. Whenever Rosie spoke about the Fraser family her feelings for Theo seemed genuine. What would cause her to kill him? Something happened in the lake house that changed everything.

'She seemed so nice, so normal,' Evelyn cries.

'Appearances can be deceiving.' Richard stubs out his cigarette. He gets to his feet and tells them he's going to the bathroom.

'At least they've caught her and she's in custody now,' Evelyn says, pouring herself a drink. 'She won't be able to hurt anyone else.'

***

Fenna goes inside to check on the children. She can't take the conversation much longer. A sound coming from further down the corridor catches her attention. She frowns.

The door to the library is ajar. Richard is in there, rummaging through the papers on Marianne's desk.

'What are you doing?' she asks.

He jumps. 'Jesus, Fenna. You scared the life out of me. I was trying to find my reading glasses. I was sure I had them a moment ago. I thought I'd retrace my steps.'

Fenna frowns. 'They're in your shirt pocket.'

'Of course.' He slaps his forehead and fumbles for his glasses, hastily putting them on. 'We're all losing our minds.'

A flash of headlights swoop through the window.

'Ah, that was quick. I ordered a taxi for Evelyn and I. It's best we get out of your hair for a while,' he says. 'Right, I'd better go and get her. Would you mind telling the driver we'll be two minutes?' Richard rushes out of the room, leaving behind the scent of cigarettes.

Fenna scans the messy desk. A drawer is open. Papers have spilled onto the floor. Her gut clenches. It's as if he was looking for something. A firm knock on the front door pulls her from her confusion. She's tired and it's been one hell of a long day. She needs to stop searching for things that don't exist.

Fenna plods down the corridor, stifling a yawn that comes all the way up from her toes. She opens the door to Giovanni and another police officer.

'Oh.' She steps back in surprise.

'*Ciao*.' Giovanni takes off his police cap. 'I'm afraid we need to search the house—'

'What's happening? Have you charged her yet?' Luke barrels towards the police officer, almost careering into the wall. He must have seen the police car come down the driveway.

Fenna tucks herself to the side, subconsciously fixing her hair and shifting in her hoodie, despising herself immediately for doing so.

'*Signore*, all I can currently tell you about the investigation is that it's moving at a fast pace,' Giovanni says firmly, drawing himself up taller.

'My brother is dead. We have a right to know, surely?' Luke raises his arms in frustration. Fenna gets a waft of his unwashed skin.

She places a soothing hand on her husband's back. 'Darling, let the police do what they need to do. They'll tell us what they can when they're able to.'

The movement calms him and he grudgingly nods, muttering something to himself.

'Julietta,' Fenna calls.

There is the sound of pattering footsteps before the older

woman steps into the entry hall. Julietta blinks when she sees Giovanni. He explains that they need to search Rosie's things for evidence.

Luke tells Giovanni to follow him to the safe to find her passport.

It's not long before another police car arrives and more officers stream out. Julietta swears and makes the sign of the cross over her chest, muttering to herself.

'W-w-what's happening? I heard a car and thought it was our taxi, ' Evelyn asks, coming to Fenna's side. She wraps a trembling arm around her waist. The unexpected touch makes her jump.

'They're looking for clues that she planned to kill Theo,' Fenna explains, shivering at the sight of so many police officers.

Evelyn stands frozen to the spot, open-mouthed.

Fenna turns to Julietta. Her expression is one of disbelief. 'We need to get the children out of here. I don't want them to wake and see this. Can you help me pack a bag, please?'

The two women hurry upstairs. Fenna rushes to Theo and Rosie's bedroom. She needs to find the notebook to show Giovanni. It's unnerving to be back in this room. It smells of Rosie's perfume, and there's a faint trace of Theo's aftershave in the ensuite. She opens Rosie's beach bag to see if the creepy notebook is still there. She told Fenna that it belonged to her dad but was that a lie? Was everything one big lie? Was she planning on murdering Theo all along? Or was it the heat of the moment?

'I don't believe she did this,' Julietta says sadly, joining her. 'She is a good girl.'

Fenna stops rummaging in Rosie's belongings. There is no sign of the notebook.

'She loved that boy. I could tell.' She wipes her watery eyes, picking up a framed photo of Theo and some famous footballer.

Fenna is about to say something when a sudden memory rushes back. Why has she not spoken to Julietta about this before?

'You told Rosie that you didn't trust this family. Why did you say that?'

The police officers' voices are growing louder in the corridor. She needs to get the children and leave but she might not get this chance to speak to Julietta again.

'Please, if you know something you need to tell the police,' Fenna pushes.

'I've always had my suspicions.' The older woman dips her eyes. The colour has drained from her usually rosy cheeks. 'The morning after Danielle Dixon went missing, I noticed the washing machine was on overnight. The family have never washed their own clothes here before, and though there was nothing in the drum, powder was spilt. It was as though someone had used it in a hurry. A few days later, Paulo complained about his garden tools. He was cross that his spade was damaged. Now, I don't know if this is all connected, but it struck me as a strange coincidence. There was something about Marianne at that time, she . . . she acted different.'

'Did you tell anyone about this?'

'No. Paulo never mentioned it again and I didn't want to lose my job. I wiped it from my mind when that teacher was arrested. Convinced myself they caught the bad guy.'

Fenna wants to tell her that she's not so sure they did.

61

ROSIE – DAY 13

Rosie lies on the hard bed in her cell. She can't stop crying. Her mind is spiralling with fear. What will happen if they don't believe her? What if she is trapped here forever? Locked away for a crime she didn't commit. The weight of her situation presses down on her. Her head spins. What is she going to do now?

Her solicitor doesn't seem optimistic. He keeps asking if she wants to call someone, but the only person would be her mum and she can't face hearing her voice. She needs to remain as strong as she can for as long as she can.

Hope is the last thing to go.

She sits up and rubs her face. *Stay positive.*

She'll be out of here soon; they will realise this is all a mix-up. They've got the wrong person. Won't they?

No one will tell her if they've pulled the Fraser family in for questioning. She has no idea if they are taking what she told them seriously.

If they think they've caught the killer they won't be looking at any other suspects, a voice in her head pipes up. The thought makes her want to be sick.

She knows she can't trust the police. They could pin this on her, use her as a scapegoat, to look like they've solved the case. Exactly like they did with her dad. She won't let that happen again. Not to her. She needs to clear her name. But how?

Who else could have done this?

She's been churning this question over and over again, yet she still can't believe anyone would murder Theo.

***

She is led to the interrogation room by an officer she doesn't recognise. He doesn't say a word. Her eyes are gritty and puffy from crying. There are no more tears. Only exhaustion. She's terrified she's going to say the wrong thing, somehow implicate herself. She's decided the safest thing is to say no comment in answer to any of the questions they have for her.

Her solicitor is waiting for her, a stack of paperwork beside him. Lucian is talking in Italian to the officer who brought her here.

She slumps into the chair, her eyes lingering on the graffiti on the tabletop. Their voices go over her head. She's too tired from a second night of no sleep to try and attempt to work out what they might be saying.

Lucian suddenly sits up. The sound of his chair scraping over the tiles goes through her.

'Carla Conti has confessed to killing Theo.'

'What?' Rosie blinks. Her heart thumps. It takes a couple of seconds for her brain to process this news.

'She was being held against her will at the lake house.' He relays what the police officer is saying. 'She is understandably traumatised. The doctors have examined her, and thankfully the physical damage is minimal.' He taps the side of his head. 'Who knows what she's gone through here though.'

'Carla killed Theo?' Rosie repeats.

He nods. 'She heard two voices arguing in English. You and Theo. When it went quiet she was terrified someone was going to kill her, so she attacked first. She killed Theo, then she ran away and hid until she realised she needed to come here and confess.'

The room tilts. Rosie grips the table to anchor herself. Her gaze follows his mouth, but her brain is not adding up what he's saying. She closes her eyes, and remembers Theo asking if she could hear noises.

'Why would Theo abduct her?' Rosie manages to ask.

He knew Carla was in the next room?

Lucian shrugs. 'All they've managed to get from Carla is that it was a man with an English accent. That's all they know so far. Like I said, she's suffered an ordeal, so I'm sure they will get more details from her when she's able to talk.'

Rosie shivers.

'The good news for you is that you're free to leave once you've signed these.' He places a thick pile of papers in front of her. 'The stars are shining down on you.'

'What? It's over?' Rosie rubs her eyes. The thought of a shower, changing her clothes, and brushing her teeth is overwhelming. Relief floods her body.

'They also found old, dried blood under the decking at the lake house, like you said.'

Rosie's stomach flips. *Danielle.*

'They are going to tear the place apart to see if they can find any trace of her.'

Giovanni knocks on the door and gestures for the other officer to leave. He looks shattered but offers a small smile when he turns to Rosie. She is too dazed to react. Giovanni and her solicitor have a brief conversation in Italian. Lucian collects his signed papers and leaves them alone.

Rosie is free to go.

'I-I can't believe it,' she stutters. 'Are you sure Carla killed him?'

'Yes.' Giovanni slips into the chair opposite. 'Theo is our prime suspect in Carla's disappearance.'

'Not knowing what happened to Danielle has eaten him up for years. So why would he abduct a girl and hold her against her will? It doesn't make sense. I don't think the two crimes are linked. Someone else put Carla in the lake house.' She presses her thumbs to her temples. 'What has Marianne said about all of this?'

'She is still in hospital. We will be speaking to her as soon as we can.'

'She knows where Danielle is. I'm sure of it.'

62

FENNA – DAY 13

It took longer than Fenna hoped, roaming around the big house, collecting the children's belongings for them all to go and stay elsewhere. She was preparing to leave when suddenly, there was the yell of voices and a clattering of footsteps before the many police cars reversed over the gravel in a hurry. A stirring in her gut told her this wasn't good news.

That was hours ago.

No one has been in touch since.

Fenna managed to get a couple of hours of sleep, in between feeding Raffi. Inhaling lungfuls of his milky warm smell was the only way she managed to calm her brain. Alba has slept through it all.

When the doorbell finally rings, Luke runs to answer it, Fenna trailing close behind.

Giovanni stands on the doorstep. He looks like he hasn't slept. 'We've let Rosie go.'

'What?' Luke shouts.

'She didn't kill your brother.'

'But—'

'He was killed in an act of self-defence. We have a confession.'

'What?'

Fenna holds on to the banister. Her legs might give way at any time. She can't take any more revelations.

'We've found Carla Conti. She's alive,' Giovanni says. His jaw tenses. 'She was being held in a bedroom at the lake house. Against her will. We believe Theo abducted her.'

'No.' Luke starts pacing. 'He wouldn't do that. It doesn't make any sense.'

Fenna gasps. 'Carla! Is she ok?'

'She will be. She's remarkably well considering she went without her medication for so lo—'

'What about Rosie?' Luke interrupts.

'We've released her. We're still in the beginning of the investigation with Carla but we're confident that *Signorina* Riley is innocent.' He looks as if he could sleep for a hundred years. 'I came to ask, how is *Signora* Fraser?'

'Like you care,' Luke snarls.

'Gerry called us from the hospital. The operation went well but she's not out of the woods yet,' Fenna explains, ignoring Luke's glare.

'We will be wanting to speak to her when she feels able,' Giovanni says.

Luke spins. 'What? Why?'

'We hope she can assist our investigation.'

Fenna's stomach flips. *The police want to speak to Marianne? When will this rollercoaster stop?*

'You're going to stoop that low?' Luke shakes his head. 'Unbelievable. She's dying. Leave my mum out of it.' He storms off.

'Please tell her that an officer will be in touch.' Giovanni offers Fenna a sad smile and turns to leave.

'Was it really Theo?' Fenna asks, dropping her voice. 'Who took Carla I mean . . .'

Giovanni hesitates for a second, darting his tired eyes to Luke who is stomping down the hallway, muttering expletives. 'It seems that way, but we don't know if he acted alone.'

***

Fenna heads to the library a little while after Giovanni leaves. She can't shake how suspicious Richard was acting. What was he looking for? Is it linked to what the police want to talk to Marianne about?

Alba toddles in after her. Earlier she asked where Uncle Theo was. Fenna had to swallow the lump that shot to her throat. She managed to distract her with a snack and avoided the question, but she won't be able to hide the truth from her forever. It's going to take a long time for this to sink in, for all of them.

Fenna pulls open the antique desk drawers but there's nothing in there other than paper clips and old takeaway flyers.

'Mama, colour,' Alba tries to get her attention.

'Not now, darling,' Fenna says, her back to her daughter. She rummages through another set of drawers, unsure what she's looking for.

Luke calls that they need to hurry up. They are going to the hospital to visit Marianne.

'Drawing, Mama. Now,' Alba cries.

'Alba, I said not now,' Fenna turns.

Alba is holding Marianne's journal, the Moleskine one that Fenna had seen her write in by the pool a few times. She takes it from her. 'Erm, no, sweetie. No drawing, that's Grandma's. Where did you find this?'

Alba starts to cry so Fenna sighs and tears out a blank page at the back for her to scribble on. She reaches into a pen pot on the desk and hands her a pencil. Hopefully that will buy her five minutes of peace. She turns her attention back to the desk.

Why was Richard in here? Why did he seem so ruffled?

Fenna pauses. She'd presumed Marianne was writing some sort of holiday diary. But what if it was more than that?

She sinks to the expensive tan leather office chair, opens her mother-in-law's journal and starts to read.

63

MARIANNE

The doctors have told me it's terminal. Richard was the first person I shared the news with. He offered to pay for a second opinion, and I know he's able to get me the best treatment money could buy, but it's too late. The clock is ticking. It's time I share my truth. Starting with the truth about what happened. The truth about that girl, Danielle Dixon.

The lake house is the place where I realised how far a mother's love goes. The boundless, unconditional devotion to a human being you created. It's the only way I can explain why I did what I did.

It was a normal holiday until she went missing. I slipped out of the house whilst Gerry and Luke bonded over a football match I'd forced them to watch, and came to the lake house to meet Richard. Like I did every time he was here. Evelyn never ventured that far. I didn't expect what I saw when I arrived.

Theo passed out in bed, half-dressed and in a deep sleep. Evidence of drugs on the coffee table. I had no idea that he'd left Croatia. The real nightmare started with what was outside on the deck. A girl I'd never seen before was lying face down on the decking. Her bare legs were mottled blue. Blood and vomit puddled together around her corpse.

It was every mother's worst nightmare.

At that point I thought Theo had a promising football career ahead of him, and I knew that if I called the police or ambulance – not that there would be any point – he would be arrested. His life would be over before it started. Whatever the circumstances, a young girl had lain dying and he hadn't helped her. I panicked. It was too late to save her and there was no way my son could go to prison. All I could do was clean up his mess.

Richard was as horrified as I was at the scene. He told me to let Theo sleep. We could make this go away.

I've agonised over our actions for years.

Richard rolled the girl's body in a rug and gently moved her into the boot of his car. I couldn't watch. We didn't know who she was. She didn't have any ID on her. We were running out of time before dawn broke and people realised we were gone. I'd told Gerry I was sleeping in the spare room with a migraine.

Richard said he would get rid of her. By this point, I was too numb to question him. I didn't want to know where he was planning on putting her. I already knew too much. Instead, I kept busy and worked on autopilot. I scrubbed the blood off the decking, flushed the drugs, and made the house sparkling clean.

Theo slept through it all.

I was about to leave when I saw his phone was on the side of the bed. It was open on a half-written text message. A long, rambling message blaming this girl for bringing drugs. Only the first part of his message had sent, something about how she made him do it.

I slipped home. Gerry and Luke had fallen asleep. No one saw me leave or return. I threw my clothes in the wash. My trembling hands stank of bleach and my palms were red raw from scrubbing the evidence at the lake house. I still can't believe I did what I did. The power of a mother's love.

Theo arrived home a few weeks later full of stories about what he'd been up to in Croatia, with photographs and a forged certificate. I never confessed that I knew where he was. We glossed over the lies.

Sometimes it's easier to stick your head in the sand.

The story was everywhere. Danielle Dixon's name would haunt me forever.

I couldn't have imagined the circus her disappearance caused. Everyone was talking about her, I was mute with fear that I would slip up. The paranoia got so bad that I went to the doctors and was prescribed sleeping tablets. I was convinced Luke and Gerry would tell something was up. Neither of them did. They put my spontaneous tears down to the menopause.

When Danielle's jacket and camera were discovered, people assumed she was in the water. We hadn't checked if she'd dropped anything. The discovery added to the theory that she went into the lake. I presumed Richard had put her on his boat, rowed into the deepest part, weighed her down, and pushed her in. But no police divers have ever found any trace of her.

I was hysterical with worry when the police announced they had Danielle's phone. Convinced they would connect Theo to her death, and Richard and my part in the clean-up would come to light. Mercifully, Richard used his contact at the police. All it took was one crooked officer to destroy the phone the moment it came in from that poor school teacher as evidence.

I've had numerous panic attacks over the years, but Richard has always managed to calm me down, in the way that only he can. I'm so grateful that he took care of things. He would never let me – or Theo – down. Richard had to protect his son. He was merely fulfilling his fatherly duty, something I am eternally grateful for.

I should have destroyed her Polaroid a long time ago. I don't know why I kept it after finding it during my clean-up of the lake house. Something inside me couldn't get rid of it. It felt too final.

Wherever he put her body, I know that he would have done it to protect me and the boys. I know he will take care of Luke and Theo, I've seen how protective he is. The lengths he will go to. I can sleep easy, knowing they will be ok . . .

64

FENNA – DAY 13

They are at the hospital. Marianne's body might be weak from the cancer and the shock of her heart attack, but she's woken up.

'How are you doing, Mum?' Luke asks, pulling his chair closer to her bedside.

'I've been better.' Marianne coughs and the painful rattle echoes around the private room. A smiling nurse stands beside the wide window, the sky is overcast with heavy white cloud. The room is chilled by air-conditioning and has a funny, tang of antiseptic smell.

They left Alba with Julietta. Fenna is glad they did as she would have been shocked and upset seeing her grandma in such a terrible way. She had no idea what to expect when they walked in. Marianne looks tiny against the plump pillows. Tubes and wires poke out from all angles. A persistent beep-beep sounds from one of the many intimidating-looking machines around her.

Raffi is in his pushchair, the nurse kindly moved a chair out of the way so they could wheel him in. He sucks his dummy and stares up at the high ceiling. Oblivious to the elephant in the room – they made a decision not to mention Rosie's name.

Gerry hasn't taken his eyes off his wife. He looks like he's aged ten years. He carefully pats Marianne's hand, mindful of the cannula in her hand.

'The doctor thinks your mum is going to be ok.' He sniffs.

All Fenna can do is match everyone's smiles, try and act jubilant at this news. But inside she's churning over what she read. Her mother-in-law's words, in her own handwriting, on pages and pages of high-quality note paper, telling her story.

Except, this was no work of fiction.

This was Marianne's memoir.

The truth about what happened at the lake house all those years ago.

At first Fenna couldn't believe her eyes. Alba's innocent singing as she scribbled on the sheet of paper faded into the background as she turned over page after page. An icy chill washed over her with each new revelation.

Richard is Theo's father. He and Marianne covered up for their son's behaviour. They put his freedom first, instead of coming clean about the young girl's tragic drug overdose. They disposed of Danielle's body, tampered with evidence, and have lied to everyone for all this time.

Marianne wanted everyone to believe they were this perfect family. But that was a lie.

Fenna had to go back and re-read each page to make sure it sank in.

It was no coincidence that I asked everyone to Laprezia during the anniversary. I suppose I needed to have my boys close to me. Remind myself I'm not a terrible human. Fifteen years on and the nightmares don't go away. Her face haunts me.

'She's still on a lot of drugs so may fall asleep quickly,' the nurse explains in near-perfect English. 'But we're pleased with her progress.'

As if on cue, Marianne's eyelids droop. She tries to fight the rest her body craves.

The nurse turns to Gerry. 'You should go and rest, too.'

He looks exhausted but starts to protest that he's fine.

'No, she's right. You should go. We can stay,' Luke orders.

Gerry reluctantly agrees and kisses Marianne's cheek before he leaves them alone.

'Will you sit with her if I go to the bathroom?' Luke asks Fenna, stroking his mum's hair, gazing at her like the adoring son he is.

Fenna nods. She waits until the door to the ensuite closes with a click before she stands up and steps towards her sleeping mother-in-law. She stands beside her bed and leans down. The smell of antiseptic hits her nostrils.

'Rosie and I found your paintings.'

Marianne doesn't move. Her bare lips part with soft snores. The medication must be strong.

Fenna shakes with uncontrollable anger. She thinks of Rosie suffering in the police station and all the lies Marianne has told. She's kept this secret for fifteen years.

'I read your journal. I know what you and Richard did,' Fenna whispers in Marianne's ear.

Any mother would protect her child, no matter the cost. The cost was that poor girl.

'You knew what happened to Danielle.' Fenna's voice is hoarse. 'You've always known.'

I wasn't thinking about her family. I was thinking about protecting mine.

Luke is humming to himself in the bathroom. She glances at Raffi in his pushchair. He is awake and alert but surprisingly still. The toilet flushes. She watches Marianne's chest rise and fall and tries to work out what to do next.

65

ROSIE – DAY 16

A tannoy announcement calls for passengers waiting to board the flight to Manchester to head to the gate. Rosie shuffles forward in the queue, her boarding card clutched in her hand. It still hasn't hit that she's leaving Italy alone.

Before she left Laprezia she visited the church and lit a candle for Dani and her dad. In a way, walking the same streets and retracing his footsteps has brought her more comfort than she expected. She's felt weirdly close to him here.

She hesitated holding the flame over a tealight candle for Theo. She came here hoping to find out the truth, and she got so much more than that.

After visiting the church, she walked to the house. *Villa Speranza*. She put her engagement ring in a sealed padded envelope and posted it through the letterbox. The CCTV cameras followed her every move. She thought she saw a curtain move but perhaps she imagined it. None of the Frasers have contacted her. She's sent messages to Fenna on social media but they remain unread. She took a long look at the house and walked away. Her chest heavy with pain and grief.

The sounds of the airport terminal bring her back to the present. She pulls her baseball cap low. Her phone rings. Newspapers have been trying to contact her, wanting her to tell her side of the story. But it's not a journalist calling, it's Giovanni.

She frowns. 'Hello?'

'*Buongiorno*, Rosie. I know your flight is leaving shortly but have you got a few minutes?' It's hard to hear him properly as a noisy group of pre-teens walk past, laughing and shoving one another.

She steps out of the snaking, stationary queue before her and presses her hand to her ear to hear him better. 'Is everything ok?'

'I'm afraid that Marianne Fraser has passed away. It happened suddenly, according to the doctors. Her heart was weak after the operation. She couldn't take the shock of losing her son.'

Her stomach clenches. The vivacious, glamorous woman who welcomed her to her holiday home a fortnight or so ago, is dead. Rosie blinks the sudden rush of tears, taken aback by the conflicting emotion this news has stirred inside.

She doesn't have time to dwell on how she feels as Giovanni is still talking. '. . . That means we didn't get the chance to speak to her about your allegations about her part in Danielle's disappearance.'

Her secrets will go with her to the grave. Rosie's shoulders sink. The tears dry up.

'Are you there?' he checks.

'Yes, I'm here.' She swallows and steps to the side to let a young family pull their large matching suitcases past.

'There's more. We've arrested Richard Taylor-Warner for abducting Carla.'

'Richard?' she repeats.

'Yes. When Carla was able to speak to our officers, she identified him as the man who took her.'

Rosie's heart thrums in her chest.

'He acted alone.'

She knows what this means. They were mistaken when they thought Theo was also involved. She turns her back on the hubbub of the airport and forces a breath from her quivering lips.

'Has he told you *why* he abducted her?' she asks after a pause.

'Carla said that it was over Marianne's journal.'

'Sorry? What? I thought you said he abducted her over a journal?' Rosie closes her eyes, sure she's misheard him.

'Yes. Apparently Marianne was overly protective with it, yelling at the staff if they touched it, so naturally Carla was intrigued at what was inside. She translated Marianne's words and realised this wasn't a diary, it was a confession. Richard, Theo and Danielle were named. But instead of going to the police with this information, Carla blackmailed Richard. Knowing how rich he is, she thought he would simply pay up.'

Rosie darts her eyes around, searching for a spare seat. She needs to sit down. Her legs are shaking with every revelation.

'. . . They arranged to meet in a remote field. But when she turned up without the journal, demanding more money, he got angry and hit her.'

The blood in the farmer's field.

'We believe that Richard panicked and put her in his lake house to buy himself some time to know what to do with her. She was kept there alone and scared. Tied up and gagged so she couldn't scream. On the night of your engagement party, she heard voices and managed to free herself, grabbing the closest thing she could to strike Richard from behind. That's when she realised she'd made a huge mistake. She'd killed Theo instead. Petrified that she was going to get in trouble, she ran away, but luckily for you her conscience kicked in and she handed herself in. Her injuries are consistent with her version of events. So does the state of the bedroom that she was being held in for all that time.'

That's why the detectives asked Rosie about the bedroom. Things start slotting into place. She shakes her head in disbelief. The whole time she was with Theo in the lake house, Carla was tied up in the next room.

'So where is the journal?' she asks.

'Fenna handed it in to me earlier today, her daughter discovered where Marianne had hidden it. It corroborates Carla's story. This is the evidence we needed.'

Rosie's heart clenches thinking of little Alba. She never got to say goodbye to the children. She itches to speak to Fenna but wouldn't know where to start.

'Clearly Marianne's terminal cancer diagnosis made her want to write things down and make sense of their crimes. She claims Danielle overdosed on drugs that night, possibly choked on her own vomit, but instead of calling for help, Richard and Marianne worked together to move Danielle's body from the lake house, and they have kept it secret ever since.'

'So Theo was telling the truth? He didn't know what happened to Danielle?' Rosie gasps.

'Who knows? We've only got Marianne's journal and whatever Richard decides to admit, to go on. He had an alibi for when Danielle went missing, but in hindsight it doesn't stand up. He slipped through the net. He paid an officer involved in the investigation to "lose" her phone. They will also be arrested.'

'I can't believe it.' She staggers over to a spare seat, beside a man wearing over-sized headphones. She hopes he can't hear a word of this conversation.

A tannoy announcement rings out.

'Do you need to go?' Giovanni asks.

'Not yet.' She swallows. 'I'm in shock. I mean, how are you feeling?' He has been working on cracking this case for years.

There's a long pause. He sighs. 'It was a slim chance that Danielle would still be alive, but I always had hope. It's silly, really. I pray we will find her body and give her a proper funeral. Her family deserves that.' Giovanni's voice falters. She can picture him trying to keep it together. 'This will also bring justice for your dad. The rumours that he had anything to do with her disappearance can finally be put to bed.'

It's a bittersweet victory. What happened that night changed the course of three families' lives forever. Rosie swallows the lump in her dry throat. Her dad's investigation led her to the truth.

Her flight is called out.

'I need to go.'

'Of course. Have a safe journey. When you come back to Italy, there's another cold case you could help with,' Giovanni says. She can hear the smile in his voice. 'Thank you again for your help.'

She says goodbye and hangs up then joins the queue. It's going to take a long time for everything he told her to sink in. She gets to the front and rummages in her backpack for her boarding pass, tucked inside her dad's notebook.

She quickly pulls it out, along with her passport to show the member of airline staff. Everyone else has boarded. She is ready to go home and never return.

66

NINE MONTHS LATER
FENNA

Fenna watches Luke unpack the final box from the moving van. It's been a rollercoaster nine months since they left Tuscany and returned to the UK to arrange two funerals. The doctors agreed that Marianne was in such a fragile state due to the cancer and her invasive heart surgery, so although her decline was quicker than they had anticipated, it was not totally unexpected.

In a way it was good to be out of the country when the news broke about Richard's arrest.

He pleaded guilty to abducting Carla and holding her against her will. Evelyn stood up for him in the media. She believes her husband is innocent. No one else agrees with her. As soon as Carla identified her attacker and Marianne's 'confession' was released, it was game over. Both Carla and Evelyn have since left Laprezia.

Despite tearing the lake house apart and re-searching *Lago Parrocchetto*, the police haven't found any trace of Danielle Dixon's body. So far, Richard has refused to comply with pleas from the police, the public, and Danielle's family to share the location of where he put her.

Following the funerals, they put their London house on the market immediately. Their debts were paid with the inheritance Luke received. A silver lining to the tragic events. They finally have everything out in the open. They've spoken about his drunken infidelity with Carla, and Fenna has had to come to terms with accepting it was a moment of madness. He promises it will never happen again.

'No more secrets,' he vowed.

She knows that everything won't be perfect, but that's fine. It's important that they work through their problems for the sake of their family.

Luke's having a lot of therapy, which is helping. From discovering Theo is his half-brother, to trying to come to terms with his mum, Theo, and Richard all having a hand in Danielle Dixon's disappearance, as well as learning that Richard abducted Carla. Who knows what he was planning on doing to her in that lake house? Her husband has had a lot to deal with. She promised to stick with him for better or worse.

And now they're back at *Villa Speranza*, but this time it's for good. Fenna had dreamt of being able to call this place home, and miraculously, it has all fallen perfectly into place.

She wipes the sweat from her forehead and places her hands on her hips. Alba is in the lounge watching TV and Raffi is having a nap upstairs – the room which had once been Marianne and Gerry's now belongs to them. It will take a while to make this house their own. She has grand designs to knock through the downstairs and create an enormous kitchen diner.

The current set-up is much too dark. Julietta has been thrilled at the idea of a bigger island.

'Right, I think that's it,' Luke says, flashing a weary smile.

It took some convincing to get this move signed off. She had persuaded him that it would benefit them all. Leave the financial stress of London life, the trauma caused by the fictitious break-in, and their monotonous routine. She explained how it would be a good way for him to get closure, how he would feel closer to his mum here.

What Richard did was unimaginable, but they had lost so much already, they didn't need to lose this house, too. Wouldn't it be good to give their children happy memories here? Of course, it's going to take time for the locals to welcome them with open arms, but she will use her Italian charm. Some short-term pain will be worth it.

'Thanks, darling. How are you feeling?' She smiles at him.

He unscrews the cap on his bottle of lager. 'A little strange. I hope we've not made a mistake.'

'Once we've put our stamp on the place it'll feel like home. Trust me.'

The stars have aligned and everything is good. It is like coming home. Fenna opens the box she carried in and carefully places a framed photo on a deep windowsill, smiling at the shot of her family. Her eyes fall to the image of Marianne that Luke must have unpacked. His loyalty runs deep.

Fenna had thought that by handing over Marianne's journal the sale value of her mother-in-law's art would plummet. What she didn't expect was that the world would clamour to get their hands on never-before-seen Marianne Fraser paintings inspired by the tragic events in Laprezia. The proceeds from the sale of the secret Danielle Dixon paintings have gone into a trust for their children. Fenna also made a sizeable donation to a missing persons charity.

There was a moment when Fenna was alone with Marianne in the hospital room and a small voice at the back of her mind told her to press her tubes. Hold them shut. Get justice for Danielle. Marianne didn't have years left to live thanks to the cancer, and Fenna could speed up the process. *Who's going to know?* She'd leapt from her chair, terrified she could think something so evil, even for a split second.

Fenna turns the photograph of her mother-in-law the other way, so she can't see her face.

She opens the patio doors to flood the dining room with fresh air and sunlight. The sound of the birds chittering in the trees makes her smile. She saw a green parakeet from the window earlier. It landed on the washing line for a few seconds. It felt like a good omen. She's become a lot more superstitious recently, looking out for signs that everything is going to be ok.

Paulo knocks on the open door, beckoning her to come outside. His face is drawn. He probably wants to talk about her grand plans for what was Marianne's eco-garden again. Something majestic will rise from the ugly blot on the landscape. The statue of that girl gave her the creeps. The sooner it's gone the better. She has contacted a local landscaping business to come and clear the death-trap outhouses in the lower gardens too.

However, Paulo seemed adamant the wildflower garden should be left untouched.

'Be careful. I wouldn't if I were you,' he'd said ominously when she'd shown him the plans. 'You should take my advice and leave it as it is . . .' He'd taken his soil-stained cap from his head and held it to his chest. There was something about his expression that had made her shudder despite the warm Spring-time breeze.

She pads to the door, breathing in the scent of cut grass and fresh lavender.

Luke's voice travels down the stairs. 'Fenna? Can you bring that last box upstairs for me, please? It's only a small one. Oh, and Raffi's woken up, I think he's teething.'

Fenna tells Paulo she'll be with him soon, his concerns can wait, right now she needs to get the house in order.

'Coming,' she replies, heading to join her family.

THE END

ACKNOWLEDGEMENTS

They say you don't choose your family, but I struck gold with mine. I don't know where I would be without their love, support and celebrations. We might be spread out across the globe, but absence makes the heart grow fonder. To my in-laws, thank goodness you are nothing like the Fraser family! To my Mum and Charlotte for our chats in Salzburg, making book-themed cupcakes, and forcing a copy on everyone you know.

To my darling John, for holding the fort whether I'm on a retreat or on deadline, and for taking us to Tuscany all those years ago. *Villa Speranza* was inspired by our holidays, none of which thankfully ended in murder.

To my children, this is for you.

Thank you to all my friends who share, support, review and buy copies of my books. You know who you are, and I appreciate every single one of you.

Thank you to my author friends, the Harrogate and Bloody Scotland crew, in particular.

A special shout out to Cesca Major for sunrise plot walks on a Welsh beach, late-night library sessions and getting lost in a field, and Izzy Broom, my roomie and voice note queen. This book would be nothing without you.

To my glorious pals in Anstey Harris's Thursday group, you don't understand how much I value your advice, cheerleading and anecdotes. Our Zoom call is a highlight of my writing week.

Huge thanks to my wonderful agent, Juliet Mushens, for always fighting my corner and for your endless encouragement. The Mushens Entertainment team are the best in the business, and I'm honoured to be part of the crew.

To the Mountain Leopard team, especially my insightful editor, Beth Wickington, who knows exactly what to say when I need to hear it. Thank you to the rest of the amazing team for their enthusiasm and professionalism, including Jenni Edgecombe, Rebecca Bader, Izzy Smith, Jessie Goetzinger-Hall, Jess Harvey and Sinead White in sales, Katrina Smedley in marketing, Isabelle Wilson in publicity, Ellie Wheeldon in control of audio and Louise Rothwell in production.

A big thank you to indie bookshops and booksellers for their support, especially Pickering Book Tree, Pritchards Bookshop in Crosby, Kenilworth Books, The Helmsley Bookshop and The Whitby Bookshop. Thanks to the many book bloggers and librarians who champion my stories. Your tireless hard work is so appreciated.

Finally, thank **you** for picking up this book. I appreciate your support, whether that's buying, loaning, reviewing or cheerleading my writing. You can get in touch with me via my website www.kategrayauthor.com, where you can also sign up to my newsletter so you don't miss any updates on my books, offers or competitions.

You can also find me on Facebook: @KateGrayAuthor or tag me on Instagram @kate_gray_author. I'd love to hear from you!

RAISING READERS
Books Build Bright Futures

Dear Reader,

We'd love your attention for one more page to tell you about the crisis in children's reading, and what we can all do.

Studies have shown that reading for fun is the **single biggest predictor of a child's future life chances** – more than family circumstance, parents' educational background or income. It improves academic results, mental health, wealth, communication skills, ambition and happiness.[1]

The number of children reading for fun is in rapid decline. Young people have a lot of competition for their time. In 2024, 1 in 10 children and young people in the UK aged 5 to 18 did not own a single book at home.[2]

Hachette works extensively with schools, libraries and literacy charities, but here are some ways we can all raise more readers:

- Reading to children for just 10 minutes a day makes a difference
- Don't give up if children aren't regular readers – there will be books for them!
- Visit bookshops and libraries to get recommendations
- Encourage them to listen to audiobooks
- Support school libraries
- Give books as gifts

There's a lot more information about how to encourage children to read on our website: **www.RaisingReaders.co.uk**

Thank you for reading.

hachette UK

---

[1] OECD, '21st-Century Readers: Developing Literacy Skills in a Digital World', 2021, https://www.oecd.org/en/publications/21st-century-readers_a83d84cb-en.html

[2] National Literacy Trust, 'Book Ownership in 2024', November 2024, https://literacytrust.org.uk/research-services/research-reports/book-ownership-in-2024